Also by Debbie Burns

Summer by the River

RESCUE ME
A New Leash on Love
Sit, Stay, Love
My Forever Home
Love at First Bark
Head Over Paws
To Be Loved by You
You're My Home

Home Is Where Your Bark Is

Debbie Burns

sourcebooks
casablanca

Published by Sourcebooks Casablanca, an imprint of Sourcebooks
P.O. Box 4410, Naperville, Illinois 60567-4410
(630) 961-3900
sourcebooks.com

Cataloging-in-Publication Data is on file with the Library of Congress.

Printed and bound in the United States of America.
SB 10 9 8 7 6 5 4 3 2 1

In memory of Hazel,
who never got to herd sheep
but who did a fine job with the kids and cats,
and for Emily,
who brought us together

"Dogs aren't our whole life, but they make our lives whole."

—Roger Caras

Chapter 1

IF ANY TWO SMALL humans or lone out-of-control canine were capable of climbing walls, Jenna Dunning's young nephews and their new border collie fit the bill. The trio raced around the dining room, circling the handcrafted rustic table for eight that Jenna's sister had special ordered from northern Wisconsin. Train whistles in hand, the boys pretended to blow on them as they ran. At two and a half and nearly four, neither of them had the coordination to make the whistles sound while running. Instead, they yelled "Toot-toot!" at the top of their lungs while the dog yipped. As much as Monica—Jenna's younger sister—wished to believe otherwise, the only calm thing about her home was the interior design throughout.

Suspecting the dog had transitioned from run-of-the-mill hyper to completely overstimulated, Jenna called out for the boys to stop, but they ignored her, immersed in their game of make-believe. They were pretending to be trains. Sam, the older of the two, was Thomas, while Joseph, the younger, was Toby.

For the life of her, Jenna couldn't keep straight which was the current favorite of several names in consideration for the dog, so she'd simply referred to him as "the dog" all evening. The boys had argued over calling him a handful of Thomas the Tank Engine characters' names, while the names Monica proposed had been rejected by both the boys and her husband. Jenna was determined to stay out of it.

The boys were in the throes of their nightly after-dinner adrenaline rush, and Jenna was in no doubt about the game ending with one or both of them in tears—which was the opposite of what her sister needed tonight. Five minutes ago, Monica had stepped out onto the patio to call one of the preschool moms who had offered to help out tomorrow. With as much as Monica had on her plate, Jenna didn't want her to come back inside to a major meltdown.

At his faster pace, the high-energy dog was triple lapping the boys, which in a sense was progress. Running in circles with his new people was a better way to get his energy out than the destructive chewing, scent marking, and occasional blanket shredding his first couple weeks here.

"Stop your feet!" Jenna yelled when the boys ignored her second request to stop running. As she stepped into their path, Sam nearly bowled her over.

Joseph, with a natural athleticism his older brother lacked, veered sideways, dodging her, and zoomed out the open doorway toward the hearth room. "No, no, Gordon, no, no!"

The dog eyed Jenna warily as he rounded the corner next. Without losing his stride, he bounded onto the table in an effortless leap. Pushing off, he landed on the far side of the room and gave his beautiful black-and-white coat a shake before zooming off after Joseph.

Jenna swore under her breath as she spied the scuffs from his claws that trailed across the center of the table. Monica and Stuart had paid more for this table than Jenna had paid for her older model Toyota Tacoma when she bought it last year.

"What is it, Auntie Jenna?" Sam's thin brows furrowed together as he raised up on his toes to peer at the table.

Jenna attempted to smooth out the scratches with her finger, but they were too deep. "I didn't think about him jumping like that." Concern populated Sam's expression, and Jenna smoothed a hand down his silky-smooth warm-brown hair. It was the same shade as Jenna's—her sister's, too, if it weren't for the highlights.

Given that the dog was now racing around the living room with Joseph, Jenna recognized that another essential training moment was lost. If she ran in and scolded him now, he wouldn't understand what he was being scolded for. Meanwhile, Sam was on the verge of tears. How many times in the last week had his mom warned that the dog was on his last straw?

In the four weeks he'd been here, the dog had racked up a costly set of repairs. An arm of her sister's adored linen sofa had been shredded in a nanosecond while the boys were watching TV, dozens of toys had been chomped including a few coveted trains, the legs of three chairs had been partially mauled, and one monitor had been knocked over while Monica watched dog training videos and a dog on-screen had barked.

Down the hall of the 3,200-square-foot Tudor-revival home, the patio door opened and closed as Monica stepped inside. Here it was, the one more thing her fifteen-month-younger sister was going to have to face tonight. At first glimpse, it'd be easy to think Monica had it all. She was a stay-at-home parent pregnant with her third child, married to a successful radiologist, and living in a gorgeous century-old home in Evanston, one of Chicagoland's most popular towns.

Jenna still wasn't sure if chaos came looking for her sister, or if it was the other way around. All she knew was that half of her own free time got swept away helping Monica be Monica. Thankfully, the parts of this that awarded Jenna endless cuddles with her nephews made helping worth it.

When Monica rounded the corner, phone in hand, it was obvious she'd been crying, and Jenna was reminded of the terrifying possibility that the lump her sister had discovered in her left breast could be cancer. Tomorrow, she was going in for a biopsy. Considering their mother had died at thirty-six after surrendering to a three-year hellish battle with breast cancer, this was a fear both sisters carried out of childhood. Genetic testing in their twenties revealed that Monica carried the gene that increased her likelihood of breast cancer, while Jenna had won the genetic lottery and didn't. Monica got mammograms yearly, while Jenna got to delay that awhile longer.

Monica's eyes widened as she walked in, clearly reading the energy in the room. "What is it?"

"Don't take him back, Mommy. Please!" With an expression lined with more anxiousness than any four-year-old's should be, Sam tugged on his mom's tight-fitting yoga tank that perfectly complemented her rounded baby belly, repeating his demand. When his mom's attention remained locked on his aunt, Sam switched tactics and dashed off into the hearth room after the dog. "Axel, no more jumping on the table. You have to promise!"

Axel. That was Sam's most recent favorite Thomas-derived name.

As she walked up for a closer look, Monica clamped a hand over her mouth. "Not my *table!*"

"I didn't realize he could jump like that." There was a guilty tone to Jenna's words that didn't need to be there. It wasn't her fault the dog had jumped on the table. Then again, he'd jumped up there to avoid her. One of the things this month had shown was that he neither trusted nor cared for adults. His saving grace—though at times it was debatable he had one—was the way he'd bonded with the boys. "I'm sure it'll buff out, Monica. I'll help you my next day off."

When Monica looked up, her gaze was resolute. "Could you drag out some books? I need to talk to Stuart."

"I doubt they're in the space to sit still for books right now."

"Put Thomas on then." This was breaking Monica's own no-electronics-after-dinner rule. "I really need five minutes alone with Stuart with no catastrophes. There's a bully stick in the pantry," she added. "Two, actually. If the dog's still hyper after he finishes the first, then go ahead and give him the second."

Jenna had no delusions as to what this talk was about. Her sister had already been fed up with the dog before finding the lump two nights ago. Plus, she'd stopped calling him by whatever name she'd been advocating for—*Racer, that's it*—and was referring to him as "the dog" with a little punch to "the."

As was typical, Monica read Jenna's thoughts even though she didn't voice them. "I know what you're thinking, and I can't take the judgment right now. I'm as worn down as a person can possibly be."

"I know you are, and I can be sorry for the dog without judging you."

"Would *you* want him?"

Surely this last bit was rhetorical. No matter how dizzyingly chaotic this month had been, she couldn't have forgotten Jenna's reaction to Monica's announcement that she'd adopted a high-energy dog while baby number three was on the way. It took Jenna's best effort not to bring this up. Impulsive as Monica could be, she needed a pass right now. She was emotionally and physically spent. It showed in the dark circles under her eyes and the fact that she hadn't showered in three days.

Maybe Jenna worked two jobs to make ends meet, but she got to go home at the end of her long days and sleep the whole night through. For the most part, she woke up restored and ready to face another day head on. Monica, on the other hand, hadn't had an uninterrupted night's sleep in four years. "Go. Have your talk. I've got the boys."

Tears flooding her eyes, Monica headed off without a thanks. Not that Jenna expected one. Thank-you's from Monica were like rain in the desert. You couldn't count on them often, but when they came, they were heartfelt and beautiful.

After telling the boys they could watch *Thomas & Friends* together for a special treat, Jenna headed into the kitchen and, after a bit of searching, fished out a single bully stick from the lower shelf of a walk-in pantry that was every bit as big as the kitchen in Jenna's apartment. In the short time it took her to return to the hearth room, the dog had begun gnawing on one of the boy's slippers. "Drop it!" Jenna warned.

She was under no delusions that he dipped his head and released the slipper because he'd spotted the bully stick in her hand, not because of her command. He trotted over and planted himself in front of her, sinking to his haunches, ears pricked forward. As far as dogs went, he was remarkable looking. Long, glossy black-and-white coat, lithe build, and long limbs. Lively brown eyes that didn't miss a trick. Soft, silky black ears that folded forward at the tips, softening his otherwise standoffish personality.

And he could sit at attention like the best of them if he had reason to.

Jenna was no dog trainer, but she still made him wait for several seconds and then sit again when he attempted to jump up and grab the treat from her. "Nope." She held the long stick to her chest. "Either you sit still while I give this to you, or we do this all night."

The dog sank to his haunches and waited this time, still as stone until her fingers opened. Then he seized it in a flash and dashed off to the corner. With any luck, that would buy them thirty minutes of calm.

"Did either of you notice that the dog was chewing on one of your slippers?" As she turned on the TV and pulled up their all-time favorite show, Sam tucked himself into the center of the couch under a cozy blanket and asked for hot chocolate. The earlier tension had left his face entirely, proving how quickly kids could move through emotions. "Did you hear my question?" she repeated.

"I don't like those slippers," Sam protested. "They make my feet hot."

"While we're training him, *all* shoes have to be off-limits. Even the ones you don't like."

"Sorry, Auntie. Can I still have my hot chocolate now?" To Sam, TV and hot chocolate were synonymous. Good thing for his baby teeth that the boys were typically only allowed one show a day.

Joseph had finally stopped circling the room and was hiding behind the love seat, red-faced and grunting, and that meant only one thing. *First turn on the teakettle, then a diaper change.*

"Yes to the hot chocolate, and, Joseph, I'll be right there with a new diaper. Don't you dare try to take that one off until I get there, you hear?" In her book, a toddler was clearly ready for potty training when he'd figured out how to take off his own diaper.

Ten minutes, one diaper change, and three freshly poured hot chocolates later, Jenna was snuggled on the couch with a nephew on each side. Joseph, who couldn't yet sit still to save himself, soon began pulling stickers off his Thomas the Tank Engine sticker book and sticking them on his arms and feet. Sam snipped at him that he wasn't going to share his stickers after Joseph wasted all his, but Joseph lived in the land of now, just like his mother, and wasn't fazed.

He pressed a serious-faced Gordon sticker onto Jenna's arm.

"Thank you, Joseph, but what if I'm someone besides Gordon today?"

With his wavy, golden curls, still-chubby cheeks, and big almond-brown eyes, Joseph was a little heart-melter. He debated her question for a moment, then grinned and yanked the Gordon sticker off her arm. "You can be Percy. Is that good, Auntie?"

Joseph was sticking a Percy sticker on her chest when Stuart walked in, his brows furrowed the same way Sam's had been earlier, an identical expression of concern lining his face, and Jenna's heart sank.

In the corner of the room, the dog raised his head, ears perked quizzically. Whatever had happened to him in his past, he was on high alert whenever Stuart was in the room. "Got a minute to step into the kitchen, Jenna?"

Did she have a minute? If she said no, would it change things?

Judging by the resolution on her sister's face when she'd walked into the room earlier, Jenna suspected the dog's fate had been set even before she'd spotted the scratches on her favorite table.

"Daddy, can you come watch Percy with us?" Sam posed the question without looking away from the screen.

"Not right now, buddy." Stuart stepped behind the couch to tousle Sam's hair. "I still need to work for another hour. But I'll be done in time to read to you later, promise."

After extricating herself from her snuggly nephews, Jenna followed Stuart into the kitchen. Because meeting his almond-brown gaze never failed to remind her that she'd loved him once, Jenna delayed the inevitable by straightening the Percy sticker on her shirt. They'd spent two years in med school together before Jenna finally admitted it wasn't the right path for her and dropped out. Now, Stuart was the man who'd married her sister and who'd managed to stick with something she couldn't and had earned the career she'd once dreamed of.

Thankfully, she neither loved him any longer nor regretted walking away from a promise she'd made when she was twelve and melting on the inside because she couldn't bring herself to walk up to her mom's casket.

And that part about not having regrets was solid.

"She's a mess, Jenna." Stuart flattened his hands on the butcher-block island and leaned forward. No surprise, he was going to jump right in. Over the course of med school, Stuart had perfected getting to the point.

"Today, she is. Once we make it through the next couple days, this whole thing should be behind us, and she'll be in a better space to handle him. You both will." Jenna was doing her best not to allow the possibility that her sister might have cancer sink in to either her vocabulary or her thoughts.

"The last few days aside, adopting him was still a mistake.

Two kids under four, a baby on the way, and a dog who might as well be hocked up on energy drinks. He's not what this household needs."

Stuart realized perfectly well that Monica should've realized this before she brought the dog home, but she hadn't, and she'd pulled them into this mess all the same. Jenna's frustration at this whole thing was about to bubble over. Shouldn't there be a wait list for these things? *Yes, I can't possibly live without this dog another minute, but okay, I'll come back tomorrow once I've had a chance to reconnect with my prefrontal cortex.*

"She's on the phone with the shelter now," he added. "Sounds like they're going to let us run him back there tonight."

"And you're telling me this because…"

Stuart frowned. "I've got a consult with a primary doctor at seven that I can't get out of, Jenna, or I'd run him there myself."

Jenna didn't need a medical degree to catch his unspoken intention. "Oh, no. I'm not driving that dog back to the shelter. I'm not going to be the one who takes him away."

Stuart frowned. "She says she'll do it. Maybe you could ride with her though? She's pretty distraught. If we wait until I'm finished, the shelter will be closed. Then we have to deal with him tonight and tomorrow, and let's face it, she could use the best night's sleep she can get tonight. Given what she's going into tomorrow."

Jenna shook her head. "If we ride together, that means we drag the boys along since you're heading back into your work cave any minute. It's going to be hard enough on them to part with him without him being dragged into a shelter right in front of them."

Stuart's brows were knit so tightly together that they could very well be stuck, but she'd been his study partner long enough to know he was playing out different scenarios in his head. "This has the potential to be one of the things the boys remember in thirty years," she added. Maybe taking the dog back had been part of the discussion practically since day two, and the boys knew it was a possibility, but that didn't mean they were emotionally ready for it.

"I know that. I do. But any way you slice it, you driving him there on your own is our best option tonight." He held up a hand. "Just hear me out. Please."

Jenna could feel the heat rising in her cheeks. At one point, she'd locked her arms over her chest, but there was no point uncrossing them. No point pretending she wasn't on the defensive. "Fine."

He dropped his voice to a low whisper even though the kids were too enthralled with the train-yard antics in the other room to be paying attention to this. "Tell the boys you have to go. Head out; drive away. After you leave, I'll make something up. I'll tell them the dog is going to a sleepover next door or something. I'll run him out five minutes behind you. Tomorrow, I'll find a way to tell them he's not coming back. I hate cats, but at this point, if I have to bribe them with a kitten, I will."

When Jenna's mouth gaped open, he held up a finger. "Seriously, Jenna, we can't even get him crated anymore. Last time we tried, it was a fiasco. He growled at me twice, bared teeth and all. And not having him crated while we're gone isn't an option. You've seen what he's destroyed when we're in the next room."

Jenna shook her head. Stuart's skirting the truth with the boys had a yucky feel, even if it saved them from a traumatic fallout tonight.

Proving he knew her as well as she knew him, he added in the same low whisper, "So, it's okay to fabricate detailed intricacies about Santa, the tooth fairy, and the Easter Bunny, but I can't stretch the truth the night before I find out if my wife has cancer?"

This was like a punch to the gut. Jenna took a long breath. "Okay. I'll do it."

Stuart crossed around the island and pulled her into a sideways hug that somehow ended up with his shoulder jabbing her in the throat hard enough to hurt. Jenna stepped back and cleared her throat hard before she spotted Monica in the hallway outside Stuart's office, sweeping tears from her face.

The part of Jenna that had taken on the role of mother in Monica's life nearly twenty years ago stirred her to go over there, give her a giant hug, and tell her she loved her. That everything was going to be okay.

Maybe it was because she knew she'd fall apart if she did, but instead Jenna turned on her heel and headed into the hearth room, pausing the TV to get the boys' attention as they scooted to make room for her again.

"Sit in the middle, Auntie, please." Sam patted the couch without pulling his gaze from the frozen image on the TV.

Because the coffee table prevented her from kneeling in front of them, she sat on top of it and leaned in, kissing their soft cheeks. "I can't. I'm sorry. I have to go. I'll make it up to you tomorrow though. Promise."

"I thought you were going to help get me to sleep!" Sam protested.

"Me too!" Joseph parroted.

"I know. I'm sorry, but remember how we talked about the things that big people have to do sometimes?"

"The unfun ones?"

Jenna nodded. "Yep, this is one of them, but I'll make it up to you tomorrow. Promise."

Sensing the change in the boys' energies, the dog had dropped his bully stick and trotted to the end of the table.

"Say bye to Toby too," Joseph said, pointing a chubby finger toward the end of the couch.

"Not Toby, Axel!"

Not either, it turns out. As soon as Jenna focused her attention on the dog, he dashed away, a flash of black-and-white fur and a raised tail. "Looks like he's not in the mood for goodbyes tonight," Jenna said before doling out a second round of kisses on her nephews.

When she returned to the kitchen, Monica was at the sink, pressing a wet paper towel over her eyes in an attempt to pull herself into mom mode, and Jenna softened at the sight of it. "I'm gonna go. I'll call you later and tell you how it goes." She grabbed her purse and headed out. If she hugged Monica tonight, they'd both be in tears.

"Yeah, okay. I'll talk to you soon."

Like Stuart had suggested, she got in her truck and drove off. The sun would be close to setting, though it was invisible behind a thick curtain of clouds that promised rain and an ample amount of it. She drove around the block, taking in the stately homes and manicured yards that made up this part of town. Stuart and Monica had been among the youngest in the neighborhood when they moved in three years ago. It had helped them get a jump on things that Stuart's family was well off and had enabled him to go through medical school without a single loan. On the other hand, Jenna would spend the next twelve years paying off her two wasted years of medical school and the additional year she spent to become a licensed radiology technologist.

She circled back around and parked three houses down. While she expected Stuart, it was her sister who stepped outside a few minutes later, half dragged by the dog as he zoomed from one bush to the other, then to the mailbox. Getting out, Jenna headed around to open the rear passenger door. She'd never been one to let stuff accumulate in her vehicles, and the back seat was bare and relatively dog-proof.

Along the short walk over, Monica was yanked after a couple squirrels in the trees and a rabbit in a bush. "The boys are okay," she said as they neared, her voice still nasal. Having spotted Jenna, the dog slowed down and dropped his tail as if realizing this wasn't a normal walk. "Stuart's showing them train videos on YouTube."

Jenna pressed her lips together to lock in an "I told you so" her sister didn't need to hear. "Look, I'm tight on time. We can talk later."

"Okay." Monica offered over a Post-it note and the dog tether that Jenna would need to attach to the seat belt. "Here's the address, and there's a woman waiting for him. I wrote her name down, but you can't go in the front. Intakes are around the back."

Jenna glanced at the address before dropping it into the front seat. "I remember where it is." It was far from the only shelter in Chicago, but it was the only one they'd ever gone to with their mom.

"I've been thinking about this whole thing nonstop the last couple days," Monica added.

"Which whole thing?" Jenna didn't know if her sister meant tomorrow's biopsy or the dog.

"All of it. Mom. Her dying when we were so little. Maybe we were older than the boys are, but we were still so young." Monica's voice quaked. "And also, how I got the gene and you didn't, and why."

"What do you mean 'why'? You got the gene and I didn't because of a random genetic lottery related to which chromatids ended up in which fertilized gametes, that's why."

Monica rolled her eyes. "You know I hate when you go all bio nerd on me."

Spoken by someone whose husband has a medical degree. "It's the process of cell division, Monica. It defines what we're made of."

Monica shook her head. "Other things more important than that define what we're made of. Remember that day when school got called off for that water-main break, and we had to go with Mom to her chemo appointment?"

So many of those days ran together, but that long day in the treatment center was etched into Jenna's brain. With no clue as to how bad the road ahead for their mom would ultimately be, she and Monica had made the most of it, making up stories about the lives of the healthcare workers, most of it related to who was secretly dating who. "Yeah. What about it?"

"On the way inside from the parking lot, you spotted a nickel on the ground and started to pick it up, but Mom told you to leave it because it was tails side up. As we walked away, you ran back and flipped it over and said it would be lucky for the next person who found it." Monica's voice pitched. "Remember how it brought tears to Mom's eyes, and how she hugged you and said you had a heart of gold?"

Jenna swallowed. Of course, she remembered. It was one of those sacred memories of her mom she kept tucked away. She and Monica had never spoken of it before. Jenna half figured her sister had been in a world of her own during that short exchange and hadn't heard it.

Suddenly Monica's face pocked with red splotches, and she burst into tears. "I ran back and picked it up while you two were hugging. It was good that you were putting out into the universe, and I picked it up. I *stole* it!"

Jenna's stomach knotted as she stared at her sister.

"Don't you see? You're fundamentally kind and giving, and I'm fundamentally flawed. *Of course*, I ended up with this gene! It's my karma. It's been coming for me forever, and I'm still doing shit like this." She pointed to the dog. "Digging my hole even deeper."

Jenna stepped forward and pulled her sister into a tight hug, Monica's round, taut belly pressing against her. "Stop it, okay? Just stop it. Tomorrow's going to be fine, you'll see. I know it."

Monica sucked in a shaky breath. "If you're not too tired, will you come back tonight? More than anyone in the world tonight, I just want my sister."

Jenna needed to get her game face on, needed to forgive her sister, to tell her that the nickel had been meant for her anyway, but her knees were suddenly weak, and all she wanted to do was get in the truck and drive away and definitely not come back. "I'll come back. Just do what you can to calm down, okay? This can't be good for the baby."

After Jenna got the seat belt tether attached, the two of them were able to get the dog loaded by sheer threat of picking him up. He leaped inside when he realized human touch was imminent. Monica took off for the house, and Jenna for the shelter.

As she drove off, she glanced in the rearview mirror and made eye contact with the dog. Jenna had a sinking feeling he knew right where he was going. "I'm sorry. For all of us. And I hope to God whoever gets you next is able to do better by you. I really do."

Soon, the rain began with a sprinkle, then fat drops of slush hit the windshield, and at some point, Jenna began to cry.

Chapter 2

THE RAIN STARTED EARLIER than predicted. As Jake Stiles inched along Ashland Avenue at tail end of rush hour, he wasn't surprised by the touch of slushiness in the fat drops splattering against the windshield. Of course, Chicago and its volatile weather-god concubine weren't done with winter yet; it was the twenty-ninth of February. In a non-leap year, one or two more snows would undoubtedly blanket the ground before winter called it a day; in a leap year, anything went.

He shifted in the driver's seat of his otherwise empty Jeep Wrangler and flipped on the wipers. Even before the rain increased from a splatter to a steady downfall swept sideways occasionally by gusts of wind as the front pressed in, traffic slowed to a crawl.

His girlfriend's voice floated from the speakers, and Jake half listened, offering the occasional mandatory reply. After a little over a year together, he'd accepted that when Alyssa wasn't asleep, interacting with her social media followers, or on her laptop with her headphones on, she was talking. She'd talked through their mutual watching of *Yellowstone*, *Mad Men*, *The Sopranos*, and Jake couldn't remember what else. In bed, in the shower, and while exercising, Alyssa talked.

If you find her so objectionable, then break up with her.

Jake drummed his fingers on the steering wheel as he stopped at a red light. It wasn't the first time he'd had the thought. It wasn't even the first time he'd had it today. She was a good person, and dating her had been great for a nice stretch. Lately, not as much.

"So, you agree?" Alyssa had likely guessed his attention had drifted off. In her defense, his struggle with ADHD had certainly predated her.

Jake cleared his throat. It was dangerous to agree when she'd caught him not listening. Last month, he'd had to upgrade their seats to first class on their vacation to Fiji because of that. Yeah, the flight had been nice, but damn, it had cost him. "I didn't say I agree. I just didn't *disagree*." Best to play it safe until he figured out what she was talking about.

With the red light seemingly stuck, Jake glanced over at the vehicle to his left. A woman about his age was driving a couple-decades-old Toyota Tacoma. The windows weren't tinted, and he had a decent view of her in the dim light of the streetlight despite the rain and settling dusk. She was shaking her head just enough to tousle her hair—brown hair was his best guess in the dim light. Her shoulders were hunched forward a bit, and her lips were pressed tight like she was bracing for a blow, but the only other passenger was an impressive-looking border collie in the middle of the back seat. The dog was staring out the window in Jake's general direction, its mouth open in a soft pant and a clever expression on its face. Longing washed over Jake. It had been entirely too long since he'd had a dog in his life.

Jake caught himself wondering what the girl to his left was upset about as he did his darndest to follow along with whatever it was Alyssa was talking about. The woman's mouth opened as she said something quick and short. Was she on the phone or talking to her dog?

Ahead of them, the light turned green, and Jake turned his gaze to the road and the fat drops hitting the windshield more vigorously each moment.

"If you ask me, it's ridiculous," Alyssa was saying. "Take tonight. If you hadn't needed to run all the way to your place, we could've shown up together. I wouldn't have had to waste money on this Uber." Her voice pulled away from the speaker long enough for her to say, "Oh, sorry. No offense."

He overheard a distant "None taken" from the driver before she began talking to Jake again.

"And the money we're wasting on two *everythings* each month—rent, utilities, parking, all of it. Honestly, it's like taking money and lighting it on fire, Jake."

Here we go again. Talk of moving in together had started just prior to their one-year dating anniversary and had since been broached multiple times. By Alyssa. Jake was far from in a hurry to take that step.

"I mean, we should try it," she added. "So what that I don't love your place? I mean, who wants to live in Logan Square when you could be in River West? But seriously, why renew my lease when rent is through the roof like this? Besides, there're things we can do to warm up your place and make it livable till we can figure out something better."

The hair on his neck pricked at the word *livable*. His place was nice. It was *better* than nice. It was home. "We've been through this. My place isn't right for two people—especially with one of them being you. There's zero closet space, remember?" Alyssa had *so* much stuff.

"There's your office." She hardly sounded discouraged. Never in his life would Jake pressure someone to live with them. "We could build a makeshift closet in there."

"I work out of that office some days, and it's not even ten by ten as it is."

"Only a couple days a week. I can hardly see how a small closet would be an inconvenience."

Jake bit his lip to hold back a retort. Her clothes and shoes took up every inch of her own walk-in closet and filled floor-to-ceiling tubs in her small basement storage unit. It wasn't all her purchases;

he'd give her that. Alyssa had more free stuff sent to her than anyone he'd ever met. Before they'd started dating, he had no idea that having an impressive number of followers on social media could do that for you.

Closet space aside, there was no way around it. The two of them were boiling toward another fight. They had been all week, and it was only Thursday. If he really was serious about breaking things off, he might as well let the tension build.

Was he serious?

Serious as a heart attack. Get on with it already.

Jake frowned. The thing about that inner voice of his was that, over the years, it had kept him out of trouble, but the trouble with *that* was it also kept him out of almost everything.

Ahead, traffic came to a stop at the next light, and Jake pressed the brake. He was disappointed not to be lined up with the girl in the Tacoma truck—and her dog. They were first behind the light, while there was a sedan ahead of him. After a handful of seconds, the sedan's driver made an illegal right turn on red, and Jake was able to pull up next to the Tacoma again.

He glanced over to find the woman wiping tears off her cheeks with the cuff of her sleeve. It was a cold, gray, and rainy evening to be heartbroken. Had someone broken up with her? Was a loved one sick? Was it her career? It wasn't every day that people looked that sad.

Over the speakers, Alyssa was repeating something he'd missed again, and this time her tone was less friendly.

"Sorry," he said. "The rain's picking up. What'd you say?"

"That we'll talk about it later. I'll see you there. You put on the suit and tie I told you to wear, right?"

Jake glanced down. Odds weren't likely that he was. For the life of him, he couldn't remember her commenting on which suit she wanted him to wear, but then again, they were his clothes. On his body. "It's a Thursday, not a weekend, and it's not like we're headed to the Ritz tonight either. My sports coat will be fine."

Her silence said everything.

Ahead of him, the light turned green. To his left, the girl gave an almost imperceptible nod, locked her hands around the wheel, and started off.

Jake spotted the eastbound SUV on North Avenue while the woman in the Tacoma didn't. Rather than hit the brakes, the driver sped up to make the light. He was headed straight for her. As everything began moving in slow motion, Jake blared his horn.

The oncoming SUV began to fishtail just before careening into the Tacoma. With a clash of crunching metal and squealing brakes, the Tacoma was flung sideways into the grill of Jake's Jeep hard enough that his airbags went off, exploding with a pop and a burst of air.

Jake rocketed forward, and adrenaline dumped into his system as the bags immediately began to deflate with a whoosh of air. His ears rang loudly, his limbs seemed disconnected from his body, and everything went into hyperfocus. His thoughts flashed to the woman and her dog. The oncoming SUV had plowed into the driver's side of the Tacoma's hood, condensing it like a pancake against the grill of his Jeep. *Please, God, let them be okay.*

Overhead, the rain continued unabated, and Alyssa's panicky scream of concern over the speakers pierced Jake's ears.

"I'm okay. There was an accident, but I'm fine. I don't know about everyone else though. I'll call you back." He dashed out of the Jeep with it still running, his phone and wallet abandoned in the center console.

In the center of the intersection, the driver who'd run the red light restarted his smoking car and threw it into reverse, rocking the Tacoma as it resettled, then, over the crunching and grinding of dented metal, attempted to take off. Jake was pretty sure the expletive he screamed after the driver was heard by every person nestled in their cars within a few hundred feet of him.

As Jake jogged around the rear of the Tacoma, a brave driver attempted to block the SUV's escape route. More steam was billowing out of its half-open hood. He doubted the driver would be able to get very far, but the panicked would-be escapist careened around the car before losing control a second time and smashing into a traffic pole.

"What the hell's wrong with that guy?" Drunk, maybe, or on something. Or possibly someone with a record desperate not to get pulled back into the system.

Jake spotted the dog first. The animal was in full panic mode, its yap piercing Jake's ears. It yanked backward as it warred with the canine seat belt that had kept it safe during the crash. As he turned his attention to the driver's side window, Jake's stomach pitched to spy blood trailing down it. The front airbags had gone off, but as old as the truck was, it didn't have side airbags. He leaned in for a better look as the rain picked up. The woman was leaning over the deflated airbag, her eyes closed. A line of blood trailed down her temple.

A car stopped alongside him, and a woman yelled out, "Hey, do you want some help?"

"Yeah, call 911." His not grabbing his phone as he got out of the Jeep showed the shock he'd been in. "Tell them we need medical attention."

"You got it."

The Tacoma's driver's side door was locked. Jake tapped on the window and leaned close. "Hey there, you okay? Can you hear me?"

She seemed to stir, but it was unlikely she heard him over the dog's panicked barks. On the opposite side, the front passenger door was pressed against the grill of his Jeep. There'd be no getting in that way. Without much hope, Jake tried the rear driver's side door and was surprised when it gave a bit. Gripping it with both hands, he yanked it open. Bent as the Tacoma's frame was, the door creaked in protest but opened halfway before it would no longer budge.

"Hey, can you hear me up there? I'm going to open your door." He needed to yell over the dog, who'd begun emitting a low, menacing growl as soon as the door opened. "Easy does it, guy. Easy does it. I'm not gonna hurt you."

The dog's bared teeth gleamed in the darkened interior, giving Jake reason to pause. Hoping to ease the panicked dog's fears, he kept talking. There would be no unlocking the front car door without being in easy reach of a distraught and powerful canine. Maybe it was because he was sitting at waist height, but the dog looked big for a border collie. "Easy, boy, just need to open that door to get to your mamma. Make sure she's okay. She took quite a hit. You too, I bet." The dog—a male—was buckled in the center of the back row. While he'd likely been jolted hard, Jake was hopeful he hadn't collided with anything the same way his owner had.

When the dog's ears went from flattened back against his head to perked forward for a second or two, Jake made his move, reaching inside with a confidence he didn't feel. Gaze averted so as not to threaten the dog further, Jake wedged his arm between the door and driver's seat, fumbling for the lock. He leaned in more, and soon he was close enough that the dog's breath tickled the rain-dampened skin on his face. "Good boy. Good boy. Almost there."

As the biting rain soaked through his blazer to his shoulders and back, Jake's fingertips brushed against the handle. Stretching a bit further, he popped the door unlocked. As he backed out, the dog let out something between a growl and a whine, which Jake took as progress.

When the front door would still hardly budge, Jake gripped the wet handle and, with all the strength he could summon, was able to force the door open. "Hey there, you doing okay?"

The woman had woken up and was attempting to tuck the deflated airbag into place. If she knew he was beside her, she didn't register it. Blood ran down her temple and cheek and dripped onto the shoulder of her jacket. No doubt, she was disoriented. Reaching in, Jake closed a hand over hers to get her attention. "Hey there. How you doing? That was one heck of a hit you took."

She looked first at his hand, then up at him and winced from the movement. It was too dark to see the color of her eyes, but her eyelashes and cheeks were still damp from the tears she'd shed before the accident.

He sank onto his heels so she could see him without looking up. "Is your neck hurting?"

Her eyes closed, then blinked open. "Maybe. My head hurts worse. What happened?"

With the road noise, he barely heard her, so he leaned in. "I'd like to check that cut of yours, okay?" Using his free hand, Jake cautiously swept the hair back from her temple. His fingers brushed against something wet and sticky. The cut was higher than her temple, up in her hair. "You got hit by an SUV. The driver ran a red light. I'm guessing you smacked up against the window here pretty hard, so it's best you sit tight until the ambulance gets here."

She nodded and closed her eyes. He knew not to move her if he didn't have to. The sharp scent of gasoline and something acrid pierced his nostrils, but the engine was dead. He didn't think there was any risk of fire, but he clicked her seat belt unlocked just in case he needed to move her quickly. Head wounds bled so much because of all the blood vessels so close to the skin—his childhood love of ice hockey had resulted in enough stitches to prove it. At the moment, he was more worried about her neck.

On the street, the woman in the passenger seat of the car idling behind them yelled out again, asking if she was okay. Over the noise from the surrounding traffic and the rain, Jake barely heard her.

"I think so," Jake yelled back without getting up. "Did you get through?"

"Yeah, an ambulance is on the way. They gave an ETA of six minutes. Do you want us to stay?"

Jake looked around as he wiped beads of water off his forehead with the back of one sleeve. No one else had gotten out, but another driver had parked at an angle behind him and put the hazards on. A few other cars were idling near the SUV, and one car had a window rolled down and someone's phone was stuck out, filming. Traffic was beginning to snake around the accident, though drivers were slowing down for a look first.

It struck Jake as bizarre that for some people, this would be entirely forgotten before their heads hit the pillow. Not for him.

"No," he answered the woman. "Thanks though." He could hear sirens in the distance.

"Okay. Be safe, and God bless you for looking out for someone else like that," she called out before rolling up her window.

Next to him, the girl stirred awake again. She looked him in the eyes first, then down at their hands. It took this for Jake to realize he still had his hand locked over hers. At one point, without him realizing it, she'd turned her hand over so that their palms were facing.

Jake had held hands with someone he didn't know exactly once in his life, at a work conference during an exercise on vulnerability and client care. He'd thought the exercise was ridiculous and had found an excuse to walk out halfway through. He didn't think that now. "I don't know if you heard that, but an ambulance is on the way. It won't be long. Until then, are you cold? I have a blanket in the back of my Jeep. A first aid kit too."

She shook her head and winced from the pain. "I'd rather you stay if you don't mind. And you're the one who should be cold. You're getting soaked. You could come sit here." She motioned to the passenger seat. Clearly, she hadn't spotted his Jeep pressed up against her Tacoma.

"That's alright. It's not that cold. Besides, I won't have to shower later." Her answering smile made him want to make her smile again. "Looks like your dog's okay." The terrified animal had stopped barking and begun alternately whining and panting instead, which was considerably easier on the ears.

"Who?"

Jake blinked as alarm flooded in. "Your dog. He's in the back seat, buckled in. But don't turn in case your neck's hurt."

"Oh, yeah. I thought it was your dog making that noise."

"No, not mine. I haven't had a dog since I was fifteen."

She looked at him again, really looked at him. "And that makes you sad?" Even before she said it, Jake was reminded of how people said the eyes were windows to the soul.

If he'd ever been asked a more personal question by someone he didn't know, he couldn't remember. "What's your dog's name?" he asked because he was out of practice when it came to being that real with anyone, much less a stranger. Then again, this was a stranger whose hand he was holding.

She blinked a few times, then her eyes fell closed. "I can't remember. He's had so many."

"Oh yeah? How many?"

"I don't know. Six. Maybe seven."

"Maybe seven, huh? That's a lot of names." Jake looked back at the dog who was staring at him, ears perked. The way the terrified animal was panting so heavily, it was clear he was stressed.

"They were trying to find one that fit. He's a mess, but the kids love him. He's my sister's."

"Oh yeah?" It was good that she was talking more. He wanted to keep her awake and conscious. "Border collies can be a handful, so I've heard."

"My sister would agree." She struggled to keep her eyes open, but at least she was talking. "My sister. She was so scared tonight. She never should've said that. I didn't want to know."

Know what? Disoriented as she was, it wasn't right to ask for clarification.

"My name's Jake. Jake Stiles. And I can see the lights from the ambulance now. It's almost here."

She was quiet for close to half a minute, her eyes closed and her breathing even, and Jake soaked up little details about her. The way the tiny lines of worry on her forehead vanished as her breathing slowed. She wore a Thomas the Tank Engine sticker on her shirt inside her open jacket. Percy maybe, or Thomas. In the dim light, it was impossible to tell its color. He wondered who'd put it there, wondered if she had kids. Just because he didn't feel a ring against his hand didn't mean she didn't have a partner. The reminder kept his gaze from lingering on the fullness of her lips and the smooth shape of her brow.

He was about to speak again—to keep her from slipping into a doze—when she opened her eyes. "Jake, huh? Another J. I'm Jenna. Two N's, no H." She shifted slightly and winced.

"It's nice to meet you, Jenna with two N's and no H." That smile again.

"Are you cold?" she asked. "There may be a blanket in the trunk. Or an umbrella."

She didn't seem to remember that they'd just discussed his not being cold or, more alarming, that she'd been driving a truck and didn't technically have a trunk to speak of. Jake squeezed her hand. "It'll be only another minute or two. Can you hear the sirens getting louder? They're almost here."

"Will you stay?" Her eyes had closed again.

"Yeah. I'm not going anywhere. Just stay awake, okay?" In the back seat, the dog with many names was attempting to lie down, and his panting wasn't letting up. They'd take Jenna to the hospital, Jake had zero doubt about that. If the dog didn't calm down, he might need to swing by an emergency veterinary hospital too. "Hey, is there anyone I can call for you?"

"I think my phone might be at my sister's. It's not in my purse. I was going back there. After. She needs me tonight."

"My phone's in my car. I can run and grab it."

Her hand tightened in his as if in answer. "Seven names, and not one of them is coming to me. That's too sad, isn't it? He deserves so much better. He's a good dog. Just nobody sees it yet."

"His name will come when you've rested a bit, I bet."

She was quiet for another short stretch before her eyes opened again. She looked at him with an expression of surprise and confusion. "What happened?"

Alarm flooded in even as Jake reminded himself that concussions could cause short-term memory loss. What if her head injury was worse than he thought? What if she was bleeding internally? "You were in a car accident, Jenna. You had a pretty hard knock on the head."

"Were you in it too?"

"Yeah, but barely compared to you."

Thank God help was pulling up. A fire truck pulled in first, its siren changing to a quick pulse before going silent. On its heels were two ambulances. Three police cars pulled in behind them. When the first EMT stepped out of the nearest ambulance, Jake waved her over. As she started toward them, a second one and two firefighters followed her.

The sight of them walking toward the car sent the dog into a fresh round of barking and snarling that was even louder than when Jake had arrived.

"Hey, Jenna, there are some EMTs coming." She was still holding his hand. "I'm going to step back so they can look at you, okay?"

Her grip tightened. "Will you stay with…with…the dog? I was supposed to take him for my sister. I can't remember the name. Everything's so foggy. But they're waiting for him."

Jake strained to hear her over the dog's barking. She wanted him to take the dog to her sister's? Even if his clothes weren't soaked, there was zero chance in him sitting through Alyssa's gala after this. "Yeah, don't worry about Number Seven, Jenna. I'll get him to your sister's."

Everything changed at once. As the first EMT stepped in, a firefighter offered Jake an umbrella. Moments later, a police officer pulled Jake aside with a never-ending list of questions for the accident report.

He wanted to stay at Jenna's side as they took her vitals, but there wasn't room, and Jake was asked question after question while the dog let the new arrivals know they weren't welcome. At one point, Jake headed back to his Jeep for his license. He needed his phone to pull up his most up-to-date insurance card. Not finding it in the console, Jake searched around and fished it off the floor. Upon lighting the display, he spotted six missed calls from Alyssa. Before pulling up his card, he shot off a text that he was okay and talking to the police and would call soon.

By the time he spotted a stretcher being hauled out of the back of the nearest ambulance, Jake had shared what he could about the accident. "Do you know where they're taking her?" When the officer gave him a look that made it clear he wasn't going to relay Jenna's private health information, Jake added, "I told her I'd get the dog to her sister."

"I thought you didn't know her."

"I had ten minutes while waiting for the EMS to get to know her well enough that she's trusting me to take her dog. I'm not going to let her down."

"Oh yeah? Well, if she confirms it, we'll let you take him. Otherwise, she'll have to get him from animal control tomorrow. Or an emergency vet, if they think he needs it, and she'll sign for the overnight charges, which aren't cheap."

Jake followed the officer over to the Tacoma. Two workers—an officer and one of the EMTs—were holding umbrellas over Jenna while she was being secured onto the stretcher. Jake stepped close so she could see him. "How're you doing, Jenna?"

Her gaze flitted his direction even though her movements were restrained by a chunky neck brace. "There he is. That's Jake."

Four people looked his way. She'd remembered his name, even disoriented as she was.

"This brace hurts my neck," she added as one of the EMTs shifted to make space for him. "But thanks for taking…Number Seven."

"Sure thing. I just need an address and a phone number."

She closed her eyes. "I hate everything about this. Especially now. And besides, I can't even remember the name." She went quiet again, like she was close to drifting off.

"We've got to get her moving," one of the EMTs said.

As soon as the stretcher started rolling, her eyes flew open. "The address is on a Post-it in there." She motioned in the direction of the truck. Inside it, the dog had stopped growling and gone back to panting heavily.

"I'll find it. And I'll get your number from them." Jake motioned to the police officers. Surely, they'd gotten her information too.

"Okay. Please tell him I'm sorry." She'd gone nasal, like she was crying.

"None of this is your fault, Jenna," Jake called after her.

He watched as she was loaded into the back of the nearest ambulance. Diagonally across the intersection, the driver of the SUV was on a stretcher being loaded into the second ambulance. He was a middle-aged man whose unruly beard and thick neck brace were visible in the streetlight. One hand was clamped over his forehead and his eyes were shut, and the image warred with Jake's anger.

As the doors of Jenna's ambulance closed, one of the officers standing next to the Tacoma turned to him. "Hey, I'm afraid you may have been assigned an impossible task. Stressed as this dog is, there's no getting near him. Not unless you want to risk being bitten. We've got a call into animal control for a snare pole. Maybe when he's free of the vehicle, he'll calm down."

A snare pole? The hairs on Jake's neck pricked. "With respect, he was calmer before you all came. I went through the back seat to unlock Jenna's door. If you give me some space, I'd like to see if I can get him unhooked less traumatically than that."

As the ambulance took off, sirens muted but lights on, three of the police officers stepped into a huddle. After a debate that had one of them shaking his head, a second one shrugged. "She gave you permission. But to be clear, you'll be doing so at your own risk."

"I know what I've agreed to, and I'm not keen on getting bit. If you'd just give me some space, I'll see if I can get him to calm down again. Besides, I need to look for that Post-it in the front seat anyway."

The three officers looked at one another as the first tow truck pulled up. "We'll give you a couple minutes," one of them said. "In the meantime, I'll get her information written down for you."

"I appreciate it." Jake headed over with enough determination to dilute any reservation over what he'd signed up for. Jenna had said he was a good dog, but added, "*Nobody sees it yet.*" What did that mean?

Jake slipped into the front seat. He took it as a promising sign when the dog stopped barking as soon as he was seated. The anxious animal's ears perked forward, and his mouth closed for several beats.

"Any chance you've seen a Post-it note around here?" Talking seemed to have helped before, and Jake needed to build up all the trust he could before he got his hands anywhere near that harness. "Why she has her sister's address on a Post-it is anybody's guess. Maybe her sister just moved. Or maybe she's not from around here."

Jake searched the seats, driver's side floorboard, and center console. Then he spotted it in the corner of the passenger floorboard. It was to an address in Pilsen, fifteen minutes or so south of here.

Below it, a single name was written. *Alice.* Next to this, *7 PM* was double underlined.

"Was there somewhere you were supposed to be at seven, Number Seven? Because that's not going to happen. Besides, I thought she was taking you to her sister's."

In the back seat, the dog whined.

Jake fished his phone from his pocket and, spying the water droplets all over it, popped open the glove box in hopes of a spare napkin. "Bingo." He dried it off, then entered the address. He'd gotten the distance right. It would take sixteen minutes to get there in this traffic, but the address wasn't to a residence. It was to an animal shelter. Clearly, Jake had gotten something wrong.

"You have any idea what's going on here, buddy?"

He pulled up the phone number and dialed. After pressing a few different options, he got a real person on the line. "Yeah, I'm looking for Alice."

After his call was transferred, Alice answered on the third ring. "Intake. Alice speaking."

His stomach tightened. *Intake.* "Hey Alice, my name is Jake Stiles. I'm a little confused, but I'm calling about a border collie who may have been headed your way."

"Oh jeez. What about him? Don't tell me he got away again?"

"No, he's right here. But I'm understanding this right? You were expecting him?"

In the back seat, the dog whined.

"Who is this?"

"My name is Jake Stiles," he repeated. "I was just involved in a car accident with someone who had him in the car with her. Says the dog's her sister's."

"Good heavens. Is he okay?"

"He's fine, I think. Nervous but fine. He was buckled and in the center seat."

"Thank goodness. If he were a cat, I'd say he's certainly used up all his lives."

"So, they were surrendering him?"

"They weren't the first; I'll give them that. Look, so long as he doesn't need veterinary care, I'll still let you bring him in. Technically, he was an adoption with them, not a foster. It's the owner's responsibility to see that he gets adequate care if he needs it, and we're too small a shelter to be able to afford after-hours veterinary services when we can avoid it."

"He's panting quite a bit. Other than that, he seems okay."

"He could be in mild shock, but I know that one. He's a nervous Nellie on his best days. And as I told that woman earlier, we close at seven. I can give you another five or ten minutes after that, tops. I have somewhere I have to be tonight."

Jake glanced back at the furry beast behind him. The dog cocked his head and whined. Some of Jenna's remorseful talk was making sense in this new light. Other things weren't.

Jake lit his phone screen to glance at the time. It was ten till seven. If he worked fast, he could request an Uber—assuming he could get the dog free from the back seat without getting bitten— and get him there in the grace period Alice was offering. Technically, this was within the realm of possibility.

"Yeah, thanks, but that's not going to happen tonight." He wasn't about to do that to a dog who'd just been a car wreck. "What time do you open tomorrow?"

"Nine a.m. for intakes, though I don't get here until ten tomorrow."

What the hell was he supposed to do now? He'd thought he'd agreed to return a dog to a person, not a shelter. This was a different story entirely. Alice gave him the name of two trusted after-hour veterinarians in the area should the dog require care, and wished him luck. Just as he was pressing End, he heard her add, "You're going to need it."

Silence hung in the air. When he looked over his shoulder, the dog's mouth was closed, and he was staring at Jake with the sharpest expression he'd ever seen a dog convey.

"Sounds like you've got two choices, buddy. You let me unhook you without a fight. We'll hang out tonight, and we'll figure out tomorrow tomorrow. Or you put up a fight, and those police officers out there will have to subdue you in a snare pole, and you'll spend the night in animal control. If I were you, I'd choose option A."

Jake headed for the back seat with bated breath. The door was still wedged half-open, and the dog growled menacingly enough to give him pause. The dog's white patches gleamed in the darkness while the black ones faded into the night. With the light from a streetlight in his eyes, Jake felt at a disadvantage.

"So, what'll it be? Spend the night with me or in the pound?"

The dog rose to all fours and tugged against the seat belt again, as if attempting to communicate how much he hated this confinement. The seat belt restraint was clipped to a D-ring that was also clipped to the back of his harness just above the shoulders. All Jake had to do was unhook the D-ring, and he'd be free. Easy enough. Where was his leash? Spotting a slim gleam of silver on the floor, Jake was thankful when it turned out to be the clip of a nylon leash. Holding it in his hands, he showed it to the dog. "Remember this?"

His question was answered with a sound once again between a growl and a whine. Without wasting a beat, Jake leaned in, intent on hooking up the leash at the same time he unhooked the harness. Alice's "Did he get away again?" comment hadn't gone unheard.

Reaching the D-ring required leaning in enough that not only were his hands and arms in easy reach of the dog's mouth, but also Jake's face. He braced himself for a warning bite or at the very least another growl, but the dog went stock-still. "Good boy," Jake repeated over and over. "Good boy." He could feel the dog's breath on his face, could smell the very doglike-ness of it. How long had it been since he'd been this close to a dog? "You like burgers? If I get you out of here without a bite, I'll get you one. Promise."

Jake and the dog sensed the moment the harness was free of the D-ring at the same time. As the dog attempted to shove past him, Jake hurriedly clipped on the leash.

Squeezing forcibly around him, the dog leaped down from the seat with a bound, landing with a startling litheness. With a look around, he shook himself off as the rain streamed down.

One of the police officers who was securing the scene with the firemen glanced over and shook his head. "Good thing we didn't have any money on you because I'd have lost that bet. If I were you, I'd stop and buy a lottery ticket on the way home. You're one lucky guy."

"Oh yeah?" Jake wasn't so sure. He was soaked to the bone, his Jeep was a big enough mess that he'd be needing a rental for an extended stretch, and an undoubtedly long night stretched ahead of him with an unfamiliar dog, and the more Jake learned about him, the less confidence he had in him. "I don't know about that, but I did promise to buy him a burger."

Chapter 3

SOMEHOW, A NIGHT THAT had promised to go in one direction now stretched out entirely in another. Jenna experienced a whole-body urge to drift into undisturbed sleep. She wanted darkness or, at the very least, considerably dimmer lighting than these overhead fluorescents, and she craved a second warm blanket now that the one draped over her had gone cold. Chills raked her body, and the shivering aggravated her pounding head.

One member or another of the hospital staff kept walking in, rousing her when she drifted off, shining lights in her pupils, checking her hand and foot strength, spouting off one question after another on a checklist everyone seemed to know by heart. What was her name, the date, did she remember what happened? Did she know where she was? Could she repeat the days of the week backward? Could she repeat the three words she'd been told earlier? How had she gotten here? Had she been alone in the car?

These last two questions made her look down at her hand and wonder if the stranger in the rain whose grip had been both gentle and immeasurably reassuring was real or a dream. Who did that for someone they didn't know? Held their hand and waited in the cold rain? At one point, she'd had a name to go with the dark hair, finely hewn features, five-o'clock shadow, and kind eyes that had been at her side until the ambulance arrived. One of the times she'd woken from a doze, the name had faded. Try as she might, she couldn't recall it. Perhaps his features would soon disappear along with it.

"There was a dog with me," she said to the med tech who was the latest to question her upon popping into the room. Jenna's own voice, heavy and thick, surprised her, and she cleared her throat. "My sister's. Do you know what happened to him? Everything's patchy, but I remember buckling him in. After the crash, I heard him back there—he sounded terrified—but I couldn't turn around to check on him. I hope he's okay."

The tech's eyebrows lifted. "A dog, huh? I'll see if your charge nurse knows anything about that. I think she talked to the police officer who dropped off your bag and a copy of the accident report earlier."

Across the room on a built-in padded bench, Jenna's clothes and bag were tucked against the corner wall. She had the faintest memory of being changed into a gown earlier. Everything from the moment she'd left her sister's was patchy at best. A collection of photos in someone else's album. Except for the pain—there was no doubt about it being hers. When she got through this, she'd never complain about an ordinary headache again.

One thing she remembered vividly was vomiting while still strapped to a gurney as the EMTs were unloading her. Being suspended upside down like that with her neck confined in a thick brace wasn't something she'd likely be able to forget. Ever. She'd been able to shed the heavy brace after the first round of X-rays, and that had made things a bit more comfortable.

"There was a guy too," she added. "Could you find out his name? Everything's a bit hazy, but I think maybe I asked him to take the dog."

"He was in the car with you?"

"No, he was there afterward."

The tech nodded as he headed for the door. "Yeah, I'll see what I can find out. Your nurse should be in soon."

"Thanks. And can you tell me what time it is?" There was a

clock on the wall, but it would require too much straining to make out where the hands were. In fact, looking at much of anything hurt enough that she'd spent most of the last few hours dozing or with her eyes closed. The cymbals inside her head clanked less that way.

"Yeah, sure. It's closing in on eleven. 'Bout five till."

"That late, huh?" As easy as it would be to drift off again after the tech walked out, Jenna needed to call her sister. She inched upward in the hospital bed and felt around for the corded phone with oversize buttons attached to the bed.

Given the big day ahead of her tomorrow, Monica should've been asleep, but she answered on the second ring, tension lining her tone.

"Hey, it's me," Jenna said.

"I've been so worried! Where are you? Do *not* tell me that was a hospital number on the screen just now!"

Jenna lifted the phone from her ear. Did her sister always talk this loudly, or was the concussion exaggerating it? "I'm okay, but if you want to know where I am, that's exactly what I need to tell you."

"You're seriously at Rush? What happened?"

"I was in a car accident, and before you ask, it wasn't my fault." Jenna hadn't been in an accident or gotten anything worse than a parking violation since she was seventeen, but the two fender benders she'd caused that first year of driving had resulted in her dad and sister labeling her as an accident magnet, which had never sat well with her.

"I wasn't going to ask that. But you're okay?"

"Yeah. They did some CT scans. I've got whiplash and a sprained wrist, but nothing's broken."

"Wow. That was no fender bender then. Thank God you're okay. You are really okay, aren't you?"

"Yeah, I'm okay."

"Your phone's here, which I take it is why you didn't call sooner.

Sam swiped it again, I guess. I caught him playing with it after I came back in."

"Yeah, I realized that after I left." Knowing she needed to say it, she added, "I guess I have a concussion too." Honestly, there was zero guessing about it. The issue was that Monica's husband had specialized in head injuries and concussions, and every time the boys so much as bumped their heads, Monica was right there at Stuart's office door. When it came to head injuries, she was determined to err on the side of caution, no doubt having heard one too many of Stuart's cases over the years.

Monica's several-second pause said everything. "I hope you've asked them to send the scans to Stuart."

"No, given how the company he works for is two thousand miles away in Seattle and has no connection to this place. But I'll get a copy of them. He can look at them later if he wants."

Monica's voice muted as she filled Stuart in. Jenna hated that she pictured them snuggled shoulder to shoulder in their king-size bed as much as she hated the fact that she could envision the way Stuart's lips would undoubtedly curl into a frown on the tails of his faint sigh before he responded, mumbling words Jenna couldn't hear through Monica's covered receiver.

Monica came back on, asking if Jenna knew the grade of the concussion.

"No, they didn't tell me." At least, she didn't think so. She opted not to add how she'd been having a hard time staying awake.

"But they're releasing you?"

"No, I'm here overnight. As a precaution only."

Monica covered the receiver for another short exchange with Stuart. "Stuart'll be on his way in a sec. I'll stay with the boys."

"No, Monica! Absolutely not." Her own slightly raised voice had the cymbals resonating loudly inside her head. "I'm fine," she added more quietly, "and there's nothing he can do anyway. I'll have a friend get me in the morning. Or I'll call an Uber." As her sister considered this, she added, "You two have an early start tomorrow. You should be asleep by now as it is."

Jenna's eyelids lowered from fatigue as she waited for her sister's reply.

"Okay," Monica said with an exhale. "But if you haven't been released yet, I want to pick you up. We'll come straight there after the appointment, and I want to see you regardless. When did it happen, by the way? After you dropped off the dog, I hope." Reading into Jenna's hesitation, Monica added, "Crap! Please tell me he's okay."

"I think he is. I think someone was going to drop him off for me." For Monica and Stuart, actually. This was the way it always went when Monica talked Jenna into doing something she was hesitant to do. It had a way of becoming her problem.

"Poor dog." Monica's voice pitched. "It's exactly like I told you earlier. Only now there's a car accident I'm responsible for too."

Jenna's head hurt too badly to expend much energy consoling her sister right now, but she forced something out anyway. "It's not your fault. It's not my fault. Some guy ran a red light in the rain. That's whose fault it is."

"Yeah, but you never should've been the one to take him."

"Can we just not do this? It happened. It's over. You need to focus on tomorrow. I need to get quiet. Call back this number in the morning when you're done, 'kay? And in case you're the one picking me up, bring my phone, please."

Monica was still teary-sounding when they hung up, but Jenna settled back against the stiff linen pillowcase. Last month, a coworker had politely pointed out Jenna had a boundary problem when it came to her sister. Probably the way the simple assertion had raised Jenna's hackles proved it was truth enough. God help her when it came to figuring out a better way to help Monica survive being Monica.

But right now wasn't the time for giving anything serious thought.

Jenna caught herself drifting off, lulled by the dull but constant pounding inside her head. They'd given her something for the pain earlier, and it seemed to be kicking in. Now, when her eyes were closed, it felt more like the party was in the next room, not bumping up against her.

She hoped her Tacoma was okay. Hoped the other driver had good insurance. She hoped the dog had calmed down and that this catastrophe would somehow lead to the fresh start he deserved.

As a dream began to take hold, Jenna found herself thinking about a pair of warm hazel eyes and the soft, caring tone of a man whose name she couldn't remember. *Please don't let him have been a dream.*

Chapter 4

DOZENS OF JAKE'S FAVORITE childhood memories were of times he'd shared with his family's golden retriever—Ruby—who'd died when Jake was fifteen. Running on the beach with her or digging together in the sand. Playing fetch. Smoothing his hand down her silky golden fur as she dozed in front of the fireplace. But none of that was going to help him get through tonight. From what his parents had shared, Ruby hadn't needed any formal training beyond her puppy phase. After a few hours with the high-energy border collie, Jake suspected his dog training skills were, in fact, pretty much nonexistent.

Clicking his tongue, he ran a finger down the mauled leg of his coffee table. "Guess I know what you were doing while I hopped in the shower earlier." Maybe he shouldn't be, but he was as impressed as he was frustrated by how much damage had been done in such a short time.

In the three hours that had passed since they'd walked in the door, the dog hadn't stopped pacing. His nails clicked continuously on the hardwood, making Jake thankful Sheila, his downstairs neighbor who was in her midseventies, was a touch hard of hearing. Actually, the dog must've settled down at least for a little while. The mauled leg of the coffee table was proof enough of that. The mid-century-modern table had been a present from Alyssa this last Christmas, and he could only imagine how well she'd take it.

When the dog glanced in Jake's direction as he passed by on another lap of Jake's condo, Jake motioned to the table leg. "Not cool." Since he hadn't caught the dog in the act, there was no training to be done here.

At least all Jake needed to do was make it through one night.

Hoping to calm the dog down, Jake turned off all lights with the exception of a few lamps and pulled up the blinds of the Georgian windows in the living room so he could see out. To a degree, it seemed to help. The dog quickly fell into a pattern of pacing three circles around the thousand-square-foot condo, then pausing as he passed one of the windows, the occasional soft whine in his throat as he stared out into the night-darkened neighborhood lit by streetlamps.

Exhaustion in the aftermath of the accident gripped hold even faster in the dim light, and Jake's eyelids grew heavy, but Alyssa was due any minute, and besides, Jake was determined to wait out the dog. Jake was under no misconceptions that if he fell asleep with the animal as wide-eyed and anxious as he was, half his place would be mauled by morning. Jake was counting on the fact that, even nervous as the dog was in a new setting, he had to get tired sometime.

At the window, the dog cocked his head sideways and his ears perked seconds before a car beeped softly as it locked. *Alyssa.*

Jake yawned loud enough that the dog glanced his way. "Isn't it about your bedtime too?"

It didn't appear so. Nor was it Alyssa's. At eleven o'clock on a Thursday night, she'd typically still be up for another several hours. In law school, Jake had been a night owl, too, but he'd since forced himself into the habit of early starts at work and even earlier trips to the gym.

The exterior entry of his building opened and then shut. As Alyssa headed up the stairs, the dog trotted to the door, a soft growl/whine combo in his throat. Alyssa knew the code and would let herself in, so Jake jogged over to intercept the dog. While he'd sat at attention perfectly for the burger Jake had ordered for him, the poorly trained animal proved to have zero interest in sitting simply because he was told to and attempted to shove past him.

Just as Alyssa flung open the door, Jake's fingers locked around the dog's collar.

Her eyes widened as she took in the dog. "Oh my gosh, you didn't say anything about him being breathtaking. Look at him!"

"Yeah, well, he goes back in the morning, so no getting attached." Seeing that the border collie's tail was wagging, Jake released him. The dog jumped up, boxing his front paws on Alyssa's chest, and knocking her against the door before returning to all fours to circle her with a thorough sniffing.

Alyssa wiped imaginary paw prints off the front of the glittery black dress inside her open coat.

Jake was about to apologize on behalf of the dog when she spoke first. "No way I'll be getting attached. No big dogs for us. But he'll make a great post." She leaned in to press a kiss against Jake's cheek. "And so will your heroics tonight, baby. Thank God you're okay, though you *couldn't* have picked a worse night to stand me up."

The hair on the back of Jake's neck pricked. Lately, all she had to do was open her mouth, and he found something to object to. This no doubt was as much his fault as hers. In this case, objections were layered into damn near everything she'd just said. But it was the last bit about standing her up that really triggered him. "Alyssa, I'm sorry you had to wing it alone tonight, but I want to make it clear that I will *always* choose helping out in a situation like the one that presented itself tonight over attending a gala."

A few years back, Alyssa had chosen one charity for each of the three causes she believed in most: making lives better for children in foster care, protecting the planet, and ending domestic violence. They'd met at a gala for one of them in January of last year; Jake's firm had sponsored a table, and he'd gotten roped into going. There she'd been at the silent auction table, ready to outbid him on a pub tour he wanted to take his brother on.

Not only had she been the sexiest woman he'd laid eyes on in a while, but he'd also been moved by how passionate she was about making a difference for her chosen charities. He couldn't say exactly when, but the rose-colored glasses had come off. They'd been different people from the start, and the longer they dated, the more he saw it.

At thirty-five, she was a little over a year older than him. She'd started her career as a freelance grant writer padded by occasional big gifts from her well-to-do parents. She still wrote a big grant or two every month, but mostly she was supporting herself—and raising money for her chosen charities—through her work as an influencer. She was damn good at it too; one of the city's best known. The thing was, she never stepped back from that role, even when she woke up in the middle of the night. Her career took the front seat in everything, and while he didn't fault her, it wasn't a life he wanted.

With a roll of her eyes, Alyssa kicked out of her heels, threw her coat over a chair, and headed for the couch, beckoning him to join her by patting the cushion next to her.

"You look great, by the way," he added as he opted to remain standing. This was no exaggeration. Alyssa could put herself together like no one he'd ever met.

The dog surprised them both by bounding onto the top of the couch from several feet away. In spite of the narrow back wall and soft cushions, he proved to have incredible balance as he stared her down, head cocked.

Alyssa's eyes widened to spy him looming over her. "Should I be terrified right now?"

Jake tugged on an earlobe. "I wish I could say no more confidently than I can." He clapped his thigh and whistled, and the dog shot off the couch, landing with an impressive litheness on the hardwood. "I think he's just really high energy and untrained, maybe even untrainable. From what I heard on the phone, he's been re-turned a handful of times already."

Alyssa turned out her lip at the last part. "I can't believe someone asked you to take their dog for them like this. Wasn't there anyone they could call?"

"She didn't have her phone, and it wasn't like she was in the space to go anywhere except the hospital after an SUV rammed into her and left her with a nasty cut and, I'm betting, a pretty serious concussion."

"She?" Alyssa shifted on the couch as the single word settled between them.

Jake still hadn't joined her, even though he'd been sitting there before she came in. "I tell you that story, and *that's* what you react to? That his owner is a woman?"

"Like how old?"

He shrugged. "Early thirties, maybe. She was bleeding, and it was dark and raining. Why?"

"Was she pretty?"

Jake dragged a hand through his hair. "What the actual hell, Alyssa? I'm not going to answer that."

Her mouth fell open an inch as she stared at him. "Jake Stiles. Tell me this, at least. Did you *know* she was pretty before you ran out in the rain to help her?"

Jake was seeing red. He stalked off into the kitchen to claim some space for himself. Grabbing the teakettle off the gas stove, he filled it with water, then set it back and turned the gas burner on high. He'd started drinking tea three years ago when he finally got it together enough to quit vaping. Three years, and he still craved that smoky rush of nicotine like it was yesterday, especially in moments like right now.

"Well, I guess that answers that." She shot up from the couch.

The dog had planted himself in the middle of the room and was eyeing them in a way that suggested he believed that if he tried hard enough, he'd be able to understand what they were saying. "This was a really important event for me tonight, and now I can't even post about why you stood me up."

"I was in a *car accident*, Alyssa. My Jeep might very well be totaled. I ran out into the rain to help a stranger who could've been seriously injured. I don't see what the problem is."

"The problem is that you ran out into the rain to help a *pretty* stranger, and then you brought home her dog. Tonight, of all nights."

Jake's hands were clenched into fists. He wanted to pound something, but there was nothing to pound. Alyssa stood in the entryway, blocking his exit to the living room, her hands on her hips and her cheeks reddening. There was no way he'd admit it aloud, but maybe, just maybe, part of the anger turning his veins to acid had something to do with the fact that, while he'd have run out in the rain for anyone, his heart likely wouldn't have sunk the way it did at fear of how she might be hurt had he not already found himself so intrigued by her for the space of two traffic lights, Jenna, with two N's and no H. But none of this was anything he'd admit to Alyssa. "I've gone to like ten of these events with you this year. What is it that was so important about tonight?"

"There're only three big galas I attend a year, Jake, and this one was the most important of the three."

"Three, huh? What about all those other things you're always dragging me to?"

"I'm not always dragging you to things, and you know very well those aren't galas, Jake. Important people were there tonight."

"And my not being there prevented you from talking to them?"

"You're not being there prevented me from…" She stopped short and threw her hands up in the air.

Jake was buzzing with adrenaline. "My not being there prevented you from what?"

"Fine. From proposing, Jake! I was going to propose. It's Leap Day, after all, a perfectly acceptable day to do that. I had everything planned out, and I'd called in favors from a dozen different people. But you didn't show up, and it was all for nothing, and now there aren't any more big galas till October."

Jake shot one hand up in the air. "Wait. Propose *what?*" Obviously, he knew, but at the same time, none of this added up.

Alyssa's jaw dropped. "You really have to ask?"

He'd certainly not seen this coming. He leaned back against the counter. "Wow."

She nodded, misunderstanding him. "Yeah, you have no idea how perfect it would've been. How much planning I've been doing."

"I'm sorry, Alyssa." He held up his hand again when she took a conciliatory step toward him. "I'm sorry your night was ruined. I really am, but it's a good thing tonight played out as it did."

Her bare shoulders squared off again. "Don't tell me you're secretly a chauvinist, Jake, because I thought you were bigger than that."

Seriously? Now she was calling him a chauvinist? "The only thing I'm going to tell is that I find it difficult to understand how two people could be in such very different places in their relationship."

Behind her, the dog had stretched out on the floor and was chewing on something. It took Jake a solid second to process that it was the spike of one of her striking five-inch heels, and the dog had done enough damage already that it was undoubtedly beyond repair. Jake wouldn't have chosen this way to do it, but it seemed as if Alyssa had two disappointments about to hit her at once.

With her gaze still fixed on Jake, Alyssa's face drained of color so fast it was as if a light switch had been turned off. "What are you talking about?"

You know you need to do it. Now is as good of a time as any. He did his best to layer his tone with compassion. "That you're wanting to get married, while I'm wanting to break things off."

She cocked her head. "What are you actually saying right now?"

He was already standing on the edge of the high dive. "That this relationship isn't working for me." When her mouth fell open, but she didn't interject, he continued. "I'm sorry, Alyssa, but it hasn't been for a while. When the disappointment settles, I'm hoping you'll agree."

"You're wanting a *break*? Is that what you're saying?"

No doubt his clarity was triggered by tonight's earlier events. Had Jenna driven ahead five feet further before the impact, tonight could've had a very different ending for her. Being there, witnessing it, had him more in tune with the frailty of the human experience than he'd ever been in his life. Right now, the only thing to do was be honest. "No. That's not what I'm saying. You may not see it yet, but there's a silver lining here. Had things gone differently tonight, had I been at your gala, I wouldn't have given you the answer you'd have been looking for, which would've ruined your night anyway. And now that it's out there, there's no going back. Not the way I see it."

Mouth still open, Alyssa shook her head. "So, you're breaking up with me?"

Jake swallowed. "I'm sorry. I really am, but yeah. I'm breaking up with you."

Turning on her heel, Alyssa spotted the shoe that was in the process of being destroyed and lunged for it with a screech. "Stupid dog!" Jake's heart went out to her before she turned and hurled it in Jake's direction. "Stupider Jake!"

He ducked just in time, and it crashed into the cabinet behind him, the spike of the heel leaving a dent in the wood. "What the hell!"

"I'm a good person, Jake, a keeper. Everybody sees it but you! My followers, they *see* me. You don't. You used to, but not anymore."

Even though a five-inch spike was just thrown at his head, he needed to be the bigger person and let it go. "You're a good person who's doing good, but that doesn't mean we fit."

"This is ridiculous." She was trying hard not to cry. As often as she talked to her followers about the importance of letting emotions flow, Alyssa hated to cry. She could get angry with the best of them, but tears were avoided at all costs. She looked between him and the dog, who'd escaped to the far side of the couch and was watching them with wide-eyed interest. "I can't believe I thought that animal was good-looking. He looks like a rat, and you can't break up with me, Jake. I'm breaking up with you! You chose somebody else's dog—a nobody dog who destroys pretty shoes—over me, and I won't stand for it."

Jake covered his mouth to hide a smile that threatened to pop up at the most inopportune time. The once-snotty kid still inside him wanted to spout off that there could be no take-backs, but he bit the words back. "Fine. You can be the one to break up with me, so long as it means you're out of here."

Alyssa looked between him and the dog and shook her head. "You two *both* belong in the pound." Grabbing her coat, she stalked toward the door barefoot. "And one of you is paying for those shoes, and I mean it!" she yelled before stepping out and slamming the door.

On the stove, the kettle had begun to whistle. Jake turned off the burner and stood there a moment, processing the surprise turn of events as the releasing steam wound down to a soft whine.

The dog trotted to the door in the abruptly silent condo, gave it a thorough sniffing, then beelined for the second heel nearest him, sank down, and began to gnaw it right in plain sight. That was when Jake started to laugh. "You and me both, buddy. You and me both."

Chapter 5

AFTER THE SHARPLY SCENTED female fled in a flurry, the dog picked up on a change in the energy coming off the man. Before the woman came, it had been clear the man had been waiting for something, which had made the dog anxious. It had turned out to be the woman who reminded the dog of a thunderstorm. The man talked to himself as he paced in the same circles the dog had paced earlier. As he circled, he rested his arms atop his head and mumbled. After some time had passed, the man settled onto the couch, leaned his head back, and closed his eyes, his energy considerably calmer now.

The dog made a point of paying heed to people's energy. It had saved him from more than a few beatings over the seasons. The man would be giving in to sleep soon, and once he did, the dog would be able to rest as well. He couldn't sleep in the same room with strangers, not while they were awake.

He didn't understand why he was here with the man any more than he understood why he'd been moving between human homes and confining cages in buildings filled with other dogs as far back as he could remember. A part of him longed to slip out the door the first chance he got and run and run and run. Another a part of him wanted to go back to the house and four humans he'd been with most recently. He could do without the anxious intensity of the woman and the calculated air of the man, but the young boys had been entertaining.

They darted about rather than parking themselves in one spot all the time like so many humans did. Their energy was always un-tainted and easy to read, and they moved through many emotions in a day. Playful, tired, angry, sad, hungry. They'd offered him bites of their food and toys to chew, and they never once swatted or kicked him or, worse, locked him in a cage. He'd even come to like their small, soft hands burrowing into his fur, so unlike his experience with other humans. Anytime an adult attempted to touch him, the dog darted away, and if he couldn't get away, he froze in place until the petting mercifully ended.

In spite of his enjoyment of the young boys, the dog had not slept well in that house. His best dozes had been during the day in a patch of sunlight while the little ones were napping. Nights were too often pierced by the cries and needs of the boys and the snapping of the man and woman as they quarreled when roused from sleep.

As poorly as he'd slept there, it had been far worse in other houses, and most terrible in the house of one man whose meanness the dog could smell through walls. And he slept even worse in cages.

More than pettings by humans who he didn't trust, more than beatings, the dog feared cages. He'd been trapped in them so many times, and sometimes for unbearably long. One of the dog's homes had become nothing more to him in memory than a cage and a swift kicking anytime he was free of it. If the dog was never shoved into a cage the rest of his life, he'd never forget his dislike of them.

If there was one hopeful thing about this new place tonight, it was free of cages.

When the man's breathing finally melted into the steady, even breathing of sleep, the dog hopped up onto the small table in front of him and gave him a thorough studying. It might not be for the dog to know why he was with this man now, but as far as humans went, this man didn't fill him with dread the way some others had. Perhaps this was in part because the man had freed him from the vehicle that was no better than a cage.

He'd even given the dog something meaty and delicious to eat that the dog had smelled humans eating before but had never been offered, and it still sat heavy and warm in his belly. He wanted another one—or two—even if they made his belly cramp as badly as the time he'd been without water for so long that when he was finally offered it, he drank and drank and drank until his stomach threatened to burst.

Stepping forward, the dog balanced one paw lightly on the couch and leaned in closer to the man. Underneath the chemical scents lingering from what the man had washed himself with earlier—apparently he hadn't gotten wet enough in the rain—his scent had an unexpected evenness to it, one that tempted the dog to trust him. The man's hands were resting on his lap, and his head was still stretched back against the couch. The tips of the fingers of one hand still smelled of the woman's blood who'd been in the vehicle with him.

When their vehicle smashed against a different one, the dog had only received a jarring, but the woman had gotten something as bad as the dog's worst beating. Her body had gone limp, and the sharp scent of her blood had stung his nose. As far as humans went, the dog trusted her enough. She often came to the house, immersing herself in the play of the young boys, and sometimes offering the dog bites of food. After the crash, strangers had taken her away. The dog wondered where she'd gone and if she was okay, but such things as these weren't for him to know.

The dog was still leaning in close when the man roused unexpectedly, sucking in a sharp breath and opening his eyes in the dim light. After jerking in surprise to find the dog so close, he cleared his throat. "Hey, there. You aren't planning on eating me in my sleep, are you?"

The dog returned all four paws to the table and stared at the man as the man stared at him.

"Know what? I'm just about too tired to care."

Abruptly stretching out across the couch, the man was asleep again within seconds. The dog watched him a bit longer, then jumped over to the padded chair nearby. He scratched at the soft fabric with his front paws and circled several times before curling up and resting his head over the side, one eye popping open every time the man stirred.

Finally, in the quiet of the night, the dog gave in to the exhaustion that had long been beckoning him.

Chapter 6

IT WASN'T A DREAM. After sunrise and her first trip to the bathroom since she'd been wheeled to a shared room whose other half was currently empty, Jenna was back in bed, her gaze fixed on the note written in small print on the back of the police officer's business card that had been paper-clipped to the accident report.

This person took your dog and wants you to call him.

This simple, declarative sentence was followed by a name, Jake Stiles—*Jake, that's it*—and a Racine area number. Her lips quirked upward even though it really wasn't news that should make her happy.

Nothing about the last twelve hours was anything to smile about, unless it was that she hadn't been hurt any worse than she had been. Now that she'd had more time to process everything, she suspected that her truck—the vehicle that was key to doing what she loved—was totaled. This was one thing. The airbags had gone off; she remembered this much. Memory of the impact itself was piece-meal, but airbags deploying meant body damage, and the truck had been edging toward twenty years old. It had been a gem find though: one owner, very low mileage for its age, and unlikely replaceable for the money she'd spent on it.

Added to this, she'd asked a stranger to take her sister's dog to a shelter on her behalf. The poor dog was probably stuck in a kennel now, his memory of the last month already fading as he waited for his next chance at a forever home.

This last week excluded, after Monica had found the tender knot in her breast, Jenna hadn't been much for prayer since her mom died. If all the praying she'd done back then hadn't worked, it really seemed pointless. Even so, she closed her eyes and said one for the dog to find his way into a perfect home. Wild thing or not, he deserved a loving home that worked for him.

Given what she'd asked Jake to do, he couldn't think highly of her. But something inside her lightened at knowing he was real. If he was real, then there was reason to believe what had passed between them had been real, too, something intimate and unspoken, hardly something she'd experienced with close friends, much less a complete stranger.

And what're you going to do about it? Ask him on a date? Because that wouldn't be weird.

Jenna pressed her fingers lightly against the Steri-Strips covering the stitches in her hair above her temple as she considered this. Why wouldn't she? Not a date but coffee—once her head stopped feeling like this.

He held your hand in the rain and waited for an ambulance with you and took your sister's dog to a shelter and you want to buy him coffee?

Okay, maybe she'd assemble a thank-you basket while she was at it. A snort escaped as some ideas of what to put in it popped to mind. An emergency raincoat. A couple flares and a roadside hazard sign. Maybe some hand warmers.

His hands were perfectly warm.

Her morning nurse walked in, interrupting Jenna's reverie. "There you are, sitting up and everything. Feeling better?"

"Much better than last night, but wow, it's bright out there." After last night's storm, it promised to be a beautiful day, but glancing toward the window had Jenna wincing like a vampire.

"That's your concussion talking. You'll want to lie low for a few days once you get home, keep the blinds pulled if you can." As she spoke, she headed over and pulled the roman shades down halfway. "No TV, no devices. They'll be discharging you this morning but not until your doctor makes her rounds. Shouldn't be long though. Enough time to order breakfast if you're hungry."

After handing Jenna a menu that had been on the far counter, the nurse took her vitals.

Home. It would be nice to get home to her quiet apartment and her plants. Jenna could nap as long as she wanted, and no one would disturb her. But, after months of being perfectly fine with the status quo of being contentedly single after another failed stab at dating, the idea of going home to no one after a brush with whatever last night's accident was—maybe not death but certainly tragedy— seemed, well, lonely.

Maybe she'd stay at Monica's a couple days instead. There was a private guest bedroom in the recently refinished basement with a private bathroom and a far nicer bathtub than the coffin-like squeeze she had in her apartment tub. Even before thinking of the boys and how their exuberant yells and train whistles would pound in her head, Stuart's concerned face popped into mind.

No, Jenna wouldn't be headed there.

She was one hundred percent over him. She just hated that she needed to remind herself of that every so often.

Jenna glanced at the clock. It wasn't even eight yet. Far too early to call a stranger and thank him for his generosity. On the other hand, it was too late to call her sister. The household would no doubt be in chaos as she and Stuart wrangled the boys out the door before Monica's appointment.

Under the covers, Jenna flexed her toes as she perused the menu. It was, at least, the perfect time for pancakes. Maybe some turkey sausage and orange juice too. In the grand scheme of things, it was a small win, but she'd take it.

Chapter 7

JAKE RESTED HIS FOREHEAD on the steering wheel of the four-year-old Subaru Forester belonging to his downstairs neighbor, Sheila. You couldn't ask for a better neighbor than one who'd let you borrow her car on a moment's notice. Even after you'd crashed yours less than twenty-four hours prior. It likely helped that, among other things, he'd been shoveling snow off sidewalks for the past three years whenever maintenance was delayed, and he'd unclogged her kitchen sink twice.

Good relationships with neighbors or not, this morning's errand wasn't leaving Jake with much to feel thankful for. He'd driven around to the back of the shelter and reversed into one of the open parking spaces. Perhaps he should've pulled in straight instead and not have had to look in the review mirror as he was parking. Then he might not have seen how the dog had begun trembling as soon as they'd pulled in. Had he not noticed this till after he'd gotten out of the car, Jake would've had momentum on his side. An object in motion stays in motion.

Less than thirty feet away, a sign over a metal door at the back of the building read "Intakes." Not a far walk. A minute at most, even with a terrified dog. Then he'd be able to get on with his life.

"It was only for one night, me keeping you." In the back seat, the dog had begun panting, and Jake was reminded of the stress the poor guy had been in last night after the accident. Even so, this wasn't his dog. Wasn't his problem.

You made it your problem when you took him in.

"My lifestyle doesn't suit dog ownership, which is exactly why I don't have one," he said, his tone the no-nonsense one he used in the courtroom the few and far times he had reason for entering one. "Long days at the office. Mandatory travel every couple of months."

The dog whined and licked his lips nervously. Jake glanced back once more. The dog's entire body had begun shaking, all the way down to his legs. He was erect, tethered in the middle seat atop a utility blanket Jake had spread out to protect Sheila's seats.

It seemed like Jake was withholding information not to admit aloud that his law firm had adopted a dog-friendly policy as a perk for getting people back in the office after the pandemic. If he acknowledged that, he'd have to follow it up with how the policy extended only to well-behaved dogs.

"From the sound of it, you're basically untrainable. You belong in the country, herding a flock of sheep or goats or whatever. You should have instincts for that. Where you don't belong is in a thousand-square-foot condo where you'd be cooped up all day. Gnawing away at every last piece of my furniture."

The dog barked once, his high-pitched yip piercing Jake's ears.

What Jake kept thinking back to was how, early this morning, he'd woken up on the couch and, before discovering the massive crick in his neck from both the accident and sleeping without a pillow all night, he'd spied the dog crowded in the chair next to the couch, asleep on his back, his back legs sticking up over the armrest and his head dangling off the front. As soon as Jake had moved, the dog jerked awake and bounded to his feet, but for those few seconds before that, he'd seemed peaceful and, well, ordinary, like there was no reason he should be labeled untrainable.

A car pulling into the lot caught Jake's attention. "Lookie here, maybe we can follow someone in. Another dog would get your mind off things, wouldn't it?"

But it was a lone woman, unaccompanied by a dog. As she passed in front of the Forester, she slowed, eyeing both Jake and the dog behind him with enough scrutiny that Jake turned on the power long enough to roll down his window. "Alice?"

"That's me. I know you told me your name, but I forgot it. I haven't, however, forgotten the dog you're bringing in."

"Jake. I'm Jake."

She gave a curt nod. "There a reason you're sitting in the parking lot looking like you swallowed a fish, Jake?"

At best guess, she was in her late fifties. Judging by the wrinkles along her forehead and mouth and the wear in her shoes, she'd worked hard most of her life. Given how he'd put money on most of it being in careers like the one she had here, he gave her a pass for her directness, but he had no qualms matching it. "You said he's been returned before? Do you remember why?"

She huffed as she stepped closer to the open window. At first sight of her approach, the dog had begun emitting a low and continuous growl that got louder the closer she came. "That would depend on which time. He's only been through here twice, but I looked up his chip last night after you called. Counting you now, this will be drop-off number seven for him. The other four were at a shelter in St. Louis."

The hair on Jake's forearms stood on end at hearing the number seven spoken in this context after his and Jenna's conversation last night and how he'd been calling the dog Number Seven most of the morning.

"And I'm guessing most of their reasons boil down to the same thing," she continued. "People come in and fall for a sharp-looking dog like him—a dog like that looks good in photos and on a leash—but they aren't thinking about the whole package. He ain't missing anything upstairs, I'll say that for him. But he's got all the energy his breed is supposed to have and some to spare. Doesn't trust people, neither, which tells me he's been mistreated somewhere along the line. Runs every chance he gets."

There it was, reason enough to pass him along to someone else who might be able do better by him. Jake didn't have time for that kind of mess...or the skill set either. "You're no kill here, right?"

"We fill up and stop intakes rather than euthanize. The only dogs ever put to sleep here are done so out of medical or behavioral necessity."

"And what constitutes a behavioral necessity?"

She tucked a lock of silver hair behind her ear, her mouth turning down in a deeper frown. "Aggression toward humans, not toward other dogs."

In the silence that followed, it was clear she heard the dog's continuous growling as well as he did. "He's scared, that's all."

Her eyebrows lifted. "You're an expert on dog behavior then?"

Jake drummed his fingers on the dashboard. He couldn't believe he was about to say this. "Do you ever foster dogs while they're up for adoption? Help them get some training in and all."

"Don't tell me you're thinking you can do better." It came out with a laugh. "'Cuz you can't. Once he's through those doors, this one won't be going anywhere till there's a landowner wanting to take him on, not after failing with this last family."

"A landowner? In the middle of Chicago. How often does that happen?" If there was one thing Jake didn't like, it was being told what he could and couldn't do. He'd put himself through law school while working full-time despite repeated warnings that it couldn't be done.

"I won't lie," she said. "It might take a while at that."

"Then let me foster him. He doesn't belong locked in a kennel. I bet that's half his problem."

Alice looked between him and the dog and pinched her bottom lip between her thumb and forefinger. "We love our foster families, but we're picky with them. A dog like him, you'll need a minimum of a six-foot fence around your yard *and* an active support network."

Jake had neither of these things. As of last night, he no longer even had a girlfriend to help out, and most of his family was back home in Wisconsin.

"You'd need to prove you're a seasoned trainer, too, or commit to getting him to one regularly."

Jake frowned. "What I can offer him is a lot better than being stuck in a kennel for God knows how long." He jutted his thumb toward the dog. "Look how he's shaking at being back here."

Alice stared at Jake long and hard. "I work intakes, not fostering. Bethany works with our foster families, and she's as overprotective as they come. I'm telling you now, you don't have a chance."

"Well, hell. That's not very helpful, is it?"

"I guess that depends on how you look at the glass you're being handed."

Jake shook his head.

"My point is you ain't through those doors yet, are you?"

Jake looked from her to the building, then back. "You mean I can just go?"

"The only thing I can tell you is what I told you yesterday on the phone." She motioned toward the intake door. "Until the dog is through that door, he's owned by the family who last paid his adoption fees. If you want to give him a shot, I suggest you work it out with them. In a couple weeks, if you're still interested in fostering him out for adoption—and you're still willing to walk that mile with him—give me a call, and I'll go to bat for you with Bethany to make it official. But not before. Now, if you'll excuse me, I came in early today for a reason, and right now, I'm not addressing it."

She turned and headed for the building, her face as stern as it had been the whole conversation, so much so, Jake wondered if he imagined the wink she offered at the last second.

The dog stopped growling as soon as she walked off, but his tremble didn't abate. Jake sat there, dumbfounded. After a full minute or two had passed, he started the ignition and drove around to the front of the building at a snail's pace, like maybe this whole thing would unfold differently if he went slow enough.

"What the hell am I doing?" He flipped on his blinker at the entrance and shook his head. He didn't have a six-foot fence. He didn't have a fence of any height. Or a *yard* for that matter.

A glance at the dog's profile in the rearview mirror showed he was looking back toward the shelter with what was likely an expression of similar confusion.

"Yeah, you have no idea how lucky you are, Number Seven. You were about as close as could be to earning that nickname of yours. By the skin of your teeth."

Abruptly, the dog pressed forward to the full extent of his seat belt, and for a split second, his cold nose brushed against the back of Jake's neck before he went back to looking out the window, his shivers subsiding. Jake figured this split-second gesture was likely as much thanks as he'd ever get, and a bit surprisingly, he didn't mind.

Chapter 8

ONCE AGAIN, JENNA GLANCED at Jake's number on the back of the business card, then at the clock on the wall. Reading it caused less strain than it had last night. Maybe the broken night's sleep had helped, or maybe the pain medicine was doing its job. In either case, she'd take what she could get.

It was a quarter to ten. She'd had breakfast, dozed, and talked to her doctor. Once they finished her release paperwork, Jenna could get out of here. If Monica didn't call before they finished the paperwork, she'd get an Uber because she had no interest in waiting around, and she wasn't in the mood to call a friend and then have to go into detail explaining what had happened.

There was one person she did want to call though. One person she wouldn't have to explain much to, and given all he'd done for her, she certainly owed him the gesture…and an apology about the dog. Picking up the corded phone, Jenna dialed his number before she could change her mind.

He answered on the third ring. "Jake speaking." Judging by the background noise, he was in a car.

Jenna's hello momentarily fled as the comforting sound of his voice washed over her, placing her right back in the dark, cold truck with him kneeling at her side and holding her hand as he reassured her that help was on the way.

"Hello?" he repeated.

Either say something or hang up already. "Hey, Jake. This is Jenna.

From last night. I found your number on the back of a policeman's card and wanted to call and thank you."

"Jenna." Something about the short pause before he spoke again warmed her heart. "I'm glad you called. I've been thinking about you. How are you? In the hospital still, I take it."

"Yeah, they wanted to keep me overnight since it seems I lost consciousness after the accident for a bit."

"That was quite the blow you took. How are you feeling today?"

"Ahh, much better than last night. It was hard to stay awake at first, which I'm guessing you noticed, but I'm much more clear-headed now."

"That's great, but I wouldn't be surprised if you're fighting fatigue for a while."

"Yeah, the doctor came in this morning and said I should plan on several naps the next couple of days."

"Naps are one prescription that aren't handed out enough, if you ask me."

Jenna laughed for the first time all morning, and pain shot across her head. Even so, it didn't wipe the smile from her face.

"Have you heard when you're being released?"

"Soon, actually. Just waiting on the paperwork."

"Oh yeah? If you need a ride, I'm like twelve minutes from Rush Medical right now. I'd be happy to swing by and take you home. Or wherever it is you're headed."

Jenna opened her mouth, but all her words stuck inside. She wanted to say yes, but would that be crazy? He was effectively a stranger.

"There's something I should tell you anyway," he added into her silence.

"Okay" slipped out before a more crafted response rose to the surface.

"Great! And I remember you saying you didn't have your phone, so I'll call this number when I pull in. No rush if you're still waiting for release. Just come out when you're ready. I'll be in a Subaru Forester. Piney green. Not mine, my neighbor's."

Jenna thanked him and hung up, warmth zinging her cheeks. What was it he had to tell her? He'd been entirely too friendly and concerned to be about to go off on her over a responsibility he never should've been handed—taking the dog in for her. This reminded her that the whole purpose of her call had been to both thank him and apologize for asking him that, but the conversation had taken a very different turn. Better to do it in person, anyway.

And why was he in a neighbor's car? Had his car been hit too? It had been so dark last night, and she'd been so out of it that she'd asked nothing about it. Or at least if she had, she didn't remember.

Moving slowly from the stiffness that had set in, Jenna headed for the bathroom to look in the mirror and winced as the bright fluorescent light buzzed on. She had bed head and no makeup, and her Irish American complexion was especially pale. Above her left temple, a thin line of hair had been shaved away for the eleven stitches she'd needed. The Steri-Strips extending from the corner of her hair disappeared into her hairline and made it appear as if she had one eyebrow raised skeptically. The only thing she had going for her at the moment was that her blue-green eyes seemed particularly bright. Perhaps the knock on the head had done it.

She splashed water on her face and used the hospital-grade toothbrush she'd been given to brush her teeth, then headed over—moving slowly to keep the headache at bay—to the bench and her bag of clothes.

Her jaw nearly hit the floor to discover how much dried blood covered her jacket and sweater. Joseph's Percy sticker was still stuck to it, and it was somehow unstained.

There'd be no wearing her sweater home. Not without looking like she was trying out for a part in a zombie apocalypse film. Her jeans weren't much better. Dried blood had pooled on top of the left thigh next to the pocket.

Because walking out of here wearing her hospital garb was likely unacceptable, she wandered down the hall to see if there might be something she could borrow. As it turned out, the hospital's lost and found was overflowing, and the med tech promised to swing by with a few options. "They've been sanitized," she added in a way that sounded like she got that question often.

Jenna thanked her and headed back to her room, refusing to think about why they might've been left behind.

By the time she'd repacked her clothes and left a message with her sister—who Jenna was doing her best not to worry about, given the circumstances—the med tech had arrived with an armful of clothes. Jenna chose a pair of sweatpants several sizes too big and a long-sleeved T-shirt that she'd wash and return at the first opportunity.

By the time Jenna had changed and signed the final release paperwork, her room phone was ringing.

"Sorry about that. Took a bit longer with traffic," Jake said.

"It's perfect timing actually. They're bringing up a wheelchair. Hospital policy. Otherwise, I'm ready to go."

"No problem. I'm parked outside the main entrance. That work for you?"

"I think so. If not, I'll find it."

"See you soon then."

Jenna's heart fluttered. Should she be doing this? Getting a ride with a total stranger when she didn't even have her cell phone to place a call should she need to? Probably not, but instinct told her it was okay. He wasn't a creep. He was the kind of guy who waited in the rain with a stranger and took responsibility for a dog because he'd been asked to.

Five minutes later, Jenna was being wheeled outside into the chilly and bright March day. As Jake stepped out of the piney-green Subaru Forester to greet her, it occurred to her that the wheelchair had likely saved her from stumbling over her own two feet. Her patchy memory of last night hadn't done him justice. He was the ogle-out-of-the-corner-of-your-eye kind of cute. Tall and lean with strong shoulders, dark-brown, almost-black hair that was a touch messed at the top, something between a short beard and a five-o'clock shadow lining his cheeks and jaw, and one of the kindest smiles she'd ever seen.

As a gust of wind swept in, the tech wasted no time retreating into the hospital, while Jenna clutched an overstuffed hospital bag, her purse slung over one shoulder. "Wow. I guess that cold front really moved through, huh?" The lake wind was as invigorating as the cup of coffee that she'd been advised to skip would've been.

"Yeah, but we're finally into March, at least. February really hung on if you ask me." He motioned toward her. "You look great though, considering what you went through…"

"Thanks." Jenna lifted her bag. "Given the stains on these, I have a better sense of how bad I must've looked last night."

"You gave me a scare; that's for sure." Jake jogged over to the car and opened the front passenger door. "I'll crank up the heat in a second."

Jenna froze in place as she spotted what was in the back seat. Not what, *who*. The dog.

"Yeah…about that." Jake dragged a hand through his hair sheepishly. "I figured it was better to tell you in person."

"I–I figured you would've taken him already. I'm so sorry…"

"It's not your fault. I tried. I just couldn't do it."

"You never should've *had* to. I never should've asked you. Honestly, everything was so hazy after I got here that I wasn't even sure I had." The dog was staring at her through the side window and wagged his tail a beat or two in recognition. Jenna stepped closer to the rear passenger door and leaned down to see him better. "I've been worried about him."

"I didn't know him before, but my guess is he's no worse for wear thanks to that seat belt."

"Thank goodness. I'm so sorry for all of it."

"If it helps, I haven't done anything for anyone in a long time that I wasn't committed to doing. I wanted to take him last night."

"It helps," Jenna said with a nod. "My sister... It ended up being a terrible month for her, the dog aside. She's got two kids four and under. I don't know what she was thinking. Actually, I do. She thought he'd help get some energy out of the boys, but things went the opposite direction."

A short laugh escaped him at this last part. "A little over twelve hours in, I can see where that could happen."

"If you don't mind me asking, what happened with taking him in last night?"

"The timing was tight. I didn't even try. Then this morning I showed up, but I couldn't get out of the car." He lifted an eyebrow. "I talked to one of the staff there though. Nothing's official, but I guess I'm fostering him for a while—given your sister's okay with it. Until he enters through their doors and the paperwork is signed, technically, he belongs to her."

"Wow. That's wonderful!" The exclamation sent pain shooting through her head, and she toned it down a few notches. "I don't see how she could be anything less than ecstatic."

"That's good—I guess." A sheepish smile lit his face, showing a set of great teeth, the sight of which made Jenna's mouth water just a touch. "Between me and you, I'm kind of freaking out about the decision."

"It's a big decision. I can see why." Jenna thought back to the scratches across her sister's expensive table. She was still standing outside the open car door, but he waved her in and waited, closing it behind her, a gesture she didn't need but appreciated all the same.

As he headed around the front of the car, she turned to look back at the dog. "Hey, boy." He was eyeing her intently. It happened so fast that she almost missed it, but his tail flicked in response. She wanted to reach back and sink her hand in that furry coat but knew he wouldn't appreciate it. He endured petting with a similar dislike to a dog on a table at the vet's office about to get its shots. "I owe you the biggest bully stick in the world, you know that? I'm so sorry I didn't see that car coming. Thank God you're okay."

As Jake sat down and started the car, Jenna was reminded that the last time she'd been this close to him, she'd been holding his hand. After buckling in and tucking her purse behind her feet, she kept her hands busy with the handle of the bag on her lap. "Want that in the trunk?" he asked. "I can run it back there for you."

"No thanks. I'm fine."

Jake grabbed his phone from the center console and pulled up his maps app. "Want to give me your address so you don't have to navigate?"

"Sure." Jenna spouted it off, and Jake's eyebrows lifted.

"Seriously? You're in Logan Square? You're like a mile or two from me. Tops. I would never have guessed that last night considering how we were halfway across town when you got hit."

"I was coming from my sister's and heading to the shelter." With the doors closed, Jenna could smell equal parts leather and pine coming off Jake, blended with a touch of nervous dog floating up from the back seat. "And thanks. For picking me up. For last night. I guess I should be more sorry about what you're taking on, but I'm not sorry for him, that's for sure. He hates crates. A shelter kennel wouldn't have been much better."

A hint of a frown formed as he headed out of the hospital drive. "That doesn't bode well for my apartment if I can't crate him when I'm gone, does it? Last night he got a leg of my coffee table while I was in the shower and a shoe while right in front of me."

Jenna bit her lip. "Maybe in this case it's better for the honeymoon to end before it really begins. He's got what it takes to be a good dog though, I'm sure of it. He's great with little kids. Supersmart too. If there's any help you need, I'm happy to do what I can. I mean it."

"Any reason you didn't want to take him on then? When your sister couldn't."

"Several." Meeting his gaze as he glanced her way after pulling onto the Eisenhower Expressway, Jenna gave a little shrug. "First, it was a sister thing. At least, a my-sister thing. I tried to dissuade her from adopting such a high-energy dog in the first place, as chaotic as her life is, and I step in more than I should most of the time, anyway. On top of that, I sort of have two jobs I'm juggling. I don't have time for a dog unless it's a couch potato, but even then, I'd feel bad to leave one alone so long."

"What'd you mean by that? You *sort of* have two jobs."

Jenna shrugged. "I have one that pays the bills that I could do without and one that I'd love to see pay more of the bills than it does."

Jake lifted a finger off the steering wheel. "Let me guess. You're a writer."

"Not even close," Jenna said with a laugh. "And why a writer?"

"I don't know. Seems like everybody's a writer these days. So…" Jake cocked an eyebrow. "You gonna tell me, or do I have to guess?"

Jenna smiled. "You most certainly have to guess now."

"Why's that?"

"Because you're so sure of yourself."

Jake made a stabbing motion toward his chest, grinning. "Ouch."

"In a good way." She brushed her fingers over his wrist. "Confident but not conceited, at least judging by first impressions."

"Thank you, though now I feel pressure to get the next guess right."

"Not on my end."

He narrowed his gaze in thought. "How about a food artist of some sort? What's the in thing lately? Boozy cakes?"

Jenna laughed. "Definitely not. I love to cook but hardly ever bake, but no, my side gig has nothing to do with food. Or booze."

"But you do make something?"

Jenna narrowed her eyes. "Depends on your definition of 'make.'"

"Candles?"

"Nope."

"Stained glass?"

"That's a jump, but no." A glance at his phone showed they had sixteen minutes till they reached her place. "Tell you what. If you haven't guessed by the time we get my place, I'll show you."

In the back seat, the dog let out a single woof that pierced the air. When Jenna glanced back, he was looking between them, ears pricked forward, an inquisitive look in his eyes. "I wonder if he has to go to the bathroom or if he's just tired of the car. He's not very patient, this one."

"He went before we headed out earlier, but I'll take him out when we get to your place, so long as you don't mind."

Jenna shrugged. "Sure thing. He's been there once before with my sister and the boys. Mostly he stayed outside in the yard and ran around in the snow."

Jake glanced her way sharply. "I thought you said you had an apartment."

"Well, technically, my place is in a hundred-and-something-year-old house. The owners live on the bottom floor. The top floor was split in two during the Depression. I share it with a resident cardiologist at Rush who pretty much only comes home to sleep. My favorite thing about where I live is the yard out back, and it's proved to be of no interest to anyone but me."

"Any chance that yard is fenced?"

Jenna nodded. "It's no Lincoln Park, but yeah, it's adequately sized and adequately fenced."

"How tall is that fence? Because I hear he's a jumper."

"Six feet, I guess. Your typical privacy fence."

Jake shook his head and a smile played on his lips. "A minute or so ago when you said if there was anything you could do…"

"Yeah?"

"I'm in a second-story condo of a building with a backyard that's been converted to garages and a handful of stone patios for the residents. There are six of us owners all together. A couple-foot-wide strip of landscaping separates the patios from the garages, but there's no fence and not a blade of grass anywhere."

"You're welcome to use my yard, but if you're looking for a place for him to go to the bathroom, from what I see of dog walkers, it's typically along the sidewalk, decomposable bag in tow."

"I'm not worried about that. I plan to jog with him, but I need a place to work him that's free of other dogs for now. You're a mile or so away. You've got a fenced-in yard. What more could I ask for?"

Suddenly Jenna's world seemed to be lining up in a very unexpected way, and her pulse raced at the idea of getting to know this person beside her better. She glanced back at the dog to find that his full attention was still homed in on them. "Dog, it seems this is your lucky day in more ways than one. But I can tell you right now, I'm going to rope off my garden before anything significant comes up." Turning her attention back to Jake, she added, "Last time he was there, he was all over it, but it was covered in snow, so it was fine."

"You garden?"

Jenna nodded.

He gave her a discerning glance. "I can see that about you."

"Is it the hospital lost and found or lack of any makeup that speaks to you more?"

He laughed. "No, there's just a calmness about you. Like a tree that holds steady in a storm. It's easy to envision someone like that gardening."

"Says the same man who just asked if I made boozy cakes." It was a deflection—her go-to reaction when something touched her unexpectedly.

Jake lifted an eyebrow. "Maybe the best thing about all this is it'll give me a chance to get to know you better."

And Jenna figured maybe, just maybe it was her lucky day too.

Chapter 9

As THE DOG DASHED from spot to spot in Jenna's backyard, sniffing along the fence line and swishing his bushy tail, Jake trailed after him. After they'd entered through a locked gate in the alley, Jenna headed inside through a back patio door to change clothes, disappearing up a flight of stairs that led to her apartment.

The yard was a good size for the area, maybe a third of an acre. Most of it was covered with winter-dormant grass, and there were just enough bare patches that, after last night's rain, he was glad he'd put down the thick utility blanket to protect Sheila's back seat on the ride home. As it was only March 1st, the surrounding garden and landscaping beds were predominantly bare or had been cut back from last year's growth.

A quaint gardener's shed stood in the corner, and Jake headed over. Judging by the thick width of the wooden board siding, it was nearly as old as the house. While the boards had likely been painted over a handful of times, they were currently a fresh shade of light moss and were lined by single-pane windows with off-white trim. Jake figured the windows were original too. No one bought single panes any longer.

The storm door at the front stood out in its newness. The top half was glass, and Jake walked up for a better look. A variety of house plants of all sizes lined shelves with grow lights hanging over the top. He recognized a few—African violets, aloe, and jade—but the rest were simply plants to him. Additional light streamed in through a solar window that had been cut into the peaked roof at one point. The shed was no bigger than eight by eight, but it was tidy and quaint, and a radiator lined the far floor, no doubt keeping the plants alive during Chicago winters.

Jake spotted a variety of empty painted pots stacked on one of the lowest shelves. Below that, lining the floor were long, sturdy benches with circular holes of varying sizes drilled along their length. They'd been designed for transport, no doubt. Jake thought of the older-model Tacoma Jenna had been driving and suspected they'd fit perfectly into the back—or would've. There was zero doubt in his mind that the truck had been totaled.

This was what Jenna did? Suddenly, he was in his Jeep next to her in the rain again at the light, watching her try not to cry and wanting to know more about her. He never would've guessed this.

"I brought a key to show you the inside, if you'd like."

As he looked over, Jake clamped his jaw tight to lock down an expression of surprise, one that likely still lit his eyes. In the couple of minutes she'd been gone, Jenna had slipped on a pair of jeans that hugged her hips and thighs and a clingy gray V-neck sweater that accented her curves and breasts and brought out her remarkable blue-green eyes. She'd brought out a jacket, too, but had laid it over a chair before walking over to join him.

He wanted to tell her she was beautiful, but strangers didn't do that anymore.

"This is what you do?" he asked with a nod toward the door.

"It is, though I can't say I started out intending to do it," she said with a shrug. "I wanted a dog but was having a terrible time keeping a plant alive, so the quest began. It's just sort of evolved the last couple of years, and it's been fun."

"It's awesome. Orders of magnitude better than boozy cakes." He liked it when what he said made her smile or laugh, liked the way it lit her eyes too.

A smile lingered on her lips. "The last couple of minutes of the drive when you still hadn't guessed, I thought it might be fun to tell you grow lights were involved, figuring you'd think I was growing the only thing most people are using grow lights for nowadays."

"You'd have been right at that."

She slipped off a coil wristband that held a single key and stepped around him to unlock the door. Jake caught a hint of something spa-like as she passed and resisted the temptation to lean in to better define it. She'd brushed through her thick, wavy hair while inside too. Aside from a hint of dark circles under her eyes and the crescent-moon-shaped stitching just visible at times arching from her temple, she looked no worse for wear from last night.

"Actually, that's what the last tenant used this place for. He was in the apartment across from me when I moved in four years ago. Not too long after I got here, he moved to Oregon to grow it for a career. He left a mess in here, and if you know anything about growing weed, it's that it smells. At the time, I was still mostly just figuring out how to keep a houseplant healthy, and I wanted to get into gardening." She shrugged. "It's evolved into this."

Jenna pulled open the door and waved him in. Jake did a quick scan of the yard for the dog first. He was standing at the edge of the patio near where Jenna had placed her coat, watching them, head cocked. "Good boy, Seven." The slightest flick of his tail told Jake he was listening.

"Seven?" Jenna asked as she stepped in behind him.

"Yeah, I meant to tell you that earlier. I don't know how much of our conversation last night you remember given that bump on the head you got."

"Bits and pieces only."

"I figured." Judging by the blush warming her cheeks, Jake suspected that one of those bits and pieces was the unexpected intimacy of that shared wait for the ambulance. "At one point, we were talking about him, and you couldn't remember his name. From what you said, your sister's family had been trying out different names, like six or seven of them, you said. Then this morning, I found out he's been dropped six times at shelters already."

Her jaw dropped. "Six! Oh, poor guy. That explains so much."

"I bet. Had I left him there today, it would've been drop-off number seven. Felt a bit like serendipity since all night last night I called him Number Seven. This morning, I've been sticking with just Seven, and I think it works. Assuming there's no objection to that from you or your sister."

"You're the one taking him in. You get to call him whatever you'd like." She fell quiet a second. "Seven. I like it. It fits him a lot better than the Thomas the Tank Engine names my nephews were trying to stick him with."

Jake chuckled. "The thing I need to remember is that I'm only fostering. Like you, I'm busy with work, and I have to travel here and there. I'd hate to leave a dog alone that much. Taking him on for a couple months and hopefully helping calm him down a bit seems like the project I've been wanting." He jutted his thumb toward the plants. "Nothing like this, but it's a start."

Jenna brushed her fingers over his arm for the quickest second. "Yeah, it is."

It seemed they both became aware of the small, enclosed space they were sharing at the same time. It was warm and bright in here and smelled of the earth, but it was also completely shut off from the busyness of the Logan Square neighborhood, and their two bodies took up most of the space not taken up by plants. Jenna stepped back and tucked a lock of hair behind her ear, but doing so made her wince.

He reached out but was quick to pull his hand back. Less than twelve hours ago, he'd been in a committed relationship with someone entirely different. If he had one hard-and-fast rule, it was taking enough of a breather between relationships, no matter how long he'd been considering getting out of the last one. Maybe romance was off the table with her, but it didn't stop him from caring. "You hurting much?"

"Not too bad. The stitches only hurt when I forget and touch my hair. My head's a little worse. Bright lights, the sun, even the dancing shadows from the trees on the way here—it's a lot to process. Those sunglasses you lent me really helped."

"I bet, and if you've had enough conversation, I can head out. You don't want to overdo it."

"I'm okay for now. The pain meds they have me on should last another hour or so, then I'll close every blind I have and bury myself under the covers for a bit," she said with a smile.

Because he was too drawn in by that smile of hers, he turned back to the plants. "So, you buy wholesale, then resell them or grow them from seeds or what?"

"Both, depending on the plant. Some are easier to start from seeds or cuttings than others."

He sank onto his heels in front of the lower shelf of terra-cotta pots and picked up a brightly painted one. It was a stunning mandala of teals and oranges painted into the shape of a flower. Other mandala-painted pots had animal or whimsical shapes. Some pots were simpler in design, a variety of bright dots or crisp, wavy lines. A few had sayings instead of pictures. He smiled at one that read "Breathe, Release, Reciprocate." Perfect phrase for a potted plant. "What about these? Where do you get them? They're great."

"That's the other half of it. I paint them."

"You painted these?" he asked, standing up with the one in his hand. "Then you *are* an artist! They're incredible." At one point on the ride here, he'd thrown the label out there, but then he'd glanced over and noticed how she was keeping her eyes closed because of the brightness of the day and fished out Sheila's spare sunglasses from the console for her.

"I paint terra-cotta pots mostly from pictures I find online." His answering look must've said "So what?" because she was quick to add, "I majored in premed and haven't had an art class since high school. I'm hardly an artist."

"You really aren't about to tell me that it's the class that makes the artist, are you? Certainly, history proves otherwise."

"That's different," she said with a wave of her hand.

Jake pulled back from debating with her, given her concussion. "Then we'll agree to disagree. So, you match the plants with pots and sell them where?"

"In season, at the farmers market off Milwaukee or at pop-up craft fairs and events. Offseason, through Instagram when I can, though that's hard because I can't ship the plants, but I do sell a decent number of pots that way."

"I'm not surprised." He set the pot down on the shelf, careful not to bump it against any others. "I'm impressed though. Very. Mind if I ask if you're running this as an LLC or as a sole proprietorship?"

"That's a little out of left field, but a sole proprietorship. Why?"

"Sorry. That's the lawyer in me." When her eyebrows lifted in surprise, he added, "Not the type of lawyer whose face you're going to see on billboards and at bus stops. I'm in corporate law. Patents actually. And as to why I asked, that's a conversation for another day, assuming you'd like to have it, and believe me, I wouldn't be trying to sell you anything."

"Okay, yeah, sure. But you being a lawyer, I can see that."

"How so?"

"Well, you're pretty to the point for starters." She laughed at something in his expression. "In a good way."

"I'm not sure my ex-girlfriend would agree with that last bit, but with what I do for a living, I've made a habit of getting to the point. I'm not surprised that it spills over into my personal life."

When a short silence fell between them, Jenna glanced toward the door. "We should probably check on Seven before he digs a zillion holes."

"Yeah, no kidding."

When they stepped out, Seven was still in the same spot on the patio, but he was stretched out on the stone, licking his jowls. They both spotted Jenna's jacket at the same time. It was on the ground, and part of it was locked under his front paws.

"Any chance you had food in one of those jacket pockets?"

Seven jumped to his feet, hackles raising, and dashed off to the far side of the yard.

Jenna made a face. "Now that I think about it, yeah."

As she hung back long enough to lock the storm door, Jake jogged over and picked the fleece jacket off the ground. One front pocket had been turned inside out, but other than that and a half-dozen muddy paw prints, it was unharmed. "He didn't eat through the material, at least."

"I wouldn't have lost sleep over it if he had. It's what I wear while I'm out here," she said, joining him. "The last thing I remember putting in one of the pockets are the treats from when he was running around out here in the snow, and we couldn't catch him for anything. I guess there were still a couple in there."

Jake raised an eyebrow. "And he helped himself."

"That's him for you. He's a counter surfer too. I've heard border collies manage their weight well, but he's all stomach and pent-up energy, that one."

He offered the jacket her way, and their fingers brushed. A jolt shot through Jake, one he didn't want to acknowledge. "Looks like other than needing to be laundered, no harm was done."

"Well, after last night, I have the perfect heavy-soil load to add to it. And he's quick like that. Training opportunities are there and gone before you can blink."

On the far side of the yard, Seven was watching intently. When

Jake looked his way, the dog dipped his head. "Looks like he realizes he did something he shouldn't have, at least. But yeah, I noticed that about training opportunities last night when he gnawed my table during the ten minutes I was in the shower."

Jenna clicked her tongue. "Sometimes it's like he's casing us."

"I hope that calculating mind of his will work in my favor eventually, but maybe that's pie-in-the-sky hope." Jake shoved his hands in his pockets. "I should go. Let you rest. Once you confirm it with your landlord, so long as your offer stands for me to use the yard, I'd appreciate it. It's perfect for what I'll be doing with him."

"Of course. You're doing a good thing for a good dog. I meant it when I said I'd like to help however I can, use of the yard included."

Jake raised an eyebrow. "I fully expect to take you up on it." He glanced over at Seven who was still observing them with a cautious air that made Jake wonder if he was braced for a beating and not yet aware that was something Jake would never give.

"Want me to run up and get a hunk of cheese or something to help you catch him? He loves cheese, and he isn't caught easily, especially when he's on the defensive like this."

Jake shook his head. "Nah, if you don't mind, I'll wait him out for a bit. Let him come to me when he's ready. I'll lock the gate when I step out."

"Sure. Take as long as you need. I'll head upstairs." Her expression seemed to fall the tiniest bit, and he could only guess that maybe she didn't want this to end either.

"Thanks, Jenna. Rest well, and text me later. Let me know how you're doing."

"I will. Once I get my phone back from my sister, that is." She held out a hand, and he had no choice but to take it. As soon as his hand closed over hers, the feeling of intimacy he'd experienced last night flooded in—just as he expected—and he didn't want to let go. Maybe she'd been looking for a handshake, but they stood there unmoving, hands grasped, as one second slipped into the next, and Jake contemplated the complete inadequacy of words, even to a man who relied on them for a living.

He was the first to break the connection, letting go and shoving his hand back into his pocket. She headed inside, and the door fell shut behind her. He listened, unmoving, as she headed up the steps until her footsteps became inaudible.

Swallowing hard, Jake turned to Seven, who was still watching him intently, and made an obvious show of picking up the leash and walking out into the center of the yard. There, he sank into a squat and waited, leash clip in plain sight. "Come on, Seven, time to go home."

———

Jenna closed her apartment door behind her and leaned against it, collecting herself. The trip up the steep flight of stairs that she shared with her neighbor had her head pounding, but this didn't account for the blood rushing through her veins or explain the smile on her face.

Aside from the plant business, life had been milling along at a steady pace for so long now. Then bam, last night's accident had been a lightning strike, and nothing since promised the same easy predictability.

Stepping away from the door, Jenna flattened one hand against her heart. The happy, bubbly feeling pressing back wasn't entirely unfamiliar, but she'd be a liar to pretend it hadn't been a long time since she'd caught herself crushing on someone the way she was on Jake.

Since dropping out of med school six years ago, Jenna had dated a whopping total of three guys, all of whom she'd met online. She still remembered how, despite their relatively accurate online profiles, her heart had sunk at least a little with each first in-person meeting. Convincing herself it was more about her own expectations than chemistry, she'd continued on to date each of them, Kyle for a month, Ben for five months, and Anu for just over a year.

Yet, if she were being entirely truthful, Jenna remembered exactly the last time she'd gotten butterflies like this. When she'd first met Stuart. Those early months of med school when it was mostly just the two of them, studying or grabbing a bite after class, before Monica walked into the picture or, more aptly, the bar where they were hanging out to celebrate the end of exam week. By the end of the night, Jenna's world split into a thousand fragments.

The part of her that never wanted to hurt like that again shot up a warning flare. Not only did she know very little about the man in her backyard, but it was safer being single. Easier to manage her two jobs, friendships, and last but not least, the space Monica and her nephews took up in her life.

Jenna kicked out of her shoes and treaded as lightly as possible to the sunroom at the back of her apartment where she did all her painting. As bright as it was outside, it would be difficult for Jake to see inside through the glass should he glance this way. Even so, Jenna hung back a few feet as she gazed down on the yard.

Jake was in the center of it, resting on his heels, leash in hand. The dog was trotting in a wide arc around him, his bushy tail lifted and his full attention on Jake. At this angle, Jenna could see that Jake was talking to him—softly, she was betting, but with enough inflection to hold the dog's attention.

Twenty bucks right now that's never going to work. There was only one thing her sister and Stuart had gotten that dog to get leashed up over this last month, and it was food.

But with this new information, it made more sense. Jenna would never fault Seven for anything ever again. Six shelters. In less than two years! It hardly seemed possible. To have family after family give up on him. No wonder he counter-surfed and battled being kenneled the way he did. Thinking of how good he'd been with Sam and Joseph despite all this had tears stinging her eyes.

Down in the yard, Jake rolled his neck slowly from side to side and lingered on the right side, making Jenna wonder if it had anything to do with the accident. On the car ride here, after he'd handed Jenna the sunglasses, they'd talked about it some. Turns out, Jenna's truck had been flung into the grill of Jake's Jeep hard enough that his airbags had deployed too. He'd insisted the damage seemed minimal and that he'd been unhurt, and hopefully this was all true.

No question, it warmed her toward him even more than the way he was taking on the dog like this, but the flutterflies—Sam's word for butterflies—had been stirring even before she'd spotted Seven in the back of the car. And now, Jenna's insides were at war, shooting off reminders of what it had felt like to fall after experiencing stirrings like this and still stirring just as wildly all the same.

Jenna was about to back away and leave them to it when Jake gave a little nod and a flick of the wrist, sending the leash clip in a tight circle. So abruptly it seemed like a trick of the eye, Seven changed course and trotted straight to him, stopping a few feet away. With a measured assuredness, Jake reached out and clipped the leash onto his collar.

As soon as he was hooked, Seven dashed to the far end of the leash and dropped into a play bow, barking at Jake and wagging his tail. Jake's face lit with happiness as he stood up. "Good boy! Good boy, Seven!" was audible through the glass.

Jenna watched them leave, Seven bucking alongside Jake like a rodeo horse along the way to the gate, and Jake letting him do it.

"What do you know?" she mumbled. "I owe someone twenty bucks over that, that's for sure." Maybe, Jenna realized, it was time to bet on possibility over probability.

Chapter 10

EYES BLINKING OPEN, JENNA attempted to get a handle on the disorientation crowding in ahead of the rush of memories of the last twenty-four hours. She was snuggled in bed under her comforter, and soft sounds of someone working in the kitchen pressed in through the closed door. For a second, her mind flashed to Jake. *Because him being in your apartment wouldn't be creepy.*

Aside from Jenna's landlords, only one person had a key to this place—her sister. Monica was the only person who could be given a pass for entering without permission. Jenna winced as she got to her feet. From the midspine up, it'd be a challenge to find a spot that didn't range from sore to darn-right painful. Clearly, the hospital-grade pain meds had worn off. She crossed her fingers that the over-the-counter stuff would do the trick, but she wasn't holding out much hope.

"Hey there," she said after peering around the corner to where her sister was working at the gas stove.

Monica gave a start. "Oh, hey, sleepyhead. I didn't hear you get up. When I came in twenty minutes ago, you were out like a light."

Jenna glanced at the clock. It was a quarter to five. She'd slept through the better part of the day without waking once. "For a few hours, at that, it turns out. So, how'd it go this morning? And yay to grilled cheese." The sight of the sandwiches in the cast-iron skillet—thick, buttered artisan bread with layers of cheese—set Jenna's mouth to watering.

"I figured in the land of grilled-cheese-worthy days, this one takes the cheese. Stuart's taking the boys to his parents' house in Lake Forest for dinner so that you and I can hang out for a while." Monica raised the hand with the spatula and rolled her eyes. "And don't even get me started on how he can't handle the boys alone at the house for a couple hours. He likes to fill up the minutes, that one."

Jenna cocked an eyebrow, then winced from the pain rippling across her stitches.

"In case you hadn't yet noticed the level of this impending deliciousness, I stopped on the way over and picked up a loaf of D'Amato's bread. I got a bag of fresh kettle chips too. And I picked up Margie's ice cream for dessert."

"Mmm. I'd say we're set then." Parched, she poured a glass of water from the pitcher in the fridge and drank it all.

"In case there was any question as to what the last couple days of worry and nausea have done to my appetite," Monica said with a nod toward the pan. "I'm making three instead of two."

Monica ate like a picky toddler when stressed, so her getting an appetite back promised things hadn't gone too awry earlier. Jenna didn't think it was her imagination that her sister looked less on edge, too, but quite possibly that was because of the cozy lounge pants and hoodie she was wearing or the way all her hair was piled on top of her head with a few lose strands spilling down her neck. "Nice. But about today—it went okay?"

"Yeah, it went alright. My boob itches and burns a little. We should get the results tomorrow, but Stuart pressed the doctor, and she seems to be leaning toward duct ectasia like she mentioned before. I kind of wish I hadn't heard that because now I've floated into the land of 'I don't have cancer and everything's going to be okay.'" Her voice pitched suddenly. "Is it too much to ask to nurse one more baby through her first year?"

Monica and Stuart weren't finding out the baby's sex, but ever since the day Monica had found out she was pregnant with baby number three, she'd been on a kick that it was going to be a girl.

"No, it isn't too much to ask." Jenna stepped close and squeezed her sister's arm.

"Enough about my stuff." Monica blinked back the tears fighting their way to the surface. "How are you doing? About last night… I never should've asked you to take him back for me. I get that now."

Jenna shrugged. "I'm okay. I have through the end of next week off work, if I need it. We'll see how it goes."

"Oh my God! Are those stitches?" Monica was really looking at her for the first time, her darker eyes lighting with concern. "What cut you?"

"Just the impact, I guess. The window didn't break."

"You should never have been driving around in a twenty-year-old truck. Stuart and I could've helped you get something newer."

"That's a hard pass on taking money from you two, and you know it." Seeing the way Monica pursed her lips, Jenna knew this meant her sister was saving the conversation for another time.

"Let me see, will you?"

Jenna cautiously lifted her hair as Monica leaned close. "It's sore today, so no touching."

"That's a lot of stitches! You hit your head hard, Jenna." Monica frowned, and a crease populated between her brows. "Did you call Dad and tell him yet?"

"How could I? You've had my phone, and besides, I slept all afternoon."

"I figured you'd have called him from the hospital."

Jenna made an effort to keep her expression unchanging. "He's got his own stuff to worry about."

"He'll want to know." Monica's mouth turned down in a frown. "He's really been trying lately. Stopping by every week to see the boys and all."

"I know. I'll call him tomorrow." When anyone asked, Jenna hardly ever let on that her relationship with her dad was anything other than fine, and the truth of it was, if there was strain there, it was on her part. He might have a new family and career that kept him busy, but he was trying. He'd lived out in Skokie ever since remarrying back when she and Monica were in college. His new family wasn't why she held a grudge though. She'd reached a place of forgiveness over how he'd drank himself out of a job in the years after their mom died. What she had a hard time getting past was that, from sixth grade on when her mom passed, she and her sister had mostly been raised by their maternal grandparents. It had been hard enough to lose her mom; having her dad shut down like that had been devastating.

"Will you?" Monica's tone carried a hint of doubt.

"Yeah. I will." Jenna meant it too.

After searching her gaze another second or two, her sister gave a single nod, and the stress left her face as quickly as it had appeared— classic Monica. She flipped off the burner but left the cast-iron skillet in place. "Couch or table, where're we eating this?"

"Couch." Jenna pulled down two of the ceramic plates she'd bought at the market where she sold her plants. She'd been adding to the collection little by little. The plates, which had been locally cast, were earthy and beautiful, and meals always seemed better on them. "Want me to put on the kettle for tea?"

"One step ahead of you. It's already hot."

"Perfect." Jenna headed for the pantry next. "In caffeine-free options, we're limited to chamomile and blueberry."

"Blueberry."

Jenna poured two steaming cups and headed into the living room where she placed them on coasters. After loading their plates with sandwiches and kettle chips, Monica followed her in. "You're still mad at me, aren't you? I can tell. You're acting weird."

Jenna had just finished getting comfortable on the couch under a blanket and had closed her eyes a second, noticing where all the stiffness had set in, but she pulled herself upright at her sister's question. "Monica, I'm not mad. I'm not feeling the greatest, but I'm not mad."

"You were mad last night. Before you got in the accident."

"I was mad at myself, if I was mad at anyone."

"For taking the dog when you didn't want to?"

"Yeah, pretty much." Resting her plate on her lap, Jenna took a bite of the sandwich and let out a groan of approval. "This is your best grilled cheese yet," she mumbled. "Delicious."

After taking her own bite, Monica closed her eyes and leaned back against the couch. "I needed this." She flattened a hand against her stomach. "Please, baby, let me keep it down." Part and parcel to Monica's belief in the baby being a girl was the fact that she'd contended with more morning sickness this time than in either of her pregnancies with the boys. "I brought the Havarti, but I used your cheddar. They should get married, those two cheeses."

"Or at least make a baby." After another bite, Jenna wiped her mouth with a linen napkin. "Hey, so, about the dog…there's something you need to know."

Monica's expression instantly crumbled. "You said he wasn't hurt!"

"He wasn't. He's no worse for wear, promise. But he's not at the shelter." When Monica looked like she was about to bombard her with questions, Jenna held up a hand and gave her a short play-by-play of what had happened—how Jake had taken Seven in last night, and how he made the decision this morning to foster him.

When she finished, Monica shook her head. "I don't get it. Why would some random guy you were in an accident with be willing to foster my dog?"

Jenna's skin pricked at the *my* rolling off her sister's tongue, given how she'd surrendered him. Then again, Monica had been his primary caregiver for close to a month, even if it hadn't worked out. "I don't know Jake well enough to answer that, but whether I should've or not, I asked him to step in last night, and he did. And I'm guessing he likes dogs, Seven in particular, or he wouldn't be doing this."

"Seven?"

"Yeah, that's what we're—he's—calling him. When Jake realized he'd been turned in six times already, he couldn't be the one to make it a seventh."

Monica shook her head in disbelief. "I had no idea he'd been turned in six times before. That's terribly sad, but also kind of vindicating."

"To know you weren't the only person he wouldn't listen to?"

"Yeah, not even close." Suddenly, Monica gave her a sharp look. "How exactly do you know all this? Your phone's still in my purse. Please don't tell me this guy is how you got home from the hospital. You said a friend was picking you up, not a stranger."

The fact that Jenna was quick to drop her sister's gaze likely said it all. "With all you had going on this morning, I figured less is more when it came to details in your voicemail." When her sister was still staring at her hard, she added, "He gave his number to the officer who did the accident report. I called him, and he was in the area. Turns out, he lives a couple blocks off California, like a five-minute drive from here."

Monica cocked her head. "First, I'd like to note that you called him from the hospital and not Dad, but we'll circle back to that another time. Second, how old is he? And is he gay?"

Jenna coughed over a mouthful of sandwich even though she knew her sister's train of thought. Monica was a firm believer that her gay guy friends were kinder than her straight ones, and no doubt this train of thought circled back to Jake taking the dog. "Ah, my age, a little older maybe, and I doubt he's gay. He mentioned an ex-girlfriend."

"This whole thing seems off." Monica pointed a finger her direction. "If he isn't gay, then clearly he's doing this because he wants to get in your pants."

"Surely you remember how hard it is to handle that dog. If that's what he was interested in—which I'm not saying I think he is—there are easier ways to ask a girl out than to foster a high-energy border collie."

"But you're clearly thinking of saying yes if he does?"

Jenna shook her head. "Are we even *having* the same conversation, because I'm pretty sure we aren't."

Monica's eyes narrowed even more. "What if he's a stalker? What if he *caused* the accident?"

Jenna groaned. "He couldn't have caused the accident." Setting her plate on the coffee table, she leaned forward and made a play-by-play of the accident using her remote and two paperbacks that she pulled from a basket at the side of the couch—at least as much of the accident as she'd pieced together, given her disjointed memory of last night. "So, see," she finished up, "it was me who was rammed into him."

When Monica reluctantly accepted this, Jenna figured she might as well get the second part of the story out there too. "Since he lives so close to here and he doesn't have a yard of his own, I told him he could use the backyard to let Seven run."

Monica blinked. "Says the girl who's always talking about boundaries. You're giving a perfect stranger free rein of your backyard?"

"I'm not *always* talking about boundaries, thank you." Even as she said this, Jenna's earlier ease with this newly formed arrangement threatened to disintegrate. What *had* she been thinking, telling a perfect stranger he could use the yard whenever he wanted? Closing her eyes, she pressed her thumb into her temple.

Reading into her silence, Monica added, "Just be on your guard, if you're set on doing this."

"I thought you'd be happy about the dog."

"Of course, I'm happy about the dog!"

Jenna settled back against the couch again. "Look, I'm going to trust my instincts here. And you know that's a lot harder to do for me than it is for you."

"Tell me about it," Monica mumbled over a bite of sandwich.

Jenna opted to ignore the side comment. "Jake's a good guy. He stayed at my side and waited for an ambulance with me. He's been nothing but polite and respectful. And as you know, he's going to have his hands full with Seven."

"Seeing how the boys couldn't wear him down, and they're nonstop unless they're asleep, I don't doubt that." Meeting her gaze, Monica held up a finger. "And fine. I'll let it go, but there's a weird energy here. That's all I'm saying."

Jenna thought back to the goodbye she'd exchanged with Jake earlier and the feeling that had bubbled up inside her as he held on to her hand for a few seconds longer than needed. Monica was closer to her than anyone else on this planet. Without fail, she knew when Jenna was two days out from her period, so much so that Jenna now set her calendar by it. Monica knew when she was mad and not ready to admit it. Knew a thousand other things too.

Maybe that's what all this was. Maybe Monica was just picking up on what Jenna wasn't ready to admit aloud yet.

Chapter 11

JAKE HEADED UP THE interior stairs to his condo for the second time in minutes, loaded down with an extra-large crate and a deluxe, memory foam dog bed and wondered if Seven had gotten into anything during his short trip to the car for the rest of the stuff. Given the way Seven's world had been shaken up so dramatically in the last twenty-four hours, the dog had been relatively well behaved in the mega-sized pet store as Jake had filled up a jumbo cart to overflowing with arguably as many nonessentials as essentials. Seven had followed along at the far reach of the leash, sniffing at various items, occasionally attempting to run off with a few, and appearing dejected when the leash prevented him from doing so.

With a bit of luck, the balls, tug toys, ropes, antlers, and variety of other chews that had made the cut today would prove more attractive than Jake's shoes or the legs of his coffee table.

As Jake pushed open the door and stepped in, Seven pounced to his feet, tail tucked and head dipped, the antler Jake had just handed him locked in his jaws. "Good boy, Seven. It's your antler. You can chew it all day long, if you want."

Jake left the door ajar as he dropped the fluffy bed on the floor and set the box containing the crate against the wall. It had been a packed day. After leaving Jenna's, he'd spent an hour on the phone talking to his car insurance company, picked up a rental—a base model Ford Edge that had him missing his Jeep but was better than Ubering or inconveniencing Sheila by borrowing her car any more than necessary—and headed to his office with Seven in tow. His coworkers had ogled over the dog while Jake packed up a few items he'd need access to when working from home the next few days.

Doubling back to shut the door, Jake pulled his phone from his back pocket. No sense pretending he wasn't hoping to spy a call or text from Jenna, but he found nothing more than a single text from his brother that Jake would respond to in a bit. On the bright side, the deluge of texts that had started coming in from Alyssa this morning—some pointed and angry, others seeming to offer space for Jake to rescind last night's declaration—had waned over the last several hours. This meant it was time to devote five or ten minutes to composing a reply that was empathetic but left no room for her to hope for reconciliation.

He was headed for the kitchen when it dawned on him how silent Seven had become. No more sounds of antler gnawing. Looking around, Jake realized the dog was nowhere to be seen. Earlier, Jake had shut both his bedroom and office doors because he wasn't sure how potty trained Seven was. Jake walked around the couch, peering under the coffee table, and even jogged down the short hallway to peer into the bathroom.

"The door!" Jogging over, Jake threw open his exterior condo door. Sure enough, Seven was at the bottom of the steps, lying on the small stoop, antler lodged between his front paws, chewing contentedly, and gazing out the exterior glass door. "Man, you're lightning fast." Jake clapped against his thigh. "Come on, boy. No going outside, and no escaping out that door when the next person walks through it. The last thing we need is you running free along the streets of Chicago."

Seven raised his head and peered up the stairs, his folded-at-the-tip black ears pricked forward in attention. His tail flicked once, and Jake clapped his thigh a second time. "Let's go, Seven. Come on."

No such luck. Jake jogged down the stairs two at time, and it must've been too fast for Seven's comfort. The dog leaped to his feet and backed into the corner of the small entryway, his antler dangling like a cigarette, the hair on the back of his neck rising.

Jake sank onto his heels. "I'm not going to take that from you, buddy, and I'm definitely not going to hurt you." Seven was intelligent. It was easy to spot in the sharpness of his gaze. Jake motioned up the stairs. "Come on. Upstairs. Let's go."

Still holding the antler like a cigarette, Seven looked between Jake and the stairs but didn't move. When Jake reached for his collar, Seven took off in a flash, bounding up the stairs in a few strides and in through the open apartment door. "And here I figured we'd made some progress after that moment in the yard earlier."

Upstairs—after shutting the door behind him—Jake went to work cutting off tags and opening packages. "You know, my brother and I didn't get this much stuff under the tree at Christmas. Combined." He squeezed the squeaker inside a nylon tug toy, and Seven perked instantly, dropping the antler and sitting up at attention. "*Oh yeah*, the infamous squeaky toy. Canine catnip. Wanna play?"

Seven's tail flicked back and forth hopefully, and Jake squeezed the toy again, dangling it Seven's way. Seven trotted in a half circle around Jake, eyeing the tug toy. After a little, he dove in, clearly wanting to grab it and dash off, but Jake held firm to the other end, hoping to entice him into play. Seven wasn't having it. Letting go, he dashed to the far end of the room and sank onto his haunches, staring at Jake expectantly.

"Hey, don't look so dejected, will you?" Jake squeezed it again. "Come on. Come play with me. A couple seconds of solid play, and it's yours."

Jake beckoned him over with a few more squeaks and calm verbal encouragement, but Seven didn't take the bait. After a few minutes, Jake switched tactics and grabbed a tennis ball. The first bounce got Seven off his haunches, and each bounce after that had him prancing closer and closer, tail raised in excitement. Before long, Seven was so amped up, he was getting as much lift as a bull in a rodeo chute. "Come on, Seven. Let's play."

Quick as a flash of lightning, Seven dove in and stole the ball midbounce, then skittered away, practically slipping on the hardwood floors, tail tucked. "That's alright. We've got more."

While Seven chewed on that ball, Jake pulled out a second one from the supposedly indestructible storage basket that would be holding Seven's multitude of toys and began bouncing that one. After a while, they fell into a pattern of sorts, Seven dashing in and stealing the tennis ball Jake was bouncing, and Jake starting up again after confiscating the abandoned one.

He talked the whole time, careful not to let too much energy creep into his tone. If he wanted Seven to learn anything about him, it was that he could be trusted. "This is what you call positive interaction, bud. Something tells me you haven't had too terribly much of it. But you might as well get used to it because what you don't know is that for the next week or so, when it comes to dinner and treats, they're being served straight from my hands. Before you know it, you'll cuddle right up to be petted, I bet."

The next time Seven dashed in to steal the ball, Jake had a split-second opportunity to offer a single pat on Seven's shoulder blade. Letting out a high-pitched yip, Seven dashed to the other side of the room and stared at him, the tennis ball falling abandoned onto the hardwood floor.

Jake frowned. "Was that really so bad?"

Seven barked and flicked his tail.

"Well, maybe it'll take a bit longer than a week, but I'll tell you right now, I won't give up on you, Seven. Somebody's got to be in your corner, and it might as well be me."

Chapter 12

THE DOG'S BELLY CRAMPED in anticipation of the tempting new kibble within such easy reach, and his mouth watered at the taste of the few morsels of kibble still on his tongue that the man had tossed his way. The man was on the floor, hand outstretched and heaped with food, beckoning the dog with his words and body language. Most of the words the dog didn't understand, but when the man wanted his attention, he used one word over and over, and the dog knew the drill. Here he would be Seven. Come, Seven. Sit, Seven. Stay, Seven. No, Seven.

Names were temporary things, and they changed wherever the dog went. The man could call him whatever he wanted, but the dog wouldn't let it become part of his identity the way he once had when he thought he'd forever be Benny, his first given name. No one had called the dog by that name in so long it carried the dust of cobwebs in his memory.

Here, the dog would be Seven until one day it, too, blended into the dust of memory. The commands the man had been using were simple ones the dog had mastered as a puppy, but it didn't make him any more eager to perform them for him. Commands led to obedience and obedience—the imperfection of it—led to pain and abandonment, or so the dog had seen time and again.

This wasn't the first time one of the humans keeping him had attempted to connect with him, had offered him treats from his hand or tempted him with fun things to chew and play with, but the more distance the dog kept, the less likely he was to get a swift kick when he displeased the man. Humans, the dog had learned, doled out praise and pleasure when he pleased them, kicks when he displeased them, and a cage when he really displeased them.

The man hadn't forced the dog into a cage yet, but he had one here now. It was at the ready, door ajar, deliciously tempting rawhide inside, waiting for the dog to sneak in and grab it—no thank you. He'd choose hunger and pent-up energy that a good chew could relieve him of over confinement. He'd choose scoldings and swift kicks in the hind end over confinement too.

He'd done his best to show the man this, but humans were slower to understand dog communication than dogs were human communication.

The man tossed another piece of kibble his way, and the dog's stomach cramped again. "More, more, more" his stomach called out.

Getting up, the dog sauntered over to the water bowl just out of reach of the man and drank his fill, though it did little to dull his hunger.

"Hey, Seven, come here, will you? Just a couple pieces. I promise nothing bad will come of it."

The dog looked up from the water bowl and licked his lips. The man's tone was as patient and even as any he'd encountered, quite unlike the man who'd nearly driven the dog out of his mind with hour after hour of confinement in a cage so small the dog hadn't been able to stand tall and lift his head. Of all the times the dog had been in a human's care before being abandoned at a shelter, that had been the only time the dog had been eager to enter one. In shelters, confinement was a given, but in those cages, there was always room enough for a good stretch of the legs or to lie sideways, and food and water were never scarce.

Earlier today, this man had brought him to the shelter where the dog had been abandoned most recently, and the dog's whole body had trembled violently at the thought of being dragged inside, but the man hadn't left him there. This was something that had never happened before.

The dog remembered the hope that had once filled him that if he was good enough, if he listened to the commands of his humans and understood them well enough, he wouldn't end up back in a shelter.

The man tossed him another piece of kibble, and the dog made quick work of it before stretching out on the floor just beyond the man's feet. Ears perked, he looked from the man's outstretched hand to his eyes and back again. There was a gentleness in the man's gaze that called to the dog to step close and let him dole out a petting, but the dog fought against it.

"Come on, Seven. You can do it. Just a little more." The man leaned forward so that his hand was even closer. The dog's mouth watered once again, and a whine slipped from his throat. "Come on, good boy."

Without getting to his feet, Seven scooted forward a bit, wriggling his body along the cool floor. The man met him halfway, his hand stretched to the full extent of his reach.

The dog flicked out his tongue, nabbing a few pieces off the tips of the man's fingers. A few went into his mouth; others fell to the floor. The dog licked them up with his tongue, then stared at the man's outstretched hand still heaped with savory bits of kibble.

"Come on, boy. You've got this."

Scooting forward a bit more, the dog took another tentative lick and nabbed a few pieces, then another one. While he was chomping the bits down, the man reached into the container at his side and filled his hand again. This time, he didn't stretch out as far, and the dog had to scoot forward for another nibble, but now that he was eating, the food proved impossible to resist. Ready to pounce to his feet at any second, the dog licked and nibbled at the kibble in the man's hand, his tongue occasionally brushing against flesh.

It had been a long time since the dog had trusted a human enough to lick his skin, but eating from the man's hand stirred up memories of his puppyhood and his first human family after leaving the safety of his mom and littermates, back when being around humans filled the dog with joy. How easy it had been then, to let his humans—young and adult alike—scoop him into their arms and burrow their hands in his fur. To press up alongside them as he dozed and savor their warmth. He would've wished to stay with that family forever—to be Benny forever—but his time with them ended in their tears and their clinging to him even as they left him at his first shelter.

The next time the man reached into the container for another scoop of kibble, he came out with a larger mound that he held in both hands, which he hardly extended forward at all. To reach it, the dog needed to raise up onto his front paws and lean in as far as he was able, so close that the man's body heat radiated against the tips of the dog's ears. The dog even grew used to the man's soft exhale brushing against the tip of his nose. He munched bite after bite, and the man proved trustworthy, neither reaching out to touch him nor offering any form of unexpected rebuke.

The dog ate the full scoop, then a second one, and the nearly insatiable hunger inside him began to dull. When he caught himself licking at the salt still on the man's otherwise empty hands, the dog startled and backed up out of easy reach. Empty hands were easy to grab him with, and this was just the time when the dog might be shoved into the cage. Wanting to communicate this, the dog glanced toward the cage, then at the man, before retreating to the other side of the room to clean his jowls along the edge of the rug.

"If that kennel makes you uneasy, you aren't going in it today, but if I'm fostering you, I've got to have it in my arsenal, or something tells me this place would never be the same."

The man got up from the floor, taking the container of kibble with him, and headed into the other room where he ran water and soap over his hands, washing away the delicious smell of kibble with that nonsensical habit humans had. When the man came back in the room, he watched him calmly a moment, rekindling the dog's unease.

"I don't know who hurt you, Seven, but they shouldn't have. It's going to be different from here on out. You'll see. You and I are going to have some fun. I promise."

The dog didn't know what the man was saying, but the tone was hopeful enough that his tail flicked automatically in response as if, deep down, he wanted to meet the man with the same amount of hope that the man seemed to have.

Chapter 13

AFTER HER SISTER LEFT, Jenna found the silence in her apartment to be pervasive. The brightness of the television proved too intense for comfort and reading threatened to stir up a headache. Still, she wasn't yet ready to call it a day, especially given how she'd slept through most of this one. Sketching new designs for her pots proved the only thing both constructive and cathartic, so Jenna sat crossed-legged on her couch, soft music playing in the background, sketching on her notepads.

She'd downplayed it earlier to Jake, but she'd loved drawing ever since she was a kid. She'd stopped in medical school—she'd basically put a stop to everything those two years but eating, breathing, going to school, and studying—but she'd picked it up again not long afterward, and those two years had been the only time since she was little that she'd not found solace in art.

At one point, she'd considered majoring in the subject in college, but hardly anybody could support themselves creating their own art, and she hadn't been willing to risk losing the joy she experienced drawing and painting in a career like graphic design where productivity would, over time, likely trump passion. Besides, back then, Jenna had still been dead set on becoming a doctor and saving the world. Or at the very least, curing it of cancer.

When it came to her terra-cotta pots, Jenna had been at this side business long enough to trust that the ones that sold most quickly were those related to the upcoming season. Several Saint Paddy's

Day-themed pots had been shipped out in the last week or so as her fellow Chicagoans geared up for Saint Patrick's Day. Since the holiday was just around the corner and she had several more out in the shed to get her through the next few weeks, Jenna figured her best bet was to focus any new designs on spring or Easter instead.

A basket of robin-blue eggs would look cute on a pot, or perhaps a string of Easter-egg garland. She could paint an impressive vintage rabbit too. Before painting anything, she polished the idea first by sketching it in a notebook. She was only half-surprised when her hand refused to listen to suggestion and began to sketch something entirely different than planned.

Border collies weren't as easy to sketch as vintage rabbits or Easter-egg garland. Neither were tall, lean guys sitting in the grass, attempting to interact with one. The next time she glanced at the clock, the better part of an hour had passed, and Jenna had three different sketches of Jake and his—albeit temporary—dog.

The fact that she hadn't yet called him even though he'd asked her to do so said as much as the fact that her fingertips were burning to snatch up her phone and press in his number. If she didn't call him soon, it would be too late. And he *had* asked her to check in, hadn't he?

Before she lost her nerve, Jenna grabbed her phone and hammered out his number on her cell. She hit Send and turned on the speaker, then set her phone on the arm of the couch next to her. As soon as it began to ring, doubt flooded in. *Seriously? Why are you calling? Didn't he say to text, not call?*

He answered on the third ring. "Jake speaking."

Jake speaking. Was that always how he answered the phone? Something about it made Jenna's pulse skitter. "Hey, this is Jenna."

"Jenna, hey. I was hoping you'd call."

Her cheeks warmed instantly. "How's Seven doing?"

"Ah, dozing until a second ago when he heard my voice. Now

he's on his feet and looking out the window. So far, I'd say he's either on or off with no middle zone. And mostly on."

"Yeah, I noticed that at my sister's. If only he'd give in and really let himself relax."

"I'm hopeful his second night here will be better. It took some cajoling, but I fed him dinner out of my hands earlier. I've been reading dog training blogs every chance I get, and apparently that helps with the bonding."

"I bet it does." His phone was on speaker, too, and there was soft music in the background, too quiet for her to tell the genre. Was that Johnny Cash, maybe? "And judging by what I saw while he was at my sister's, I'm sure that wasn't easy to do."

"It took about a half hour or so, but I finally wore him down. What's clearly not helping matters is the kennel I bought earlier. I've got it set up in the room so he gets used to it. You warned me, but he really hates them, doesn't he?"

"Yeah, he does."

"He keeps looking at it like it's going to snatch him up."

"Aww. Poor puppy."

"I'm hoping he gets used to this one. It was the biggest they had. I think I could just about nap in there. I'm working from home the next couple of days, but I have to be in court next Friday, and there's no taking him with me there."

"Well, let me know if I can help somehow. I'm likely off all week next week because of the accident."

"Thanks. I may take you up on that. How's your head, by the way?"

"It's okay. I slept most of the day, then my sister came over and made everything better with grilled cheese." She said it with a laugh, one that Jake returned. She fell quiet a second, savoring the sound of his laughter as it pressed into her space and envisioning the energy of it sticking on to whatever it hit like little dewdrops.

"Grilled cheese can do that, can't it?"

"This one was made on D'Amato's bread, and it was pretty close to perfect."

"Now I want grilled cheese."

"There's a half slice left. If I don't get the midnight munchies, I'll save it for you. If it's still your plan to work with Seven out in the yard tomorrow, that is."

"I'd love to, if your landlords say they're okay with it."

"I should've started with that. I texted them earlier, and yeah, they're good with it. I knew they would be. Like I said earlier, the yard has pretty much been mine to do with as I wish the last couple of years. It was a barren and overgrown mess when I started, so they've had no complaints."

"I bet not."

Silence sat between them for the first time since the call started. Jenna glanced down at her notebook only to see her most recent sketch of Jake and Seven staring back up at her. Guiltily, she snapped it closed.

"Did you pick up a rental yet?" he asked into the silence.

"A rental? Oh, no. The truck was old enough that I had liability only. Now I'm wishing otherwise. Obviously."

"Not to sound like a lawyer, but the driver that hit you was intoxicated. He had full coverage, thankfully, but it wasn't his first DUI. It had been several years since the last one, but he got that one reduced to a nonmoving violation earlier. Expensive but not impossible to do. My point is that you're entitled to a decent settlement, all things considered."

"You found all this out from your insurance company?"

"Not all of it. You'd be surprised by the information that's readily available if you know where to look."

Jenna's heart raced faster. If he'd looked up the other driver, had he looked up her too? If so, what had he found?

"Now you're wondering if I looked you up too," he said into her silence, his tone playful.

Jenna bit her lip. "I suspect you did. Thankfully, I don't have anything to hide."

"No, you don't. You've got a nice Instagram account though. Plants N Pots by Jenna. It's got a nice ring to it."

"Thank you, but no fair," she said with a laugh. "I can hardly even glance at a screen right now, even if I knew where all this readily available information was hiding."

"Then to even the score, I'll have to shake my ghosts out of the closet for you."

Heat zinged Jenna's skin. "Only what you want to share." She reached out and brushed a fingertip over the edge of her phone, wishing he was sitting next to her.

"I should admit I'm seldom called to share much beyond what's easily skimmed off the surface."

Jenna processed this, hoping he'd say more. "A lot of people get by that way."

"My ex-girlfriend would tell you I'm one of them."

Jenna pressed a hand over her chest. Her heart was racing even before he mentioned his ex-girlfriend again. Once again, it was singular and carried a lot of weight. A red flag? Maybe. Maybe just a yellow one.

"What I'd like," he said, "is to make you dinner."

Jenna blinked in surprise at this unexpected turn in the conversation. Whatever color flag she'd picked up on, dinner was something she was willing to commit to. "Oh yeah? Dinner is always nice. Especially when it's homemade."

"Assuming I can cook, right?"

"Your words, not mine."

"I'd ask when you're free, but how about we circle back to that tomorrow once we see how you're feeling?"

Maybe Jake didn't tend to go deep, but he was hands down the most direct person she'd ever met. "Yeah, sure. Makes sense." Another silence fell between them, and Jenna figured it was time to hang up. "Tomorrow then."

"Definitely."

"If I'm not out in my shed when you get here, text me, will you? I'd like to see Seven. And I'll text you the gate code in a sec so you have it." In what she hoped was a playful tone, she added, "And if by chance one of those ghosts you're going to share over dinner is that you're secretly a career criminal, you should know the house and both apartments have different entry codes than the gate, and there's a camera down there too."

Jake chuckled. "If it helps, other than minor traffic violations and underage drinking in college, I've never broken the law."

"It helps."

"Good. Sleep well, Jenna."

"You too."

Jenna hung up and clamped both hands over her mouth, letting the conversation sink in. He'd be over tomorrow, and he'd invited her to dinner. A man she hadn't known existed just a little over twenty-four hours ago. "Jake Stiles, I certainly didn't see you coming, but you've got my attention. That's for sure."

Chapter 14

WHEN SEVEN PROVED TOO wary to approach, Jake pulled a tennis ball from the backpack he'd packed and bounced it on the floor. A smile lit his face at the way Seven's tail instantly relaxed and his ears pricked forward in interest. Underneath that aloof exterior was a dog who wanted to play. "Come on, Seven. Trust me. This is going to be fun. Promise."

Before sunrise this morning, they'd gone for a three-mile walk/jog combo—jogging three or four blocks, then walking one during which Seven got to sniff and explore to his heart's content before they took off at a jog again. By the end, Seven had not only gotten the hang of the routine, but he even seemed to like it. As for Jake, while he'd expected to miss his typical morning routine at the gym, the time outside with a dog by his side had been refreshing.

For the last few hours, Seven had been surprisingly well behaved, chewing on a variety of synthetic and natural bones and antlers and occasionally pacing a few circles around the front room but allowing Jake to get in some focused work. Maybe it was a Saturday, but all the prep for next week's court case still awaited him, and he'd taken most of the day off yesterday. Now, it was nearing noon, and Jake needed to get Seven out again before two back-to-back virtual meetings this afternoon.

The dog's sharp gaze locked on the ball Jake was bouncing, but he refrained from dashing in to capture it like he had yesterday. "A couple steps forward, one step back. That's okay, bud." Putting the ball away and opening the door a few inches as an enticement, Jake sank down to his heels and held the leash in plain view. "You know you want to go outside. No sense pretending you don't."

Five feet away, Seven sank down and stretched low on the floor with a soft whine as he watched Jake intently, his tail flicking back and forth. It took a minute for Jake to notice the way the dog's bright-chocolate gaze occasionally flicked toward the backpack, and he'd lick his lips nervously after doing so. "Is it the backpack, bud? Think there's something in it that might get you? I promise it's full of things you're going to love."

Jake carried it out of sight into the kitchen. As he did, Seven made a dash for the cracked-open door, nudging it open with his nose. Jake lunged for his collar just as the door swung open. Seven's terrified yelp as Jake grabbed hold had his heart sinking to his toes. "Seven, I'm not going to hurt you. Ever."

While he intended to refrain from touching the dog until he'd earned his trust, after Jake clipped on the leash, he rubbed the top of Seven's head between ears that instantly tamped downward. "Is this really so bad? It's what we humans call a bit of affection. It's my hope that you'll come to see its merits."

Judging by Seven's look—which reminded Jake of Ruby's look of resigned consent whenever he'd given her a bath—that would be a long time coming. "There. All done."

Jake circled back for the backpack and offered it out in Seven's direction. Tail lifting in alarm, Seven took a tentative sniff before scooting back to the full reach of the leash. "I've got nothing but Frisbees, balls, treats, and water in here for you, bud. You'll see."

As soon as they were outside, Seven seemed to forget about the backpack slung over Jake's shoulder as he sniffed and scoped out his surroundings for something to chase. Jake pulled out his phone to text Jenna that they were on their way, then settled in for the mile-and-a-half walk mostly along California Avenue. A cold front was expected to roll in later, but for now, the weather was mild, the sky was bright blue pocked with puffy gray clouds, and the walk was enjoyable.

Seven's leash manners were better than Jake would've expected for a dog with his history, which basically meant he didn't pull every single second. Really, he only pulled when he spotted a rabbit in the grass or a squirrel or bird in a tree. Other dogs on the opposite side of the sidewalk proved to be of minimal interest, as did people and cars.

Hearing his phone beep with a new text, Jake slipped it from his pocket. It was Jenna.

Perfect. I'm out in the shed. See you soon.

The timing of it was decidedly less than ideal, but Jake couldn't deny how much he was looking forward to seeing her again today. Downtime between relationships—and a sufficient amount of it—was his cardinal rule, but a voice inside his head argued that this was different. He hadn't gone looking for her. Even so, their worlds had collided hard enough that it was as if he was setting off on an entirely new orbit, high-maintenance border collie in tow. And it was an orbit that every single part of his being told him should have a Jenna in it too.

The ever-logical, left-brained lawyer in him clung to the possibility that, once the last of the adrenaline from the accident wore off, she'd lose some of her appeal, but that certainly hadn't proven to be the case yesterday when he'd been standing out in the yard with her, her hand locked in his. His whole body had hummed with the same kind of electricity that guided him through closing arguments the few and far between times he ended up in a courtroom, reading the energy on the faces of the jury rather than following a pre-rehearsed script. *Trust this*, it promised.

While lying awake last night, he'd decided to give himself a pass on this cardinal rule of his. He'd keep sex off the table, but he was going to let himself get to know her. And he hoped she felt the same way.

Along the walk, Jake was encouraged to spy Seven glancing up at him occasionally. Who ever said the dog was untrainable?

When they made it to the alley behind Jenna's, Seven began to prance ahead at the far end of his leash, his mouth gaping open in a pant. "Clearly nothing's wrong with your memory." The back privacy gate had already been unlocked and was resting slightly ajar, so Jake headed in. The yard was empty, but the storm door to the shed was propped open. "Hey, hey, we're here."

Jenna appeared in the doorway of the garden shed, a smile lighting her face. "Hey there. Glad you made it. How was last night with him?"

She was in jeans and a snug hoodie that hugged her hips, and on her feet were a pair of garden clogs with bright flowers. She'd donned a pair of gloves and had a small, leafy plant cupped in one hand. Unexpectedly, the sight of her reminded Jake of the last time he'd been at his parents' weekend cabin in northern Wisconsin, sitting by the lake barefoot with no cell reception and not a thing to do and realizing that he was as happy as he'd been in a very long time.

"No accidents and nothing was devoured," he said with a grin, "so I'd call it a win."

"I was hoping he'd give you an easy night."

After shutting the gate behind him, Jake asked Seven to sit. Once he'd repeated the command a few times, accompanying it with a closed fist, Seven reluctantly sank to his haunches. He flattened his ears and licked his lips nervously as if bracing for another petting.

When Jake unhooked his leash, Seven dashed off at a sprint, circling the yard twice before slowing to a trot to sniff here and there along the edges of the privacy fence. "You know, I think he'd move just that fast if he was able to slip out the front door of my building."

Leaving the bag and leash on the grass, Jake headed over to the garden shed and stopped a few feet from where Jenna was leaning against the frame of the door. Her thick brown hair was pulled back in a loose ponytail that covered her stitches. Were it not for the slight bruise leaking out from her hairline onto her temple and the hint of dark circles under her eyes that hadn't been there the night of the accident, she wouldn't look like someone who'd so recently taken a hit to the head.

"I'd like to think he knows you're doing a good thing for him."

"Me too, but I'm skeptical. I picked up a cozy dog bed for him yesterday—memory foam and all—but he hasn't done more than sniff it yet. Last night, he slept on the hardwood in the hallway, just outside my bedroom door. I swear, every time I woke up and looked his way, he had one eye open watching me."

Jenna laughed. "If it helps any, my sister and her husband had a trainer come to the house a couple times. They were told his inability to relax is half his problem. It did seem like he calmed down some while he was with them, just not a ton."

"Well, I can't say I know what I'm doing, but I'm pretty stubborn, and I'm determined to wear him down."

Jenna's answering smile lit her eyes. "Well, *I* can't say I've ever known a dog who deserves it more. I'm pulling for you."

"I appreciate that. I put a call into the shelter in St. Louis where he was returned several times before he ended up in Chicago. The trainer who worked with him is supposed to give me a call. I'm hoping at the very least to get a handle on what happened to him."

"That's a great idea." Jenna brushed a gloved hand across her forehead, leaving behind a thin trail of potting soil. Before he realized he was going to do it, Jake swept it away with the base of his thumb.

"So, how about you?" He returned his hand to his side, clenching his fist as a flush warmed her cheeks. "How's your head today?"

"Much better than yesterday, thanks. Staying off screens is helping. So are a lot more z's than I typically get."

"Good. Very good."

Jake wondered if she was thinking about the dinner invitation he'd mentioned last night. Rather than broach it her with it first thing, he nodded toward the inside of the shed. "I take it you're potting new plants today."

"Yeah, for next Saturday's market on Milwaukee. It's the first one of the season. I'll miss the truck, but my sister promised to take me. There's a playground nearby that the boys love."

"Good that you won't miss it. You know what's funny? Now that you mention it, I'm pretty sure I've seen your booth before. I typically swing by that market every few weeks to buy fresh herbs and veggies. Though before meeting you, my interest in plants was limited to edible ones."

Jenna smiled. "It's a start, at least."

He nodded toward the plant with vibrant lime-and-dark-green-striped leaves in her hand. "What's this one?"

"Gorgeous, isn't it? It's a lemon lime maranta. People call them prayer plants because their leaves fold up at night."

Jake's eyebrows lifted. "Oh yeah. I thought it looked familiar. My mom had one when I was a kid. Fascinating the way some plants move to follow the sun—or for the lack of it, I guess."

"My mom had one too. She had a sunroom full of plants, actually, but her maranta was one of the ones I remember most. Its folding leaves seemed a lot more miraculous before I learned in biology class that it was just some well-timed cell division."

Jake grinned. "But still cool. So, you and plants… You get your green thumb from your mom then?"

Her expression fell almost imperceptibly. "Sort of. Back when I was a kid, my sister and I desperately wanted a dog for Christmas one year, but we got plants instead. Once we'd proven we could keep our plants alive, a dog was supposed to be in our future." She nodded toward Seven who was thirty feet away and growling softly at something on the other side of the fence. "My sister's failed adoption with him was the closest either of us has gotten to that. The shelter was having a special adoption day at a pet store next door to where she was picking up a curbside order. It was love at first sight till she realized he was multiplying the chaos in her home rather than helping wear the boys down."

"I can imagine that being the case." He nodded toward the shed. "So, you wanting a dog but needing to know you could keep a plant alive first really was what started this?"

"Pretty much," Jenna said with a shrug. "That was a little over three years ago now. Turns out the plant I had bought was a zebra plant, one of the hardest to keep alive indoors, and while trying to figure it out, I caught the plant bug."

Jake motioned to Seven who was still sniffing along the fence line. "So, how come you never got the dog as a kid?"

Jenna dropped his gaze and transferred the plant from one hand to the other. "My mom got sick that February after we got the plants—Christmas cactuses. Turns out they're like weeds and almost indestructible so long as they get the right amount of sunlight and water, but my sister and I still managed to kill them in the aftermath of her diagnosis."

Jake winced. "I'm sorry. That must've been tough."

"It was." Jenna shifted feet. "I don't usually tell people that."

"If it makes a difference, I'm glad you told me." Jake could tell by the look on her face that whatever happened with her mom hadn't had a happy ending. Her eyes went glossy, and she blinked a few times too many for it to be a coincidence.

She lifted the plant. "I should get this in a pot, and I know you have a dog to train."

"Sure thing. I'm here though, if you ever want to finish that story."

Jenna stared at him hard for a second or two before saying okay, and Jake found himself thinking of how her blue-green eyes were the exact color of the shallower ocean waters he'd seen last month in Fiji.

Turning, Jake headed across the yard as Seven was beginning to dig alongside a fence post. After whistling to get the dog's attention, Jake called out, "No digging," and grabbed a couple tennis balls from the bag. He bounced one of them off the ground high into the air, and Seven's head cocked sideways as he watched it rise. His ears perked forward, and that fluffy tail swished back and forth.

Catching the ball in the air, Jake bounced it again, this time higher, and Seven let out a single excited yip.

Funny, Jake realized—and also not funny—how two very different beings had entered his world at the same time, and it was turning out that both of whom seemed to require the same thing from him—trust. And Jake would be damned if he wasn't intent on earning it.

The next time he caught the ball, he held it out a few seconds before throwing it diagonally about twenty feet or so from Seven. Sure enough, the dog took off at a sprint, dashing after the ball as it ricocheted against the fence, then catching it in his mouth, and sprinting away like he'd caught something special.

"There you go, Seven. Attaboy!"

Jake bounced the second ball and called to Seven to get his attention. Seven dipped into a play bow for a second or two before dashing to the far side of the yard with the urgency of an animal whose tail had caught fire.

In the grand scheme of things, a single play bow wasn't much, but it was a start, and Jake would take what he could get—with the canine who was growing on him, and with the woman who, if Jake were being totally honest, had unintentionally laid claim to a piece of his heart before they'd exchanged a single word.

After finishing up potting a few additional plants, Jenna stepped out of the garden shed to watch Jake work with Seven. Given how the dog had avoided Stuart at all costs the whole time he'd been at his and Monica's house, Jenna wouldn't have expected to see this. Seven was playing with Jake, from afar, but she'd still call it playing. His mouth gaped open in what looked like a grin as he awaited the next ball, and his bushy black-and-white-tipped tail wagged back and forth like a feather duster attacking a shelf of dusty library books.

It was as if he'd realized something good could come out of humans that wasn't limited to dinner or treats. His keen-eyed gaze was zeroed in on Jake as he bounced the ball high into the air and caught it, delaying the next distance throw by a few beats while Seven danced in place in anticipation. The ball Seven had chased after most recently was abandoned at his feet, and he showed no interest in gnawing it. For him, clearly, the reward was the chase.

"It probably goes without saying, but I'm impressed."

Jake grinned. "I really think half the battle with him is going to be giving him the opportunity to release some of that energy."

"I bet you're right."

"Can you imagine what it would feel like to run like that? Like you're leaving gravity behind."

Jenna shook her head. "Mmm...no, I can't. Running and fun haven't commingled in my vocabulary since I was like four or five, but he's built for it, that's for sure."

"No running, huh? I'm betting you do something, though, because I'd have a hard time buying gardening will keep you in that good of shape." He held up a finger, grinning. "To be clear, I meant that respectfully."

Jenna resisted the urge to glance down at her hips and thighs as the compliment settled in. Because it was easier than admitting to herself that he'd noticed her body—the curves, muscle, and padding that helped get her everywhere she needed to go without complaint—she attempted to answer in the nonchalant way of one human who exercised talking to another. "Potting plants is no more calorie burn than a sink full of dishes, but gardening's more work than sedentary hobbies, which is helpful. However, given my love of snacking, I'd say what's worked most in my favor has been not having a vehicle since I left for college. Until I got the truck last year, at least."

Jake cocked an eyebrow. "You went without a car for over a decade? With *these* winters?"

"Yep. I used public transit in winter months, but in warmer ones, I biked or walked everywhere."

"Impressive. I've known several people who've given up a vehicle at one point or another. Most didn't even make it a full year."

"Vehicle ownership certainly has its conveniences; I'll give you that."

Looking away for a moment, Jake threw the ball in the opposite direction from the one Seven was anticipating. "Yeah, it does, but seriously, I'm impressed."

Jenna thanked him as Seven dashed full speed across the yard while chasing down the new ball.

Jogging over to the backpack, Jake pulled out a handful of brightly colored Frisbees. "Maybe I shouldn't push my luck, but it'd be nice to see him add some precision to that speed."

"Are you thinking of agility classes?"

"Once I can get him leashed up easier. Want to join?"

"I'd love to watch, but he really looks like he's on the cusp of something transformative with you. He wouldn't even get caught in the same room with my brother-in-law, if he could help it. The whole time he was there."

A dark look passed over Jake's face. "That's not the only thing that points to abuse at some point in his past. I just hope he decides it's worth giving people another chance."

"I have faith he will, starting with you."

Jake cocked an eyebrow. "I'll do my best not to let either of you down."

Having caught up with the ball, Seven trotted over with it until he was about ten or twelve feet away and dropped it onto the grass. Looking up, he stared intently as Jake tapped the bright-red Frisbee against his knee. As he watched, Seven's head tilted back and forth like a metronome.

Rather than throw the Frisbee clear across the yard the way he had the tennis balls, Jake sent it on a short, gentle trip in Seven's direction. Scooting sideways at it came toward him and landed at his feet, Seven tucked his tail and let out a yip. As he pranced in an arc around it, Seven looked from Jake to the Frisbee as if attempting to decipher if this was a new form of reprimand.

"That's for you, boy." Jake readied the green one next. This time, he aimed a little away from Seven and threw it a touch harder. After a second of indecision as it passed nearby, Seven bounded after it with the enthusiasm of a bull attempting to buck off its rider. Once again, he stopped a few feet from it in the grass to glance back uncertainly at Jake.

Jake had a red one ready. "Come on, Seven, this is for you. Go get it."

He threw it a bit harder and a little farther away. Seven ran after it, barking and wagging his tail. When it landed in the grass, Seven was brave enough this time to step in for a sniff and to clamp a paw over it before backing away like he'd encountered a rattlesnake.

"He's really the cutest." Jenna headed for the first two abandoned Frisbees and one of the nearby tennis balls and carried them to Jake, who only had a yellow Frisbee left in his hand.

"Thanks."

Their fingers brushed in the exchange, and a rush of warmth radiated out from behind Jenna's ears and jaw as his touch stirred up the memory of the security that had swept over her the other night—in spite of the pain and chaos—as he'd held her hand.

The voice of self-doubt crept in on the memory's heels, reminding her car accidents weren't how you met people. This wasn't how someone entered your life with any permanence.

Jenna sucked in a breath. She was no different than Seven, unsure of whether to stop a ball that was already rolling.

On Jake's fourth Frisbee throw, Seven ran alongside it the last few feet. He could've caught it easily, but he didn't seem to understand that this was the point. Instead, as it landed and rolled at an angle across the grass, he pounced on it, wagging his tail, and letting out a single bark.

"Mind if I take some video of this? He's so cute."

"Go for it. It'll be a good marker for his progress." Jake sent another Frisbee sailing his way, and Seven dashed alongside it.

Once it hit the ground, Seven was ready to attack. He pounced on it with his front paws before hesitantly taking it in his mouth and trotting in a victory circle with it sticking straight out in front of him, a saucer of bright blue clamped between his teeth.

Laughing, Jake called out, "Good boy! Good boy, Seven." He sent the red one sailing across the yard, though this time he aimed a bit further way. Dropping the one still in his mouth, Seven sprinted after it, this time knocking it out of the air just before it hit the ground.

Likely it was little more than the joy of the sprint, but soon there was no question as to whether Seven was having fun once more. His bushy tail wagged back and forth, and his mouth gaped open in an easy grin. Looking at Jake, he barked once,and bounded forward.

"Yeah, yeah, I get it. You want another one. Here it comes."

As the red one sailed across the yard, Seven made a dash for it, running alongside it for a few strides before snatching it out of the air with his teeth. Perhaps he'd grabbed it on instinct and was surprised because the act of capturing it caught him off-balance. He rolled in a circle on the grass but popped up onto all fours quickly, shaking himself off, the shiny red disc still clamped between his teeth.

Jenna was ecstatic to have caught the whole thing on video. "Adorable *and* impressive!"

Jake threw a few more Frisbees and continued showering Seven with praise as he went after them. Each time, Seven seemed to grow more and more comfortable with the fact that this new game was, in fact, a game that was safe to play with unbridled enthusiasm, and he started to catch the Frisbees in midair with more and more confidence.

When Seven had run enough that he was panting heavily, Jake paused the game to pour water from a bottle into a plastic take-out container that he pulled from the backpack. Seven trotted over but was hesitant to approach until Jake stepped back a foot. Then he lapped up the water, nearly drinking the bowl dry.

If someone had told her he could make this much progress in a little over a day, Jenna wouldn't have believed it. "I think this is what he's been missing all along, a relationship with a human he can trust and an outlet for all that energy of his."

Jake headed over to stand next to her, shaking his head lightly as he smiled. "Can you do me a favor and continue to remind me that I'm just fostering? Because of all those reasons I had for not getting a dog these last several years, not a one of them has changed."

Arching an eyebrow, Jenna said nothing. Instead, she pulled up the first of a handful of short videos she'd taken and stepped closer so Jake could see the screen. As closely together as they were standing, their arms brushed a few times, and while doing her best to pay attention to the videos, Jenna found her attention warring with the desire to lock in that smell of leather and pine.

While filming, she'd moved the camera back and forth between Jake and the dog. She'd caught Jake's expression of surprised delight after Seven caught a Frisbee in midair for the first time, like a kid opening a favorite Christmas present. She stood next to him, seeing what he was. She hoped he realized it, too, how perfectly the two of them fit together.

"What I'd rather remind you of is how good you two are together," she said as the last video finished.

Without stepping back, Jake looked up from the phone and locked his gaze on her. In the sunlight, his hazel eyes were vivid green outlined in brown and accented by thick, dark eyebrows and his short beard. Just a foot or so separated his mouth from hers, and Jenna wondered what he'd do if she closed in that distance until their lips were touching. Would he kiss her back or step away? Something about the look in his gaze told her he'd lean into it the same way she wanted to.

They were both startled by Jenna's phone abruptly blasting out the first few lines from Maroon 5's song "Payphone" that her sister had programmed to play as the ringtone whenever she called.

Jenna nearly dropped her phone as the world flooded in. "I need to take this. It's my sister. I've been waiting for her call."

Jake stepped back. "Yeah, sure thing."

Jenna headed across the yard for a bit of privacy, her pulse skittering. Monica no doubt had been staring at her phone all day, willing it to ring or for an email to come in, alerting her that the biopsy had been read. Until Jake had showed up and the happy buzz that filled her around him had offered a bit of distraction, Jenna had been on edge too. Working in the garden had eased some of her tension. Smelling the soil and working the roots loose in her hands before repotting the plants had, as always, grounded her. Now, the anxiousness slammed back in with the force of a horse galloping at full speed.

"Hey there." Jenna pressed her ear to the speaker, willing her tone to carry a lightness that had entirely fled.

"It's not cancer!" Monica blurted out, a blubbery-sounding mess.

Jenna folded forward as relief swept over her. She closed her eyes and let out a giant exhale, tears flooding in. "Thank God!"

"It's duct ectasia. For certain." Monica paused to sniff loudly. "I'm getting a round of antibiotics, and if it's still hard and sore, then I'll get it removed after the baby comes."

"Thank heavens, Monica. Now you can just relax and soak up the rest of this pregnancy."

"I know I said I didn't care," Monica continued so fast she cut her off, "but I don't want to lose my boobs. I was prepared for this to be it, for the choice to be made for me—and maybe worse—but now I don't have cancer, and I'm back to having to decide again. Is it wrong to think that's worse?"

Jenna took a second to process her sister's rapid-fire words. "I get what you're saying, but you don't have anything to decide right now. You're still a few months shy of thirty, and you have a human life inside you. That's all you need to think about right now."

"But this isn't going to go away. Mom was thirty-three when she was diagnosed, and I have the gene mutation. I'm more likely to get it than I am not. That's *never* going to go away."

Swiping tears from her cheeks, Jenna took a breath. This right here was life with Monica most of the time. One drama to the next without a breather. "An elective mastectomy isn't your only path forward, remember."

"But it's the best one." In the background, the boys' bickering escalated, and Monica sniffed back her tears. "Joseph won't take his nap, and he's being a little monster. I'm going to drive around for a bit and see if I can get him to fall asleep that way. What are you doing? Can I come pick you up?"

Jenna glanced across the yard where Jake was throwing the Frisbee for Seven, and Monica took her hesitation as refusal.

"It'll be a half hour before I can get there, so you've got a bit," Monica added. "And it'll just be for an hour or so. We can take the boys to the P-A-R-K. Or out for I-C-E C-R-E-A-M."

"Yeah, sure thing. I'll be ready."

Slipping her phone into her pocket, Jenna headed across the yard. After throwing another Frisbee, Jake turned her way. He didn't say a word, but the look on his face made it clear he realized that something big had just played out.

"My sister went in for a biopsy yesterday." Her voice sounded steadier than she'd have expected. "It's not cancer. Thank God. But in the comedown from all the worry, she's a mess. We've all been on edge this last week, waiting to figure out what was going on with her."

He nodded slowly. "I bet that's been rough for everybody. Do you need a ride over there or anything?"

"Thanks, but she's going to load up the boys—they're two and four—and come pick me up." She shrugged. "It's a long story, but the short of it is she's a bit of a mess more often than she isn't."

"And you're the big sister." He didn't have to add "helping keep her together" for her to know that's what he meant.

"I guess you could say it's my other part-time job," she added with a shrug even as a smile crept back onto her face. "She's my sister though. I love her and my little nephews more than anything. But I'm working on better boundaries with her. Her not actually having cancer promises to make that road a bit easier."

"I bet so." On the other side of the yard, Seven was staring their way expectantly, the green Frisbee abandoned at his feet as he panted. Jake jutted his thumb in Seven's direction. "I suspect I've got my own learning curve headed my way with this one."

Jenna laughed, and the lingering tension from the phone call fled. "I'd argue otherwise, but I bet you're right."

Jake threw one more Frisbee in the opposite direction so that Seven had to dash the full length of the yard to catch up with it. It hit the ground and started rolling on its side just before he caught up, and Seven snatched it up, his tail lifted in pride or excitement or both. "Now to tell him it's time to get going," he said with a laugh.

"Cross your fingers he sleeps through my meetings this afternoon, will you?"

"Are you taking him into your office?"

"No, these are virtual, and I'll start out next week from home, too, but like I said yesterday, I'm in court all day this coming Friday, so I'll have to get him in that crate sooner or later."

"Like I said, if you need help that day, let me know."

"I appreciate that. And about that dinner we talked about… I'm heading up to my parents' house in Racine tomorrow, so what about Monday night? My place. No stress whatsoever. The only thing you have to do is show up."

"Yeah, sure. Sounds good."

He bent down and picked up the backpack, hiking it over one shoulder. "What do you like?"

Without him having added "to eat" at the end of that, Jenna's imagination traveled to something entirely different than food, and she swallowed hard. "I'm allergic to shellfish, but other than that, I like pretty much everything."

"Good to know. And what about different ethnicities? Any to steer clear of, because I run the gamut when I cook."

"No, but the fact that you asked has me excited to try your cooking."

"Good." A half smile lit his face. "I'll do my best not to disappoint."

"Same." Jenna caught herself blinking a few too many times after this left her tongue. *Of all the ways you could've responded, that's what came out?*

Jake didn't seem to mind. "You won't."

Because she was having a hard time holding his gaze all of a sudden, Jenna looked over at Seven. "I should probably get going. My sister will be here soon."

"Yeah, sure thing. No need to wait us out. No telling how fast I'll be able to get him leashed."

"See you Monday then."

"Yeah, see you Monday."

Jenna headed inside with her insides buzzing like she had both hands planted on the plasma globe at the Museum of Science and Industry. In those dizzying and painful seconds after the crash, as she'd struggled to come to grips with what had just happened, she'd never have expected it might lead to anything like this.

Chapter 15

JAKE GLANCED AT THE clock. It was just after six, and his Monday had flown by. Dinner wouldn't be done at six thirty when Jenna got here—assuming she'd arrive on time—but it wouldn't be long afterward. After all his talk about liking to cook, he'd ended up choosing something that wasn't overly time-consuming: chicken piccata with sides of roasted veggies and smashed potatoes.

His workday had been too packed putting out one small fire after another to give much thought to cooking anything tonight that he hadn't already mastered without relying on a recipe.

Seven didn't realize it, but he should be thanking his lucky stars Jake had been able to order curbside pickup for the grocery items he hadn't had on hand, therefore relieving Jake of the need to battle locking the dog in the crate in order to run inside the store.

The dog would need to get used to the kennel soon enough and, seeing how Seven had yet to so much as creep inside the propped-open door to snatch the giant rawhide or supposedly irresistible peanut chew waiting for him at the back of it, Jake had doubts about coaxing him in easily.

Rather than begin that battle the first time today, he'd loaded Seven into the rental during his lunch hour and run by for the grocery pickup after a short stop at Jenna's. Seven had gotten to chase down a dozen balls and Frisbees, but that hadn't been enough to dampen the dog's energy level this afternoon.

After that, Jake had risked being late for his one thirty client call to drop off a bag of Alyssa's things that had still been in his apartment, tucked into drawers and closets. He'd suspected she was home but having neither the time nor inclination for a face-to-face conversation while she was undoubtedly still simmering, he'd left it at the door rather than knocking. After getting back to his place, he'd texted that he'd dropped it off. Hopefully he wasn't being overly optimistic that she was getting the closure she needed when she did nothing more than text him back the middle finger emoji.

Finished browning the chicken, Jake transferred the slices to a plate and added the garlic to his favorite cast-iron skillet and let it soften before adding the wine—Sauvignon Blanc—and boiling it until it was reduced by half. As he was adding the chicken stock, lemon zest, thyme, capers, and bay leaf, he glanced over to find Seven standing in the middle of the wide entryway between the kitchen and living room. One of Jake's running shoes was hanging loosely from his mouth. When Jake met his gaze, Seven wagged his tail hopefully, and a laugh erupted before Jake could tamp it down. Sometimes this training thing was hard to do with a straight face.

"Let me guess… You want to go for a walk, huh? What I want to know is how'd you get the coat closet door open? Because I'm ninety-nine percent sure I had it soundly shut, given your affinity for shoes."

Rather than knobs, Jake's interior condo doors had aged bronze lever sets that could be opened with the simple downward press of a hand—or paw—but Jake wasn't ready to give Seven credit for having worked that out already. Until proven otherwise, Jake would stick with the belief that the door had been ajar.

For the most part, Seven had been fairly well behaved these last couple days, chewing only on his toys and antlers, though he still paced circles around the front room with an unsettled intensity Jake had never witnessed in a dog.

He'd caught Seven gnawing on the coffee table leg again earlier this afternoon and had stepped forward to stop him with a firm "No,

Seven" that he intended to follow with an attempt at redirection, but the terrified dog had dashed away into the corner, letting out a howl/whine combo that nearly snapped Jake's heart in two. How long would it take for the dog to trust that Jake was never going to hit him?

"Sorry to be a buzzkill, but I've got a bit longer before I'm finished in here, and that shoe isn't for drooling on. How about you let me get this in the oven, then I'll run you outside for a quick walk before Jenna gets here?"

As if he understood, Seven dropped Jake's cobalt-blue and white-trimmed shoe onto the hardwood floor at his paws. His bushy tail continued swishing slowly back and forth in that semi-hopeful wag of his, like he wasn't ready to admit he wanted to play even though inside he was bursting to do so.

Lowering the gas flame on the stove, Jake headed for the shoe more casually than he'd approached the table leg gnawing earlier today, and Seven did nothing more than back up a few steps at Jake's approach. In the grand scheme of things, it was a small victory, but Jake was taking what he could get.

After returning his unharmed shoe to the closet and firmly shutting the door, Jake pulled out a Nylabone from Seven's toy basket. Seven looked at it with the same displeasure he'd given the piece of broccoli Jake had tossed him earlier. Turning away, Seven headed to the windows to stare out into the street below, and Jake went back to the kitchen with a chuckle in his throat.

Once the broth returned to a boil, Jake returned the seared chicken to the skillet with a pair of long-handled tongs, then set the skillet in the oven next to the stoneware dish of veggies that were already roasting. Last to finish up were the smashed potatoes, but he'd already pre-boiled the baby potatoes and simply needed to toss them with olive oil, crushed garlic, salt, and pepper before smashing them onto a quarter sheet pan using the bottom of a round glass. After sliding them in the oven on the lower rack, Jake set the timer.

Everything would be ready close to the same time, thanks to a bit of finagling with desired cooking temps and placing the dishes in the oven at different times. After he wiped his hands on a towel, Jake glanced over to call Seven from the window, only to find the dog was staring him down again, this time from a bit further away, Jake's shoe dangling from his mouth once more.

Jake cleared his throat to suppress a hearty laugh. "Well, that settles that. You can open doors." This time, Seven lowered Jake's shoe to the hardwood with surprising gentleness, then stepped back, that fluffy tail wagging hopefully. "And there's gotta be five pairs of shoes in there, yet you realize exactly which ones I've been wearing when I take you on a run or to Jenna's."

Jake glanced at his watch. It was closing in on six thirty, and he was one of those cooks who put things he no longer needed away as he worked rather than saving it all for the end, so the kitchen wasn't a disaster, even though it was far from immaculate. Hopefully, Jenna would forgive him a little mess in exchange for a more contented dog.

Jake headed over for his shoe and found that this time it was the left, while last time it had been the right. "At least they're equally slobbered on, huh?" Picking it up off the floor, Jake realized this was one of those times he really needed the advice of a trainer. Was it better for Seven's growth to focus on what he was doing wrong—going for Jake's shoes—or what he was doing right—attempting to communicate his needs, a step toward trust and connection. Until convinced otherwise, Jake opted to go with the latter. "Slightly damp at the heels or not, I wasn't going to wear my running shoes on a date—even though that's not what I should be calling this."

Jake headed for the closet and opened the door, and Seven trailed five or six feet behind, watching him hopefully. After returning the sneaker to the rack, Jake gave his shoes a once-over. He'd stay in the jeans he was already wearing but change into a shirt that didn't smell like he'd been cooking. He kicked out of the Nike athletic sandals he'd been wearing around the house and put them on the rack too. "What do you think? Boat shoes or loafers? No to the oxfords, given how we're staying in."

He glanced back at Seven, whose head was slightly cocked and his ears perked forward.

"Loafers it is." Jake slipped them on, then jogged back to his room to pull on a clean Henley and tossed his T-shirt into the laundry basket. When he came out, Seven pranced by the front door. "If you've been trying to tell me you have to go to the bathroom, I'm gonna feel really bad."

Jake made quick work of grabbing the leash, a couple treats, and a few pet waste bags and knelt by the front door after Seven backed away at his approach. He held up the leash the way he'd been doing, making it clear what he wanted Seven to do.

After quirking his head from side to side a few times, Seven let out a single, ear-piercing bark and bounded forward. When Jake reached for his collar, as always, every muscle in Seven's body seemed to tense as he froze in place, waiting for the click of the leash onto his collar. As soon as he heard it, Seven backed off a few feet and shook himself like he'd just gotten a bath.

"Come on now, Seven. Is a little bit of human contact really so bad?" Seven's pressed-back ears and lowered head expressed that it was. "Watch it now, or I'm going to start telling people you have a flair for the dramatic."

As Seven trotted down the stairs a step or two ahead of him, it hit Jake how it had been a long time, a few years maybe, since his mood had been this light and hopeful. Funny, but up until now, he'd only been thinking about how this fostering thing could make a difference in Seven's life, not about how it could make a difference in his.

—⁓—

The twelve-inch potted plant in Jenna's arms—a vibrant Christmas cactus in its second bloom that would be easy to care for—proved heavier and heavier the further down Milwaukee she made it. The matching saucer for collecting water underneath the pot was in her shoulder bag, and Jenna was half-tempted to slip the plant in there for a block or two as well to give her forearms a breather.

Jake had texted earlier, offering to pick her up, but Jenna had declined, commenting on how the walk over was just what she needed. What she hadn't counted on was what the breezy afternoon was undoubtedly doing to her hair. It would be a wild mess by the time she got to his place, and she hadn't thought to grab a hair tie.

In her back pocket, Jenna's phone buzzed for the second time in a row, which meant her sister was calling. Monica was the only one to consistently call back if her first call wasn't picked up. Knowing she'd keep calling, Jenna moved to the edge of the sidewalk and set the pot down before pressing the speaker button to answer the call. Her arms thanked her for the breather.

"Hey, what's up?"

"Wanna come over tonight? Stuart can run over and get you if you don't want to Uber. He wants to see how you're doing anyway."

That's a hard no. "Can't. I have dinner plans tonight."

"With who?"

"Whom."

"Seriously, you're correcting my 'whoms'?"

Technically, her lack of them, but Jenna figured her sister wouldn't appreciate the comment. "To answer your question, with a friend."

"Which friend?"

Contemplating her reply, Jenna closed her eyes and rolled her neck in a circle in hopes of mitigating a tinge of whiplash.

Monica jumped in before Jenna came up with an answer that her sister was likely to receive well. "You're such a liar. You're seeing the guy from the accident, aren't you?"

"I didn't realize there was a disclaimer as to how long I have to know someone to call them a friend."

"When you want to get in their pants, then they're called a potential love interest, not a friend."

"Considering I haven't given a thought to his pants, then I was right with the label I've granted him." *You've given a little bit of thought to his pants, or at least what's under them, haven't you now?*

Monica huffed. "Where're you meeting him?"

One of the cars passing by was blaring music through open windows, and for a moment, Jenna couldn't hear anything other than the Kid Laroi and Justin Bieber belting out the lyrics to "Stay." Jenna turned away from the street, taking her phone off speaker and pressing it to her ear. "Not far from my place."

"Not far from your place...like *his* place? You seriously aren't going to a stranger's house, are you?"

Jenna pursed her lips. Maybe her sister was irritating her so much because she was right. "If memory serves, you went home with Stuart three hours after meeting him."

"Ouch. And maybe so, but you'd known him a whole semester, so I knew he was safe."

Jenna checked herself. This was not a fight she wanted to have. Besides, she and Monica could go down rabbit holes of who did what faster than anyone she knew. In the background, Jenna could hear the boys starting to fight, and Joseph's escalated pitch warned that tears weren't far behind.

"Can you just trust me, please? I'm not jumping into anything tonight, promise. And I have a phone on me, obviously. If it makes you feel better, I'll text his address."

"Fine, but the boys got a bunch of new books from the library, and they wanted you to read to them."

"Aww, sweet. Tell them they can bring their favorites when they come over Saturday night for me to babysit."

"Fine, and since it's been so long, if you end up getting L-A-I-D tonight—which I'm not saying you should—just remember that new-relationship ecstasy is shockingly short-lived."

"How is it you're both ten steps ahead and prophesying doom at the same time?"

Monica snorted. "If that's not a tagline for untreated anxiety, it should be, and yes, I know that's what I have, but I'm still on the boat of belief that it works in my favor."

After they hung up, Jenna checked the distance remaining to Jake's condo before tucking her phone into her pocket. It was less than three blocks from here, but she'd have to cross the street and head down California. Given the rush-hour traffic and steady stream of cars passing by, Jenna determined to wait for the pedestrian crossing signal at the lone traffic light she still needed to pass.

As she hoisted the pot, a wave of doubt crept over her. A thank-you present for what Jake was doing by taking Seven on like this wasn't out of line, nor was giving him one of her potted plants. What she was doubting was the pot she'd chosen. After seeing how Seven was making such great strides Saturday, Jenna had found herself sketching both dog and caregiver again last night. She'd woken up at first light today, tired and headachy but unable to sleep any longer, and she'd decided to paint her favorite of the sketches on a pot for Jake—one without Jake in it because that would've been too much. *Obviously.*

After a two-hour midday nap during which she'd slept like the dead, she'd glazed the pot and set it in front of a fan to dry. It was of Seven sitting on his haunches, head cocked at an angle and ears perked forward, his paw on a lone red Frisbee in the grass. If Jenna was a reliable judge of her own work, she'd captured a somewhat realistic touch of that charismatic expression of his.

Still, Jake had only committed to fostering him. If Seven proved too much for him—*please, please don't let that be the case*—this gift could turn into a sad reminder of a failed attempt.

But it was too late to back out. Jenna spotted someone waving at her from the opposite side of the street, just over a block ahead. That someone was Jake, with Seven at his side, sniffing the base of a light post.

Hoisting the pot in one arm, Jenna waved back. Because the traffic was too loud for him to hear her, she pointed toward the intersection ahead where there was a crosswalk. For Jake, that was only twenty or so feet behind him. Suddenly, the pot felt weightless as Jenna continued along on her side of the street as nerves threatened to get the best of her. *What if he does want sex tonight? And what if that's all he wants?*

At the intersection, Jenna used her elbow to press the pedestrian crossing button, and before her nerves got the best of her, it was time to cross. After confirming the cars were stopping, she stepped into the crossing lane. Halfway across, a gust of westerly wind picked up, whipping the leaves of the cactus. Jenna felt grains of potting soil flicking against her cheeks at the exact second one landed in her left eye. It was big enough—and painful enough—that her eye immediately began to water.

Because Medusa hair wasn't bad enough.

As she neared the other side, left eye closed tight as tears streamed out from behind clamped lids, Seven must've realized he knew her because he yipped a couple times in greeting. Under different circumstances, this would've made Jenna's day.

"Hey there," Jake said as she closed in the last few feet to the sidewalk. "Looks like you've got a fan. He had to go to the bathroom, so I figured we'd head this way and see if we could spot you." After a pause, he added, "That's not the glare of the sun causing you to squint like that, is it? You okay?"

Jenna shook her head. "Can you take this a sec? It's for you. Obviously." Jenna was too busy bending over to block the wind while attempting to blink the obtrusion out of her eye to notice Jake's reaction, but his tone said enough.

"Damn, Jenna. This is incredible! You nailed that expression of his perfectly. Thank you! It's really well done. And earlier today I was thinking about how I don't have a single plant in my place."

While still doubled over, Jenna offered out a reply. "You're welcome, and if you want more green in your space, you know where to come."

"Yeah, I do." After a pause, he added, "Any luck?"

"Not yet." Whatever was in her eye *hurt.*

Jake's hand closed over the back of her arm. "Hey, let's step over this way out of the wind. If I can see what's in there, I can get it out."

"I think I may have got it." Such a lie, clearly. She could hardly open her eye, and tears were still streaming down it.

With the pot in one arm and the leash around the wrist of the hand holding onto her, Jake guided her to the front of a two-story building out of the direct wind. Before she realized it was going to happen, he set the pot down and stepped close. "Really? Because you look like you're hurting. Can you look up for me?"

He was so close they could be dancing, and Jenna savored the warmth radiating from his body against hers. His thumb brushed over her lower lid, and despite the pain in her eye, Jenna's breath stilled at the experience of his touch. "I see it, and I think I can get it, so long as you don't move."

As she held still, Jake lowered her lid with one finger and used another to sweep out the offending object from the white of her eye. "There. Looks like it was a grain of sand, of all things."

Jenna blinked, and relief swept over her. "Wow, that's better. Thanks. And the offender being a grain of sand isn't actually that random."

"Is there sand in the soil?"

"Yeah, the Christmas cactus is one of those plants that needs good drainage and does better when you mix the soil with sand. Though this is the first time I've managed to get a grain of it in my eye."

She did her best to dry the tears still clinging to her cheek and lower lid without smearing her makeup any more than it undoubtedly already was. *So much for looking better than when I was wheeled out of the hospital.*

Just as Jake was leaning down to pick up the pot, Seven was lifting his back leg to scent mark it. "Hey, Seven, no!" It was a firm no, but his tone was far from harsh.

Even so, Seven bolted to the end of his leash and tugged against it, tail tucked tight against his hind end like he was bracing for a blow. Jenna was afraid he'd get away, but his collar proved tight enough not to slip over his head, and Jake held fast to the leash's handle. "Easy, bud. It's okay. I didn't mean to scare you." He kept speaking in an easy, low voice until Seven stopped fighting the leash.

Letting out a breath, Jake sank onto his heels and held out his hand. "It's okay, Seven. You just can't pee on my new Christmas cactus. It's one of a kind. Plants N Pots by Jenna."

The comment brought a smile to Jenna's face, and at the same time, Seven's tail relaxed even though his ears remained tamped back against his head.

Still resting on his heels, Jake glanced up at Jenna. "Someone along the line treated him quite poorly, it seems." He shook his head, and Jenna glimpsed the anger over this injustice boiling under his surface. "If I could communicate just one thing to him, it's that I'm never going to hurt him."

"If you keep doing what you're doing, eventually he's going to get it; I'm sure."

Jake pulled a treat from his pocket and extended his hand, the treat resting in the center of his palm. Seven's ears instantly pricked forward, but he didn't budge a single step forward. On the street, a steady stream of cars passed by, but Seven didn't so much as glance toward them, even when someone yelled "Pretty dog!" out an open car window. A bird landed in a tree overhead, and Seven glanced upward for a second or two before returning his gaze to Jake's outstretched hand. After another few seconds went by, Seven let out a soft whine.

"Come on, boy. A couple steps and it's yours, but I can't wait you out too long. Dinner's in the oven, and we've got to get back, or Jenna's going to think I can't cook. We don't want that, do we?"

Jake slid the treat down his hand and caught it between the tips of his fingers, raising it out that way, and Seven abruptly sank onto his haunches like he'd been asked to sit. With too much distance separating them, Jake stood up and stepped forward, while Seven remained sitting at attention like a sentinel. This time, when Jake offered the treat his direction, the dog snatched it from the tips of Jake's fingers.

"Good boy, Seven." As Seven chomped the treat, Jake picked up the pot, holding it in one arm and the leash in the other. "What I don't want is to force him to do things—other than not chewing up my stuff—but that's all the interaction with people he seems to have had."

Jenna stepped into stride alongside Jake as they headed toward his apartment. "I think you're right that that's all he knows—obedience and punishment for the lack of it—or that's what's been driven home the deepest. But he's only two or so. I have faith he'll figure out that this companionship thing isn't so bad, as long as you have the patience to wait him out."

Jake cocked an eyebrow. "Is this the right time to own up to a lifetime of struggle with ADHD and a track record of having a terrible time waiting for anything?"

From his tone, he'd clearly made peace with this fact about himself, so Jenna didn't feel bad about the laugh that tumbled out. "After seeing you with him Saturday, I never would've guessed that."

"Yeah, well, after struggling through undergrad, I knew I'd never get through law school without some significant changes. I took a year off school and figured out how to help myself move through some of the most challenging symptoms. I wouldn't say I've mastered the whole thing, but life is less of a struggle now. Hopefully this experience with him won't prove I don't have the patience I thought I had."

"Well, I don't know that much about ADHD, but I've seen you with him enough that I'm sure there's an opportunity for a win-win here." Jenna waggled her eyebrows. "You helping Seven learn how to trust, and him helping you continue to expand your capacity for patience." The way Jake looked at her before he spoke, Jenna worried her words had offended him.

"I just heard a podcast about that the other day, about how you can't change someone or something with being changed yourself. Maybe it's a bit esoteric, but it struck a chord."

Seven, who'd been trotting just ahead of them and occasionally pausing to sniff a myriad of bushes and lampposts glanced up suddenly, as if their conversation had piqued his interest. He barked at them once, a single yip that was loud even among the surrounding noise.

Jenna nudged Jake in the arm. "Sounds like it struck a chord with him too."

"You think? That kind of sounded like 'fat chance' to me."

Jenna laughed along with him. "One thing's for sure. You two are made for each other."

"Yeah, well, I'm just glad you're coming along for this ride, however crazy it proves to be."

When she met Jake's gaze, his mouth pulled into a small, private smile that hers automatically reciprocated, and happiness radiated down to her toes. She wasn't going to be the one doing the work, not like Seven, and not even like Jake, but that thing he'd said about changing and being changed… She wanted to step into that arena, too, however it played out.

Chapter 16

Toward the end of an incredible dinner, Jake's phone began to ring out from the windowsill behind the kitchen sink. On vibrate, it rattled obtrusively against the ceramic tile, overriding the soft classical music that played over his portable Bluetooth speaker. The first time it rang, he said he'd call whoever it was back later, but one call rolled into another, reminding Jenna of her sister when she was being persistent, and making her wonder if Jake also had a Monica in his life.

Aside from this distraction, the evening had been going great. The conversation had an easy flow to it, and none of the first date-that-might-or-might-not-actually-be-a-date awkwardness poked its ugly head. Jake really did know his way around a kitchen, he was a gracious host, and his place was a wonderful combination of clean and inviting but also lived in, which Jenna appreciated.

Upon getting here, Jake had put the Christmas cactus on the side table next to his couch after Jenna advised him it would be best kept out of direct sunlight. Although Seven forwent any further attempts to scent mark on it, as soon as Jenna and Jake had sat down at the table to eat, he leaped onto the couch to give both the pot and plant a thorough sniff.

Since then, he'd mostly been gnawing a sturdy new rubber chew toy that Jake had asked Jenna to stuff with small treats as he set the table earlier. "I'm hoping it buys us thirty minutes of focused, nondestructive dog so that we can eat in peace," he'd said with a laugh. The toy was designed so that when Seven bit down hard enough in the right spot, one or two of the small treats would drop out of a hole in the bottom.

Even a room away, Seven proved every bit as entertaining as dinner and a movie as he worked the new toy. Perhaps Jenna shouldn't have been surprised, but it didn't take him long to master it. She'd just taken another bite of the mouthwatering chicken when Seven clamped the bright-blue toy between his teeth, tilted his head in an awkward angle, and began to shake out the treats so that they fell one by one in a continuous stream at his feet rather than letting go of the toy to snatch up a single one at a time.

"Well, I guess he's got that one solved," Jake said with a chuckle. "During my meeting this afternoon, he figured out which was the most productive way to roll a treat-dispensing puzzle ball in ten minutes too."

"Oh yeah? You can see how intelligent he is in the way he looks at you."

When Jake's phone began to vibrate for the fourth time, Jake sat back in his chair. "Whoever that is isn't giving up. I didn't think to put it on Do Not Disturb. Excuse me a sec, will you?"

He headed into the main part of the kitchen and pulled his phone off the windowsill. Jenna spotted the dark look that flashed across his face as he glanced at the screen. Figuring it wasn't her business, she returned her attention to Seven, who'd dropped the toy and had it clamped under one front paw as he gobbled up the last several treats with the speed of an anteater.

Jake lingered at the sink, likely reading voicemails that had been converted to text. "Hey," he said, his voice lifting, "one of those calls was from a St. Louis area code. I've been playing phone tag with the trainer at the shelter where Seven's from. Mind if I return her call before she leaves for the day?"

"Go for it."

Jake pulled a small notepad and pen from one of the kitchen

drawers before returning to the table. After pressing Dial with his cell on speaker and setting it between them, he sank onto his chair and pushed his mostly empty plate back enough to fit the notepad in front of it.

By the third ring, someone picked up. "High Grove Animal Shelter. Tess Redding speaking."

"Hi, Tess, this is Jake Stiles. I just missed your call."

"Oh, hi, Jake. I'm glad we're connecting."

Across the room, Seven stopped midchomp and looked toward the table where the phone rested. Jenna wondered if he was reacting to the particular voice on the other end of the call or if it was simply the sound of a human voice coming out of a tiny object that had gotten his attention.

"Me too. I'm reaching out to see if you remember a dog who moved through there—apparently several times, with the last one being about nine months ago. I left his microchip number in my last message. I'm hoping you still have those records."

"You're in luck. We keep our animals' records ten years after they've been adopted out. I looked him up before calling you. He's a young border collie, right?" When Jake confirmed that he was, Tess continued. "He should be a little over two now. I can't remember what you called him in your message, but he went by a few different names while he was here."

Jake glanced at Jenna. "Given the number of times he was supposedly turned in, I'm not surprised by that. In any case, we're calling him Seven. By the way, a friend of mine—Jenna—is here with me, and she may have some questions for you too."

"Sure thing," Tess said. "Either of you feel free to fire away, and Seven, huh? I like it. Seven's a lucky number, and way better than the unfortunate nickname that stuck after one of his failed adoptions."

"Oh yeah? What was that?"

"I was an advocate for not making it official, but the first few people who adopted him from us were quick to return him. Some of us here started calling him Turnstile after that."

Jenna clamped a hand over her mouth as Jake chuckled. "I could see that. So, he really did move through there four times?"

"I have his record pulled up, and yeah, unfortunately. Since you're calling me, and you're clearly not who adopted him last, I'm guessing he's been surrendered five times now, huh?"

"Actually, it's six. I'm fostering him now to keep it from being seven, which is how he got his name."

Tess clicked her tongue loudly enough that it carried over the speaker. "And I would've sworn the woman who adopted him last was committed to keeping him forever. She went through several weeks of training with him before taking him home, and they seemed like such a match. I checked in with her after thirty days too. She said she thought they'd gotten through the thick of it and were bonding. She was supposed to bring him back here if it didn't work out."

"Well, I can't say how he got here, but his last two shelter stays have been up here in Chicago."

"Chicago? Wow. Well, in the grand scheme of things, it's not that far, I guess."

With the attentiveness of a dog who'd spotted a rabbit in a bush, Seven trotted over to the table, his attention still homed in on the phone. Planting his front paws on the table like they had every right to be there, he stuck his nose against the edge of the phone and sniffed, the hair on the back of his neck bristling as he did.

"It's safe to say he remembers your voice," Jenna said. "He's zeroed in on the phone."

Tess's drawn-out "Aww" rolled over the speaker. "Hi there, good boy. It's okay. You're not coming back. At least, I hope you aren't." Seven's ears perked forward, but he dropped down to the floor once more and backed up several feet. After a slight pause, Tess added, "If ever a dog has needed to land in his forever home, it's him."

"I agree," Jake said. Two thin creases abruptly lined his forehead. "But I have to tell you, I'm only fostering him. With my work schedule and his activity needs, I doubt I could make it work long-term. I am, however, committed to this fostering thing leading to that."

"If it helps, we've found that foster families are every bit as important as adopters when it comes to helping our animals find their forever homes."

"Thanks. He's pretty jaded when it comes to trusting people. My hope is to build up rapport with him along the way, even if he's not one to let his guard down. At all. Which is why I'm reaching out to you. Jenna's going to be helping too. Any advice you can give us is welcome, along with his history, if you can share it. We have the sense he's been abused. It'd be helpful to get an idea how far back that goes and how severe it might've been."

After glancing back and forth between Jake and Jenna, Seven trotted over to the front windows, staring out onto the street as if in search of the voice on the other end of the call, the hair on the back of his neck still bristled and his tail sticking out behind him. Jenna couldn't tell if it was from excitement or fear.

"I can help with both of those. I can't give names, obviously, but I can give you a rundown of his history here, which'll make it clear why he's slow to warm up to people."

"That'd be great."

"Okay, my guess is it's best to start at the beginning. Hold on a sec. I'm going to put you on speaker and pull up those notes."

Jake looked at Jenna and lifted a brow. "Whatever it is, at least we'll know," he whispered. As he listened, he'd been doodling on the pad in front of him, and a collection of precise squares, triangles, and squiggly lines began to fill the small paper.

Jenna smoothed out the linen napkin that was folded on her lap. The part of her that experienced an urge to change the channel anytime a nature show threatened to stir up tears wasn't fully convinced she wanted to learn the dog's history. Then she looked over at Seven, and resolution set in. Whatever had happened to him, she and Jake needed to understand it.

"He was just shy of eight months old when he first came in," Tess said over the speaker. A chorus of barks erupted in the background, but they were muted enough to still hear her okay. "I don't think I met that family, or if I did, I don't remember, but the reason for his surrender says only one thing. Divorce. I have a coworker who could tell you the exact percentage of divorce-related surrenders off the top of his head, but we certainly get our fair share of animals for that very reason." She fell quiet again. "Let's see. He was only here a little over a week that first time, and that includes the mandatory time in quarantine. The first family to adopt him returned him after one long weekend with him, so we basically counted that as a failed trial and got him back on adoption row ASAP. The second family kept him just over a week, and that was when he got the nickname I was telling you about. Let me check those notes as to why they surrendered him."

As they waited, Jake stopped doodling to split one of the smashed potatoes still on his plate in half and take a bite. Comfortably full, Jenna sipped her wine.

"Well," Tess continued, "that family's reason for surrender is exactly what you might expect of anyone returning a less-than-a-year-old border collie—too much energy. Even though he was so young, it's shelter policy that any dogs who're returned twice or more are marked for special attention before they're adopted out again. That means he didn't make adoption row as quickly that next time. That's when I started working with him one on one. He's as smart as dogs come. I'll swear by that. He just didn't know what to do with all that energy of his."

"I can imagine, given how energetic he still is more than a year later."

Tess was quiet another few seconds, but they gave her the space to answer. "Looks like he spent close to two months with us that time. The couple who adopted him… I remember talking to them. The guy said he grew up on a farm and had worked with border collies before. The girl hadn't, and she was the one who really seemed over the moon for Turnsti—for Seven, I mean. Since he was a three-time surrender, a staff member went to the house before he was placed with them. The house and couple checked all our boxes—big, fenced-in yard to run in, among other things. But try as we might, we don't always know." Tess let out a breath.

"I'll spare you the details, but he came back to us about six months later, only it wasn't an owner surrender that time. Seven had been taken by police order to the city pound. I guess the next-door neighbors had called animal control a couple of times, but it wasn't until they caught the man who'd adopted him on video that animal control was able to step in. Thank God they scanned this chip and called us, and we were able to get him back. That poor doggo got the spa treatment after that, and he needed it."

Jenna blinked back tears, and Jake shook his head, clearing his throat. "It was physical abuse then?"

"That and neglect. From what the neighbors shared, he spent a good deal of the six months he was with that man crated—turns out he and the woman parted ways soon after they adopted him, and unfortunately it was the man who kept him. On top of the neighbors' testimony, some of Seven's teeth are more worn down than they should be at his age, so we think he did a decent amount of gnawing on metal—and obsessively licking his paws." Tess sucked in a breath, and when she started next, her tone was more upbeat. "But he was young and resilient, and the important thing is we got him back."

"Thank God," Jenna said, her stomach tightening at the thought of what Seven had endured.

"He was here that time for close to six months as well, and

everybody doted on him as much as he would let us, which basically means we gave him tons of treats and lots of exercise but hardly any petting since it seemed to add to his stress rather than relieve it, and shelters are notoriously stressful environments for dogs."

"I've been trying the last few days, but he clearly prefers not to be petted," Jake said.

"Except for by my nephews," Jenna added. "They're four and two. They were part of Seven's most recent family. After he was there for a couple of weeks, he'd let my nephews put their hands all over him. But the whole month he was with them, he never once let my sister or her husband touch him. It was like they didn't bond a bit."

"Huh. Well, his relationship with the young boys shows he's capable of trust, at least. I suspect he's just really jaded. Understandably so."

"I can see that," Jenna said.

"He's still young, so don't give up hope. Border collies are long-lived, and he's not much over two." Jake and Jenna murmured in agreement as Tess continued. "So, I have few questions for you as well, but before moving on, I'll finish up his history here. Like I said, he spent about six months with us that last time. Once he was available for adoption again, he was the picture of health, and his coat looked great. But he's such a pretty boy, we didn't want anyone getting drawn in by his looks and not thinking about his story or the work he'd require, so we didn't list his picture online and only allowed people who inquired about him after reading his story—and who had experience with high-energy dogs—to meet him. When he left that last time, we really thought we'd found his forever home. Since he didn't end up back here, I can't tell you what happened."

"I'll call the shelter up here again tomorrow and see if I can find out anything they haven't already told me. If I find out anything, I'll let you know."

"That would be great. I'll add it to his notes. Oh, and Jenna, was it? Can I ask what happened regarding your sister not keeping him?"

"It is, and sure." Meeting Jake's supportive gaze, Jenna reminded herself that her sister's failure with Seven wasn't hers to own. "My sister came across him at a community pet adoption event and fell in love with him. When she found out he was from a shelter my mom had taken us to as kids, she thought it was a sign that he was meant for her and her family, and she jumped in headfirst, so to speak. Neither she nor her husband had ever had a dog, and not only does she have two kids under four, but she's pregnant and due with baby number three in a few months."

"Oh wow. Yeah, I can't see Seven being a good fit for her family under those circumstances without having a slew of support lined up."

"Unfortunately, she didn't, and her world is just so busy. He's a great dog though, and I fully support what Jake's doing."

"So, you two are stepping in to foster him?"

"Technically Jake's fostering him, and I'm helping, but yeah."

"Okay. Any other pets in the house?"

"Nope," Jake said with a wink. "Just a sharp-looking Christmas cactus. How is he with other dogs though? I'd like to take him to a dog park, but he doesn't seem interested in the dogs we've passed on the street."

"I looked up his temperament before I called, and it's pretty much what I remembered. He can mostly take other dogs or leave them. He doesn't enjoy ones who are too forward in their play, but he was fine in enclosures with calmer dogs. He loves to run though. That's his jam."

Jake and Jenna both smiled at once. "Yeah, we noticed," Jake said. "I've got him chasing down Frisbees. I was thinking about signing up for agility training."

"Perfect! I can't think of anything better than constructive play for him. Actually, I can think of one thing, but I bet it'll prove just as challenging."

"What's that?"

"The way I see it, you should think of meeting Seven's needs like a balance scale. He's one of those dogs that it's easy to say, 'Give him plenty of exercise and he'll be fine,' and he does need that, but he also needs connection and reacclimating to human touch again. Even if it's limited to when you hook and unhook him from a leash at first, if you can create a few quiet, peaceful moments every day to run your hand down his back from head to tail, even if he doesn't love it, I'm positive he needs it. Feeding him out of your hands, offering him treats, gently brushing him, sitting on the floor with him, those kinds of things."

Jake nodded slowly. "Thank you, Tess. I think that's exactly what I needed to hear."

"Yeah, well, I wish you both the best with him. He's one of those dogs who's going to make you work for it, but he's worth the effort. I don't know any trainers in Chicago to recommend, but I can ask around. And with him especially, I'd make sure whoever you find practices positive-reinforcement training only."

"Absolutely. No question there."

"You know, I'd be happy to do a few video sessions with you until you connect with someone up there. You can schedule them on High Grove's website. If nothing's available when you need it, just reach out to me again, and we'll figure something out. Seven's one dog I'd do just about anything for."

Jake raised an eyebrow. "Thank you, and the more I get to know him, the more I agree with you."

After hanging up, Jake looked from Seven, who was still over at the window but staring their way expectantly, to Jenna. He shook his head as he dropped the pen to the table, processing the conversation.

Given how undefined this thing between them was, she reached out with a confidence that surprised her and closed her hand over his. "I didn't get to say this earlier, given the sand in my eye and all, but that plant is hardly a sufficient thank-you for what you're doing with him."

Jake flipped his hand over so that their palms were pressed against each other. "You don't have to thank me. I'm just glad you're helping, however you're able. It's daunting, but less so with you in the picture."

"Thanks." His words brought a smile to her face. "I'd like to think I'd have gotten to the shelter and changed my mind as well. I was so mad at my sister that night that I was hardly letting the experience in, but I'm sure it would've sunk in eventually, what taking him back actually entailed."

Jake cocked an eyebrow. "Trust me, when you pulled into that lot, it would've sunk in. He was shaking in his boots. Figuratively speaking," he added with a smile. "But what you said about being mad at your sister… Is that anything you'd want to talk about?"

Their hands were still entwined, and the warmth radiating out from his no longer seemed separate from the warmth in hers. Even so, his offer made her want to pull away and sit back in her chair, but she took a breath and waited out the temptation. If the last decade had proved anything, it was that the Jake Stileses in this world didn't come around often. Hardly ever, in fact. "Is yes *and* no an answer?" she said with a soft laugh.

"When I was a kid, I'd have said no to that, but the older I get, the less black and white everything seems."

Jenna nodded slowly. "The thing is, to tell you why I was mad at my sister, I'll have to tell you about my mom. How about we clean up first though? My sister's always joking about how there's table talk and then there's couch talk, and I can't say she's wrong about that."

When Jake agreed, Jenna's belly flipped like she was standing on a board at the deep end of the pool, something she rarely did. Unlike her sister, Jenna was one to test the water, first a toe, then the feet and ankles. It could take a full ten minutes before she got her hair wet, if she did at all.

But maybe there was a time to stop worrying about a little bit of momentary discomfort and just start swimming.

Chapter 17

JENNA SWEPT A LOCK of her hair back from her face and winced almost imperceptibly, reminding Jake of the line of stitches hidden there. Seated as she was on the opposite end of his couch, facing him, legs crossed, and a throw pillow tucked in front of her, she had a vulnerability he'd not seen since he'd been next to her in the rain waiting for the ambulance. But this time, reminiscent of the yin-yang symbol, a strength encircled that vulnerability, keeping her spine straight and her shoulders back.

"You don't have to tell me anything you're not ready to."

They'd cleaned up the kitchen together, and just once had he closed a hand over the small of her back while stepping behind her. His hand still felt alive from the touch.

"It's not something I talk about—hardly ever, in fact. But I do want to tell you." She pulled in a breath that lifted her shoulders. "She died, my mom. You probably got that the other day."

After admitting he had, Jake left her the space to continue. Seven was stretched out on the floor on the opposite side of the room, watching them. He'd been lazily licking his front paws, and his eyelids were growing heavy, but every time either of them moved more than an inch, his head popped up and his ears perked forward in alert.

"It was breast cancer," she continued. "My grandma had it but wasn't diagnosed until she was in her late fifties, and she recovered. My mom was just thirty-three. I was nine, and my sister was not yet eight. I told you how we were wanting a dog for Christmas but got those cactuses instead. Well, my mom was diagnosed in January. I guess she felt the swelling under her arm sometime in October, but money was always so tight in our house, and she wanted to wait for the new year because she hadn't come close to touching her annual deductible, and Christmas was coming." She shook her head. "The gift of hindsight, right? I didn't find out about that until I was in my twenties, but I swear, since I heard it, it's been hard not to wonder if those two months could've saved her life."

Seeing that she was giving him the space to respond, Jake figured the best thing to do was meet vulnerability with vulnerability. "I grew up just outside Racine, and when I was twelve, we had the day off school for Presidents' Day. A couple of my friends wanted to go to a movie—*Shanghai Knights* had just come out—but the rest of us wanted to play hockey. One of my buddies fell through the ice that day. It took a long time for the EMS to get him out. He survived, but he was never the same. I think about that day often, about what he'd be doing right now if we'd gone to the movies instead."

Jenna stared at him as one breath blended into the next. "Then you know. It's easy to think our pain is one of a kind, but so many of us carry it."

"That's true, but I didn't mean to get you offtrack."

"You didn't." Jenna looked over at Seven, who had just fallen into a light doze. "My mom had this sunroom full of plants and no furniture but a single, cozy chair. She liked to read in there on her days off. Each one of those plants was healthy and beautiful. I don't know how she knew so much about caring for them, but she did. After she died, I watered them, but either not enough or too much because just about every last one of them was wilted and brown by the time the house was sold."

The image of a young girl with big blue-green eyes attempting to take over a responsibility like that tugged at him.

After she cleared her throat, Jenna added, "Less than a year later, my sister and I went to live with my grandparents out in Tinley Park. My dad started drinking—or at least using it as a crutch—when my mom got sick. He was never abusive or mean to us like you hear about some people, but he withdrew inside himself. He lost his job and moved into an apartment to be closer to his new job on the other side of town, and my sister and I hardly saw him."

"That had to be rough, after losing your mom."

"He'd take us to dinner once a week. All the talk was pretty superficial though, how's school going and whatnot." She shrugged. "We had amazing grandparents, at least. I miss them every day. And my sister and I had each other, there's that. We never got the dog, but our grandparents had three cats." Jenna made a face. "Cats are great, but theirs were older, and two of them were always throwing up, and the other one hated everyone but my grandma, so much so that when he got the inclination, he'd chase us across the room, trying to bite us. I think my sister and I had both had our fill of cats by the time we left for college."

"I could see that," he said with a chuckle. "So, a couple years ago, you decided you wanted a dog but figured you needed to take care of a plant first." He nodded toward the plant she'd brought him. "Which led to Plants N Pots."

Jenna shrugged. "If the shoe fits…"

Nodding, he added, "And your dad. How is he now?"

"Better, I think. While we were in undergrad, he got sober and met his second wife in AA. She's twelve years younger, and they have a couple kids who are a little older than my nephews. They live in Skokie, and I can't say I see them much, but I'm happy for him. He's reconnected with my sister the last couple years, seeing how their kids aren't far apart in age. I think it's been good for her."

"And you?"

Jenna shrugged. "My dad and I aren't super close, but I'm okay with it. I'd like to think I don't hold any grudges, but I probably do," she said with a dismissive laugh. "So, how about you?"

Jake narrowed his gaze. "Were we finished talking about you?"

"I'm not sure there's much else to say." Looking down, she fidgeted with a frayed string of yarn at the edge of the pillow. He stayed quiet on purpose to see if she'd fill the space, and she did. The glasses of wine on the adjacent coffee table were being ignored, but so far this hadn't been the conversation for casual drinking. "Losing my mom was hard. The kind of hard that defines you. At her funeral, I promised myself I'd become a doctor and help cure the world of cancer. I held on to the dream for a while, but it didn't materialize. *Obviously.*"

"But you do work as a radiology technologist."

Jenna cocked her head. "Hardly curing the world of cancer, but I needed to pay the bills, and the hours are good. I did major in biology in undergrad and worked relentlessly and got accepted into med school. Two years in, I realized the whole thing was just about killing me. My heart wasn't in it anymore. Maybe it never had been. If I'd listened to what I wanted to do rather than what I felt I needed do, I'd have majored in art most likely. Though I don't regret my undergrad degree. I probably wouldn't regret those two years in med school, either, if I wasn't paying so much for them in loans." She laughed off this last bit before tossing the pillow his way. "That's pretty much my entire life story. Can we talk about you now for a bit, please?"

"Yeah, we can do that." She'd taken off her shoes upon arrival and Jake had moved them to the closet to keep them out of too-easy reach for Seven. Now, she tucked her knees into her chest, locking her hands around the backs of the thighs of her skintight jeans. Jake cleared his throat and reminded himself not to think about how much he appreciated the view, even though images of those legs would no doubt be keeping him awake tonight. Resting the pillow on his lap, he leaned over for a swallow of wine. "I can imagine those loans being a pain. I bartended throughout law school so that I didn't have to take out as many loans as I would've otherwise. I hope never to be that sleep-deprived again in my life."

Jenna smiled sympathetically. "I bet, and how'd you end up in Chicago over Racine? Was it school or work, or something else? And I love Racine, by the way."

"Racine's nice, and it was law school that first brought me here. That, and I wanted a stab at living in a bigger city, and I'd always liked Chicago. My undergrad was at UW-Madison. After that, like I told you, I took a year off to figure out how to better manage my ADHD, then, after my third go at the LSAT, I managed to score high enough to get into Chicago-Kent. The school had a big draw for me. While I was growing up, my dad owned a small machining business. He could turn out a great product but, ultimately, he ended up filing for bankruptcy and lost it. He didn't have the knowledge to run the business side of things and owed a lot in back taxes. I started out in business law because I wanted to be able to help people like him, but I migrated to intellectual property law when I was a year in."

"Sounds complicated."

He shrugged. "So does med school."

Jenna laughed. "It was, and that's a bummer about your dad losing his business."

"It was humbling, for certain. It took my parents close to a decade to recover financially, and they live pretty modestly. My mom has worked in the front office at the elementary school my brother and I went to for the last, I don't know, twenty-five years or so. I'm thirty-three, and she started there when I was in third grade. My brother was in fifth."

"That's sweet. What about your dad? What he'd end up doing after that?"

"I guess you could say that losing his business worked out okay in the long run. He got to continue to work around machines, which was his passion. One of the companies who bought some of his equipment hired him, and he stayed there until a couple of years ago. He was turning sixty and wanted something less physical. He got a job at a library not far from the house. He walks to work and sits behind a counter checking out books all day, and he's happy. They both are. They're still in the house I grew up in too. People don't do that anymore, not our generation anyway."

"No, they don't, do they? I loved that about living at my grand-parents' house. There were still boxes of my mom's baby stuff in the basement and her high school yearbooks in her old bedroom closet. It helped me feel connected to her when I really needed it." Clearing her throat, she shifted back to a cross-legged position again.

The movement was enough for Seven to pop his head off the floor and glance her way. Once he seemed to determine that neither of them was about to move from the couch, he settled his head back onto one paw, his eyelids heavy. Jake didn't think it was his imagination that the dog was starting to relax a bit more now that he'd spent a few nights here.

"How about your brother? Are you close?"

Jake shrugged. "Yeah, we're close. Different, but close. He's in Racine still but downtown. He got my dad's gift for tinkering with things. When we were kids, he was always taking our stuff apart to see how it worked. Like me, he has ADHD. He went to college initially to major in engineering but didn't finish. Now he works as a machinist, and in his free time, he brews beer in his garage. His wife's not crazy about the smell of hops in the house, but the two of them balance one another out well enough. She's pregnant too. With their first. About seventeen weeks along, I think."

"Nice. That'll be fun, and good that they aren't far from your parents."

"Yeah, my mom's excited. That's for sure."

"You and your sister," Jake said, circling back to what had first started this conversation. "I take it you're close, given what you both went through."

Jenna blinked a few times. "Yeah, we are, which I guess can be both good and bad. She can be pretty impulsive and darned sure of herself at the same time." She nodded toward Seven, who popped his head up instantly. Realizing they were both looking his way, he lumbered to his feet with a yawn and walked over to the window. "Like when it came to adopting him. She can't always pull back enough to see a bigger picture. Maybe we're all like that some, but I really see it with her."

Before Jake could respond, she gave a light shake of her head and continued. "I'm only fifteen months older, and I lost my mom, too, but—the way I remember it, at least—so much fell on me after she died. My sister, she's supersmart, smarter than me, but she just kind of stopped growing up, stayed in the baby role. Having the boys to care for is changing that though. Every parent needs some help with little ones—they're so all-consuming—but she's doing it mostly on her own, and I'm proud of her. And I don't want to be resentful about water that should be under the bridge, but sometimes she'll say or do something, and that frustration just kind of bubbles up."

Jake dragged a hand over his mouth, his stubble pressing against his fingers. His stomach tensed at the thought of how she might take what he was going to say, but he knew he needed to say it anyway. "There's something I've been wanting to tell you."

Jenna shifted in her seat, and Seven turned from the window to face them. "Yeah, sure. Anything."

"The other night, just before the accident. It was raining and nearly dark, and we were both headed down Ashland. A couple lights before you got hit, I don't know why, but I looked over and noticed you. And Seven. We were idling there, waiting for the light to turn green, and you were illuminated by a streetlight, and I could tell you were sad. Really sad. The kind of sad people don't like to let themselves get."

Tears welled up instantly, bringing out the blue in her eyes. "My sister was upset about surrendering Seven, and she confessed this stupid story from our childhood back before our mom died when there was so much competition between us. I don't know why, but it just hit me right in the gut." A few stray tears slid down her cheeks, and she brushed them away. "I wasn't drunk or focused on a podcast or looking at my phone, but I keep asking myself if the wreck would've still happened if I hadn't been crying. I thought I was paying attention, but I didn't even see him. Maybe I did at the last second, but I don't remember the impact. The last thing I remember is the light turning green and starting to go. I don't think I looked left."

"Jenna, that guy was over twice the legal limit for alcohol, driving too fast for conditions, and he ran a red light. You didn't do anything wrong."

"Except for not looking left and right before I went."

"When you're at a stoplight, it's a best practice, not a law."

Jenna nodded and wiped under her eyes. "I know." She'd quelled her tears and was back in control. "But thank you. We were clearly still alongside one another when I was hit, then, given how I hit your Jeep." When Jake nodded, she added, "Did you see him coming?"

The fact that he dropped her gaze likely said enough, but he admitted that he had. "But I didn't tell you that to make you feel like you should've. Had I not been paying attention to you, I doubt I would've seen him either."

She swept her hair back in one hand and gave a little shake of her head.

"Jenna, I'm telling you all this because I think you should know that it was you who had me running out of my Jeep so fast after the impact. Those couple blocks we inched along at those lights..."

Jake shook his head. "I can't explain it, so I'll just leave it at that. It was you I was running to." Jake motioned to Seven, who was fully awake again, his head cocked like he was trying to figure out what was playing out between them. "It isn't why I kept him rather than leaving him at the shelter; that was all him. But this..." he said, waving his hand in a circle between the three of them. "I don't know. Given that you've offered to help me with him, because I've asked to use your yard, it didn't feel right not to tell you that."

Jenna blinked a few times, then abruptly braced one hand on the back of the couch as she leaned toward him. Jake met her in the middle, their mouths connecting with a heat that threatened to stop all blood flow to his brain. He locked one hand around her neck and the other around her hip as they raised up onto their knees, their bodies pulling together like magnets. Instantly, the world fell away until it was just lips and tongue and the soft grazing of teeth and the perfection of her body against his.

As the kiss deepened, a memory pressed in of a game of "If You Had To" that he'd played with friends in undergrad. "If you had to give up one for the rest of your life, would it be sex or kissing?" he'd been asked on one of his turns. It'd been easy to throw kissing out there without a second's hesitation. He'd gotten a pillow chucked at him by one of the girls there who he'd gone on a couple dates with.

If someone were to ask him that same question right now, he'd have a hard time answering, even if ultimately the answer was the same. Kissing Jenna felt like coming home and stepping into a hot sauna at the same time, heating his blood and simultaneously making him want to laugh with that strange feeling bubbling up his throat. If it was joy, it had been entirely too long since he'd experienced it.

His hand slid over the rise of her ass, and he pulled her closer. His lips left her mouth to explore her neck and sternum. *No sex or anything close to it.* Had he promised himself that? Surely, he hadn't. Not when it was so obvious how good they'd be together.

Over at the window, Seven began to growl, deep and low and incessant. Jenna pulled away first to look his way. The same second that Jake realized the direction Seven was staring—at the door—he heard the footsteps clomping up the stairs. Definitely not the couple next door. "Oh, crap. Hang tight a second, will you?"

Jake hadn't thought about changing the entry code to the lock on his door, even though Alyssa knew it, because never in a thousand lifetimes would he let himself into her place post-breakup. Apparently, that courtesy didn't extend the other direction. Jake heard the soft beeping of the keypad just as he lunged toward the door. Seven beat him there, the low growl still in his throat, which came as a surprise until Jake remembered that the last time Alyssa had been here, Seven had witnessed her screaming and throwing shoes.

"I wouldn't try opening that until I get this dog restrained," he yelled, pressing against the door with the flat of his hand as Seven backed just out of reach of him. "Buddy, even if we don't like 'em, we don't growl at visitors." Jake was about to ask Jenna to grab the leash out of the coat closet when Alyssa started up on the opposite side of the door.

"Jake Stiles, you bought me this swimsuit in Fiji! Maybe the rest of that stuff is mine, but not this. I don't want your gifts. Not when you're throwing our relationship away!" Her voice was muffled by the door, but there was zero doubt Jenna was hearing every word.

She'd stood up from the couch and was headed their way. With Seven so focused on the door, Jenna was able to catch him by surprise. She locked a hand around his collar, and he stopped growling immediately, shifting his back end away from her as he tucked his tail and flattened his ears against his head. After meeting Jake's gaze, Jenna nodded toward the door. "I'm guessing you probably want to take whatever this is outside."

"I'm sorry. For this..." He jutted his thumb toward the door.

"And for not explaining sooner. I was getting to it, promise. And I will," he said. "I'll explain everything. When I get back."

Jenna nodded, her gaze filled with what seemed like concern but not anger. "Okay. Once you're outside, I'll let him go."

As he stepped outside to confront Alyssa, Jake promised himself that whatever it took, he was going to get this thing right with Jenna. Nothing had meant as much to him in a long time.

Chapter 18

NIGHT HAD FALLEN AND, since Jenna's earlier walk to Jake's, the temperature had dropped fifteen or twenty degrees. Thankfully the wind had died down, or Jenna's teeth would be chattering. She pulled her jacket tighter, her footsteps resounding on the concrete sidewalk beneath her. Earlier, she'd chosen a longtime favorite jean jacket for its looks rather than its warmth, and while it had been sufficient on the way here, her insulated puff jacket would've been a better choice for the walk home.

As her thoughts circled back to what had played out in Jake's condo fifteen minutes ago, she did her best not to let the sadness press in, even as it threatened to. She'd rather cling to the memory of Jake's lips against hers and to the words he'd spoken before the intimacy of the night had collapsed rather than the visual of the raven-haired goddess she'd caught a glimpse of from Jake's living room window after the two had tromped down the steps and outside to talk.

Jenna had walked over there to stop Seven from growling, not to peer at the unexpected visitor. Of course, someone as good-looking as Jake would want someone as put together as that. Hadn't this theme played out in Jenna's life before?

That bulge pressing against you while you were kissing earlier didn't seem like he was too put off kissing you, did it?

"Are you cold?" Jake asked as he rejoined her. Seven had just hurled himself headfirst into a hedge and sent a handful of birds flying off into the night, and Jenna had walked a few steps ahead.

At Jake's suggestion, they were taking a string of quieter side streets back to Jenna's place so they could talk without the road noise pressing in. This first street, Rockwell, a little west of Jake's place, was new to her, and Jenna eyed the stately houses along it, the many lamps in the windows warm and welcoming. One of her favorite things about Logan Square was the varied architecture of the century-old homes; nothing here looked cookie cutter.

"A little. I'll warm up as we walk."

The sidewalk was narrower here, but they were still able to walk alongside each other.

"Want my jacket?"

"So that you freeze?" she said with a laugh.

"I've got too much adrenaline flowing through my veins to be cold for quite a while." Even though Jenna held up a hand in refusal, he tugged off his jacket and draped it over her shoulders. His was lined and warm and felt like the warm hug she was craving after the emotional slap of an ex-girlfriend attempting to barge in during a first kiss—or a string of first kisses, to put it more accurately.

"Thanks."

"Look, Jenna, unless you have any specific questions, I'll just start talking, and you can stop me whenever you're inclined."

He'd apologized for the second time when he'd come inside five minutes later, but the energy in the room had irreparably changed, and Jenna didn't want whatever he was about to explain to dull her memory of that remarkable kiss or the intimate conversation that had played out just before it. It had been her request to cut the night short. "Yeah, okay."

Before he even began, one question was at the top of her mind—how long had Jake and his ex-girlfriend been broken up—but Jenna wanted to hear him out first. She slipped her arms into the sleeves of his jacket and pulled her hair out from underneath the collar.

"Given how I asked you to my place and made you dinner,

I can see where it might be tempting not to believe me, but the first thing I want you to know is that I didn't plan on kissing you tonight—or sleeping with you, or anything in between. Not that I'm not interested." The first easy smile played on his lips since before the interruption. "I'm guessing I made that pretty clear a little while ago, but if I've had one steadfast rule since hitting my midtwenties, it's downtime between relationships to get my head together."

"Makes sense."

Jake dragged a hand through his hair. "I wasn't looking for you, Jenna, but our worlds collided all the same, and I don't want to pass up this chance to get to know you."

Jenna smoothed her lips together as she took this in. He was clearly laying down some cards, and as private as she tended to keep them, they matched her own. He hadn't phrased it as a question, but she found herself agreeing anyway.

The sidewalk was narrow enough that Jake's arm pressed against hers as they walked. Seven's leash was in his opposite hand, and for now, the inquisitive dog was trotting just ahead at the far reach of his leash, pausing occasionally to sniff at one thing in the darkness or scent mark on something else.

"I figured you had someone significant in your recent past because you've referred to an ex-girlfriend in the singular, and most people in their thirties don't have only one ex."

"Yeah, well, that was the timing of it more than anything."

"How long ago did you break up?"

Jake dropped her gaze. "Not soon enough. I'd been thinking about it off and on the last couple of months. We went to Fiji together at the end of January, and it should've been a great time, but I remember this one evening walking along the beach as we took in this incredible sunset. I suddenly just knew with such clarity that I wasn't supposed to be there sharing it with her." He shrugged. "Ever since, it was me processing that and being slammed at work and not wanting to deal with it and then getting really irritated with both myself and her that nothing had changed.

"Then Thursday night came, and I hadn't gotten to it yet. I was headed to meet her at one of these fundraisers she loves going to, and I was angry. Angry at half of what she said. Angry at myself for not breaking up with her earlier. Then the accident happened, and I took Seven rather than meet up with her at the gala. That brush with the potential impermanence of life, seeing the way you were hit... I'll just say after that, there was no putting it off any longer. Even had I not gotten out and talked to you."

Seven had stopped in his tracks and was sniffing excitedly at something unseen along the narrow strip of grass between the sidewalk and curb, and Jake and Jenna had turned to face each other on the sidewalk. The streetlight shone on one side of Jake's face, reflecting in his eyes. Maybe the cold was sinking in or maybe he was a bit on the defensive, but in either case, he'd shoved his hands in his pockets.

Even if he'd already intended to—which judging by his earnest expression, she believed—he'd broken up with his girlfriend after waiting with Jenna in the rain for the ambulance. Even though she wasn't entirely sure this was a good thing, her heart leaped at the thought. Whatever it was that had occurred between them, she hadn't been the only one to feel it.

"Turns out," he added, "she and I were in very different places in the relationship, although what I told her outside tonight stands. I think she has a predetermined goal for how she wants her life to play out, and she was trying to squeeze me into that mold to check off boxes at the right times rather than giving honest thought to whether I was the right person to do those things with. I get she's still processing the breakup, but I suspect she's working through anger over being a few rungs further down on her life plan. Like I said, I told her as much outside earlier, but I'm not sure she's in the space to hear it yet."

"And what about you?"

"The only thing I regret is not breaking up with her sooner." He rocked back on his heels and made a face. "Actually, that's not true. If I had, I wouldn't have met you. Or Seven."

Jenna took in a breath as the randomness of this whole thing sank in. Had she refused Stuart's request, had she seen the driver coming, had Jake listened to his intuition sooner, had he left for his event a handful of seconds sooner or later than he did. How precarious this thing called life was. "Jake, whatever happens, I'm really glad we met, but from what you just shared, something happening between us right now is the opposite of what you're looking for."

"I might not have been looking for you, but here you are all the same. I can't change that. I don't *want* to change it."

"What *do* you want then?"

Jake brushed his fingertips along one side of her cheek. "I guess you could say that answer depends upon where the blood's flowing at the moment, but even when it's all flowing north, I still want you in my life. I want to get to know you." He paused, shaking his head. "No, I want more than that. But when I don't check myself, I can move fast, and given how we met just five days ago, I know I'm moving fast. On top of that, I'm asking for your help with this handful of a canine, and that has the potential to complicate things."

"I offered the help, kind of the same way you offered me this jacket."

His answering smile melted the heaviness that had been in his gaze. "Yeah, well, you look better in my jacket than I do, so it's a win-win."

Jenna fought back a whole-body urge to press her lips against his once more. "Maybe then we save the debatable stuff for later. I think the important thing here is that we keep the lines of communication open and maybe keep brakes on a bit."

"Yeah, okay. Agreed." His smile dropped into something more intimate. "But if I seem to forget how to apply them, will you?"

Jenna bit her lip, but the smile slipped out anyway. "I think I can do that."

"Just to be clear, I won't be handing out demerits or anything if you forget too," he said, making her laugh again. Enticed by Seven, who was pulling at the leash in attempt to get walking again, Jake took her hand, and they started down the sidewalk once more. "In all seriousness, thank you. For not holding a grudge about that interruption earlier, or about me not explaining this sooner."

Seven stopped straining against the leash now that they were making progress again, and Jenna fell quiet for the space of several footsteps before she replied. "I loved someone once who didn't love me back. Technically, we were never more than good friends, but I still loved him. I don't know if he knew it or not, but it doesn't matter. He got swept away by someone else before I worked up the nerve to tell him. It cut me to the quick."

"I can imagine it would."

"Yeah, well, even though it took me awhile to get there, I'm thankful for the experience now—for several reasons, and the biggest one is for me. I think that was a life experience I needed to have, to love someone and not be loved back. I wouldn't have wanted him to be with me because of my feelings for him. If it isn't mutual, there's nothing there. Not really. Hopefully Alyssa will be faster to see this than I was."

"Thank you for putting it like that. I needed to hear it, and I hope so. She's a good person—just meant to be with someone else."

The last of Jenna's insecurities about Jake being over his exgirlfriend drained away. "Since we're pulling out our skeletons tonight, you might as well know I didn't get as clean of an exit from the guy I was telling you about as I'd have liked. It made getting a clean slate a little more of a challenge."

Meeting her gaze, Jake raised an eyebrow. "How so?"

"For the last four and a half years, he's been my brother-in-law."

Jake's brows nearly disappeared into hairline. "You're telling me the person he met was your sister?"

"He was my study partner in med school. We went out with a bunch of people one night to celebrate the end of exams. Half the group was so exhausted that one drink knocked 'em out, and the group thinned out pretty fast. I'd just ordered a second drink because I wanted to get tipsy enough to tell him how I felt. I figured if he didn't feel the same way, I'd have the Christmas break to lick my wounds. Then my sister showed up because of a gigantic fail of a first date, and she needed to vent." Jenna shrugged. "And that's all she wrote. A few hours later, she was going home with the guy I'd been trying for the better part of a month to tell that I loved him."

Jake shook his head, wincing. "Oh, Jenna, that sucks. Please don't tell me she knew?"

"I think at one point I thought she should've, but no, I hadn't told her. It came out later. They were on again, off again for a couple of years, and they got married while he was in residency. She was pregnant with my darling nephew, and honestly, they're just about opposite enough to make sense." She nudged him in the arm. "In case you're wondering, their relationship wasn't why I quit med school. If anything, I stayed in that full second year because I wanted to be certain of my motivations for walking away. I did expand my study partners though," she added with a laugh.

"I hadn't gotten past the part about your sister marrying a guy you'd been in love with, but I'm glad that's the case."

Jenna shrugged. "Like I said, when it's not a good fit for both, then it's not a good fit."

"No wonder you've been so levelheaded about Alyssa showing up like that."

"Quite possibly."

Hands still locked and fingers laced together, Jake tapped the back of her hand lightly against the side of his jeans. "So, what happens now?"

Jenna shrugged. "Hmm. The way I see it, you walk me home but don't come inside. This week, you hang out in the yard with Seven as much as you want. I'll be off, so that'll be nice. Then Friday I can babysit Seven part or all of the day as needed while you're in court, and maybe this weekend we got out to dinner or something, keeping the conversation going and the brakes applied as we get to know each other better, and you get the distance you need from your breakup. How's that sound?"

Seven had stopped to sniff the various toy fairies and accompanying knickknacks some children had set up along the thick roots at the base of an old tree, and Jake and Jenna were facing each other again.

"I like it." Jake's crooked smile pulled up the side of his cheek with the dimple. His gaze dropped from her eyes to lips, and Jenna had a hunch what he was going to ask just before he said it. "You didn't say anything about kissing though. Where does that fall on the spectrum of getting to know one another while still applying brakes?"

Jenna shook her head adamantly. "Sorry, but seeing as how I've already had a taste of how incredible that is, I don't think I can be trusted to answer that without considerable bias."

Jake's smile widened. "Same. How about we vote on it then? Yes to kissing now, and copiously at that. No to waiting a few weeks and letting the tension build."

"Hmm, that's a hard one, Mr. Stiles. Perhaps you could offer me a quick reminder before I make my decision?"

Even before Jake leaned down and pressed his lips against hers, Jenna knew what her answer was going to be.

Chapter 19

EVEN THOUGH SHE WAS only moving between her top-floor apartment and the backyard, each time Jenna headed outside with Seven on Friday, she leashed him up. Getting him leashed took considerable patience and cajoling, but Jenna didn't think it was her imagination that he shied away less and less from the short pettings she doled out before unhooking him.

Dropping to her knees on their fourth trip outside so far today, she sank beside Seven and lowered the canvas tote carrying two newly painted pots to the ground next to her. Anticipating another petting, Seven flattened his ears against his head, making Jenna chuckle. "You're such a sweet boy, Seven, even when you're up to no good like earlier."

Jenna ran her hand down his head and along his back and soaked in the feel of his long, silky fur and warm body underneath. He only seemed to get anxious when she neared his hips and tail, so Jenna stopped at the middle of his back for now, imagining if one day she'd be able to do so from tip to tail without him minding. Miracles never ceased.

"It hasn't been such a bad day, has it?" He'd been anxious when Jake—who'd looked darn sexy in the suit he was wearing for his court case—had dropped him off early this morning, but for the last hour or two, he'd relaxed some. "According to that trainer in St. Louis, you need these pettings as much as anything."

After several gentle strokes, Jenna buried her fingers in the thick hair around his neck and scratched, working her way underneath his collar. She must've hit a sweet spot because Seven unexpectedly leaned into her touch and one back leg thumped in the air. Like a perfectly normal, average, run-of-the-mill family dog. Too surprised for words, Jenna simply scratched as Seven continued to lean into it. She worked her way up and down his neck, and before long, something between a grunt and a groan escaped him, making Jenna laugh.

As if realizing he'd let down his guard, Seven abruptly side-stepped out of reach. Staring her in the eye, he barked once and wagged his tail.

"I'm sorry. I don't speak dog, but you seem to be saying both yes and no at the same time." Seven looked pointedly across the yard as if reminding her that this was his time to be free. "Yeah, yeah, okay. Enough petting for now. God forbid we overdo it, and you become overly domesticated. We wouldn't want that now, would we?"

Jenna stood up and Seven, anticipating her next move, sank onto his haunches and crooked his neck so she had easy access to unhook his collar. "Don't let anyone tell you you're not a smart one."

Once unhooked, Seven bolted away, dashing around the yard with the speed and excitement of a dog who hadn't been free to do so in weeks rather than the ninety minutes since they'd been out here last. Hoisting her tote, Jenna headed for the garden shed.

Although she still had the weekend ahead of her, she dreaded returning to work next week. Not only would she be staring at a bright screen most of the day, but she'd also be going without the midday nap that had proven more enticing than a midday cup of coffee all week. As she unpacked her two newly painted pots, Jenna debated rather to repot the succulents she hoped to take with her to the market tomorrow or wait until later this afternoon. The now-familiar headache that popped up every afternoon since the accident was pressing in, and nothing took care of it like a nap.

Jenna had left the storm door propped open to keep an eye on

Seven as she worked, and a movement caught her eye. The dog stood in the doorway. Without a single paw past the threshold, he sniffed the air, nose lifted. It was the first time all day he'd shown any interest in what Jenna was doing when she stepped inside here.

"Hey, boy. Did you get your zoomies out already?" Seven wagged his tail back and forth, head tilted. "Fair warning, it'll be naptime soon, so soak up the outdoors while you can."

Jenna returned her attention to her potted plant stock, deciding if she had enough ready to take with her to tomorrow's pop-up market or if she needed to do some potting this afternoon. Preseason as it was, traffic would likely be light. When she looked back at Seven what seemed like just seconds later, he had one of the spider plants that had been on the shelf nearest him clamped between his teeth and was wagging his tail hopefully. Even though it was in a cheap plastic pot from the wholesaler, it was still not something he should have. Jenna pointed to the floor and did her best to sound authoritative yet not terrifying. "No, Seven!" She pointed to the ground. "Drop it, boy."

Seven backed up, plant clamped between his teeth, and dipped into a play bow.

"Seven, this isn't a game. Drop it!"

With a wag of his tail, Seven bounded away, turning his head to see if she was following, as if enticing her to play. He'd done this with the boys at her sister's house, snatching up their toys in hopes of getting them to play, and before labeling Seven as untrainable, Monica and Stuart had been working with the boys on the "drop it" command as well as getting them to replace whatever off-limit item he grabbed with an acceptable dog toy. As far as Jenna knew, this was the first time in the last month that he'd attempted to play with an adult, with the exception of what Jake had been doing out here with him this last week, but Jake had been initiating that play, not Seven.

As the wound-up dog bounded further into the yard, tail

wagging and hopping along like the Easter Bunny, Jenna clamped her lips together to hold back a laugh. If he wanted to play, she'd play, but first she needed to save her plant from further harm. Out of the corner of her eye, she spotted a tennis ball resting in the empty center hole of the patio table. One of the other occupants must've seen it and stuck it there while passing between the garage and the house.

Heading over, Jenna grabbed it and bounced it at her feet. Dipping his head, Seven dropped the spider plant on the grass in front of him and barked loudly, fluffy tail wagging in excitement.

Not wanting to miss out on another potential training moment, Jenna kept Seven's attention on the tennis ball while heading his direction. When she got close enough, she swept the plant off the ground and held out both for him to see. Seven impatiently waited through a few firm noes when she held up the plant and some encouraging yeses when she held up the ball.

Before throwing the ball for him, she returned the spider plant to the potting shed and closed the door. There'd be no selling the plant until some of the broken leaves regrew, but no real harm had been done, and spider plants weren't toxic to pets, so no worries there.

Fixated on the ball in her hand, Seven bounded along beside her just past arm's reach. Once the shed door was closed, he barked excitedly. "You win, Seven. Let's play."

Jenna threw the ball across the yard, and Seven dashed after it. Progress wasn't always a straight line, she reminded herself. Sometimes it was the accidental savoring of neck scratches and the snatching of off-limit items in an attempt at play, and she'd take each and every bumpy opportunity he'd give.

Chapter 20

THE DOG JERKED AWAKE from a noise outside, the remnants of a dream clinging to him. He'd dreamed of the man with the calm demeanor who'd reintroduced the dog to the joy of intentional play with humans, and now the dog wanted more. More, more, more. Play called to him the same way food did. Perhaps he wanted it too much. The man had left the dog here with the woman for long enough now that the dog wondered if his stay with him was finished.

Given how the man's scent still clung to the woman's skin after their mouth-on-mouth exchange at her doorstep this morning, the dog was hopeful to see him again. It was one of the dog's least favorite things about humans, how unclear they were about their departures. Arrivals were easy. They were here. Departures, less so.

Not sharing his concerns, the woman was dozing on the couch half-hidden under a blanket, her breathing even and slow.

The dog got up from where he'd been napping on the rug and walked over to the water bowl that had been brought over from the man's home along with a selection of antlers and other chews that seemed to be solely for the dog's use. Aside from on these things and on the woman, the man's scent was nowhere else in the woman's home, and the dog suspected they weren't mated pairs like some humans the dog had stayed with.

With his last family, the dog had come here once before. The scent of that woman was strong in many places here, and the scents of Sam and Joseph clung to the lower portions of the walls and windows where their busy hands had touched, but those scents were more faded than the mother's. As entertaining as the young boys had been, the dog no longer wished to return to their home. There, the dog had been continually bracing for an eruption like he'd experienced in other homes—pieces of furniture and angry words hurled with the same force.

Finished lapping up water, the dog trotted over to where this woman was dozing. Human families were more complicated than canine ones, but from the similarities in their scents, the dog sensed the two women shared the same blood and had been raised together like the two boys. This woman—Jenna, as her people called her— was calmer than her sister, and the dog preferred her company.

Propping his front paws on the edge of the couch, the dog sniffed along her hairline. Her wound was healing, but the rich scent of blood still clung to it. The smell of the sweet treat she'd eaten before curling up on the couch still carried on her breath. Hoping to snag some for himself, the dog dropped to all fours and trotted into the kitchen, sniffing along the counters and nudging the pantry door with his nose to find that it was tightly closed. No food had been left out within reach, and the lid on the trash proved locked.

Disappointed, the dog lapped up some more water before remembering the treats that had been in the woman's jacket earlier. Had she given him all of them? The jacket had been hung beside the door, and the dog trotted over, his mouth watering. Sure enough, one of the pockets still held a few. After tugging the jacket free from the hook, with a bit of finagling, the dog worked the treats out from the pocket with his nose, one by one.

Afterward, he sprawled across the floor and chomped on an antler, hoping to ease the anxiousness that had set up in his jaw for a good chew. The comforting sensation of his teeth crunching down on the antler soon made the dog want to doze again, and his thoughts returned to the man, to Jake. "Seven," he was still calling him, making him long to answer to it. Seven, Seven, Seven.

In the dog's dream earlier, he'd been running alongside the man as they'd been doing in the still dark of early morning, but there had been no leash tethering the dog to him. Even so, the dog had been running as contentedly as could be alongside the man on the long stretch of sand that flanked the endless water at the beach where they'd run yesterday as the sun was rising. In the dream, the dog had even slowed his pace to match the man's. Dreams were confusing like that. The dog had no memory of running beside any human that way. Perhaps he had once as a puppy, but those memories were too faded now to parse out.

The dog had never been to a piece of earth as enticing as that one—oh, the smells that radiated up from the sand! Then there was the water. It stretched out endlessly and smelled of the fish that swam in it. If the dog ever got the chance to run free there, he'd never be able to contain his excitement to run alongside a human at their considerably slower pace. He'd run and run and never stop.

Tired and wanting a soft spot to doze, the dog spied the empty end of the couch just past the woman's feet. The rug and stiff-sided chair weren't nearly as tempting as the couch for a short doze. Sleeping as she was, she wouldn't even know he was beside her. Eyelids getting heavy, the dog abandoned his antler and made his way to the couch, moving stealthily so as not to wake her. He circled a few times and curled into a tight ball, but even so, the bottoms of her feet were still within easy reach. As he was beginning to doze, the woman shifted in her sleep, and suddenly the bottoms of her socked feet were pressing gently against his back.

Lifting his head, the dog watched her for the rise and fall of several of her breaths. Her sleep continued on, peaceful and even, and he remembered the way her deft fingers had felt as they scratched the hard-to-get places underneath his collar.

He'd never once slept this close to a human, but his choice was to abandon the comfort of the couch and warmth of her feet for the unwelcoming floor or the stiff chair. After another few breaths, the dog allowed his head to come to rest on his front paws once again and his eyes to drift closed.

Only this once.

Chapter 21

THANKS TO THIS YEAR'S warmer-than-average winter, jogging with Seven on the sidewalks just before sunrise this week hadn't proven to be a treacherous jaunt over packed snow or black ice. While Jake hoped the warm weather was here to stay, that wasn't likely. Nine days into fostering, he was no closer to getting Seven in his new kennel. This meant taking Seven to work with him next week on his days in the office. It meant skipping the gym or leaving him unsupervised at home. Or forcing him in the kennel, something Jake wasn't ready to do.

Last night, he'd caught Seven standing at the edge of the open kennel door, gazing at the rawhide inside, but he still wasn't tempted to step in and grab it. Perhaps he believed if he did, the door would close behind him, trapping him inside. Jake figured even for dogs, some ghosts were harder to leave behind than others, and he wasn't ready to force Seven to face this one.

With the luxury of an unscheduled Saturday morning stretching out before them, Jake loaded Seven into the rental and headed further north to Lakefront Trail. His jog with Seven the other morning had included a quarter-mile stretch near North Avenue Beach, and Jake had been eager to return after seeing how intrigued Seven had been by the water.

After unloading from the rental, Seven must've caught the scent of the lake on the breeze because he grew excited enough to start prancing in place. Even so, Jake started them out at a walk, giving Seven a chance to go to the bathroom and sniff around a bit.

Quick on the uptake as the dog was, it hadn't taken long for him to pick up on the routine: walks were for sniffing and scent marking, while jogging was for just that—jogging. Once Seven had done his business and they'd backtracked to the nearest trash can, Jake took off at a slow jog on the paved trail that stretched out in both directions until it disappeared along bends in the lake. Craving green space that was considerably more abundant an hour and a half north of here in Racine, Jake headed north on the path away from the city rather than south toward it.

As Seven settled into the pace of the jog, his energy shifted to the calm and attentive focus of a working dog who was being given something to do, neither pulling against the leash nor—for the most part—attempting to stop and sniff at various spots along the trail.

Out here by the lake, the wind was sharp and cold, considerably colder than around the condo where the houses and trees offered a windbreak, and Jake's throat burned, but he pushed through it until the sensation dulled.

"When it comes down to it, I guess you've been bred to work, huh?"

At the sound of Jake's voice, Seven glanced up before returning his attention to the trail ahead of them. Because the dog was doing so well with it, Jake was pushing him longer and longer between walking breaks, stopping somewhere between half- and three-quarter-mile stretches to walk, sniff, and do whatever he wanted to do.

After jogging thirty minutes out on the trail, Jake turned around, heading back toward the car. At the close of an hour, they'd covered close to six miles at a jog with a handful of stops along the way. Aside from a steady pant, Seven looked like he was just getting started. "You could run circles around me, that's for sure."

As for Jake, the steady lake wind and temps still in the low- to midforties had about numbed him through.

After gazing toward the beach, Seven wagged his tail hopefully at Jake. "Yeah, yeah, you want to play in the sand. I get it. Let's get some water first. And I'll grab a jacket."

Water fountains—for people and dogs—were still shut down for the winter, but Jake had planned accordingly and had ample water in the trunk. He'd brought along a few Frisbees, too, but now that it came down to it, he wasn't ready to tempt fate and let go of Seven's leash.

Over the years, he'd seen people using long lead lines for these kinds of things. He'd hoped to come back with one next weekend until he remembered that next weekend was the Saint Patrick's Day parade. Given the throngs of people who'd be pouring into the city for it, he'd steer clear of downtown Saturday with Seven for certain.

After Seven lapped up two bowls of water and Jake grabbed a jacket that would do little to cut the lake wind, they left the parking lot and headed down the open white sand flanking the lake that reflected today's bright-blue skies. Tail lifted like an Arabian horse, Seven pranced at Jake's side like a kid at an amusement park with too many rides at his disposal. Laughing, Jake reached down and ruffled the hair on Seven's lower neck and shoulders, and Seven didn't even wince at his touch.

"As cute as you are, I'm just not ready to let go of this leash. God only knows where'd you'd run off to."

The beach was all but empty except for some sporadic walkers bundled in coats. Jake walked along with Seven just above the swell, his eyes watering from the sting of the wind, until Seven stopped abruptly and started digging with an unexpected ferocity.

"I hope it's buried treasure." Jake had no doubt it was something interesting, judging by Seven's excitement.

Ears pricked forward, Seven continued digging with the determination of a dog on a mission, kicking sand into a wide spray behind him. Squatting alongside him, Jake pulled out his phone to snap a picture and send it to Jenna. After Seven had dug down the better part of a foot, his nails scraped against something that sounded hard and hollow like plastic.

He let out an ear-piercing bark but didn't lose a beat in his digging. "What is it, Seven?" Seven barked again and stopped digging, leaning close to sniff at whatever he'd uncovered.

Jake leaned closer to investigate, but his phone rang while still in his hand. The call, a FaceTime request, was from Jenna, and he clicked accept. "Hey there. You busy selling plants?" She had a worn-in Cubs hat on, her hair was pulled back, and a wide smile lit her face, her white teeth shining.

"Well, I wouldn't say busy, but I've had my first customer. She bought an orchid. I remember her from last year."

"Nice. Not that I know a lot about tropical plants, but isn't it a bit cold for orchids?"

"Fair question. All the plants I brought today should be fine for a few hours in the midforties and up. Plus, I'm set up along the wall of the concessions out of the wind, and the sun's shining. But I'm betting it's a good deal chillier where you are. You look cold."

"Especially after cooling off from a run," Jake said with a laugh. "Honestly, I can't feel much of anything right now." This close to the water, his teeth were nearly chattering.

"Well, there're some food trucks here, and one of them is a bagel truck if you'd like to swing by. They have the best coffees."

"Ah, now two things at the market are calling my name," Jake said with a wink.

Smiling, Jenna blew him a kiss. "So, any idea what he's found?"

Returning his attention to the hole at his feet, Jake shook his head. At its widest, the exposed portion of Seven's find was maybe an inch thick. It was dark-green and sculpted—a well-muscled thigh, Jake realized. Further down, a two-toed foot was sticking up out of the sand.

"Look at that." Jake flipped the camera so that it was facing out and aimed at the center of Seven's freshly dug hole.

"Please tell me that's not an animal."

"An anthropomorphic one, but a toy," Jake said with a laugh. He rotated the camera toward Seven, who was digging a bit less exuberantly now that he'd begun unearthing it. "It's crazy he smelled it buried so far down."

"So, what is it?" Jenna asked.

"Hold on a sec. He's almost got it out, and you can see for yourself." To help Seven out, Jake reached in and pulled the plastic foot out of the sand enough that he'd have something to grip onto. Sure enough, the leg was still attached to the rest of the doll, and Seven needed to tug hard to free the rest of it from the sand. Once he had, he held it gripped in his mouth, his head sticking up high.

"Is that a Teenage Mutant Ninja Turtle?" Jenna asked with a laugh. "It's bigger than Seven's head!"

"That it is. Too bad it's missing an arm. It's Michelangelo, and I'm pretty sure it's a collectible."

"I wonder how long it's been buried. And who left it there."

"Who knows," Jake said. "But I don't think Seven cares." They both laughed as Seven trotted around at the full reach of his leash, a sandy green plastic Ninja Turtle hanging from his mouth.

"No, I don't think he does." Jenna stuck out her lower lip playfully. "I can't believe I miss him so much after spending the whole day with him yesterday."

"Yeah, I'm finding that he grows on you like that, but if you're serious about wanting company, we'll swing by."

"Definitely."

"Not that it's a game changer or anything, but didn't you say your sister was going to be there?"

"She dropped me off with all my stuff and went back home. She's coming back with the boys after lunch once it warms up a bit, though I appreciate how you clarified that," she said with a laugh.

Jake chuckled. "I'd love to meet her. I just wasn't sure how the boys would handle seeing Seven again."

"True, but we've got three hours or so before they're back, so no issues there."

"I'll see you shortly then." Hanging up, Jake glanced over at Seven, who'd settled onto the sand and was chewing Michelangelo's foot. Jake couldn't imagine how the dog was tolerating all the sand still clinging to the toy getting in his mouth, but he didn't seem to care. Jake would offer him another drink of water once they got back to the car.

"Come on, Seven. Let's go. And you can bring along your special treasure." And for no reason other than that he wanted to hear the sound of it leaving his lips, Jake added, "We're going to pay my girlfriend a visit."

—⁓—

Jake's visit to the market was a bit like him getting a first glimpse inside her imperfectly organized cabinets and closets. This thing Jenna was doing with her painting and the plants was deeply personal, but here at the market was where she stepped into the public eye and offered her shiny dream out for everyone to see. Maybe that's why it had been easier to show him inside the secluded space of her garden shed, the cozy nook where the dream was still nestled in the space of privacy. If he paid attention here, he'd no doubt see the way some of the early-season shoppers averted their gaze when passing her table.

Not everybody was in the market for a well-potted plant; Jenna didn't mind. Many of the other vendors had a following of their own. Given how a rising tide floated all boats, she'd never batted an eye over how much business other people brought in, and an upside of this was that most customers left having purchased from more than one vendor.

Since she started here last year, Jenna had found that enough people connected with her potted plants each day that she went home with a smile and a nice chunk of money. Even so, she couldn't help wondering what Jake would think of all this.

She studied him as he stood on the other side of her table and checked out her competition, Seven at his side. A small line had formed at the Nobody's Got Nuts like Bernie's table even before Bernie had finished setting up, and Margie's Honey Butter Is Better Than Sex table tended to be another vendor to get the earliest sales. One of last season's newcomers, Candles by Claire Voyant, promised to be a steady hit as well. While the owner's first name was Claire, her last name was Wheeling, not Voyant, but the play on words had helped distinguish her earthy candles from other candle vendors occasionally selling here. Claire's locally sourced, soy-based candles were blended with white sage, lavender, rosemary, or cedar. Jenna had a cedar candle in her living room and a lavender one in her bedroom. Another one of her favorite booths to support was the Sole-Mates vendor whose imperfectly matched but coordinating socks were made with materials from recycled cotton remnants. In fact, she probably owned a different-colored pair for every day of the week.

"Lots of vendors here for this early in the season." Jake turned her way once more. The quick but firm kiss he'd greeted her with from across the table had sent a burst of happiness down her limbs that she was still savoring.

"Yeah, last year was my first season here, but from what I remember, the preseason pop-up events started out strong, then died back a bit until the weather really warmed up."

"Makes sense."

After greeting Jenna with a shrill bark when he realized who was on the other side of the table, Seven had turned away and was sniffing the air, his tail flicking hopefully back and forth.

It hit Jenna that all last year here or at the more sporadic craft fairs she'd participated in earlier than that, she'd never had a love interest—or his dog—pay a visit while she was working. Anu had certainly had ample opportunity to come here with her, but if the weather at all cooperated, he golfed every Saturday. Perhaps, Jenna realized, the fact that he hadn't carved out a single visit in all those months they'd been together had been sign enough he wasn't for her.

But Jake was here, his assertion that her colorful table of potted plants looked remarkable still ringing in her ears. He stood across the table from her. The skin of his cheeks above his stubble was still pink from his run in the lake wind, and his lips had a redness to them that made Jenna ache for another kiss.

Jake nodded toward Bernie's table on the opposite side of the lot. "So, ah, not to get too personal, but can you attest to Mr. Bernie's claim? I'm starving."

Jenna laughed. "If you're starving, then you need more than a bag of cinnamon-roasted pecans or almonds. Like I said earlier, the food trucks won't disappoint." She pointed toward the south end of the closed-off parking lot where a small crowd had gathered to take advantage of the various offerings. "And since you asked, I don't know if he has any ready yet, but Bernie's butter toffee pecans are close to sinful. I could be talked into going home with a bag of them today if you'd like to try them."

Looking down the row of tables, Jenna searched for any sign of Mandy, the vendor whose goods were at the table to her left, and spotted her on her way back from the food trucks. "My table mate for today—Mandy—is going to watch my table when she gets back so that I can run over to the food trucks with you. Bud's Bagels would be my suggestion based on who's here today. If you haven't had one, trust me, you can never go wrong with a Bud's Bagel."

Jake clamped a hand over his stomach. "I'm sold." He looked over at the table next to her. "Mandy sells dried herbs, huh?"

"Offseason. When she's here. Come May, she'll be selling bundles of fresh herbs, and thriving ones at that."

Mandy was halfway across the lot, a large coffee in one hand and a folded wax-paper sandwich bag in the other. She was the first to say her short legs had never slowed her down. Jake's brows lifted as he looked at Mandy more carefully. "I actually remember her—and the Brewers cap. I've bought from her before."

"Oh yeah? Small world." As Mandy neared, Jenna offered an introduction. "Mandy, this is Jake. He was just saying he remembers buying from you before."

"That right?" With Seven having caught the lion's share of her attention, Mandy shook her head. "Look at that pretty boy! I've wanted a border collie ever since seeing the movie *Babe* when I was a kid. Actually, at first I wanted a pig, not a dog." Mandy raised a finger playfully and winked. "Growing up in Lincoln Park and literally having a yard the side of a postage stamp, I was pretty quick to figure out that wasn't in my future, so I switched to asking for a border collie instead. What is it now, close to thirty years later, and sadly I'm no closer to getting one that I've ever been. My husband's a stickler for couch-potato dogs, and he came with two of 'em."

"Couch-potato dogs have their merits too," Jake said. "This guy was on my bed at five fifteen this morning, one of my sneakers dangling from his mouth," he added. "I'm getting the sense it'll be a challenge for him to understand that we don't have to wake up early on weekends."

Getting up from her chair, Jenna crossed in between the two tables to join them. "Aww. Granted it's probably less sweet when it's you who's being woken up, but it's still sweet. He's really wanting to connect with you."

Jake raised an eyebrow. "That's my hope. I got up and took him for a short walk, then went back to bed for another hour or two, and he refrained from gnawing on a single piece of furniture this time."

After trotting over to give Jenna a quick sniff, Seven refocused on Mandy, eyeing the bag in her hand, his tail wagging hopefully.

"Not a chance," Mandy said. "Cute as you are, big guy, I'd fight you for full rights to my lox bagel. I haven't had one of these in close to five months."

Jake shifted Seven's leash from one hand to the other. "Jenna's been talking the bagels up, and I'm sold."

"You won't be disappointed, promise. And they have day-old bagel bites for dogs too." Mandy turned her full attention to Jake—and away from Seven. "You know, I think I remember you too. Anybody ever tell you that you look like Adam Levine?"

Glancing over at Jake, Jenna blinked. Now that Mandy had thrown it out there, she could see a similarity that extended beyond the dark hair and lean torso. Perhaps in the shape of the face or his hazel eyes.

"Nobody who's ever heard me sing," he said with a serious enough expression that made Mandy laugh. Heading behind their tables, Mandy motioned them on. "I've got your green babies, Jenna. Sit at the picnic tables while you eat, if you want. I promise I'll holler if I get busy."

As they headed off, Jake closed a free hand over Jenna's back, and a rush of happy warmth flooded over her. This thing with Jake was real. Something about his showing up here made that clear. And even though everything was still so new and undefined between them, there was an easiness to this that in Jenna's experience usually took a much longer time coming—if it came at all. "I'm glad you're here."

"Me too. This thing you're doing is awesome, and a cool way to spend a Saturday." His hand left her back to lock with hers, and their fingers entwined.

The back of Jenna's hand brushed against the side of his nylon joggers and against his outer thigh, bringing her attention to all the parts of him she'd hopefully get lucky enough to explore at one point or another. But right now wasn't the time to think about that. "Thanks, and yeah, it's a good way to spend a Saturday morning. Especially when the weather holds out."

Jake's brows furrowed. Jenna was about to ask him what was wrong when he continued. "You know, recognizing Mandy like that got me thinking. The night of the accident—you remember what I said about looking over and seeing you a few blocks before you got hit?"

Jenna leaned against him playfully. "That would be hard to forget, even for a girl recovering from a concussion."

He smiled. "The thing is, I wonder if some part of me recognized you. Now that I'm here, I'm certain our paths crossed at some point last year. Even if I didn't buy anything from your table, I'd have spotted you at one point or another."

"I'm sure, but what about it?" By the way he was quick to glance downward, this was the first time he seemed anything other than sure of himself, making Jenna wonder what was coming.

"Just that maybe it helps explain why it felt like everything stopped—or needed to stop—when I looked over at you. Because I don't believe in fate, Jenna." He said it with a laugh, but it didn't mask the earnestness in his tone. "Or any of that other stuff."

At the mention of "other stuff," the word *soulmates* popped into Jenna's mind, but she wasn't about to voice it. Besides, she didn't believe in that stuff either. That was her sister's job, to turn everything that happened into a sign or a part of her destiny or a message from her higher self, the "I can't help it that I fell for your best friend and study partner—we're meant to be" exacerbations that sometimes made Jenna want to bang her head against a wall.

Even though what came out next wasn't Jenna's typical MO, it was the most vulnerable she'd been in a long time. "I don't believe in that stuff either, not really. Even so, I remember the first time I saw you...or can remember seeing you, anyway. Everything around those couple minutes is patchy, but it was dark and cold and everything hurt and Seven was making so much noise and you were this stranger who was holding my hand. None of it made sense, but I looked over at you, and you had this concerned expression on your face that absolutely didn't fit the chaos of the moment, and I remembering thinking, 'What did I do to earn this?'" With a shrug, she added, "Yeah…mostly, I'm still thinking that."

Jake stopped, and since Jenna was holding his hand, she stopped too. Seven glanced back, his ears perked and his head cocked. "That's what I keep asking myself. Every morning."

When he brushed his lips against hers in a way that conveyed all the emotion she could see building in his eyes, Jenna was half-tempted to wish for a way to bottle up the experience and keep it forever. Something told her that if such a request were granted, it would most certainly back up the train of life and stop other important moments from coming. Instead, she determined to savor it while it lasted, and when the kiss ended, small smiles lit both their faces.

"Maybe the answer to that is we both did the same thing—everything and nothing." Jake motioned toward the sun that had popped out between thick, patchy clouds. "Maybe we just soak up the sun and not worry about how long it's going to be out."

This time, Jenna was the one to step in for a kiss. "I can get on board with that. Most definitely."

—⁓—

Arms loaded with two coffees, three bagels, and a bag of treats for Seven, Jake headed for one of the open picnic tables that was in the sun and waved at Jenna, who was walking Seven around a clump of trees. Earlier, while Jake had been waiting for the bagels, Seven had gotten so excited about something in a branch above him that, for a moment there, it had looked as if he was attempting to master Tree Climbing for Dogs 101.

The irony didn't escape Jake that he and Jenna were having the intimate conversations they were having while—until a few minutes ago—he didn't even know how she liked her coffee. Even so, that never-quiet inner voice of his wasn't doling out his typical warnings. In fact, if it was saying anything, it was, *Go on, jump. It'll be okay.*

Maybe there really was a first time for everything.

"Well, he likes squirrels," Jenna said with a laugh as she and Seven walked up, Seven practically dragging her along. Jake didn't doubt the dog hoped some of the food in Jake's hands was for him. "Good thing dogs don't have retractable claws. For a second there, I thought he was going to pull me up that tree."

"No kidding. Good thing for my furniture too. He likes to dig before he settles in for a doze, I've noticed." As Jenna took a seat on the bench opposite him, Seven hung back a few feet, eyeing them both before homing in on the wax-paper sandwich bags. He was panting from his encounter with the squirrel, and there was a gleam of excitement in his eyes that almost looked like straight joy.

"You know, going back to what we were talking about earlier," Jenna said, "about fate and all. If one *did* believe that kind of stuff, it'd be a nice way to think about how all the things that happened to Seven were actually leading him to you."

Jake's forehead tightened as Jenna's words sank in. "Yeah, minus the fact that I'm just fostering him." Even though she didn't voice it, Jenna's expression made it clear she thought Jake should've said something entirely different. "Not the answer you hoped for, huh?"

"If you ask me, you two belong together. Not that I'm pressuring you," she added with a sly smile that called his attention to her mouth and had him itching to reach across the table and kiss her. "You need to do what's right for you. I get it."

"Most of the time, I don't think I'm very good at knowing what's right for me, though I've gotten better at figuring out what's *wrong* for me—faster than I used to anyway."

"Maybe it's okay to not know anything more than that what you're doing with him right now is making a difference. An important one."

Seven pressed in then, planting his front paws on the bench next to her and leaning in to sniff the bags of bagels. Catching Jake's gaze, he bounded back from the table like he was about to scolded, but Jake didn't think it was his imagination that it wasn't with the wild-eyed fear he'd shown earlier in the week.

"You know," he said, "I think if dogs could speak, one of the things they'd tell people is less talk, more action…and more food. Seven, for sure." Sorting the bags, he passed the one marked BC, short for Breakfast Club, in Jenna's direction.

"At least he's a quick learner. All you had to do was shake your head, and he hasn't yet tried getting back up on the table for the food."

"He is a quick learner. I'll give him that. For some things. When I put away my shoes, I tell him no as I close my coat closet door, but anytime he wants to go outside, he's quick to flick the handle with one paw and swipe one of my shoes. He's not chewing on them, just carrying them around and letting me know what he wants to do. What he wants *me* to do is more like it."

Jenna made a face. "Please tell me you recognize how cute that is."

Jake shook his head and chuckled. "Yeah, but I can't say it bodes well for him accepting that I'm the alpha in this relationship. Hey, I meant to tell you, I scheduled a tour of an agility and training center over in Des Plaines Wednesday evening. Wanna come along?"

"Yeah, I'd like that. I'm back to work next week, but I'll have evenings free."

"It's a date then," Jake said and gave her fingers a squeeze.

"Yes, please," she said in just a suggestive enough manner that Jake was compelled to get to his feet, lean over, and kick-start the best kiss of the day, which Seven interrupted with a high-pitched bark.

After pulling away, Jenna brushed her fingers down the side of Jake's face. "While I could do that all day, I think someone's telling us he's as hungry as you are."

"You'd never guess he had breakfast already," Jake said, settling back onto his bench seat.

Jenna lifted a brow. "I can't blame him. I'm kind of hobbity like that sometimes too. Those second breakfasts are the best."

Jake laughed. "You're a pleasure, Jenna. I mean that."

"Thank you, and likewise. So, what'd you end up choosing for you?" Motioning toward the third bagel, she added, "Or which two, I should say."

"Mandy made that lox bagel sound worth fighting for, so I figured I'd give that a try. The extra one is a dessert bagel. Chocolate hazelnut cream with toasted almonds and banana."

"Oh, I had that once. It's delicious."

Under Seven's watchful eye, Jenna had been pulling out her sandwich from its bag but stopped to look at something that had caught her interest.

Over at the edge of the lot, a new vehicle was parking behind the other mobile vendors. Rather than a full-size truck, this one was a modern cargo van, narrow and easy to drive but tall enough to stand up inside the cargo area. The graphic on the side read *The Bearded Barber*. Underneath that was a pen-and-ink profile of a bearded man, and below that, a pair of scissors and a tagline that read, "On-the-run cuts, shaves, and trims."

"If we're talking about what we want, or at least what we'd wish for if we could, I'd have to say one of my big ones is what just pulled in."

"A mobile barber truck or a more heavily bearded boyfriend?" Jake savored Jenna's soft laughter that followed his quip.

"What you've got going on there is pretty sexy, if you ask me." Jenna's flirtatious look heated Jake's blood. "The first one, without the barber part."

"For your plants?"

Jenna nodded. "It would be so much easier. I could bring a bigger selection, and the sensitive ones would be protected from the weather. Plus, I could travel all around town."

"Why don't you then? That'd be awesome."

"Because they're anything but cheap. I looked into it before buying the truck. I couldn't even get close to justifying the numbers." She shrugged. "Maybe in seven or eight years when my med school loans are paid off."

Jake rubbed his temple and forehead as his ADHD kicked his thoughts into overdrive, the words threatening to tumble out in a rush. "Not to go all defense attorney on you again, but after that accident, you've got a payout coming to you." He held up a hand before she shot him down. "I get you don't want to sue. But that man was fully insured and drunk. You lost a truck, suffered a concussion, got a crapload of stitches, and a dog that had already been through hell went through it again—for a short time, at least. You've got money coming to you, Jenna, and you don't have to take the driver to court or even get a lawyer. Hell, I'd be happy to make a few phone calls on your behalf. Just know that your situation isn't necessarily what it was a year ago when you bought the Tacoma."

Scooping the back of her hair into one hand, Jenna looked from Jake across the park to the van. "What's your best guess of what I could walk away with? *Without* a lawsuit."

Jake dragged a hand over his mouth. "Over 50K. Likely closer to a hundred."

Seeing the way she blinked a few times was proof enough that it was a bigger number than she was prepared for. Wanting to give her the space to process this, Jake opened the bag with the day-old hunks of bagel that had been basted in beef broth then dried overnight, and Seven whined like he knew they were for him.

"Sit, Seven."

With zero hesitation, Seven sank on his haunches and sat as still as the gargoyles lining Randolph Tower near Millennium Park. After Jake opened his palm and offered over the largest bagel chunk, Seven escaped to the far edge of his leash and hunkered down on the grass to munch it into pieces.

Next, Jake slid his own bagel out of its bag and took a hearty bite. Mandy hadn't been kidding. It was worth fighting a dog over, and maybe a human too. "Damn, that's good," he said when he finished a second bite.

Jenna grinned. "I'm glad you think so."

"Sorry if what I said upset you just now."

She nodded. "I'm okay, just a little in shock, I guess. That much money would be a game changer. With more time and a truck like that one, I really think I could make a go of this business. It always just felt like such a catch-22. At least, until now."

"Would you quit the clinic then?"

"Not for a while. I'll drop down to three days a week in a heartbeat though, if my finances ever warrant doing so. It'd be great to have Fridays off. There's almost as much that goes on in this city on Fridays as Saturdays."

Jake lifted his coffee her direction in a toast. "Here's to that coming your way sooner than you think."

Jenna had just tapped her cup against his when something over by the vendors caught her attention, and her eyes went wide. "Oh crap. Speaking of things coming our way sooner than we think, Thing 1 and Thing 2 are running this way."

Glancing over his shoulder, Jake spotted two little boys running their direction full tilt, the smaller one moving at a considerably slower pace than the older one. A well-dressed blond brought up the rear at a walk as she yelled at them to be careful.

Well, it seemed he'd be meeting Jenna's family after all.

Chapter 22

HOW HUMANS COULD IGNORE food that was right in front of them was beyond the dog's comprehension. Hungry for more of those mouth-watering treats, the dog wriggled in place in hopes of getting Jake's attention, but his efforts were interrupted by the familiar sounds of Sam and Joseph calling out in play. They were here, running across the grass toward him. A rush of conflicting emotions sent shivers raking across the dog's body and a fresh pant over his tongue. Did this mean he'd be leaving Jake? The dog's whole body began to quiver at the thought.

Sam, the older boy, reached him first, smelling of sweat from the exertion of his run, his hands and mouth smelling of cheese crackers, and the salty dampness of recently shed tears clinging to his eyelashes. "Axel! You're here! I didn't know you'd be here!" His small hands worked their way into the dog's fur, and the dog went still. He looked over at Jake to find that distress lined features that had so recently been relaxed and easy as he and Jenna talked.

The dog was so desperate to know what the boys' arrival meant that panic disoriented him. If he went back to living with the boys, their father would most certainly lock him in a cage again.

When Joseph reached them, he hurled his small body against the dog. "I missed you, Toby!" His chubby fingers locked around the dog's ear, and the dog skittered backward, accidentally pulling the toddler off-balance. He fell to the ground, and tears budded on his eyelids. The dog leaned in and licked the boy's cheeks until a laugh erupted from him.

Jenna helped pull Joseph to his feet and then planted a kiss on the top of his head.

Sam pushed in. "Auntie Jenna, how come you have Axel?"

Kneeling at Joseph's level, Jenna spoke to the boys, her tumble of words lost on the dog, but her calm tone and demeanor comforting. Even so, shivers continued to rake his body.

Picking up on his unease, Jake unhooked the leash from where Jenna had tied it to the table and wrapped the end around his wrist, offering his own calming words the dog's way. "Good boy, Seven. Not a thing for you to be worried about, bud."

While the dog didn't fear the boys' touch—not even Joseph's, despite the way his small fingers sometimes tugged on his hair hard enough to pinch—he didn't yearn to lean into it the way he had when Jenna had scratched along his neck and under his collar the day before. With the young boys, the dog had always given more than he'd received.

It was different than in his recent life with Jake. Jake had been offering the dog more than he'd been demanding from him, so unlike the people in the dog's other homes.

Jake lifted the bag of treats off the table and sank down so that he was level with the boys but used his body as a buffer between them and the dog. "How'd you two like to give Seven a treat?"

"Me first! Me first!" Sam said, cutting off his little brother, and Joseph burst into full-fledged crying. Jenna lifted him into her arms, talking about sharing and taking turns and other things the dog didn't understand.

Sam extended his small hand for a treat. "Why are you calling him Seven?"

"Because Seven's a lucky number and a lucky name." Jenna returned Joseph, who'd stopped crying again, to his feet.

Joseph shoved out his small hand too. "Is our doggie lucky?"

Jenna looked at Jake, a thin crease splitting her eyebrows. "I certainly think so."

Jake had a treat in his hand, and the dog sank onto his haunches and licked his jowls even as his body continued to tremble. Nothing he was witnessing made it clear who'd be taking him home from here.

If it was Jake—if Jake gave him another chance—the dog would do better. He'd listen more; he'd stop chewing on the leg of that piece of furniture that tasted so divine. He'd do his best to stop swiping left-behind morsels off the kitchen counters when Jake wasn't looking. Sometimes the dog did that even before he realized he was doing it, so quitting it wouldn't be easy. He'd even go by Seven, if that's what Jake wanted.

"I'm sure you've fed him treats before," Jake said as he placed a small piece of the savory treats on each boy's outstretched hand. "Just keep your hand flat while he takes it from you."

To prove how good he could be, the dog waited at attention until Jake nodded that he could take the treats, then snatched them up with quick flicks of the tongue that made the boys erupt into laughter.

He was still munching when the boys' mother walked up. His whole body started trembling even harder at the sight of her. Aside from a lot of angry words aimed in his direction and too much time trapped in that crate of theirs, nothing so bad had happened to the dog in that house to have his body trembling so heavily, but it was beyond his control. Perhaps it had to do with the fact that while there, the dog had constantly been bracing for something worse to happen, given the way the man and woman so often snapped at each other when the boys were asleep or in another room. The dog had been so tired there, so on edge. He didn't ever want to feel that way again.

With Jake, the dog had been sleeping deeper and for longer stretches than he could remember. A few times, he'd even let down his guard enough that Jake had moved through the room without the dog so much as stirring.

"Mommy, Mommy, we want to take Seven home again! Did you know his name was Seven now? And can't we take him home again, pleeeease?" Sam said as Joseph dug his small fingers deeper into his fur.

Their mother was too busy greeting Jake to listen, so Sam repeated his plea over and over until he had her attention.

There were two deep lines of worry above her eyes when she looked the dog's way. "Well, this is perfect timing, isn't it?" She hoisted Joseph onto her hip and pressed a kiss against his cheek. "Remember how Mommy's doctor said having a dog with as much energy as Seven wasn't a good idea for me right now? Remember how you and Sammy have your new train table now instead? Think of how much *fun* you've been having with it."

"It's not as much fun as Seven!" Sam crossed his arms, and his whole body tensed like wire.

His mom's shoulders lifted, then fell as she heaved a big sigh. "Sammy, this is not how we show our best selves to Auntie's new friend, is it?"

The dog looked from Jake to Jenna to the boys' mom, desperate to understand what was happening. Were they arguing about him? Sidestepping directly in front of Jake, he barked and wagged his tail. When Jake looked his way, the dog whined.

"It's okay, Seven. It's alright, buddy." Jake looked at Jenna. "He really seems worked up. Maybe I'll take him for a quick loop around the park to see if he settles down."

Jenna nodded. "Yeah, that'd be good. Boys, we'll see Seven again in a few minutes, and maybe you two can play on the playground for a bit, huh?"

In a flurry of commotion as the food was packed away, Jake led the dog off toward the other edge of the park where there were more squirrels than people. Jake sank down next to him, and the dog didn't even scramble away when Jake ran his hand down the fur along his side. "Seven, good buddy, no need to get so worked up. Nothing's changing. You're coming home with me."

The dog didn't understand Jake's words, not most of them, but he trusted his tone and his gentle gaze and the reassuring touch of his hand. Jake wasn't sending him away. The dog would get another chance. Another chance to run on the sand by the water. Another chance to play chase in Jenna's big yard. Another chance to eat dinner out of Jake's hands. Shoving forward, the dog swept his tongue across Jake's face, from his chin to his nose, the thick stubble tickling the dog's tongue.

"Aww, Seven," Jake said, wiping his face. "I thought I'd never see the day."

The dog pressed in again, dousing Jake in a few more licks. He was also getting another chance to get used to his newest given name. Seven. This time, the dog wanted to make it stick.

Chapter 23

By the time the last of the unsold plants were loaded into the back of Monica's Traverse, the boys had gone from teetering on the edge of meltdown mode to swimming in it. Refusing to climb into his car seat, Sam planted himself on the curb, arms crossed as he whined about all the things he hadn't gotten or been able to do over the course of the day. Joseph was red-faced and blubbering amid a full-scale toddler tantrum and had thrown himself on the grass. Monica attempted to lift him, but he was a thirtysomething-pound deadweight and doing his best to counteract her efforts, so Jenna took over. Monica didn't need to strain like that this far into her pregnancy.

While Seven's name hadn't come up in the last two hours, Jenna knew the boys hadn't forgotten about their encounter with him or their hopes of bringing him home. The topic would no doubt be revisited again at home. Jenna was betting around bath time, when the boys were most prone to reflection. For now, more immediate things had their attention, like the cupcakes they hadn't been allowed from the cupcake truck or the crocheted dinosaurs for sale four tables down from Jenna.

As Jenna hoisted Joseph up into the Traverse, something about the way his body torqued in struggle struck her funny bone, and she did her best to lock down a smile. Spent as the little guy was, he'd likely think she was mocking him. Leaning in, she planted a kiss on his forehead, which was hot from exertion.

While she'd gotten him into his seat, she was never going to get the buckles snapped until he stopped arching his back. Pulling his favorite stuffed-animal crocodile out from the travel bag, Jenna tapped him on the knee to get his attention. "Joseph, want your Crocky?"

At first, his expression made it clear he'd continue to fight her, and he shoved Crocky away, but then, just as abruptly, he lunged for it right as Jenna was about to slip it back in the bag. "I want Crocky!" Still in a crying jag, Joseph hugged his favorite worn and slightly soiled crocodile against him, and Jenna was able to wedge her fingers in between the boy and his crocodile to snap the buckles closed. Mission accomplished.

"Aww, what sweet cuddles you're giving Crocky."

Eyes damp with tears and chubby cheeks splotchy red, Joseph gave a nod. "Crocky likes hugs." And just like that, he'd transitioned from monster toddler to endearing but exhausted toddler who no longer rejected touch.

Jenna wiped his cheeks dry and planted a kiss on top of his head. "I think he especially likes hugs from you."

On the other side of the SUV, her sister had convinced Sam to climb in as well, but he was still sulking. While Sam had moved away from his daily naps, Jenna wouldn't be surprised if he dozed off on the way home today right along with his younger brother.

Monica had brought the boys earlier than anticipated with the understanding that Stuart would swing by before lunch and take them home, but he was on call today, and that hadn't happened, and now, this. Not that Jenna was surprised he hadn't shown up. Stuart only put in a handful of forty-hour workweeks a year, two of which were over Thanksgiving and Christmas. The rest of the year, aside from a couple not-quite week-long vacations, he put in more hours than Jenna did at both her jobs.

Given how Monica had been the one to go to bat for baby number three, this mostly solo-parenting thing seemed to be working out for her. This was how it had been at Jenna and Monica's house when they were kids, too, only their dad's career had been on the manual labor side of things.

Finished with Joseph, Jenna climbed into the front passenger seat and collapsed against it, savoring a few seconds to herself while Monica passed out graham crackers and sipper bottles before she climbed into the driver's seat. "Thanks for making today happen," she said when her sister got in and closed the door. "It meant a lot to make this first day of the season."

"That's a no-brainer," Monica said with a wave of the hand. "I wouldn't have let you miss it. And you did good. That's less than half of what we brought back there. Maybe a third."

"Yeah, it was a nice start. Several of my buyers were repeat ones from last year too."

"Nice." Monica slumped against the steering wheel a second or two. "Pretty please will you come home with me for a bit? Stuart will still be locked in his office, I'm sure, and your plants'll be fine in the trunk."

The boys overheard and echoed the plea for her to come home with them.

"I was going to go home and crawl under my covers for a bit. Given how I'm going back to work next week, I'm going to miss my newfound nap habit."

Monica stuck out her lower lip and blinked her eyes. "You can nap on my bed, if you want."

"That's a hard pass on that one, thank you."

"You can nap on my bed, Auntie Jenna," Sam pleaded. "I'll be *real* quiet. And give me the remote, Mommy. I wanna watch Daniel Tiger."

Joseph drummed the backs of his ankles against his car seat. "Me too! Me too!"

Monica waggled a finger. "Sammy, do we say, 'Give me,' or do we say, 'Please may I'?"

Sam dropped his shoulders as he let out an exaggerated breath. "Can I have the remote *please*, Mommy?"

Not one to hold out for perfection, Monica passed him the remote—Jenna figured her sister would give up on hoping for her kids' natural use of *may* before too long—and by the time they'd made it a quarter mile out of the park, the theme song to *Daniel Tiger's Neighborhood* rang out in the back seat. Jenna suspected that, at four, Sam knew how to work the Traverse's Infotainment System better than she could.

Monica reached back and tapped Sam on the tip of his sneaker. "Turn it down, please, so Mommy and Aunt Jenna can talk." Whether he did a smidge or not, Jenna wasn't sure, but Monica let her request go as the boys fell into that cathartic quiet of overtired kids given food and television. "I'm starving," she added. "Think about what we can make for a late lunch or order in, will you?"

Had she actually agreed to go to her sister's, or had her wish being so outnumbered made any decision moot? With Monica, everything but a very clear no was a yes. "Okay, but I had a big breakfast earlier with that bagel sandwich."

"The one you enjoyed with your *boyfriend*," Monica added, dragging out the word *boyfriend* to several times its typical length.

With the boys and customers in earshot earlier, Jenna hadn't gotten more than a "Well, I can see why you're so taken with him" from her sister before they'd gotten swept onto another topic entirely.

"So, other than the chaos surrounding your first impression, what'd you think?"

Monica raised her eyebrows. "What I said earlier. He's a cutie, that one. But I think the more important question here is what do *you* think?"

Jenna took a second or two coming up with an answer. "That it feels like I'm floating when I'm around him."

"Well, I haven't heard you say anything like that in a long time.

Maybe never, now that I think about it." Monica let out an exaggerated sigh. "You know what I'd give to feel that again? There's no floating on clouds when you're parenting kids under five…unless it's when your babies are asleep maybe. But not about your partner. Certainly not someone who's so married to his work."

Jenna didn't know what to say to that, but Monica didn't stay quiet for long. When she dropped her voice, Jenna had to lean in to hear her over the rear stereo system.

"Maybe it's fatigue and ligament pain talking, but sometimes I worry it was a mistake to try again. I know I'll love her when she gets here, but seriously, with *three* of these, I'm going to need another sister. As it is, the one I have looks like she's going from busy to even busier now that Mr. Dreamy is in the picture."

"I'm always going to make time for you and the kids. You know that. But, Monica, you can't do it all. With Stuart as busy as he is, I really think you should consider a nanny. You've got the funds for it. A couple days a week, at least." When Monica pursed her lips in thought, Jenna added, "I know Mom did it by herself when we were little, but it was a different time. And she wasn't managing the same crazy schedule you are."

"Yeah, maybe. I've been thinking about it." Monica dropped her voice lower even though the kids couldn't hear her. "Sometimes I think Stuart works so much because it's easier than parenting the kids."

Jenna glanced back at the boys. Sam was transfixed by the screen in front of him, munching on his crackers. Joseph had dozed off already, a half-eaten cracker stuck to his bottom lip, his mouth open, and his thick eyelashes wet from the tears he'd shed. "I don't know if it helps any, but I've only kept in touch with a couple people from my med school days, and neither of them have even started *trying* to navigate a family around their careers."

"It's just that he really didn't want number three." Tears stung Monica's eyes. "And now he sleeps with his back to me."

Jenna blinked. "Would a date night help? The boys can sleep over, if you'd like."

"I don't know. Maybe. It hasn't been great since this," she said with a motion toward her belly, "but it got worse when I failed so badly with the D-O-G."

Jenna blinked. "When it failed or when you brought him home? Because if I remember correctly, you said Stuart was super pissed the D-O-G was there in the first place."

Monica shook her head abruptly as she slowed down to make a right turn. "He blew off some steam like he always does, but it was different when the D-O-G left. Like he blamed me for scarring our babies forever for taking him away, especially given how this whole scare of mine turned out to be benign."

"Have you talked to him about this? Because I can't see this being the thing he's mad at, if he's mad and not just stressed or exhausted."

"I hate it when you do that."

The abrupt change in her sister's tone had Jenna sitting up in her seat. "Do what?"

"Act like you know him better than me."

"I'm fairly certain I'd have said the *exact* same thing just now if you had married someone who was a stranger to me."

"Look, whatever. I don't wanna fight. My point to this whole thing is maybe the boys are right. Maybe we should try again."

Alarm flooded Jenna. "Try again with *what?*"

Monica rolled her eyes. "The D-O-G, obviously."

"What are you talking about? He's Jake's now."

"You said he wasn't even officially fostering."

A rush of panic had Jenna's fingers growing numb. "What are you even saying? That doesn't make any sense."

"You saw these two this morning. How sad they were. And the three of them were so good together."

"First, five minutes ago, the boys were just as sad over not getting cupcakes, Monica. And second, is that why you called me crying almost every day you had him? Because they were so *good* together?"

Monica shot her a look before focusing on the road. "What's gotten into you?"

"Sev—the D-O-G is who's gotten into me, that's what. He and Jake are great together. Really great. They belong together."

"Until he gives him up."

Jenna clamped her hands around her knees. "I don't think he's going to do that."

"Are you saying you think he's going to keep him?"

"I could see things moving in that direction. It's only been a little over a week."

"So, you honestly think the D-O-G is better with some random guy you just met than with us?"

Jenna cleared her throat. "In just over a week, Jake has sought out Seven's old trainer for advice. This morning he took him to the lake for a long run, and he's signed up for agility classes. He's teaching him to catch Frisbees and working on his manners and everything. Yes, I *one hundred percent* think he's better off with Jake than he was at your house when no one could hardly find a minute to work on getting him to sit at attention, and the extent of his exercise was shutting him in the backyard with no one to play with him."

Monica's mouth had fallen open and took a few seconds to close. "Wow. Well, I see whose side you're on. I guess new relationships will do that, huh?"

"I'm on *Seven's* side, Monica. Him being in your house was a mistake from day one. The boys loved him, and he was good with them, but he didn't fit in your home. Trying it again wouldn't change anything. Trust me."

"So much for putting me and the boys first."

Her sister hated being told no, and Jenna largely left her to figure out her life for herself, but on this she would take a stand. "He's not what you need. A low-energy canine possibly, if you need one at all. A kitten maybe. But nothing right now works, too, if you ask me."

Angry red splotches had blossomed along Monica's neck, making it clear how upset she'd gotten. Jenna shot a glance toward the back seat to find that her and Monica's talk had caught Sam's attention, and he was staring their way quizzically. "What are you talking about?" he asked.

"Just Mommy and Auntie stuff," Monica said, readjusting her hands on the steering wheel. "Did you finish your crackers? And what's Daniel Tiger doing now?"

Monica's attempt at distraction worked. Sam's attention was caught by his show again while an uneasy silence hung between Jenna and Monica, thick as dense fog. Jenna stared out her side window, wondering if she could have found better words to help her sister see that Seven was exactly where he needed to be.

Chapter 24

AN HOUR AND A half later, Jenna was a passenger in the Traverse once more, heading home, only this time the driver was Stuart. No doubt, he'd picked up on the clipped conversation between sisters and noticed that Jenna was largely hanging out with the boys, because he'd not even hesitated when Monica asked him to drive her back instead.

Jenna had shot invisible arrows in her sister's direction at the question, but Monica hadn't been looking her way, intentionally, of course. With Stuart, conversation always came easily, but Jenna still avoided being alone with him whenever she could.

While the worst of the Saturday traffic had eased up by this time of day, Stuart navigated the slower neighborhood streets rather than hitting Milwaukee. Stuart was the type to add a handful of miles and minutes to his commute to avoid sitting at any unnecessary traffic lights. He'd been this way in med school, and his work-from-home career had made him even more traffic averse.

In med school, he'd driven an eight-year-old Infiniti G35 that had been passed down from his mother when she'd gotten a new one. Jenna had traveled countless places alongside him, often with their elbows touching. There'd been dozens of trips out for coffee or late-night jaunts for fast food or simply to get out of the city to find a quiet place to study for a few hours. Countless times, people had assumed they were a couple. More than once, when their fingers brushed across the table, Jenna had made that assumption too.

Back at the house, he'd asked about her concussion and the insurance claim, offering advice with that respectful bedside manner he'd acquired. He'd asked about her first day back at the market too. Perhaps that was why the silence weighed so heavily now. They'd already talked about all the easy stuff.

The sun had been out for most of the afternoon, shining on all the bright blades of new growth and buds, promising spring, but had ducked back behind the clouds. Maybe that's what they could talk about, the weather. "I guess they're calling for snow next weekend."

"Yeah, I heard that too. I figured we wouldn't make it out of March without another big snow or two."

"Yeah, except next Sunday is the parade."

"I thought about that. Hopefully the storm'll roll in after it's over. You're going, right?"

"Yeah, I'm planning on it." Both Jenna's parents had Irish roots, but her mom's side of the family was more closely connected to them, and aside from a handful of years when the parade had been canceled due to excessive drunkenness and then again during the pandemic, they'd participated every year that Jenna could remember, all the way back to when she'd needed a stroller to make it through the long parade route. Some people counted on seeing their extended family at the holidays. Now that her grandparents were gone, Jenna often only saw them each year at the parade, and this was thanks to a great-aunt who organized the Walsh family float every year.

Stuart drummed his fingers on the steering wheel. "I guess whatever that was back at the house will be all said and done by then, right?"

Jenna shifted in her seat. Stuart should know by now to leave well enough alone when it came to arguments between Jenna and her sister. "Likely, but no guarantees."

"I'm starting to think she's right about the baby. That there's no doubt about it being a girl. Monica wasn't nearly this on edge with the other two."

He seriously wasn't about to make this about hormones, was he? "With the other two, she didn't have two kids under five to care for all day. There's a big difference between caring for one small human and two."

If Stuart picked up on the defensiveness in her tone, he didn't acknowledge it. "Tell me about it. From right about five o'clock every night till eight or so, our house is about as peaceful as a bar fight."

"If you're both doing your best, maybe it's time to call in some help. A couple moms at my work use the same nanny service, and they have great things to say about it."

He rested his arm on top of the center console. "I'm open to that. I'm open to whatever she needs, except canceling this vasectomy. I will *not* do this a fourth time." After clearing his throat, he added, "Sorry if that was too much information."

Blinking away an unwanted image of Stuart's testicles getting the old snip-snip, Jenna cleared her throat. "When things cool off, I'll bring up the service with her again."

"That'd be nice. So, I take it that was what set her off?"

It didn't escape Jenna's notice that Stuart was assuming Monica was the one to get pissed, not her. Jenna was the steady one; she and Stuart were similar that way. The ones not to rock the boat. "I'll let her tell you."

Stuart ran a hand over his mouth and chin. "Whatever it is, she's really been riled up about you this week. About the accident." It wasn't like Stuart to press a personal topic, which made it clear something deeper was troubling him. "Keeps insisting it's all her fault."

"It isn't her fault, and I'm fine. Really. I keep telling her both those things. Other than the fact that I'll never not look both ways at traffic lights again, I'm okay."

"Yeah, I can imagine you being tense in cars for a while." He motioned to the street ahead of him, and his mouth pulled up in that same small smile as when he'd gotten a nearly impossible question correct. "Minimizing big intersections for you this afternoon."

Surely, he realized she remembered how congested intersections all but had him breaking out in hives. "Thanks."

After a handful of seconds had passed into the better part of a minute, Stuart was the first to speak. "It's that guy you've met that's got her unsettled, if you ask me."

Jenna shifted in the bucket seat. "What about him?"

A flush heated Stuart's cheeks, proving how out of his element he was to pursue this conversation. Clearly, having it meant something to him. "Everything, I guess. How you met—a car accident. How he was so quick to take the dog for you. How fast things are moving."

Jenna held up a hand. "Things aren't moving that fast, thank you. And his taking the dog was the result of extraordinary circumstances. I'm sure if I'd hit him up in the grocery store with the very same question, I'd have gotten a different answer entirely."

"Yeah, I know, it's just the way she lost her mom—"

"I lost her too. Just saying."

"I know, but she was just so young." Jenna was about to interject that fifteen months hardly made a difference when it came to losing a mom, but Stuart pressed on before she could say anything. "I'm not saying it's right, but you filled—and continue to fill—a really big space for her. She gets threatened when she thinks something might pull you away from her."

"I'm not going to pull away from her, but I *am* working on better boundaries with her. Not that it's been easy. That's why she's mad today, if you want the truth."

"I suspect that's something everyone in her orbit has to do, especially people like you and me."

Jenna stared out the passenger window, letting Stuart's words settle in. Most of the exteriors of the houses they were passing were still winter drab, but several were decorated with bright-green wreaths and had shamrock and rainbow decorations in windows or in the landscaping.

Stuart's comment stirred up a memory of him saying something similar a long time ago. This had been a few months after he and Monica first slept together, when it became apparent that the two of them were, at the very least, going to be an on-again, off-again couple and possibly something more. "We're the same, you and I," he'd told Jenna with a sheepish shrug of the shoulders. "Without the gravity of something bigger tugging us along, we'd likely get stuck in one spot and never go anywhere."

She thought of Stuart the last several years. Maybe Monica's gravity had drawn him in, but it wasn't without a nearly continuous struggle. If he was intentionally sleeping with his back to her, Jenna bet it had something to do with this. From what she could make of things, he always seemed to be the one attempting to apply the brakes and failing. On a thousand different household purchases to gatherings he claimed they didn't need to hosting progressive dinners and block parties on his only night off to the third child he apparently hadn't wanted to have.

Even though it immediately gave her a bad taste in her mouth, for a handful of seconds, Jenna allowed herself to imagine what their life would be like if she and he had gotten together instead. Wrapped up in a new relationship as she would've been—and an important one to her at that—Jenna most likely would never have taken the opportunity to look deeply enough within to realize that medical school was no longer right for her.

They'd both be doctors and immersed in their careers and hardly taking time to look up at the world around them. Plants N Pots would never have come to be. Jenna almost certainly never would've settled in her beloved Logan Square, seeing as how Stuart had never envisioned living anywhere else but Evanston. Who knows who

Monica would've found for a partner instead; someone similar to Stuart, no doubt. But the boys wouldn't exist, nor the little human growing in her sister's belly who'd someday soon be as familiar to her and as distinct as Sam and Joseph.

She'd never have met Jake—whatever ended up happening between them—and he wouldn't have connected with Seven.

It was hard to explain the tears stinging Jenna's eyes as she kept her head turned toward the window and blinked them away. They certainly weren't tears of sorrow; she realized that much. For the first time in her life, without being caught in someone else's orbit, she'd drifted off and found a path of her own.

"What you said just now about being in her orbit," she said when she was finally composed enough to respond to his comment. "Until you said it, I didn't even realize it myself. I'm not in her orbit anymore, and I think she's sensing that. Not because of Jake. Not because of anyone but me. It doesn't mean I won't be there for her. I'm just not in anyone's orbit anymore. Anyone's but my own, and I like where it's taking me just fine."

She doubted Stuart fully understood what she was talking about, but Jenna didn't care. For the first time in a long time, she was exactly where she wanted to be.

Chapter 25

JAKE GLANCED AT THE time displayed on his dashboard and tapped his thumb against the steering wheel, Alice's words the last time he'd seen her in the shelter parking lot coming into mind. *"In a couple weeks, if you're still interested in fostering him out for adoption—and you're still willing to walk that mile with him—give me a call and I'll go to bat for you with Bethany. But not before."*

Alice had known this was going to get hard. She worked at a shelter, of all things. Seven wasn't the only high-energy dog who'd moved through there, and he wouldn't be the last.

In the rear of the rental, the metal-on-metal sound of the boxed-up kennel bouncing as he drove over bumps and made turns had been grating on Jake's nerves on the way to and from work. Belted into the back seat, Seven didn't seem to notice the sound as he stared out the window, anxious for something besides being closed inside Jake's office with him all day at work where the only window had been too high for him to see out of and where the "oohs" and "aahs" every time Jake took him outside for a quick break had had Seven tucking his tail tightly against his hind end.

Yesterday, while working from home, Jake had attempted to get Seven kenneled for a short trial run. When it came to everything else, the dog was making strides, and Jake had been hopeful to have earned enough trust with him that they could build up Seven's tolerance to the kennel ten or twenty minutes at a time.

Jake had walked him over to it after coming inside from a long afternoon walk while Seven was still leashed. As soon as he realized the direction they were headed, he'd tugged and pulled hard enough that he nearly slipped his collar. Jake had kept trying, projecting as much calm as possible, but when he noticed the way Seven had started to tremble uncontrollably and had even urinated on the floor a touch, he'd stopped immediately. Later, he'd packed up the kennel to take it back to the store.

That was all there was to it. Jake was never going to kennel this dog.

Now, Jake would focus on short stints of alone time in the condo instead—starting tonight, Jake's first dinner out with Jenna.

Attentive as ever, as Jake turned into the strip-mall parking lot off Diversey Parkway, Seven immediately sensed the change in routine and stared at the row of stores straight in the direction of the pet store where they'd come the morning after Seven's first night with Jake.

"Remember this place? Can you believe it's been two weeks since we were here? How it can feel both so much longer and shorter at the same time, I don't know, but it does."

After he parked, Jake transferred the big rectangular box from the trunk to a cart, then got Seven out of the back, wrapping the leash handle securely around his wrist. "Considering you've never placed so much as one paw in this kennel, I'm swapping it out for a camera." After a short pause, he added, "Let's be real here—so that I can watch you chew up my place while I'm gone."

Leaving the kennel at the front register while he shopped, Jake hurried Seven along the aisles, making quick work in his choice of a few new chews, a treat puzzle that promised to keep dogs busy for hours, and a pet camera. If there was any way to make a success of Seven's first time alone in Jake's condo tonight, it had to start with making time for a long jog around the neighborhood first, and Jake had left work later than intended.

When they made it back to the register, no one was in line, and Seven immediately sank to his haunches like a perfectly behaved dog, leaving Jake in zero doubt he remembered being given a couple treats by the checkout guy last time.

"What a good dog!" the girl behind the counter exclaimed when she looked over and spotted Seven sitting at attention. "Mind if I gave him a treat?"

Jake said that he didn't, and from the opposite side of the counter, she ogled over Seven, claiming he was the most striking dog she'd ever seen. When he caught the bite-sized treats in midair that she tossed his way, she even clapped.

As she scanned Jake's items, he pointed to the kennel in the cart at the end of her register to remind her that he had a return. It turned out that she hadn't yet learned how to do returns and they needed to wait for the manager, who took her time walking up from the back, and Jake could feel the tension at the lost time mounting inside him.

As he waited for the manager to process the return, Jake spied a display of colorful pet tags on the other side of the counter. "Help your pet return home" promised the ad at the top.

Lifting a bone-shaped one off the hook, Jake fiddled with it. Maybe in a couple weeks he'd think about it. Who got a pet tag for a foster dog?

Looking down, he caught Seven's gaze, and Seven wagged his tail, no doubt trying to communicate his desire for another treat.

"Oh, look, I think he wants one!" The girl cheered like Seven had just jumped through a hoop. She was standing behind her manager, her attention on anything but the return. Clearly, she'd have to learn the return process another time. "They're on special this week too. At twenty-five percent off."

The manager glanced over and spotted the tag in Jake's hand. "We have a machine that does them right here."

"Oh yeah? Maybe next time." For some reason, guilt tugged at him as he slipped the tag back onto the hook. "Wait, how long does it take?"

The manager shrugged. "Well, nobody's in line ahead of you, so just about as long as it takes you to type in your information."

Next to him, Seven yipped loudly, and the girl clapped again. Really? She couldn't have worked here that long to be this excited about a few tail wags and a bark.

Jake rubbed his lips together. "I guess we've got time for that." He reached for the bone-shaped tag again and started to lift it off the hook but spotted one in the shape of a four-leaf clover on the opposite end of the row. "Actually, this one is more his style."

—⁓—

As they waited for their food, Jake took a swig of his beer, an IPA, before entwining his fingers in Jenna's once again. Even though they'd held hands enough these last two weeks that the act had a natural feel to it now, Jenna had a sense that Jake was holding her hand right now at least in part to lock himself down from pulling out his phone to check on Seven. When he'd asked her to dinner tonight earlier this week, he'd planned to have Seven crated for an hour or two. Instead, the dog was roaming loose in Jake's condo.

They'd both walked to get here, meeting about halfway between their places on Milwaukee at the Chicago Diner. It was one of Jenna's favorite restaurants and, given how a large slogan on the back wall read "Meat Free Since '83," she was happy to find out he liked eating here too. She only knew a few nonvegetarian guys who ate here without being forced to by their partners.

"So," he said, "one more day, and you'll have been back at work a full week. How are you feeling?" Despite the tension visible in his shoulders and the set of his jaw, Jake slid his thumb back and forth across her palm, and Jenna got the sense that, right now, he was a man at war with himself, wanting to be here, yet not fully unplugged from what he'd left behind at his condo.

"Pretty much back to normal," she said as the steady sensation of his thumb moving along her palm proved almost hypnotic. Underneath the table, their ankles touched, and that was nice too. "Monday was long, but every day since has been easier." She squeezed his hand gently. "You know, it's perfectly fine with me if you need to check on him again."

A crease formed between his brows. "I appreciate that, but if I do pull up that camera again and he's eating my couch, it'll just ruin our date. Better to wait and let whatever happens happen."

He'd pushed their date back a half hour to ensure that Seven got a long dinnertime jog, a bit of playtime, and a full dinner before he headed out, but Jenna hadn't minded. It gave her some time to unwind after getting home.

Their server dropped off Jenna's chocolate peanut butter shake, promising their food would be up soon. Jake's eyebrows lifted at the sight of the drizzled chocolate and peanut butter inside the tall clear glass mounded with vegan whipped cream. "I can't say I've ever tried one of their shakes—some things just feel like they wouldn't be the same without dairy—but that looks amazing."

Jenna offered it his way. "Want to try it? I don't think you'll be disappointed, though I usually wait till after the meal before I start, so it's not so frozen."

Using the long metal spoon, Jake took a spoonful and nodded. "Really good. I don't know why I'm surprised. I can't remember being disappointed in anything I've ordered here."

"Have as much as you'd like. I usually never order the shakes here unless I split them with my sister, but as I'm back to walking just about everywhere without my truck, I'm hoping my hips and thighs will give me a little bit of grace this time." Jake made an obvious point of leaning to the side to glance underneath their small table for two at the side of the restaurant and raising an eyebrow. Jenna's jaw dropped an inch before a surprised laugh bubbled out. "Should I be feeling judged right now," she added, "because I kinda am."

"No, not judged. Admired. Appreciated. Not judged." When Jenna dropped his gaze, he leaned in and lowered his voice. "You have great hips, and even nicer thighs." He added, "And beautiful eyes and a fantastic mouth," into the silence hanging between them, which made all Jenna's blood pool south. "If you want me to stop there, I will, but there's some really nice real estate in between I could talk about too."

Heart racing, Jenna's mouth pulled a little *o*. Yeah, there'd been a whole lot of kissing this last week and a half, but this was new territory, and she could see the hunger in his gaze. Good thing the tables on either side of them were currently empty. The table spacing in here allowed for anything but private conversations.

To Jenna's relief—and disappointment—the server was walking up again, this time with their dinners. "Here you go," he said, sliding the Reuben and hand-cut fries in front of Jake and the sweet-potato tofu burger and side salad in front of her. "Let me know if you need anything else. I'll check in again in a bit."

After thanking him, Jenna met Jake's gaze. This intensity was something she'd glimpsed in him before, but it was the first time it had been fully directed at her.

"What is it?"

Jenna shrugged. "I don't know; maybe I don't know how to receive compliments, because I'm working really hard not to deflect everything you just said by reminding you that we aren't supposed to be doing this yet."

Letting go of her hand, Jake sat back in his chair and took a long drink of his IPA before nodding slowly. "When I'm less than settled, I can be direct. Sometimes too direct. It doesn't really change anything though. Even if I don't say it aloud, I like you. I like sex, too, and eventually I'm looking forward to liking sex *with* you."

Uh, yes, please. Jenna folded her napkin on her lap. "Maybe it would help us both to talk about a time frame for 'eventually.'"

Neither of them had touched their food yet, but Jake picked up a fry and raised an eyebrow, a half smile bringing out his dimple. "You first, Jenna Dunning. What kind of time frame is your eventually?"

Her full name sounded nice on his lips, sending her blood south again. Jenna wondered what he'd say if she asked how fast they could get back to his place, but even as the thought crossed her mind, she shoved it away, fighting to answer with something other than her hormones. "We met two weeks ago tonight—we collided, technically—and you were still in the process of breaking up with someone. Sticking with public places another few weeks could be helpful. I loved going with you last night to the training center for Seven. Having him with us in the car was probably helpful in that regard too."

Jenna meant it about last night; she'd had a great time watching Seven's first session with a trainer. Afterward, he'd gotten to sniff the Astroturf and various agility props throughout the ring before chasing down Frisbees and even running up and down a few pyramid-shaped platforms and bridges at the promise of the treat waiting for him on the other end.

"This is the first time we're without him, isn't it?" Jake popped the fry into his mouth, nodding as he chewed. "Maybe that's why all I could think about a few minutes ago was all the things we could do with that dairy-free whipped cream."

Jenna laughed heartily, and the tension that had arisen between them fled. "That's an eventually that's much further down the road, just FYI."

Jake grinned. "Especially while there's a potentially destructive dog hanging loose at my place. He'd have time to eat through the walls if I let myself get started with that."

Jenna held up a hand. "Don't tell me if you're serious. I won't be able to eat a bite. Besides, it's your turn. What's your eventually?"

"Well, a couple minutes ago, my answer was however long it took us to get back to my place. But you're right. We need to take our time getting there. I like you. A lot. I don't want to do anything to jeopardize that."

They locked hands again in the center of the table. "Thank you," Jenna said. "And I like you too. So…public places for a while longer yet, sounds like. Or my backyard; that's pretty public."

Jake narrowed his gaze playfully. "How about your potting shed? Is that public enough?"

Laughing, Jenna shook her head. "You can call me out for changing the subject if you'd like, but before I forget it about it, would you like to bring Seven by the parade Sunday? If you don't think it'll be too much for him."

"The South Side parade?"

"Yeah, my mom's side of the family is Irish. We have a float in it every year. My great-aunt organizes it."

"That's awesome. I love that parade, and hell yeah, if you're in it, I'm there. Do you need a ride?"

"We have to get there super early to line up, so I'll ride with my aunt. Maybe you could give me a ride home though?"

"Yeah, sure. And since Seven will be in the car with us, we're safe there. Not that I have any real experience with it, but I swear it's a bit like parenting, fostering him."

"I can imagine that." Jenna wondered if Jake realized it yet, how deep he was in with Seven. Looking from the outside in, it was so easy to see—his hearty laughs last night at some of Seven's antics, the way his eyes lit up when talked about him, the way he made time to meet the dog's needs even if that meant putting off his own.

Jake Stiles was falling in love with that dog.

More than Jake's sex appeal, more than his bedroom talk or his incredible cooking, it was his capacity to love that misunderstood dog that had Jenna falling so deeply herself.

Chapter 26

SINCE MOVING TO CHICAGO, Jake had been to the South Side Irish Parade more years than not. A couple of his buddies were hanging out today at a pub in the South Side a few blocks off Western from sunup till last call, but he wouldn't meet up with them today, not with Seven in tow. He was here to see Jenna in the parade, and he'd keep as much distance from any potential craziness as he could.

While his Irish roots on his mother's side had been muted down over the last couple generations, he adhered to the belief that everybody was Irish on Saint Paddy's Day. Most years, he'd come dressed in green—right down to a pair of green plaid pants so tight in the crotch that every time he wore them, he swore it was his last—and drink enough Guinness to not be hungry the rest of the day.

Unlike the downtown parade that attracted a couple million attendees and participants with its impressive floats and the dyed-green Chicago River, this one was considerably easier to navigate. Even if it got a bit crazy at times—he'd fielded more than one potato being hurled his direction over the years—for the most part, families could bring their kids and canines and have a good time here. While Jake wouldn't have set foot with Seven downtown yesterday for the big parade for anything, he was hopeful about this being a good experience for the dog.

Seven jumped down from the back seat of Jake's Jeep—which was back from the body shop and good as new—and sniffed the air cautiously. "What're you smelling, bud? All the chaos you're about to be nose to nose with, or the snow up in those clouds?"

Forecast or not, there was no question a sizable snow was coming. The smell in the air, wet and crisp, was unmistakable. Anywhere from five to nine inches was being predicted, depending on the way the storm ended up moving through. The temps this morning had started out in the midforties but had been dropping steadily while the clouds darkened. Jake wasn't going to be surprised if once the snow started, it dumped on the city fast and hard. Thankfully, meteorologists were predicting it would likely hold off until the parade was over, but if it didn't, the one thing you could say about most Chicagoans was that they knew how to drive in the snow.

In the back of his Jeep, Jake had both a coat and the green plaid pants, and he lingered a moment, debating on each. He was wearing a long-sleeved thermal under a bright-green hoodie, jeans, and a pair of green high-top Converse Chuck Taylors. His crotch itched at the thought of the pants, and he was getting here late anyway, so the plaid pants just weren't happening this year. As for the coat, he only planned on being out here an hour or two, and he was warm enough in what he was wearing for now, so he decided against both.

After shoving a couple waste bags in one pocket and a handful of treats in the other, Jake shut and locked the door. "Ready, bud?" Back at the condo, Seven hadn't seemed a fan of the green-clover-print bandanna Jake had tied on him, dropping to the floor and rolling over onto his back as if it itched, but Jake hadn't fallen for it, not with Seven's thick coat. During the car ride here, Seven seemed to have forgotten about it, and Jake refrained from straightening it a touch over his shoulders in the event that doing so brought it to his attention once more. Against Seven's glossy black-and-white fur, the triangular patch of green was a good complement. "You look real sharp, good buddy, though next year I'm getting you one of those leprechaun hats."

Next year? You're just fostering, remember?

He *was* just fostering, but it wasn't his imagination that Seven was making progress. In his couple hours of unsupervised time during Jake and Jenna's date the other night, the only thing Seven had damaged was the kitchen towel hung over the oven handle. He'd shredded that to pieces—no doubt because it smelled like food—but otherwise, Jake's place had been unharmed. Even that tempting table leg hadn't taken on any more damage.

There was no question about it. The dog was trainable, so long as his caregiver put in a lot of time and TLC.

Before he and Seven got too close to the crowds and the parade, Jake pulled out his phone and texted the location of his parked car to Jenna, who'd be riding home with him this afternoon. The parade had started in Beverly at 103rd and Western, but he intended to watch it a few blocks from where it ended in Morgan Park at 115th. Given how there were upward of a hundred different participant groups—various floats, bands, cars, dancers, and walkers—and Jenna's family was toward the back, it would be a while yet before she got there.

The parade had started at one o'clock, and it was just after one thirty. While parking in the city was hardly ever a breeze, on days like today, it was a good half-mile walk from most anywhere to the parade route, but Jake hoped the trek would help Seven wear off some energy and acclimate to the noise and crowds they'd soon be in the throes of.

For the first few minutes of the walk, Jake and Seven encountered only a handful of people, and most of those were associated with the various stores, pubs, and restaurants they were passing here in Morgan Park. Jake was encouraged by the way Seven did no more than prick his ears at the people who called out to him.

Beautiful, gorgeous, stunning, pretty, handsome. Eventually, Seven got it all.

The closer they got to the noises of the parade, the less Seven strained against the leash to pull ahead, but his tail was still relaxed, which meant he wasn't too nervous at the promise of what lay ahead.

As they passed a pub, a group that was clad entirely in green from head to foot and seated at a table outside next to a propane heater beckoned them over, but Jake declined. "Sorry, he's not much for attention, and even less for affection," he called out, raising his voice so they'd hear him over the speakers. "Life hasn't always treated him that well."

"Ahh, a true heartbreaker then," an older man called back. "This is for him, but you're welcome to wear it for him." He tossed Jake a large green bead necklace with a pint for a medallion. "Be sure he gets some Guinness tonight, son!"

After thanking them, Jake headed on, draping it over his neck and chuckling. "You know, buddy, one of the things I love about you most is how your looks are totally wasted on you."

It took the better part of a block for Jake to realize he'd thrown a four-letter word out there that after nearly thirty-four years on this planet, he was still quite hesitant to use: love. Given the way he'd been brought up, the odds weren't in his favor of it ever rolling off his tongue. He couldn't remember the last time he'd told his parents or brother he loved them—or heard those words from them either. Decades, likely.

It wasn't that they didn't; it just wasn't something that had been spoken much in the Stiles household. Certainly, this had been one of Alyssa's biggest complaints over their year together. "You'll throw out your love for that restaurant but not for me," she jabbed at him once, chasing the words even further down his throat.

As if he'd picked up on Jake's line of thought, Seven turned and looked up at him, that calculating expression in his gaze.

"Yeah, okay, so maybe 'like' would've been better suited just now." When Seven barked, Jake laughed. "Don't blame me, bud. Aren't you the first to show how Rome wasn't built in a day?"

———

From where Jake and Seven were hanging back on the grass twenty feet back from the corner of 113th and Western, Jake spotted the two bead-wearing mules with spiky-green manes that Jenna had texted him about earlier when she'd gotten in line for the parade. "She's getting close, bud," Jake promised Seven. "Not long now, and we'll head home."

And it would be none too soon. It was colder than Jake had realized when he first stepped out of the Jeep, and snow flurries had started up, whipping about on the wind even though it was still a couple degrees above freezing. While Jake was damn cold and wishing for his coat, he still hoped any real accumulation would hold off a bit longer.

The thin crowd of parade goers in front of them hollered at the mules, snapped pictures, and took videos. Thankfully, everyone in the immediate vicinity had proven to be a relatively tame bunch to watch the parade with. This last half hour, Jake had gone through all the treats he'd brought along, and darned if he wasn't giving Seven an A+ for his behavior so far.

Other than sitting at attention when Jake asked him to, Seven had remained standing, though he didn't seem overly anxious, just alert and watchful. He'd even tolerated a dozen up-close ogles by the kids nearby, and his patience with them had worked in his favor. A toddler had spilled her take-along container of Goldfish crackers, and Seven had snarfed them up while the kids watched and laughed.

After all the treats and Goldfish, Seven had to be thirsty. A mom sitting in a camping chair nearby had offered Jake a bottle of water from her family's cooler, but in this environment, Seven had either not been thirsty enough or relaxed enough to drink from Jake's hand. Jake wished he'd grabbed the backpack that he'd packed with a jug of water and a bowl, but he'd offer it to Seven as soon as they got back to the Jeep.

Jake sank onto his heels and dragged a hand along Seven's back. "How do you feel about stepping into the thick of things for a minute or two to wave at Jenna?"

Seven abruptly pressed forward and swiped his tongue straight across Jake's mouth and nose, making Jake wish he'd hung on to the water bottle for himself, but Seven's response seemed like confirmation enough.

Jake headed toward the family who'd given him the water. "Hey, mind if we step in front of you for a minute or two? I'd like to wave to my girlfriend. She's about to pass by."

The group consisted of a dozen people, young and old, standing and seated in camping chairs and wrapped in blankets, but the parade had been going on long enough that they easily made way, waving Jake ahead of them with smiles and calls of "Go right ahead."

Keeping the leash tight, Jake led Seven in front of them, noticing the cautious way the dog first eyed the metal barricade blocking off the street. By the time they made it up there, the mules had moved on, but a handful of people on horseback were passing by. Seven cautiously stuck his head between the metal bars and barked at the horses, the hair on the back of his neck standing on end, making everyone around them laugh.

"Hey, there she is, Seven!" Jake spotted Jenna sixty or seventy feet down from them. She was with a group of people of various ages, waving to the crowd. Sam was at her side, one hand locked in hers.

Jake watched for several seconds, aware of the way adrenaline flowed through his body at the sight of her. The truth of it was, he'd have hung out here for much longer than this just for a glimpse of her. She was in jeans and an Irish wool sweater and wearing a glittery miniature-sized leprechaun hat—not that different from the hundreds of participants who'd passed in the last half hour, but sight of her still sucked his breath right from his lungs.

Even though it was unlikely she'd hear him over the group of kilted men with bagpipes fifty or so feet behind her, he began waving and calling out her name.

Seven looked up at him questioningly, as if attempting to decipher what had caught his attention. "It's Jenna, bud. You'll spot her in a minute."

When she was fifteen feet way, Jake called her name a second time. This time, she looked right at him, and recognition lit her face.

"Jake!" She passed care of Sam off to an older man walking at the front edge of their family float and jogged Jake's way, her cheeks pink from the cold and her eyes bright. Her hair was in a loose braid with green ribbon woven in and sparkly clovers pinned in several places. "I was worried I'd miss you!"

"We weren't going to let you," Jake said with a laugh.

As she neared, Seven barked loudly, his tail wagging.

"Oh, sweet Seven, now I don't know which of you two to hug first," she said with a laugh.

"Don't be daft! *Kiss the lad, lady!*" a drunken man called out, his words slurred. Judging by his over-the-top accent, he was likely not Irish, but even so, the declaration created a ripple of laughter all around.

"Oh, believe me, I plan to do just that," Jenna shot back in the man's direction, her blue-green eyes sparkling. Careful not to knock off her hat, she slipped off the longest necklace from around her neck. Instead of green beads, it was composed of letters, spelling KISSMEIMIRISH multiple times over. "I saved this one for you," she said with a laugh.

As she draped it over his head, Jake pulled her in for an open-mouthed kiss, and the crowd erupted into cheers. Maybe it had nothing to do with the encouragement, but Jake pulled her closer, closing one hand around her back, and his tongue slid against hers before they pulled apart.

A few disappointed jeers rolled over the crowd as they pulled apart. "More kissing!" someone yelled.

Waving them off, Jenna kept her focus on Jake. "I've seen it a hundred times over the years, but I've never kissed anyone in the crowd before. I guess there's a first time for everything."

"That's the sexiest thing you've said to me yet." He pressed his lips against hers one more time. Her hands and lips were ice cold, and he wanted to offer her body heat that he suspected he didn't have. "You're freezing."

"So are you," she said with a laugh, her cheeks and tip of her nose red. "I thought walking would warm me up, but it hasn't." Pulling something from her back pocket, Jenna bent down to greet Seven, who'd barked again as they'd kissed. "This is for you, sweet boy," she said, offering him a treat through the bars. "The group ahead of us is giving them out to people with dogs."

"Nice. You still meeting me at the Jeep when you're done? I doubt you saw where I parked yet, but getting here late like I did, I'm a ways out. I could head toward 115th and walk with you."

"That's okay. It's always a swarm of people down that way as the parade dumps out. And cell service will suck. I doubt we'd ever find each other." Jenna glanced toward the group she'd been walking with, but they'd moved on past them now. "If I didn't need to say goodbye to everybody, I'd find a way over this barrier right now."

"I'll lift you over in a heartbeat, if you want."

Jenna's eyes seemed to say yes before she gave a light shake of her head. "While that's the sexiest thing *you've* said to *me* yet, I've got to swing by my aunt's car and grab my stuff. Besides, I need to say goodbye to everybody. I won't be long though. Promise. We'll go get the biggest hot chocolates ever." Closing both hands over the sides of his face, she stepped in for another kiss, and the drunk Irish impersonator down the way called out for tongue. Jake felt Jenna's laugh reverberating inside his mouth, and he wanted to remember it forever.

Lost in the adrenaline of the experience, he'd been ignoring the putt-putting sounds of the miniature cars with their lawn-mower engines as they grew louder, even though Seven had reacted badly to the first group of them that had passed by. Too late, a bugle horn blared from close by, piercing their ears, making both Jake and Jenna jump. Jake had the leash wrapped around his wrist so that it couldn't slip out from his fingers in the event Seven caught him off guard, but in the space of the snap of two fingers, Seven bolted backward with enough force that the leash was yanked clear off Jake's wrist.

Seven was loose.

Jake turned with a start, ready to lunge for the leash as Seven continued to bolt backward in panic, but a stranger shoved in front of him, attempting to do the same thing, impeding Jake but not moving fast enough to catch the leash.

"Hey, somebody grab that leash!" Jake yelled after Seven skittered away from the stranger who'd lunged at him.

His tail tucked tightly between his legs as he continued backing away, Seven looked at Jake for a split second before his attention was caught by several strangers abruptly closing in on him.

"Wait, give him some space!" Jake yelled when he saw the panic flooding into Seven's gaze. Whether anyone heard him or not, he didn't know because an entire pack of miniature cars was descending upon them on the other side of the barrier, and no one could hear anything any longer.

As Seven bolted down the street away from the parade, Jake realized just how badly he'd been playing with fire, and a fear gripped him worse than anything he'd experienced in a long time.

Chapter 27

SNOWFLAKES STINGING HER CHEEKS, Jenna checked her phone for what must've been the tenth time in the last few minutes. Given how patchy cell service was in the crux of the crowd, it was likely pointless to expect a text from Jake right now. What if he hadn't caught up to Seven, and the terrified dog was still on the loose? Her belly in a knot, she did her best to not to crescendo into worry over the various dangers awaiting a dog running loose in the city, especially given how tens of thousands of cars would be hitting the streets in the next hour as attendees attempted to get home ahead of the front pressing in.

As he'd chased after Seven, Jake had yelled over his shoulder for her to still meet him as planned, but Jenna wished she'd have clambered over the steel barricade and run after them rather than continue on the last couple blocks of the parade. *Jake's a runner,* she reminded herself. *I'd have slowed him down.*

Judging by the well-meaning jeers and several "What a cutie!" exclamations when she'd caught up with her family, close to half of Jenna's thirty or so cousins, aunts, uncles, and family friends participating in the Walsh family float today had witnessed her PDA with Jake, but no one seemed to have noticed that Seven got away.

As the parade slowed to a crawl, Jenna scanned the crowd ahead of her. She'd forgotten about the backup at 115th as those who still had beads and trinkets left over slowed their pace to toss them to the crowds clamoring for more. A brisk wind whipped about, sending a slurry of snowflakes in all directions, making Jenna shiver harder in spite of the body heat pressing in from all around.

While most of the group had taken turns riding up on the flatbed trailer and walking, Stuart had walked the whole time while pulling his family's wagon. For the last half hour, Joseph had been curled up in it under a blanket, fast asleep. A few minutes ago, Sam had gotten back on the low-bed trailer and was sandwiched in between a couple of his second cousins. They were using a green plaid blanket over their heads as a tent and occasionally sticking their heads out in an attempt to catch snowflakes on their tongues.

After she worked her way over, Monica brushed Jenna's arm. "Hey, I saw how Seven ran away. He's going to be okay. I'm sure of it."

Tears instantly stung Jenna's eyes. Prior to this, they hadn't spoken more than a handful of words to each other in the last eight days. With a dozen family members here who neither of them had seen all year adding to the commotion of the parade, both sisters had other things to focus on besides the fact that they were still holding grudges after last weekend's fallout. Until now, Jenna hadn't realized how much this had been wearing on her. Frustrating as her sister could be at times, Monica was her person, and tears of relief at this olive branch burned her eyes. "What if Jake hasn't caught him yet? All these people are about to get in cars, and half of them are drunk."

"Hopefully not the drivers." Monica looked round as if this was sinking in for the first time, and her lips puckered into a slight frown. "And if he hasn't caught him, Stu and I will load up the boys and drive around looking for him. You can ride with us. We can ask everybody else to drive around, as well."

"Thanks. Only I think I'll stay on foot." A few tears slipped over her lids. "It's my fault Jake brought him here in the first place. I never should've mentioned it. Seven did so good at the training center this week that it seemed like a good next step. That stupid man with the horn!"

"I don't know if it helps, but I doubt that man even noticed Seven was there. I think everyone in a half-mile radius was looking right at you and Jake. Those were some serious fireworks going off."

Jenna's cheeks were too numb to flush further. "I'm kicking myself. Trust me."

"Don't beat yourself up. That's not what I meant." Monica touched her arm again. "Sometimes things just happen. And sometimes it takes a while to realize something good comes out of them."

Jenna couldn't imagine anything good coming from this. She checked her phone again and blinked in surprise to find a missed call and two texts from Jake had actually come through. Even with her phone on loud, she'd not heard it in this crowd. The first text was the location of his car. The second nearly had her knees buckling.

> Almost had him but some drunk guys scared him off. Now I lost him. Call me when you can.

Jenna clamped a hand over her mouth. Ahead of her, the parade had come to a complete standstill. "He doesn't have him yet. I gotta go. It'll be a half hour or more before this clears up. I can't wait that long." Even though she was back to having zero bars of reception, she typed in a quick reply and attempted to send it several times only to receive Not Delivered notifications each time. "Crap! There's no service again." She slipped her phone into her back pocket as a wave of unease threatened to get the best of her.

"What about your coat and your stuff? Didn't you leave it with Aunt Bridgette? It's freezing, and your lips are nearly blue as it is."

"I'll be okay," Jenna insisted, scanning for the best path through the rapidly condensing crowd.

Monica locked a hand over her arm. "Let me get you one of the blankets from the wagon, at least."

"By pulling it off Joseph?" Jenna raised an eyebrow, and when their eyes met, Monica's lips quirked into a smile.

"I can see when I'm arguing a lost cause. I'll grab your stuff from Aunt Bridgette, and we'll call you when we get the boys loaded."

After asking Monica to say her goodbyes for her and to explain what had happened, Jenna snaked through the crowd and over to the line of steel barricades separating the parade route from the spectators. Within fifty or so feet in either direction, there wasn't a single break in the metal fence line. Jenna headed for the nearest spot where two barricades were joined only to realize that the way they were designed, it would be nearly impossible to separate them at any place other than at the end or beginning of the line.

Ignoring the catcalls from a handful of college kids who were too drunk to realize she was too old for them, Jenna attempted to lodge the two barricades free, but doing so created a ripple and clanking that extended down several barricades in both directions.

"Hey, you can't be doing that," someone called out from not far behind her.

Jenna turned to find one of the police officers on her side of the barricade making his way over. "Sorry. I need to get over. There's a dog running loose in the streets because of me, and I need to help find him." She pointed ahead of them. "And I can't wait to wade through that."

"All the same, these barriers are like dominoes, and you can't be taking them apart."

"Hey!" one of the college kids yelled, "You were the one making out with that guy back there." This set off a chain of remarks and hoots that did nothing to further her plight.

"I saw that dog run off." A few feet down, a kind-looking woman lifted a camping chair over the top of the barrier. "Step up on this, and we'll help you over."

When Jenna saw that the officer wasn't going to object, she took the chair and braced it firmly on the ground next to the barricade as someone else set another one up on its other side.

The police officer reached out to offer his hand, and Jenna took it. The crowd was noisy on the other side and pressing in close, and she was glad to have him standing next to her while attempting this. It was harder than it looked, balancing on a camping chair, but after a bit of effort, Jenna hoisted a leg over and planted her foot squarely in the center of the other one, and once her other leg was over, getting down proved far easier than getting up. "Thank you all. I really do need to help find this dog."

Both the police officer and the woman wished her luck at the same time, and Jenna thought how if Monica had been standing here, she'd surely have said "Jinx."

By the time Jenna had wedged her way through the dense crowd of spectators, enough adrenaline was coursing through her that for the first time in the last few hours, she no longer felt the cold pressing in. Even so, the flurries were falling fast enough now to collect on her sweater at the tops of her shoulders and the mounds of her breasts.

She kept moving a full two blocks to get some distance from the crowd before reaching around to pull her phone from her pocket, only to grasp an empty pocket. She flattened both hands against her back jeans' pockets, then her front ones. It wasn't here. She clamped a hand against her mouth as she scanned the ground behind her. This wasn't possible.

It could've fallen when she was climbing over. *Or one of those dozens of people bumping into you could've been someone stealing it.*

Jenna began to run back toward the parade, even though doing so made her throat sting from the cold. If she'd lost it while she was climbing over, surely someone would've seen it fall. Wouldn't they have?

This wasn't her. She didn't lose her phone. She'd *never* lost her phone. Jenna was the one to show up on time, to come prepared with everything she needed. She didn't lose things or get pickpocketed in crowds because she wore her stuff in a zipped cross-body bag against her chest. Except for on parade day—the one day this year she'd let her ego get the best of her because she wanted to look good and not look weighted down by a cross-body bag. Assuming she'd be surrounded by people she trusted, she'd brought nothing more than her phone and hadn't thought twice about slipping it into her back pocket. Only now she'd lost it, and she'd separated from both Jake and her family.

This wasn't happening.

By the time Jenna made it back to the spot where she'd crossed over the barricade, her throat stinging from running in the frigid air, the crowd was changing. Some people had left while others had pressed in, hoping for more of the trinkets being handed off at the parade's end, and just about everybody left was drunk. "Hey, can I get by, please? I think I dropped my phone. Has anyone seen a phone?" she called over and over.

"Hey, I gotta phone for you! Right here."

Jenna glanced over and was only half-surprised to find some wasted guy flashing her, his junk shriveled from the cold and anything but worth advertising. One of his friends shoved him, asking if he wanted to get arrested. "Sorry," the friend called her way. "We'll pummel him into bits if he tries that again."

"When he sobers up, maybe tell him with a model that worthless, he shouldn't be advertising it to anybody," Jenna shot back before walking on, a "Well played!" trailed after her.

The woman who'd offered her the chair was nowhere to be seen. She was *not* a pickpocket, Jenna promised herself, not that helpful woman. No, it had either fallen to the ground, or someone else had swiped it.

She walked the area back and forth several times before giving up. When they heard what she was looking for, a few people asked if she needed to make a call, but none of them ended up having any service. Finally, she gave up.

"I don't know what to do," she said to no one in particular.

She had no idea where Jake was or where he'd parked. She no longer knew where *anyone* was. But she *did* know where her sister and Stuart had parked—most of her family had parked within a block of one another, and she'd spotted the Traverse earlier. With the kids and the wagon, Monica and Stuart would be moving slower than she could—assuming they didn't hop into the back of the float once her uncle made it out of the quagmire at the end. Determined to catch up with them, Jenna worked her way free from the crowd and fell into the thin stream of people heading off.

Even while alternating between a jog and a brisk walk—her throat burning the whole time—it took a full twenty minutes to get there. She needed to backtrack almost to the start of the parade while weaving through the crowd, but she moved fast enough to keep the cold at bay as more and more snow tumbled down, the flakes thick and wet, sticking on the branches, railings, bushes, and grass and, eventually, the sidewalk and street.

Finally, she made it to 105th and Oakley. The Traverse was gone, marks from its tires having left unmarred tracks in the little bit of snow that had collected alongside its tires. Exhausted, cold, and thirsty, Jenna could barely keep herself from collapsing to the ground in a sob. Could it really have only been an hour or so since she'd been standing there kissing Jake and thinking how beautifully life had fallen into place?

In the now-dense snow that dumped from the sky, Jenna figured time had to be playing tricks on her. A single hour couldn't flip everything on its head so fast, could it?

Didn't the accident prove it could?

All the same, she'd lost her phone, couldn't get a hold of her sister to tell her, and had no idea where Jake might be. And worst of all, Seven was quite possibly still out there somewhere, running and lost and even more afraid than her.

Chapter 28

As HE WALKED UP to his Jeep for the second time in twenty minutes, Jake dragged a hand through his snow-soaked hair and pulled in a long breath. The adrenaline that had been carrying him through was waning, and the fatigue of uncertainty was creeping in.

His gaze fell to the tracks in the snow that surrounded his Jeep. Even this second time, the sight of them had tears stinging his eyes, had his knees close to buckling. It wouldn't take much for the sobs to rip through him, but crying wasn't something Jake had done in years. It wasn't something he allowed himself to do, just like using the word *love*. Maybe that's why he'd held off getting a dog so long; you could keep people at bay much easier than you could dogs.

And now this. Even as he wanted to shove away the reality of it—to not feel it—there was no denying how deeply the dog had worked his way right past all Jake's barriers, and for the first time, Jake saw how he may have worked his way past some of Seven's, in return.

Navigating unfamiliar side streets and alleys, the dog had made his way back here. To Jake's Jeep. He'd circled it a few times, the leash trailing at his side and leaving a trail of its own. Judging by the messy prints on the driver's side window, Seven had even planted both front paws up there for a look inside before he took off again.

In the first ten minutes or so after Jake had lost his grip on the leash, he'd spotted Seven twice and had been close to catching him, but both times the terrified dog had scurried away before Jake could grab the leash. The first time, one of the departing parade goers had tossed a beer can at a friend and missed, and it had skimmed across the street loudly in Seven's direction, beer spraying.

The second time, after spotting Seven barking at him on the other side between cars, Jake had stepped into the middle of the street to stop traffic for fear of Seven getting hit. As far as Jake was concerned, the only approaching driver had been way too far away to warrant the severity of the horn blowing that had proceeded, sending Seven bolting off down the street once again. Jake had made this opinion clear by unleashing a few choice expletives in the driver's direction before he took off after the terrified dog.

Jake had wanted to believe Seven had been running away from other people more than from Jake, and these footsteps cemented it in. Seven hadn't been running from him; he'd simply been terrified.

"Let me find you and get you safe, buddy. I'll never fail you like this again. I promise."

After spotting Seven's tracks here, Jake had trailed them for a couple blocks as they veered between the sidewalk and the grass before they disappeared at 111th and South Longwood Drive. Had someone managed to catch hold of Seven's leash and pull him into a car? Or had Seven weaved through traffic and come out somewhere on the other side or even further down on the same side, but Jake had not found the tracks?

Locking his hands along the edge of the roof, Jake leaned forward and pressed his forehead against the window of this driver's side door. As he pulled in a breath, he swore he could smell Seven's wet-dog scent still clinging to the glass.

What was he supposed to do now? Hang around here and hope Seven circled back again? Get in the Jeep and drive around in hopes of catching a glimpse of him God only knew where?

Pulling out his phone, Jake checked for a call he hadn't heard come in only to confirm it wasn't there. Even so, he placed another call to Jenna. Once again, it went straight to voicemail.

Clearly something had gone wrong for her not to have shown up here or to respond to any of his texts or calls. While the parade had still been going on, with so many people congregating in one space, her phone had rung and rung until it eventually went to voicemail—a sign of the patchy service in the thick of the crowd. But not anymore. Now calls were going to voicemail. *Maybe her battery is dead.*

Only she was supposed meet him here. How long did he give her? It was snowing heavily now, and Seven's tracks would be covered over soon. It was almost a quarter after four, and he'd last seen Jenna around two thirty, maybe a little after. Thinking back to that kiss and the look in her eye, he couldn't fathom that she'd had a change of heart about meeting him. Something had come up.

"Whatever it is, she's not coming, or she'd have been here by now."

Resisting the urge to relieve some of the tension inside him through a swift kick of the door, an action he'd regret later, Jake headed to the rear of his Jeep and opened the tailgate. His thick hoodie, Converse shoes, and jeans were soaked from the snow. He stripped out of his hoodie, leaving his mostly dry thermal on, and grabbed the jacket and plaid pants. Maybe they were tight in the crotch, but at least they were dry.

Sight of the backpack he'd packed with water and more treats for Seven had his stomach tightening.

Shutting the tailgate, he headed to the driver's side door, got inside, and wedged the soaked Converses off his feet. He turned on the ignition and set the heat to high—his fingertips had gone entirely numb, and the rest of him wasn't far behind—then moved his seat back as far as it would go. Snow covered the windshield, blanketing him in what had become a quiet late afternoon. He stripped out of his jeans and pulled on the plaid pants, even though doing so while still so wet was a bit like getting dressed right out of a shower.

"Tell me how I find you, Seven. Do that for me, will you?"

He had a dozen friends he could call on to help scour the streets with him, but could he really ask them to head out in this? His brother—who drove an F-150 and who'd do anything Jake asked him to—lived an hour and a half away. Even though Jake itched to place a call to him, he refrained.

Instead, he pulled up the number for the shelter, hoping they hadn't closed early and that Alice would be there. It ended up taking a few minutes to get her on the line, but she was there, and her somewhat crass, no-nonsense tone proved to be an unexpected comfort as it washed over his speakers.

"Hey, Alice, this is Jake Stiles, the guy who's been fostering Seven—the border collie who's been through there a few times."

"Yeah, I remember you, but if you're calling to tell me you want to bring him in, let me just tell you right now we're closing early because of the front. They're calling for nine to eleven inches now."

Of course, they were. Would Seven be roaming the city in anything less? "I'm not bringing him in. Now or ever. But I need your advice."

"Oh yeah, what's that?"

"He got loose—my fault entirely—but I remember you said he's done that before. Do you have any thoughts as to where he might go?"

"Well, that's a shame. I'm sorry to hear that, and I'm sorry not to have better advice for you, but he's a wild one, that one. You can't expect him to circle back any more than you can expect him to be headed anywhere in particular. The last time he was loose, he was roaming free a good couple of days before he was picked up. He'd made it a good thirty miles that time, if I remember correctly."

Jake's heart sank. "If someone picks him up and checks his chip, will it lead them back to you or to the family who adopted him last?"

"I can't say for sure, but we gave the family the information to register him in their name when they took him. My guess would be they hadn't done it yet. Lots of people don't."

"Well, I'll check in first thing tomorrow, but you've got my number in case someone calls about him, right?"

"I do. You're saying you still want to foster him?"

"No, I'm not. I don't want to foster him anymore. I want to adopt him. And he *did* circle back, just so you know. I'm on the South Side, and I took him to the parade. I shouldn't have, but I did. He got scared, and I lost my grip, but he circled back. He was just too afraid to come to me, and when he couldn't do that, he came to my car instead. I just didn't get here fast enough. I'm saying this because I think you should know he's *anything* but a lost cause. He's the smartest dog I ever met, and the gentlest one too."

It went so quiet on the other end of the line that Jake wondered if the connection had dropped, then a muffled barking in the background proved otherwise. "Well, Mr. Stiles, after so many years in the business, it's few and far between, but some dogs still surprise me at times. Some people too." Jake was clearing his throat when she continued. "I hope you find him. Before the snow gets deep and this cold front really presses in. I'll put a notice on Lost Dogs Illinois for you and throw up a few pictures. Where on the South Side did you last see him?"

"His tracks disappeared at Longwood between 111th and Monterey. He's got a green bandanna on, and he's dragging a leash."

"Oh yeah? Eventually that'll get caught on something, and he'll lose it, if he hasn't yet. They usually do, anyway, but I'll make mention of it on my post, and I'll leave your number as the contact."

"I appreciate it, Alice. I do."

"And if it helps any, unlike a lot of 'em, this one seems to have a good understanding of how important it is to steer clear of cars. Or maybe he's just lucky. Guess he's got that going for him too."

Jake flicked on his wipers and sent the snow cascading off his windshield. The world had gone so rapidly from the gray-brown of late winter to a blanket of soft white, it was disorienting. "That he does, Alice."

Chapter 29

OUT OF THE SNOW and away from people, Seven stretched out in the dim light underneath an overhang between two buildings. He'd sought refuge here once before. Before Jake. Before the family before Jake. He'd slept a whole night here that time, and not a single person had noticed him. It had been even colder then, and the heat coming out the vent next to the building had helped fight the deep chill that had set up inside him.

He hadn't meant to run off this time, not from Jake. The blaring noises and clambering from all around and the people lunging for him had been too much, and Seven had run and run and run until he could no longer hear Jake calling his name even as he missed the comfort of hearing it as soon as the sound faded.

Unlike other times he'd run before, the running hadn't filled Seven with joy this time. Perhaps this was because of all the running he'd been doing with Jake—along the sidewalks or along the vast stretch of water by the sand or even in the yard or inside the expansive building where he'd chased down Frisbee after Frisbee as his heart pounded with the joy of it.

Now that he was tucked safely back here where no one would spot him, the fear that had been driving him onward faded, and his limbs and body became his to notice again. When he'd run off, he'd been thirsty and scared and dragging a leash. He'd been hungry too. He wasn't hungry anymore. His belly bulged from the food he'd gulped down after finding a treasure trove of it in a bag alongside the road. The bread had been stale, but the meat stuck to it had still been so tasty he'd wolfed it all down along with bits of the paper clinging to it, even though doing so had dried out his mouth and tongue even more and left him longing for more than the mouthfuls of snow he'd eaten afterward.

His paws stung sharply from whatever coated the pavement, melting the snow into water and clinging to his paws as he ran. His neck, throat, and the backs of his ears hurt from earlier when he'd jumped over a tall fence to get away from two strangers beckoning him from inside a car. The leash had gotten stuck, trapping him against the fence, filling him with wild panic and making it hard to breathe as he'd jerked from side to side until his collar finally slipped over his head, and he left it behind. The discomfort around his throat occasionally stirred up a cough, but the sound was soft and foreign to his ears, as if it wasn't his cough but another dog's.

As Seven watched the snow out past the awning tumble from the sky in its hurry to pile onto the ground, his eyelids grew heavy. He burped from the food sitting heavy in his belly and licked his lips before lowering his head onto his front paws. Exhaustion overcame him, and soon he dozed, dreams of Jake and Frisbees and the comforting chair where he liked to sleep passing over him like thin clouds on a windy summer day.

Sometime later, the shivers that had taken over his wet body woke him as did the ache in his belly, alerting him that in his hunger, he'd eaten something he shouldn't have.

He'd only moved through this part of the city once, and he didn't know what lay between here and the endless water to the east or to other places he'd been, like Jake's or Jenna's or the family's home from before or the shelter where he hoped never to have to go again. He didn't know how far any of these places were from here or what might get in his way if he tried to reach any of them—wide stretches of busy roads or buildings that rose up so high they disappeared into the clouds, or people who might very well lock him into a cage if they caught him—but he trusted instinct would guide him if he pressed on. The thought of doing so had him shaking from more than the cold.

Even so, Seven rose onto his four paws and shook himself off, spraying a mist in all directions from the not-yet-evaporated snow that had fallen on him earlier. Each paw burned and his belly ached, but he belched and licked his lips, knowing that even if he threw it up, if he encountered another bag of discarded food like the one he'd gobbled up earlier, he'd devour it all the same.

Stepping tenderly on his sore paws until walking on them dulled the pain in them, the dog headed along the pathway to the edge where snow was blowing in. So much snow tumbled from the sky, Seven feared it would never stop. The city had gone quiet, like it was sleeping, too, not a person in sight and the normally busy streets mostly empty of cars.

Stepping out into the snow, the dog gazed around him, licking at the flakes landing on his nose. Maybe the snow was playing tricks on him, or maybe his earlier dreams hadn't fully faded because he could almost hear Jake calling his name.

He didn't know how he'd get there, but he knew where he was going all the same.

Chapter 30

IT HAD BEEN A crapshoot, attempting to find where Jake had parked, given how she'd taken nothing more than a split-second glance at the location he'd shared with her before losing her phone, but she was giving it her best shot. The longer she was out here, the more likely it was that either he was gone or her chances of connecting with him were less than walking around a corner and spying someone out sunbathing in this snowstorm.

He'd met her at 113th and Western, and his parked Jeep had been somewhere northeast of there, but in this cold, each block seemed not only farther and farther apart but also painfully desolate after the parade goers departed seemingly en masse.

If only she'd memorized Jake's number! He still had a Racine area code, and she'd memorized a handful of the other seven digits, but not all of them and not in the right order. She'd ducked into a bustling and rowdy pub earlier and used the hostess's cell phone to try a couple different variations but with no luck. They'd either been nonworking or wrong numbers. She'd also left a message on Monica's cell after she didn't pick up. She'd explained what happened and promised to call again once she either connected with Jake or gave up looking for him.

Her numb fingers clenched into fists and buried deep in her jeans' pockets, Jenna rounded the corner of 112th and Hoyne and scanned both sides of the street, some part of her still holding out hope to spy Jake's Jeep idling next to the curb, Jake and Seven waiting inside.

Nothing. "Seeeveeen!" The call was swallowed up by the falling snow that seemed to stop the sound from carrying, but she kept calling for him anyway.

The one thing she'd done right today was wear her warmest wool socks and thermal long underwear, but her cute leather combat lace-ups were soaked through, as were her clothes. Her toes stung, and everything else had gone numb. Tears meandered down her cheeks with less hurry than the dripping of her nose in this cold.

"Seven! Here, boy! Here, Seven!"

The snow was picking up, and it was nearly dark. Disorienting as the cold and tumbling snow were, Jenna could only guess as to the time, but she needed to face the facts. Wherever Jake was, it was impossible to believe he'd still be waiting by the curb for her to show up.

Most of the mom-and-pop businesses in the area were closed, and she would not be walking up to someone's house asking to use their phone, but she'd passed a food mart a few blocks back on Longwood that had still been open. The second she admitted to herself she was giving up, her already-depleted energy fled like a drain plug had been pulled. Each step back in the direction she'd come was like walking in deep sand.

This section of the South Side mostly consisted of houses dotted with restaurants, pubs, and mom-and-pop businesses, nearly all of which were decorated for Saint Patrick's Day, and the shiny green ornaments, wreaths, and lights stuck out in contrast with the snow, but when out of the corner of her eye, Jenna caught a swath of blue wrapped around the cap of a post of someone's privacy fence, something about it stopped her in her tracks. It looked like the handle of a leash. A blue leash. Like Seven's.

Finding energy she didn't know she had, Jenna burst into a run as she crossed the street. The house was dark inside, and it didn't seem as if anyone was home to object or for her to notify, so she crossed the grass over to the fence, the snow crunching under her boots as she walked. It was a five-foot wooden privacy fence with capped posts every eight or so feet, and there, on the third cap over, was an inch-wide blue strap that on one side was half-covered with snow.

It seemed impossible she could've spotted it from the opposite side of the street in such heavy snowfall, and she reached out with trembling hands. Sure enough, it was the handle of a blue nylon leash dangling just inside the fence. Maybe it belonged to the family who lived here. Maybe they hung it here so they could hook up their dog and head straight out the gate, but Jenna pulled it over anyway. Her heart both lifted and sank to find a collar attached. Both collar and leash were a bright, crisp blue and hardly worn in, not weathered at all, and the leash handle was double lined. Just like Seven's. The quality was obvious in the stitching and the smooth, thick nylon. Jenna remembered her sister mentioning the independent store where she'd bought them only a month and a half ago. Turning it in her hand, Jenna spotted several long white hairs stuck at the edge of the snap where it joined the nylon.

Rising up onto her toes, she peered over the side and into the yard. "Seven! Here, boy! Are you in there, Seven?" It was a small backyard with little more than a covered grill, a collection of empty planters, and a tall stack of wood, all of which were covered in snow.

It took her a moment to spot them, but once she did, there was no mistaking them for anything else. A line of tracks now mounded over with additional snow led across the yard to the back side of the fence in front of the alley.

"Seven!" she yelled as loudly as she could.

Her only answer was the muted silence of the falling snow. Even the wind had stilled.

He hadn't stayed, but Seven had been here. Maybe it wasn't much, but it was the best Jenna had. Draping the leash and collar over her shoulder and shoving her frozen hands back in her pockets,

Jenna looked up and down the street to see which way would give her quickest access to the alley.

As she headed down to the sidewalk, the snow crunching underneath her, the shiny gleam of green metal dangling off the collar caught her attention. Lifting it, Jenna blinked in surprise to spy a clover-shaped tag that read "Seven" on the front in a big, playful font. She'd had no idea Jake had bought this, but it had to have been put onto the collar by him, seeing how he'd given Seven his name.

When she turned it over, tears flooded her eyes. There, in a smaller version of the same font, was Seven's name once again, Jake's address, and a Racine-based number. Just waiting for her to find it.

Chapter 31

STILL BAREFOOT AND WITH his heat cranked up to high, Jake drove around block after block, inching down alleys and occasionally pulling into parking lots to scan for tracks in the snow and rolling down his window to shout Seven's name every couple of minutes. He didn't know this area that well, but he drove in a grid, moving farther and farther out in each section before heading back to where he'd lost Seven's tracks at 111th and Longwood to start over again in another direction.

Spying an empty parking space alongside the curb that was otherwise lined with cars, Jake pulled in and shifted into Park, then reached for his phone to pull up the map of the area that he'd been using as a reference. *Leave no stone unturned.* Seven was out here somewhere. Jake had checked with both animal control and the police; the dog hadn't been picked up yet. Snowing as heavily as it was, it was likely he was hunkered down and waiting out the storm. If Jake didn't find him first, someone would spot him tomorrow after the front passed and people ventured out again.

Alice's comments about Lost Dogs Illinois had given Jake an idea. He only knew one person in Chicago who could be in instant contact with enough people around here to rapidly spread the word about Seven. The only problem was she couldn't stand him. Setting his reservations aside, he'd texted Alyssa earlier that Seven was lost and out in the storm and asked if she'd be willing to post a picture and notification on her Instagram account for him.

She'd responded fifteen minutes later, asking him to send a few pictures and commenting that while Jake might not deserve any favors, no animal should be wandering the streets in this storm.

A few minutes later, she'd sent a screenshot of her post which included a close-up of Seven and its accompanying blurb, one that had given Jake a hearty laugh.

> Hey friends, no need to tell me about turning the other cheek... My exxxx (yeah, the one I've told you about) lost his dog (yeah, the one he basically dumped me over). Karma talk aside, this poor pup is lost in this storm and needs our help. Text this number if you spot him please!

She'd posted a carousel of the pictures he'd sent and listed Jake's number followed by the intersection where he'd lost track of Seven's paw prints. Ever since, the texts had been steadily coming in, and a handful of calls too. Each time his phone dinged or rang, he glanced at his dashboard multimedia display, hoping to spot Jenna's number or get a positive lead on Seven. So far, no such luck.

Jake figured this might prove to be the impetus he needed to finally get around to changing to a Chicago number. At the very least, once Seven was found, he'd need to keep his phone on Do Not Disturb for a couple of days until the popularity of this post died down. So far, he'd gotten at least a dozen "Asshole" texts and twice as many "Poor pup/Good luck" wishes. A clairvoyant had called after having a vision of Seven curled up by Garfield Park Conservatory. Four people had texted asking if Jake was on any dating apps yet and if so, which ones, and one person had texted simply "Marry me."

Adding to Jake's unease, Jenna still hadn't called. "She's with her family. Whatever this is, she's okay."

Still idling alongside the curb, Jake closed his eyes and pinched the bridge of his nose. It was close to twenty miles to his house from here. Seven had trekked the three-quarters of a mile back to his Jeep on his own. Was there any chance he'd try to get to Jake's place next? Should Jake abandon his search here and head there instead?

Two or three inches of snow had already fallen, and the roads were a slushy mess but easy to navigate in his Jeep. Given how Jake hadn't prayed in forever, it struck him as odd how the "Please, God" one-liners kept floating through his head. *Please, God, let Seven be okay. Please, God, let me find him. Please, God, let me be heading in the right direction. Please, God, let Jenna be okay.*

As his phone dinged with a new text, Jake cleared his throat before pulling it up.

> You have the best smile. I've had such a crush on you forever.

Swiping Delete, Jake took a long breath. "This isn't working." The wipers pulsed, sending the new-fallen snow cascading off the windshield. He stared out ahead, hoping for a clearer answer than the indecision floating through his head. The snow fell fast enough to have a dizzying effect. Given the blanket of clouds and the snow, it was nearly dark already, even though sunset wasn't for another forty-five minutes.

A hundred or so feet straight ahead, a solitary figure was headed down the sidewalk, the first person Jake had seen out walking in this in a while. At first, it was hard to tell if it was a man or woman or what direction they were walking, but something about the gait had him sitting straighter in his seat. A woman. Walking his direction. Then she passed directly under a streetlight—a woman wearing a small green hat and a light-colored coat or sweater with a blue strap hanging over her shoulder.

Jake threw open his door and bellowed out her name even though the dense falling snow sucked it right up. "Jenna!"

He unhooked his seat belt and, leaving his door wide open and the Jeep running, dashed out barefoot. After the first couple of strides, his bare feet no longer registered the sting of the snow underneath them, and he cursed his too-tight pants, but he kept running, closing off the distance between them. "Jenna!"

She stopped moving a few seconds as if registering that someone was running straight at her, then abruptly burst into a jog too. When they met, she fell into him, burying her face in his chest as he locked his arms around her. "I didn't think you were real." Pressed against him as she was, her words were muffled.

"You're soaking wet, Jenna."

"And you aren't wearing s-s-shoes." She said it with a laugh, but her teeth chattered wildly.

"I've been calling you."

"I lost my phone."

Pulling back a little, he lifted her chin so he could look her in the eye. He saw it then, how cold and exhausted she really was. "Have you been out in this the whole time?" As she nodded, his gaze fell on her lips. They'd gone entirely blue. "Come on, let's get you warmed up."

He lifted her into his arms without warning. She'd been walking this whole time; he didn't need to carry her the last hundred feet, but he wanted to. She stiffened in surprise, but after a stride or two, she relaxed into the sway of his walk, her shivers reverberating against his torso. He pressed his lips against her temple, the sweet scent of whatever it was she put in her hair filling his lungs and comforting him better than any blanket he could've been offered.

"Why aren't you wearing s-shoes?"

"Because my shoes and socks were soaked—like yours, no doubt. It's warm in the Jeep. We'll get you warmed up in no time."

"That'll be nice," she said, her teeth still chattering. She lifted the blue strap off her shoulder, only it turned out not to be a strap after all. "I f-found this a couple streets over. Seven's collar and leash. The handle got stuck on a fence p-post, and he wiggled free of it." She pointed at a quiet pub not far past his Jeep. "I was heading in there to call you. Because of this." She held up the dog tag he'd picked out earlier this week while waiting for the manager to finish his return of the kennel. "I almost had your number memorized, but not q-quite."

Tears of relief stung Jake's eyes, but he cleared his throat and blinked them back. There was a second spot now where Seven had definitely been. Added to this was the fact that Jenna had been in the area the whole time. They had to have been circling each other as they searched for Seven. Maybe he was hanging around here, too, and in one of these circles, they'd find each other just like this.

It was a hope worth holding on to.

―‿‿―

"Let's get that soaked sweater off before you get in, at least."

Jenna lingered by the open passenger door of the Jeep. Jake was right. Her sweater was soaked through, the wool weighed down from the snow melted by her body heat. Teeth chattering, she started to pull it off but felt his hand on her arm and raised her arms, allowing him to pull it gently over her head instead. The leprechaun hat came off along with it; Jenna had forgotten she was still wearing it.

"I think I could wring this out, if I tried." He smiled, then nodded toward the long thermal she was wearing underneath it. "How about that? Looks like it's soaked too."

Jenna looked down. Underneath her soaked thermal long-sleeved crew was nothing but a bra, one of her favorites even though she hadn't expected anyone to see it, most especially Jake. "It'll be f-fine."

"My coat's in the back seat. What about wearing that instead? It's warm and dry." As she was debating her options, he popped open the back door to grab it and deposit her sweater.

If she took a seat and stripped out of her shirt inside the Jeep, would he make it around to his seat fast enough to spy the little muffin-top that would undoubtedly form over the top of her jeans when she sat down? *It's not like he didn't just carry you a hundred feet a moment ago, is it? He knows you like your grilled cheese with an extra side of cheese.*

Not that there was much call for stripping down outside the car either. But it was dark and snowing heavily. Everyone in a hundred-yard radius was either home or tucked away inside the pub. Deciding to go for it, Jenna grabbed the bottom of her shirt and slipped it over her head. Afterward, she stuck out one arm, then the other, for Jake to slide his jacket over her shoulders.

Once it was on, she pulled her soaked braid out from underneath the collar. The jacket was too big, but soft inside and smelled of leather and pine, and Jenna never wanted to take it off. When she looked up at Jake, his gaze wasn't even close to meeting hers. "Shouldn't you at least be pretending not to stare?" With her shivering jaw, her words were broken into segments.

"Should I?" Blinking, he looked up from her breasts, his mouth quirking into a hint of a smile. "You're so damn beautiful, whatever etiquette's been engrained in me is conceding to all the blood draining south."

A broken-by-shivers laugh erupted at this. "Mr. Stiles, if my teeth weren't doing th-this," she said, pointing her jaw, "I'd kiss you for that."

The answering look in his eyes had her insides swelling with hope. He leaned in and pressed his lips gently against hers. He started to pull away but changed his mind and leaned in again, his mouth opening against hers and his hands closing around the bare skin of her waist inside the jacket. Jenna's hands closed over his shoulders, her fingers melting the snowflakes collecting there.

The moment lasted just long enough for Jenna to marvel at how nothing had felt this unequivocally right in a long time as when they kissed. When they pulled apart, Jake pressed his forehead against hers. "If we didn't have a dog out there who needs us, I'd warm you up and let you do a whole lot more of that."

The warmth lighting inside her had nothing to do with the jacket she'd just been lent. "How about we take a rain check—or a s-s-snow check—because that s-sounds pretty good to me too."

As Jenna stepped away to climb into the Jeep, he stopped her. "What about your pants? How wet are they?" His expression had grown serious again in light of the bigger concern they were facing of finding Seven. "Though I'm afraid the only thing I have to offer you in that department are the ones I'm wearing, but they're god-awful tight in the crotch and pretty wet now too."

Jenna laughed again. "My pants are fine, but I was absolutely going to ask the story behind y-yours."

Jake pressed a kiss against her temple. "How about I tell you as I drive us to where you found that leash?"

"Sounds like a plan."

Chapter 32

JENNA CURLED UP ON the floor in front of one of Jake's living room windows and wrapped herself in a mound of blankets, watching the Jeep's taillights disappear into the dense snow. While it was arguably a little more than a sliver, this window had a wider view of the sidewalk down below than the other and was Jenna's best chance to catch sight of Seven should he instinctively know how to navigate the eighteen or so miles between here and where he'd last been spotted—and want to return.

He wants to be found. He wants to be here. I know it.

When she hadn't stopped shivering once in a full thirty minutes, Jake had driven her here. He'd been right about it making sense to split up, except now he was driving around in this mess alone, and the storm showed no signs of relenting.

"I'll check every half hour," he'd promised. Since Jenna didn't have a phone, they'd run her by her place so she could grab a change of clothes and her iPad. Thank God for technology. She'd be able to make calls and check her texts while using Wi-Fi calling.

While dropping her off, he'd run inside long enough to give her his Wi-Fi code and change into sweats and a gray-green hoodie that brought out the green in his hazel eyes and made Jenna wish circumstances were different and he could stick around awhile so she could lose herself in their depths and maybe a little more.

Jenna pulled up the Find My iPhone app for the second time since logging on to the Wi-Fi here, hoping for new results. Someone had likely pulled out the battery because her phone didn't show up anywhere. Pausing often to glance out the window toward the empty sidewalk below for signs of Seven, she filled out the form to report her phone as stolen. Not for the first time tonight, she said a prayer of thanks that her photos—priceless ones of the boys, images of her artwork, painted pots, and plants and, new to the mix, of Seven— were backed up on the cloud. At least she hadn't lost those.

Afterward, she pulled up Instagram. Jake had shared how he'd reached out to Alyssa in hopes she could help him find Seven, and before leaving, he'd given her Alyssa's Instagram handle so she could track the comments in case someone spotted him. "I don't know if there's ever a good time to talk about exes, but, if it helps any, there's no nostalgia on my end; I doubt on hers either. But if there's one thing Alyssa does well, it's get the word out, and right now Seven needs all the help he can get."

Jenna didn't blame him. She'd have done the same thing. Even so, as she pulled up Alyssa's handle, she thought back to her nine-year-old self opening the kitchen junk drawer after Christmas and finding an envelope stuffed full of receipts for all the wonderful things Santa had brought. Maybe Jake had been ready to leave Alyssa, but he'd still spent a full year with her. It had been a significant relationship, and diving down into the rabbit hole of all things Alyssa would no doubt hurt.

The first thing that caught Jenna's eye as the account pulled up was the endearing close-up of Seven from Alyssa's most recent post. The second thing was Alyssa's number of followers. Upward of nine hundred thousand. Not too far a cry from a million. Alyssa was an influencer, one who was only following 133 people herself. Jenna's 1,860 hard-earned Plants N Pots by Jenna followers had never seemed less significant.

As she skimmed through Alyssa's older posts, Jenna could feel the voice of self-doubt poking its ugly head, but maybe that shouldn't come as a surprise. Didn't this happen to just about everyone poking around on someone else's social media feed? Even as Jenna reminded herself that half these photos had been taken with filters and most had likely been staged, she also recognized that this voice of doubt had deeper roots.

It warned how relationships founded upon the adrenaline of car crashes and surrendered dogs had no staying power. *You're not even close to his type,* it promised. *Bookends need to match.* Jake was a lawyer who'd been told more than once he resembled a rock star. With Alyssa's dark hair, smoky eyes, full lips, and coordinating accessories, she'd looked like a coordinating accessory herself. The proof of it was right there, further down on her feed. A dozen or more photos of them at fancy events peppered it, as did selfies in remote and picturesque locations. The intimacy of a close-up of Jake dozing in a hammock in a remote tropical paradise stabbed Jenna right in the gut, so much so that she needed a moment to collect herself.

You're thirty-one years old. Everyone you meet is going to have a past.

Clearing her throat, she pulled up the post about Seven and started scrolling through the comments. The post had only been live less than two hours, and there were already hundreds of comments. Dozens upon dozens of them were from people remarking how kind and beautiful Alyssa was and how Jake never deserved her. Some were flat-out propositions. A handful of people asked if she knew if Jake was on any dating apps. The ones about Seven were mostly well-wishes and prayers and people promising they'd watch out the window for sight of him, while a few were by people reflecting on the breed being anything but an easy one, and a few others were by people reflecting on their own experiences with lost dogs.

Jenna was scanning the sidewalk below through the dense snowfall for sign of Seven when her iPad rang out. Spying her sister's number on the screen, she pressed the speaker to accept. "Hey, I was about to call you."

Monica's shriek filled the quiet room. "Finally! I don't care how good the sex is, nothing is worth you not checking in like this. Is Seven okay? Did you find him?"

"I couldn't check in because I lost my phone. Actually, it's looking like it was stolen." Her jaw had finally stopped chattering enough for her to speak without sputtering, at least. "But more importantly, we haven't found him yet. Jake's still driving around looking for him. I'm at Jake's place watching out the window in case he comes back on his own."

"That sucks—about your phone and Seven. I really hoped he was toasty warm and dry by now."

"Yeah, me too."

"But good idea about keeping lookout for him there. I've heard stories of dogs traveling a lot farther than that to get home. We'll do the same in case he comes here."

He won't, Jenna thought but refrained from saying. Seven's panicky behavior at the arrival of her sister and the boys at the park last Saturday was proof enough of that.

"Well…" Monica said, hopefulness lifting her tone. "What do you think? It's the universe stepping in; I know it!"

"What're you talking about?"

"You seriously didn't see my texts?"

Biting back a defensive reply of how she'd been out walking around in this storm all evening, Jenna pulled up her texts app and opened her sister's texts. "I haven't so much as glanced at a text since I last saw you. I really just got here." Monica's most recent text was a close-up of a kitten's face, its blue eyes wide and its pointy ears perked forward. There was a carousel of other images, too, in the kids' arms and up against Monica's cheeks. "When did you get a kitten?"

"We didn't get her. We found her! This afternoon. While we were out looking for Seven and trying to get ahold of you. She was in an alley under this disgusting old sofa next to a dumpster." Jenna was still processing this when she added, "Tell me you see it. You *have* to see it."

"See what?"

"Her markings."

Jenna swiped to the close-up photo. The kitten was black-and-white with black ears and a larger patch of black over her right eye than her left. The white of her chin and neck was disrupted by a single circle of black directly under her nose and mouth. "She's a cutie, that's for sure, but see what?"

"Jenna! She looks just like Seven! Don't you get it? We were *meant* to find her. All week, we've been going back and forth about the boys missing Seven and maybe getting another dog or a cat, and there she was, and she looks just like him. That expression. You *cannot* tell me you don't see it."

The pattern of color was the same, more black on top, more white underneath, Jenna would give her that, but other than that, Jenna could mostly just see what appeared to be an overwhelmed black-and-white kitty with big blue-gray eyes, but maybe it was something you had to see in person to pick up on. "Poor thing was out in this weather, huh? She looks so little and frail."

"She doesn't act it though. Not now that she's eaten and warmed up. We're guessing she's about ten weeks old, but yeah, she'd have frozen tonight. No question. We'll get her to the vet tomorrow, but she's got a voracious appetite, and she even used the litter!" After a slight pause, she added, "We stopped at the pet store on the way home."

"That's sweet, Monica. Really sweet."

"Yeah. This was meant to be. I know it. The boys even agreed on a name, and Stuart and I are good with it."

"The boys picked it? Let me guess." Jenna circled through a few Thomas the Tank Engine character names that she'd committed to memory. "Bertie?"

"Close. Rosie."

"Aww. I like it."

"Yeah." Monica fell quiet for a second. "I'm really sorry I've been an ass this week. I just don't want to lose you."

"You aren't losing me. Ever."

"I know. I *know* that. My head knows that." She dropped her voice. "Even if you are having great sex, and I'm not."

"First, I'm not having sex. Not yet. Second…" She drew a blank as her thoughts trailed off, imagining her and Jake having sex and what it might be like. She cleared her throat. Where had she been headed with this? "Maybe there is no second. But in any case, you aren't losing me. Promise."

When Monica spoke again, it was obvious she'd teared up. "Thanks. The truth is, I know we don't deserve to keep Seven after the way I quit on him. I knew it last week too. Just like I know he deserves someone like Jake who isn't going to do that to him. When he finds him, we're having a party to celebrate. You three can come to dinner. Seven and Rosie are going to have to get to know each other anyway, so we might as well jump into it."

Jenna bit back a myriad of skeptical retorts. Didn't her sister realize she and Jake had only officially been dating a couple weeks? There was no guarantee Jake had entered her life with the sort of permanency that warranted introducing the two animals to each other, even though doubting it had her heart aching.

"You two *are* going to make it," Monica added, knowing exactly what Jenna was thinking. "I know it just the same way I knew Stuart was the person I was going to raise kids with the very first night I laid eyes on him."

Most of the time, Monica seemed to live in a world of complete faith and zero practicality. Sometimes this was frustrating as could be. Other times, Jenna would give just about anything to live right there beside her. "I hope so."

"I know so. Before you know it, you will too."

For a second or two, Jenna debated confessing the insecurities that had flooded in upon pulling up Alyssa's Instagram account but decided against it. Before tonight, Jenna had figured Jake was as practical as she was, but when they'd been standing by his Jeep earlier, she'd caught something both hopeful and knowing in his gaze that had reminded her of her sister; she just hadn't been able to put her finger on it until now. Whether it was a leap of faith or instinct, it was the same thing that first-year hummingbirds had to have when starting out on their migration over the endless gulf on their way south to Mexico. Maybe they couldn't envision what was waiting for them on its other side, but they trusted it was there all the same.

How was it so easy for some people to believe in something—their own instincts even—when everything was so new and unproven?

If it worked for newbie hummingbirds, why couldn't it work for Seven and lead him right to this door? In the same way, why couldn't it work for her and Jake?

Why couldn't it?

As soon as she asked herself this question, a soft smile pulled at her lips. "So, this celebration dinner you're talking about... What would you like me to bring?"

Chapter 33

JENNA JERKED AWAKE. SHE must've slipped into a doze while staring out into the snowfall. It was damn mesmerizing. She dragged a hand over her face and let out a yawn. A quick check of her iPad showed it was after midnight. If sentry duty was making her sleepy, it had to be worse for Jake, who was still out driving in this.

Around ten o'clock, a comment on Alyssa's post about Seven had stirred up hope and changed where Jake was searching.

> I saw him!!! I called out for him but he ran off. He was walking straight down S. Paulina at W. 35th!

The woman had called Jake as well and, after talking to her, he believed it was a credible sighting. Prior to this, Seven's last known location—where he'd gotten free of his collar and leash—had been twenty miles south of here. Jenna had guessed as much right off the bat, but pulling up Google Maps had confirmed it. As of this new sighting, he was ten miles closer than before.

This wasn't random. Seven was making his way home.

Getting up from her spot on the floor by the window, Jenna stepped into Jake's several-sizes-too-big slippers and coat and headed out of his condo, leaving the door ajar and clomping downstairs in the too-big shoes. Earlier tonight, she'd set out bowls of Seven's food by both the front and back entrances, hoping he might linger by the door if by any chance she missed his approach.

Opening the door, she brushed as much as she could of the new-fallen snow off the kibble and scanned for paw prints but didn't spot any. No tracks were out there but her own and Jake's from earlier, which were now snow-covered and hardly visible. After doing the same thing at the back entrance, she returned to the front and stepped outside, but first left the rug hanging out the door so that it wouldn't close behind her. Jake had told her the door code, but in case she remembered it wrong, she had no interest in getting stuck outside in the cold for a second time in one night.

She walked down the gangway to the sidewalk lining the desolate street, the too-big slippers sinking deep into the snow, the crunching sound as unexpectedly comforting as the snowfall itself. Far down to the left, a snowplow was crossing at an intersection. Jenna cupped her hands to her mouth. "Seeeveeen. Here, boy. Here, Seeeven!" Because she didn't want Jake's neighbors throwing darts at her, she kept it to a few calls, then trudged back inside before the cold really began to sink in.

She shut the exterior entrance behind her, kicked off the snow from her slippers, and trudged up the stairs. Inside Jake's condo, she kicked off the slippers, hung up his coat, and headed for the kitchen to heat water in the kettle, thankful Jake had a decent selection of teas. Normally, if it was much after the lunch hour, she went for herbal teas, but tonight called for caffeine.

Before heading to the bathroom, Jenna checked for a missed call. Jake should be checking in again soon. He'd found Seven's prints exactly where the woman had indicated seeing him and had followed them for over a mile before losing track of them again at Mariano's parking lot in Riverside Square that was in the process of being plowed. The last time they talked, nearly an hour ago now, he'd been circling it, trying to pick them up again.

Jenna was just leaving the bathroom when her iPad rang out, and she jogged over to answer it. "Hey there! Any luck?"

"Not an ounce. His tracks don't pick up anywhere, I tell you." Frustration peppered his tone, and he sounded a bit hoarse. "Dumpsters line the building behind the shopping center, and his tracks circle a few of them, but the service road alongside them was plowed too. I guess he traveled down it, but the strip mall butts against Bubbly Creek, and there's a line of hedges and trees at the back edge of the property. I got out and walked some of it, thinking maybe he went down for a drink, but I never found any tracks. I doubt he stuck around here. I've been yelling for him nonetheless."

"I was just outside doing the same thing."

"Oh yeah?"

Jenna pulled the shopping center up on Google Maps. "Jake, Marino's is a bit east of the trajectory between where he was spotted on Paulina and here, but technically, it's about a half mile closer to your place than where he was last seen."

"Yeah, I was thinking the same thing. The only problem is that just north of here is the Chicago River. The only way he would've been able to cross that anywhere close to here is over the Ashland Avenue Bridge, and I can't see him doing that. Last week, I couldn't get him over a ten-foot-long pedestrian bridge over a dry creek at a park without him trying to bolt."

Jenna closed her eyes at the thought of Seven trekking over a bridge as big as the Ashland Avenue one, and she did her best to keep her fear out of her tone. Jake didn't need her adding any tension to his experience. "There are pedestrian crossings on both sides of it," she said. "I've used them more than once, on foot and on a bike. If he wanted to get across badly enough, maybe he would try it."

Jake let out a sharp breath. "It'll kill me if he's headed home, and he gets hurt along the way."

Tears stung Jenna's eyes. "Hardly anyone's out in this. He's got that going for him, Jake."

"Yeah, I keep telling myself that."

"All we can do is trust him to take care of himself. He's been loose before and been okay."

He was quiet for several seconds before responding. "Yeah. He has."

"What if you came here for a bit, and I headed out for a while, so long as you trust me to drive your Jeep in this."

"Thanks for offering. I do trust you, but I can hold out a while longer. I'll head to the bridge though. As fast as it's snowing, it's hard to tell, but the tracks that I have seen could very well be a couple hours old. Some of them have been so covered over, they're almost impossible to spot. If he did cross that bridge—if he's coming home—he could be miles past it by now."

"He very well could, which is why I keep watching out the window." The kettle began to whistle, and Jenna jogged over to it, taking the iPad with her. "You said to make myself at home, so I'm making a cup of tea."

"Great. What kind?"

"Something with caffeine."

"I think I have both green and black. In the cabinet to the right of the stove."

"I remember from before, and I'll go with black. Watching the snow fall is darn near hypnotic."

Jake chuckled. "Yeah, it is. I stopped and got an extra-large coffee earlier."

"I bet you needed it." Jenna immersed a tea bag into a mug of steaming water and laid the tag over the side. "You know, I was thinking earlier about something I read when I was a kid. It was about a dog who traveled across most of the United States to get home to his family after he got lost while they were on vacation. He crossed mountains and deserts and rivers. I remember crying like a baby to know that a dog could love his family that much." Jenna's soft laugh stirred up the tears that were still so close to the surface, and she dabbed at the corner of her eyes. "It was one of the things I added to my arsenal about why I wanted a dog so badly."

"Bobbie the Wonder Dog, right?"

"Yeah, that's him."

"I read an article about him a couple years ago. Pretty incredible feat, close to three thousand miles, I think."

While the tea steeped, Jenna returned to the front window, iPad in hand. Jenna was about to bring up how Bobbie was some breed of collie, too, when something caught her attention—not movement, but tracks. They trailed along the sidewalk and joined up with hers at the entranceway of the building. They weren't human footprints, either, but animal tracks, the best she could tell. Raising up on tiptoe and pressing her forehead against the window, Jenna peered downward, finding the bowl of kibble barely in view. Nothing was there, but the tracks led straight to it. "Jake, there are tracks leading right up to the door! And they weren't there just a couple minutes ago, I swear!"

"Dog tracks?"

"I think so. I can't tell from here." She ran for the door and shoved into her still-wet boots rather than Jake's slippers in case she needed to trek out further into the snow this time. "The call will drop as soon as I step out of the range of your Wi-Fi, so I'll call you back when I get inside."

"Sure thing, but I'm on my way now. I'll see you soon."

Jenna grabbed the coat Jake had lent her and dashed down the steps so fast she nearly lost her balance. Over nine miles! Could he really have made it here that quickly in snow this deep?

She threw open the door to find a bit of the kibble had been tossed over the edge of the bowl, and the prints in front of it were most definitely canine. Rather than heading back up the walkway, they wove through the landscaping along the side of the condos.

Following them, Jenna jogged around the side, the streetlights casting an uneven glow along the landscaping. She fully expected to spot him standing by the back door as she rounded the corner, but he was nowhere in sight. His tracks led right to it though, then off into the back parking lot.

"Seven! Seeeven!"

Jenna took off in their wake, terrified she'd lose track of them, but nothing aside from the street had been plowed around here yet, and his prints were the only thing breaking up the virgin snow. They led behind a second building then, as a fence blocked the way, toward the street again. Jenna's feet turned to ice in her still-wet shoes, but she pushed ahead faster, the snow deep enough to work the muscles in her legs.

It wasn't until Seven's tracks veered sharply alongside Rockwell that Jenna realized where he was heading—straight toward her place. Perhaps he'd smelled her scent on the kibble, or perhaps he was drawn to the yard where he'd played with Jake dozens of times, but he was heading along the same path he and Jake traveled every afternoon on their way to play in the yard. Jenna squinted ahead in the darkness beyond the streetlights, attempting to catch a glimpse of something aside from falling snow.

Cupping her hands, she yelled as loudly as she could. "Seven! Here, boy! Here, Seven!"

She'd just broken into a jog when a movement in the distance caught her eye. Something a few hundred feet ahead had just stepped out from behind a tree and was watching her, and Jenna caught the reflection of a pair of eyes in the beam of a streetlight.

"Seven!"

That was when she heard it, clear as day. A single, high-pitched bark.

"Come here, boy! Come here, Seven!"

She could make him out in the darkness now, a shaggy black-and-white dog jogging toward her, tail wagging and mouth gaping open—somehow completely ordinary and miraculous at the same time.

Seven had come home.

Chapter 34

JAKE HAD BEEN DRIVING so long his eyes were playing tricks on him. He blinked hard and looked again. It wasn't a trick of the eyes. Ahead of him, off to the left, two figures were walking in the dark along the sidewalk, and not any two figures, a woman and a dog, side by side, no leash linking them. Maybe he was the luckiest person on earth because he'd be damned if it wasn't his dog and his woman, as much claim as he might be able to lay to either of them.

Not wanting to scare Seven off, he closed in the distance to them slowly. They turned at the same time, and Jake pressed the brake, coming to a slow stop in the middle of the street. He'd be damned, too, if hot tears weren't flooding his eyes. He slipped the Jeep into Park and opened his door. After skittering off several feet further from the street, Seven circled and faced him again.

"Hey, Seven, it's me, bud." His voice cracked wildly as he stepped out. He'd be damned even more if he wasn't about to start blubbering like a little kid. Tears streamed down his face, and he made no move to stop them, even before Seven barked and bounded toward him.

Jake sank onto the backs of his heels as Seven dashed out into the otherwise empty street, pressing in close and dousing Jake's face in licks as sobs raked Jake's lungs, his chest heaving. There was a dreamlike quality to the whole thing that peaked when Seven didn't pull away as Jake draped his arms around his neck and buried his face in his soaked fur, his hands brushing against the soaked green bandanna still around his neck.

When Seven's warm tongue eventually found Jake's ear instead of his cheek, Jake pulled back a bit, laughing as the tears continued to flow. "I was so afraid I'd never see you again, bud. I'm so sorry I let go of that leash." He dragged the back of one hand over his face. "Thank God you've got more lives than the average cat. Thank God you found your way home."

Jenna had stepped into the street but was giving them some space. When Jake glanced her way, she was wiping tears from her face too. He couldn't remember the last time anyone had seen him cry, just like he couldn't remember the last time he'd cried with this much gusto. "Look at me, blubbering like a baby."

"Don't say it like that. It's one of the most beautiful things I've ever seen, the connection you two have."

"Where'd you find him?" he asked because he'd never pull himself together if he responded to that remark. He dragged his sleeve over his face as he stood up and cleared his throat. Sticking close, Seven trotted around him in a circle. Later, when Jake could say it without falling apart, he'd find a way to tell Jenna that, judging by the way the two of them had been walking side by side like that without a leash, Jake wasn't the only one Seven shared a connection with.

"He was headed down Rockwell. Toward my place after he didn't find a way in at yours."

"Oh yeah?" Jake looked down at Seven, noticing the exhaustion lining his features. He was soaked and shivering and favoring one front paw. Jake motioned toward the Jeep. "Want to get in, Seven?" He headed for the rear passenger door and pulled it open, and Seven wasted no time clambering in, although he was spent enough that Jake needed to give his back legs a boost.

After he closed the door, Jenna smiled encouragingly. "He's worn out, but he's okay. That's all that matters."

Jake pulled her into a tight hug, fresh tears stinging his eyes. He wanted to thank her, but the words stuck in his throat under threat of more tears.

"It's over now."

"Yeah," he said, clearing his throat. "Come on, let's get him home."

The final block to Jake's building and around to the parking lot in back was a quiet one, with nothing more than the sound of Seven's exhausted panting filling the car. It was an odd feeling, opening the back passenger door after parking and letting Seven hop down without a leash, but as soon as he was out, the exhausted dog beelined for the back door, making Jake's eyes sting with tears all over again.

They trudged up the stairs, Seven in the lead, and Jake waved Jenna on ahead of him. Once inside, Seven went straight for the water bowl and took a long drink, then collapsed in the middle of the floor, sprawling out on his side. He even let Jake cut away the bandanna without so much as flinching.

"If that's not the face of exhaustion, I don't know what is," Jenna said as she tugged out of her own boots.

"Twenty miles. Through the snow. It's hard to believe."

Jake pulled a space heater from the bottom of his closet, plugged it in, and aimed it in Seven's direction before grabbing a towel to dry him off. Seven was soundly asleep even before the water in the kettle began to boil.

"I don't know about you, but this time I'm going for decaf," Jenna said with a laugh.

A smile tugged at Jake's lips. "Me too." He stood over Seven a minute or two, towel still in hand, watching him as if he might disappear if he looked away.

"It's over now," Jenna repeated.

Nodding, Jake walked over to his kitchen counter and leaned against it. His sinuses and throat felt swollen and raw. How foolish he'd been to think tears were something he'd left behind with his childhood. His body could produce them as readily as ever; he'd just kept at bay the one thing that brought them to the surface—love. Tears stung his eyes again, and he blinked them away. "If he hadn't come back... If we hadn't found him..."

"But he did." Jenna strode over and wrapped her arms tightly around him. "Jake, it was my fault you were there today. And I distracted you with all that kissing." This part tumbled out with a choked laugh. "But you aren't blaming me, and no one is blaming you. He's here. He's safe. He wants to be here. We know that now. We didn't know it before."

"You're right. I know. It's just...terrifying." Leaning his forehead against the top of hers, he closed his eyes and took a few intentional slow breaths. "I didn't tell you earlier, but I called the shelter. I told Alice this thing I was doing with him is over." Just as Jenna pulled back and her eyes went wide in alarm, he smiled. "I'm adopting him."

"Oh Jake, thank God. You two are meant for each other."

"The irony is, I don't know who I'm adopting him from, your sister or the shelter, but it doesn't matter. I'm in it for the long haul with him. He isn't going anywhere. Neither am I." His lips brushed hers, softly at first, then harder. She shifted in his arms, and their bodies pulled together like magnets. "And I'm really hoping neither are you."

Jenna pulled back just a touch and traced a finger over the ridge of his jaw. "Tonight, or more generally speaking?" she asked, a smile playing on her lips.

"Both. Everything."

"Everything?"

She was smiling now, but he wasn't. "All that talk earlier—the joking and the not joking—about me wanting to take it slow? On my part, that was fear talking. And right now, I'm coming off a night of feeling more fear than I've felt in a long time. While I was driving around, it hit me that most of the time fear is exactly the thing that's holding me back."

"I've been there too."

"Maybe clarity follows on the heels of terror, but I know what I want now."

Jenna looked over at Seven. "Something tells me he knows it now too."

"I'm hoping you do too."

Jenna met his gaze again and nodded slowly, her smile returning. "I know what I want, and it's pretty much right here in this room too."

"That's good, because I want it all, Jenna. No holding back anymore. With him. With you. I want it all with you. All your everythings."

Jenna's mouth fell open an inch. "I'm pretty sure that's the most romantic thing anyone's ever said to me."

"Oh yeah? That's good because it's darn sure the most romantic thing I've ever said to anyone. I can promise you that."

Jenna bit her lip, but a laugh tumbled out anyway. "So, where do we go from here?" Seven jerked awake and lifted his head off the floor to look their way, his ears pricking forward. As if whatever he saw satisfied him, he dropped his head again and began drifting off once more.

Jake hooked a finger over the top of her jeans above the belly button. "The shower, I'm hoping. After you finish your tea and I text Alyssa that he's been found so she can let everyone who's watching out for him know he's safe."

Her mouth fell open an inch, and Jake had just enough time before she replied to wonder if he should've kissed her again before bringing up the shower. After glancing over at a sleeping Seven, she looked at Jake, and a smile tugged at her lips. "You should definitely shoot off that text, but maybe we can save the tea for later."

And Jake hoped that, where Jenna was concerned, he had a lot more surprises coming his way.

—⁓—

At some point, it had transitioned from very late to very early, and Jenna was still awake, curled in bed next to Jake, a smile playing on her lips even with her eyes closed. Every time she began to drift off, her thoughts stirred up again, and there was nothing to do but lie awake appreciating the sensation of his solid form next to hers, the steady rise and fall of his chest, the nearly inaudible sound of his breathing as he dozed, and his smooth sheets against her skin, the scent of his detergent pleasantly foreign to her nose. His hand, resting over her hip, twitched in his sleep, and Jenna made a wish that the city would be all but shut down tomorrow. How wonderful would it be to have another whole day to get to know one another in this way?

It hadn't surprised her that they were compatible physically. The promise of that had been there these last few weeks, building until the moment was right. He'd told her he wanted all her everythings, and later, this most recent time he'd been inside her, he'd told her he loved her. Crazy as it was for them to be spoken so early, the words had tumbled out of Jenna right back, and there was no denying they rang with a deeper truth than she'd felt in a long time.

Soon after, Jake had dozed off, leaving Jenna to savor the experience of lying next to him as he slept. She did her best not to wake him and lifted onto her elbow to look out the side window on the opposite side of the bed. It was still snowing, but it was hardly more than a dusting now, and the flakes were no longer in such a hurry to reach the ground.

A sound down the hall caught Jenna's attention. Seven was awake. She was debating getting up to check on him when he ambled down the hall and stood in the doorway, eyeing them in the darkness. Something was hanging out of his mouth that gave Jenna a start until she got a closer look and realized it was Michelangelo, his still-favorite toy more than a week after its discovery.

Jenna was wondering if he needed to go to the bathroom after all the water he'd drunk upon coming in, when he surprised her with a running jump onto the bed.

He stood at the foot of it, eyeing them in the darkness for several seconds, Michelangelo dangling out of his mouth from one foot. "Good boy, Seven," Jenna whispered.

After dropping Michelangelo nearby, Seven circled and circled in place, then curled up between her and Jake's feet, draping his head over Jake's ankles and his tail over Jenna's. As he drifted back to sleep, his body heat radiated through the blankets and sheet, warming her feet and ankles. It was unprecedented, Jenna was almost certain, him wanting this level of connection with people, which meant each of the three of them had entered new territory.

As far as Jenna was concerned, this was perfectly fine with her. They'd figure it out together.

Chapter 35

UP NEAR LOYOLA PARK just off Lake Shore Drive, the breeze was softening the late-June temps, and had she not had somewhere important to be, Jenna wouldn't have minded working at this pop-up craft fair another several hours, soaking up a perfect summer day by the lake.

Having only owned the vehicle for a little over a month, she was still getting used to everything about the new-model, high-roof Ford E-Transit van that she and Jake had transformed into a mobile version of Plants N Pots by Jenna. Inside, the walls had been decked out with custom built-in shelves in a variety of sizes and hanging grow lights, and the sides and back on the outside had been professionally painted with her new logo as well as her own paintings of her potted plants. Driving it in Chicago traffic wasn't the most fun thing she'd ever done, but she was getting used to it, kind of like driving a mobile billboard around.

To help draw in potential buyers, Jenna had invested in an assortment of whimsical plant stands that she set up outside the van at events to showcase some of her best plants and pots. Not only were the metal and wood stands helping sell her wares, but people had proven interested in buying them as well, so she'd added them to her expanding retail list.

Today had been her fourth event with the van, and packing up was more seamless each time.

"Taking off?" Carla, a woman selling ceramics over at the folding tables, asked while on her way back from the specialty ice cream truck.

"Yeah, I'm heading out to see Seven in his first agility and herding fun show this afternoon."

"Oh yeah? Wish him good luck for me. And whereabouts are you working next weekend?"

"Actually, I'll take next weekend off. Jake and I are getting out of town for a long weekend over the Fourth and heading up to Voyageurs National Park for some camping and canoeing—with the dog, so we'll see how he likes canoes."

"Oh fun. Well, I'll see you around, I'm sure."

"For sure." Jenna jutted her thumb toward the van. "Now that I have this, I plan on doing a lot more events this year." She'd dropped down to three days a week at the clinic, which had opened up her schedule, enabling her to commit to more, but Jenna's big goal was to dive into Plants N Pots by Jenna full-time next spring. The thought still seemed completely out of reach at times, but then again, so had owning a truck like this one. While she never would've wished for the accident, good things had certainly been born from it.

Several of them.

After loading up, Jenna had just enough time before she headed out to swing by a vendor selling specialty dog and cat treats. For Seven, Jenna picked a peanut-butter-flavored doggie doughnut with Greek-yogurt-based icing and bacon bits for sprinkles, and for Rosie, she chose a bag of heart-shaped catnip treats. Now four months old, Rosie was a veritable rocket ship of energy most of the time—and enough like Seven that Jenna had given her sister credit for the comparison she'd made that first night they found her. The good news was that a high-energy kitty was a lot more manageable in Monica's busy household than a high-energy border collie had been.

Earlier, Jenna had bought a bag of the boys' favorite cinnamon toast popcorn for later this evening. Jake was coming over to help babysit the boys overnight. Hopefully, it would give Mom and Dad an easier evening and night with Clary Mae, who'd joined the world three weeks ago and who'd been breaking hearts ever since.

Maybe Jenna was leaning into this trusting-the-heart business her sister was always going on about because she hadn't even blinked an eye when Monica had been right about Clary being a girl. "When you know, you know," Monica had insisted, and Jenna had never agreed with her more.

An hour later, Jenna made her way onto the bleachers, content in the crowd of spectators assembled for the fun show at a popular agility farm an hour west of the city. Whether Seven would prove to be a good sheepherder remained to be seen, although he'd certainly perked up the handful of times he'd been in an arena with sheep so far. The trainer Jake and Seven had been working with insisted the dog had both the intelligence and instinct for herding, but right now, Jake wanted to focus on agility competitions with him, a sport Seven enjoyed as much as Jake.

Today would be Seven's first timed agility trial. He'd passed the American Kennel Club's Agility Course Test, and Jake had gotten him registered to compete in agility events. Today's event was open invitation, and it didn't take Jenna long to realize that however Seven ended up doing today, he almost certainly wouldn't be the worst.

As she was getting seated, small dog breeds were still finishing up their first round in the agility arena, and a miniature dachshund entered the arena with her handler. Just the sight of her trotting in confidently with her head and tail held high had people laughing. The jumps were currently set at their lowest level, but other than that, the course was the same for dogs of all sizes. After starting out in the wrong direction, the dachshund got redirected and did an admirable job the first half of the course, jumping poles, dashing through tunnels, and crossing the seesaw, but at the weave poles, she stopped and sniffed, then squatted in the middle to urinate on the Astroturf, which sent a roar of laughter through the audience. Afterward, she was considerably less interested in finishing the course, but she trotted around after her owner, sidestepping most of the jumps and doing an impressive job of hauling herself up and over the steep A-frame planks, which sent the crowd into wild applause. While the announcer had poked fun at her mishaps as she moved through the course, he'd done it in a congenial way and, at the end, encouraged the crowd to applaud her for her spirit, which they did.

Slower paced from the start, the corgi who followed her proved more consistent throughout, tackling each obstacle with the same focused intensity and generating a good deal of praise from her owner as well as from the audience. The last of the small dogs was a Jack Russell who was too ramped up to wait for the starting bell and dashed through the exit of the nearest tunnel and over two jumps before his owner got him corralled and started him over, but once he got going, he was impressive to say the least.

Next, there was a short break while the jumps were raised, and then it was time for the larger dogs to move through the course. Jenna pulled out her phone and texted Jake good luck and added a kiss emoji even though she doubted he was paying attention to his phone. He was somewhere behind the scenes on the opposite side of the large arena, waiting with Seven.

Spying a new text from her sister, Jenna opened it to find a reminder to get Seven's debut on video, and Jenna texted back that she would.

The first dog out after the jumps were raised was a black-and-white husky who took the course at a trot but did everything his owner asked, moving over the seesaw, the pause table, and the A-frame planks with steady determination, but then he lost interest in the final two jumps and trotted over to sniff the judge's pockets, making everyone laugh. Next up was a yellow Lab who popped out of the first tunnel, then circled right back around to run through it again and then attempted to head back inside it in the opposite direction before her owner was able to get her attention and get her moving through the course again. The announcer had a lot of fun with her.

Laughing, Jenna clamped one hand over her mouth. At least there were other newbie dogs here today too.

When she finally spotted Jake and Seven entering the big arena from the far side, Jenna's heart skipped in her chest. However Seven did out here today, she'd forever be proud of them both, Jake for not quitting on him when the rest of the world had, and Seven for giving Jake a chance right back.

When Jenna lifted her phone to start videoing, she spotted a new text from Jake.

Glad you made it! Love you and see you on the other side.

Maybe because Seven was the first border collie up, and border collies had a reputation for being good agility dogs, the crowd fell quiet as Jake and Seven walked over to the starting circle and got still, waiting for the referee to give the go-ahead.

Just as he should be, Seven was alert and keyed in on Jake, waiting for his signal to start. As soon as he got it, Seven bolted out toward the center of the arena, missing the first jump entirely, and the crowd let out a disappointed "Awww."

But Jake was quick to get his attention and Seven circled back, watching Jake's signal for where to head next. From that moment on, the two of them worked together, Seven sailing over jumps and Jake running at his side, signaling which obstacle to jump or scale next, each of which Seven did with ease. This gave Jenna a sense of how deeply the two of them had bonded. More than that, they'd become a team.

Even though she'd seen them practicing together dozens of times, Jenna had never seen them so coordinated, so in tune with each other. Seven moved through the weave poles with the grace and fluidity of a true canine athlete and scaled the seesaw without the slightest hesitation. It was what drew crowds, a border collie with the athleticism and focused attention to make moving through the course appear effortless, and when he was finished, the crowd went wild with applause.

Jake knelt down, and Seven ran into his arms, wagging his tail. He licked Jake's chin as Jake wrapped him in a hug. After this, Jake looked toward the bleachers for the first time, scanning the crowd. Jenna, who was still on her feet, let out a whoop and blew him a kiss. Grinning at her, Jake stood up and closed one hand over his heart, and Jenna knew just what he meant.

His cup runneth over too.

"There you go, folks. That's what it's all about!" the announcer blurted into the microphone. "Even with that mishap in the beginning, my bet is that we've just seen our winning time today, and it's by a first-timer named Seven, of all things. But it says here that's for good reason. Folks, believe it or not, this dog circled through shelters six times before finding his forever home. Would you believe that? Well, I for one will say he's a lucky-number Seven at that."

While Jenna couldn't agree more, she'd counter the claim with one of her own. She and Jake were just as lucky. Likely even luckier.

Sometimes home is wherever you land and family is whatever you make of it.

Read on for a short excerpt of
Summer By the River, now available
from Sourcebooks Casablanca.

Chapter 1

THE OVEN TIMER WAS buzzing when Josie pushed through the swinging door into the kitchen. It was hard to believe two hours had sped by since she'd placed the six trays of blueberries into the commercial ovens to dry them out. With the tea garden hosting their first wedding, there'd been no doubt it would be a whirlwind of a weekend, but Josie hadn't expected this craziness. She'd been going nonstop since dawn, and her empty stomach was grumbling in protest.

She was loading the last of the trays onto the baker's sheet pan rack when the doorbell rang, its melodic chimes resounding through the old mansion.

Leaving the oven mitt on the kitchen counter, she headed down the hall toward the front. She was almost to the door when the back screen door thwacked open.

"Moooooommm! Mommy?" Zoe called, her tone brimming with the demanding urgency of a six-year-old.

"Up front, babe. Someone's here."

Josie checked out the side window before unlocking the door, proving old habits never die. She ran through a mental list of the expected guests. She'd thought everyone who was coming had arrived. The crowded back terrace certainly made it seem so.

This guest was alone, and just the kind of guy whose presence instinctively stirred up female hormones. He was taller than Josie by half a foot and, judging by the fit of his jeans and black T-shirt, in good shape. He was older, too, but not by much, early- to mid-thirties maybe. His eyes, bright blue-green, warred for attention with a broad smile accented by the short, brown stubble on his cheeks and chin.

Zoe zoomed down the hall and smacked into Josie, plastering her petite body into the back of Josie's leg. Half-hidden, she peered around Josie's hip at the visitor while muttering something about the two boys she'd been building sandcastles with.

"Hang on a second, Zo." Before returning her attention to the man, she ran her hand over Zoe's long chestnut hair, her fingers raising a few of the baby-fine ends by her forehead like little exclamation points. "Hi. You're here for the wedding?"

The stranger's easy smile widened at her question. "Well, that depends. If you're the bride and you're still taking offers, I could be tempted to throw my name into the hat."

Josie worked to keep her jaw from falling open. Did guys really say things like that anymore? She was a bit out of touch—by design—but she was pretty sure they weren't supposed to.

Zoe tapped Josie's arm, demanding her attention. "Did you hear me, Mommy? Those boys aren't sharing."

Josie scooped Zoe up at the same time the man offered his hand.

"My bad, sorry." Clearly, he'd picked up on her lack of enthusiasm for his compliment. "I'm looking for Myra Moore. I believe she's expecting me. I'm a freelance journalist working on an article for the *New York Post*."

A rush of lightheadedness flooded her. *A journalist?* She attempted to readjust Zoe, who was too big to be held any longer, on her hip. "Why?" she managed to get out, forgetting about his white teeth and blue-green eyes.

"I'm in town researching a missing person and what might be an unresolved murder. I'm hoping she can help me find the answers I'm looking for."

Josie's muscles went rigid. *No, no, no. Not like this. I'm not ready.* Her mouth gaped, but nothing came out, and her vision went from spotty to almost completely gray. Her arm locked around Zoe's slim torso as she struggled to remain standing and alert.

Swaying, swaying. Was it the room swaying or her?

She smelled the stranger closing in around her before her spotty vision could process it. The woody, sweet scent of sandalwood filled her nostrils, the one concrete thing she could process.

She might as well have been a doll in *The Nutcracker*. She could feel Zoe sliding off her body and onto the floor and the man stepping closer, and she could hear their muffled talking but couldn't process the words. She struggled to stay conscious—to tell him to back off—but words wouldn't come. Then she was in his arms and he was carrying her, and her vision was clearing from gray to spotty again.

The next thing she knew, Josie startled to find herself lying on the couch in the front parlor when she hadn't even realized he'd set her down. She startled even more to find the stranger hovering over her, staring. Had she passed out? It hadn't seemed that way, but the last couple seconds—or minutes—were disjointed.

Movement in the entryway caught her attention. Zoe was pulling Myra, the tea garden's eighty-year-old owner, into the parlor and tugging on her skirt. Myra's faithful Corgi-Pomeranian mix, Tidbit, trailed in at her side.

"You won't believe it, Myra!" Zoe chirped. "Mommy's eyes were fluttering like butterflies and I thought we were going to fall and this man catched her and carried her all the way over here."

Caught. The word rose to Josie's lips reflexively, even though she couldn't voice it. The irony didn't escape her that she was worried about Zoe's grammar at a time like this. Somehow, she forced herself to sit up using limbs that reacted like boiled noodles.

The stranger cleared his throat and directed his words to Myra. "Sorry, ma'am. I let myself in. Your, uh, this woman fainted—sort of."

"Heavens." Myra leaned over and pressed her palm across Josie's forehead. "She's been running herself ragged the last few days. Zoe, be a dear and get your mom a glass of water, will you?"

Zoe gave Josie a questioning glance. "You're all better now, Mom, right?"

"I'm fine, baby." Her words come out squeaky, barely audible.

If Zoe had been distraught to see her collapse like that, she seemed to be processing it fine now. "Make sure nothing happens till I get back." Then she dashed out of the room and down the hall.

"You all right, Miss?" the man asked.

Josie dropped her gaze to the floor and repeated that she was fine.

Standing beside him, Myra offered him her hand. "I'm Myra, and this is my house. Bob phoned just now and said you'd be coming. I'm afraid I've forgotten your name."

"Carter." The man took Myra's arthritic hand with care. "Carter O'Brien."

"It's nice to meet you, Carter. Once I see to Josie, I'm happy to answer your questions." Myra sank onto the sofa next to her. Tidbit scooted back to make a running jump to clear the couch with his short legs, then nestled down between them. "You all right, dear?"

"I'm fine." Josie kept her hands folded across her lap as Tidbit sniffed her arm. *How could Myra know he was coming and not tell me?*

Like a rabbit frozen in the grass, she waited for him to proceed with whatever devilry brought him to her doorstep. She couldn't imagine how he knew. All she could think was it had to have been the shady man in Chicago who'd forged her and Zoe's papers. The process had been complicated, to say the least. But Josie and Zoe Waterhill were legitimate people now. Falsified, maybe, but legitimate. They had social security numbers and birth certificates. Josie hadn't been comfortable using the man's services, but she would never have been able to register Zoe for school otherwise.

But what might it have cost her?

Carter squatted in front of her, balancing on the balls of his feet, resting his forearms against his thighs as he eyed her in concern. "When I was growing up, I had a cousin with low blood sugar. My aunt kept orange juice on hand. It helped when she crashed. If you have any, I'd be happy to get you a glass."

"Do be a dear and try, will you?" Myra answered for her. "If Linda, the kitchen manager, isn't in the kitchen, Zoe will show you where the glasses are kept. It's down the hall and to the right."

He nodded and headed down the hall toward the back of the house. Josie finally noticed the gaping-open front door. His bag—most likely a laptop case—was still abandoned on the stoop. A ridiculous urge flooded her to grab it and run for the river where she could toss it into the gray-black water in hopes it might carry its secrets into the abyss.

But even if her spent legs would obey, there'd be no point. Whatever information he had in there was surely backed up somewhere else. No, whatever Armageddon he was bringing was already rushing her way.

Beside her, Myra swept aside a lock of her hair and brushed her thumb over Josie's cheek. "I know what you're thinking, Josie. I was coming inside to tell you about the call and heard him as I walked in. I'm sorry for the scare it has caused you, but you've got it wrong. The wind that blew him here has nothing to do with you."

Josie searched Myra's gentle eyes for the truth since, for the first time in over five years, she found herself doubting her words.

Acknowledgments

Writing a book is like embarking on a road trip. Even if you know just where you're headed, the journey will surprise you. When I started *Home Is Where Your Bark Is*, I anticipated that I'd devote much of the story to Jenna's relationship with her sister. Then Seven came into the picture, and soon he was driving the car, at least as much as a plucky border collie is capable of doing so. All my characters began to revolve around him, and even the boundaries Jenna eventually established with her sister were put into practice to help meet Seven's needs. Looking back, it's obvious that Seven was the perfect center for this tale, and I couldn't be happier to have told his story.

Dogs like Seven—ones with high energy and a history of abuse or neglect—often don't fare well in shelters. Their anxiety heightens, and soon they're even more challenging to adopt. Foster caregivers can make all the difference for animals like Seven. They're dealing with escape artists, counter surfers, reluctant potty trainers, and vandals. It isn't a job for the faint of heart. For everyone reading this who has given it a whirl, whether you succeeded or couldn't go the full mile or became your foster animal's forever home, know you're making a difference.

Thank you to my editor, Deb Werksman, whose love for Seven parallels mine. Deb, your sage advice across so many stories has been invaluable. Here's to nine books together, each of which is stronger for your guidance. Thank you to Susie Benton, Alyssa Garcia, Jocelyn Travis, and so many more at Sourcebooks and

Sourcebooks Casablanca who are integral in bringing books like this one to readers.

Jess Watterson, thanks for believing in me and in that first shelter story. Who would've guessed what it would lead to? Here's to many more unique endeavors together. Lori Foster, I knew of your generosity beforehand, but you have my deep gratitude for giving *Home Is Where Your Bark Is* a read and embracing this story (and Seven) as you have. Thank you to my critique partners Cynthia J. Bogard, Susan Coventry, and Susan Steggall for their insight and feedback on this manuscript. Thank you to my friend Laura Lytle who helped with all things Chicago, morphing it from a city I love to visit into a home for Jake, Jenna, and Seven. Thank you to Amanda Heger, my friend and fellow author, who's always up for a writing date or to commiserate on the highs and lows of author life. It wouldn't be the same without you.

Lastly, thanks to my daughter, Emily, who was integral in bringing our slightly toned-down version of Seven into our family. Hazel, our border collie, had thirteen wonderful years with us after her rough start in life. Hazel and her littermates were found in a trash bag on a busy roadside before they were brought into a shelter. As a puppy, Hazel challenged everything I knew about being a dog owner; as an adult dog, she kept us all in check; and as a senior dog, she was the example of grace in motion. It's an honor to have been one of her people.

About the Author

Debbie Burns is the bestselling author of heartwarming women's fiction and love stories featuring both two- and four-legged stars. While her books have earned many awards and commendations, her favorite praise is from readers who've been inspired to adopt a pet in need from their local shelter.

Debbie lives in Saint Louis with her family, a thoroughly spoiled rescue dog, and two Maine Coon cats who ought to be named Pete and Repeat. When she isn't writing (or reading), you can find her hiking in the Missouri woods, working in her garden, or savoring time with family and friends.

Website: authordebbieburns.com
Facebook: authordebbieburns
Instagram: @_debbieburns
BookBub: authordebbieburns

Also by Debbie Burns

Summer by the River

RESCUE ME
A New Leash on Love
Sit, Stay, Love
My Forever Home
Love at First Bark
Head Over Paws
To Be Loved by You
You're My Home